SPECTER

ZETA TRILOGY
BOOK 3

ROB GRAFRATH

First edition June 2025

Cover design and chapter heading art by Gabrielle Grafrath

Paperback ISBN 978-1-953470-08-9

Hardcover ISBN 978-1-953470-09-6

Published by Ourania Publishing

1

———————————

THE WRAITH QUEEN

Boom-boom, *boom-boom!*

The drums are back.

The Wraith Queen twisted in her warped throne, straining against the chains binding her arms and legs. Her gossamer-cloaked head slammed against the throne's back in frustration. Was there no way to cover her ears?!

Ears? She didn't have ears!

Her cackle echoed in the stone room, then silenced as abruptly as it had started. If she had eyes, she would weep.

Nope, no eyes, either!

Another laugh, then silence.

Yes, it was all *so* funny. Not funny-ha-ha but funny-*strange.* Nothing made sense anymore. Well, at least she still had a mouth.

Boom-boom, boom-boom, boom-boom!

She took a deep, rattling breath, filling herself up until she was sure she'd burst, then let out a screech. It felt good. If she couldn't stop the drums, she'd drown them out.

No, don't ignore them. Find them. Send adventurers off to stop them.

Finding things was easier now that she had mastered the skill of casting her all-seeing eye across her domain. Her attention descended to the underworld in search of the drums. Wraith-pooches were sniffing around at the jagged, rocky border to their realm again. They flinched at her great screech as it echoed through their plane. The whole pack scampered back into the dark abyss with their tails between their legs.

She finished screeching and then shouted at the creatures. "That's right! You better run, you mangy mongrels! It serves you right for coming so close to the material plane!"

They were sorta cute, though.

But not as cute as *larvae!* She returned her gaze to the material plane and cast it upon the insectoid hive mound engulfing the base of Castle Interra. There they were, hard at work — bumblebees as big as boulders, anthropomorphic army ants, and best of all, massive maggots — those milky white fly-babies were her favorite! Cute, cute, CUTE!

The Wraith Queen's wandering eye scoured through the winding hive tunnels on a maggot hunt. Where were they? She dove deeper. Minutes later, she emerged into a massive tunnel packed with pale insectoid eggs. So many eggs! They could've filled a coliseum!

The tunnel was more expansive than any she'd seen the insectoids dig in the past. Plunging down the cavernous tube, following its descending twists and turns, she found its creator. Before her loomed the biggest grub she'd ever seen — big enough to gobble up entire buildings in its pincers.

"By Maahes's mane, what are you?!" she called out at the thing.

The grub wriggled, causing the tunnel to rumble. Bits of dirt and rock tumbled down, half-concealing it.

The Wraith Queen laughed, tickled by this pathetic attempt to hide. "You can't hide from the omnipresent queen bitch of Interra, you stupid grub! Keep it up, and you'll cave in the whole place and squash those eggs back there. Hey, did you undermine The Day Queen's tower? Is that what made it fall?"

Rumble, crunch, tumble went the tunnel as Mr. Monster-Grub wriggled and jiggled in his hidey-hole. Now, he was completely buried. Which, of course, hindered The Wraith Queen's omnipresent view, not one iota.

"You will cease this infernal digging and hold still! You'll make the whole city collapse at this rate!"

Boom-boom, boom-boom!

"Earthquake! No, it's the drums again. If it's not one thing, it's another!"

Her view rose to a vantage point high above The Night Tower. She had put up with this cursed racket for weeks now. If she could track the pounding drums back to their source, maybe she could shut them up.

What a joke. She may have been omnipresent, but she was utterly powerless. Her only power was her influence, but these days, her subjects had dwindled to a paltry few. With so few adventurers in her realm, the Curse of the Night Queen (or Wraith Queen — take your pick) would never be lifted.

It was no wonder they had abandoned her, with the state it was in.

Below her lay the ruins of Castle Interra, engulfed by the ever-growing insectoid mound. Only The Night Tower still stood — The Wraith Queen's seat of powerlessness and personal prison. Small fires burned like flickering stars in the darkened ruins of Centra City. Its only occupants were squatters, adventurers, and the rare hold-outs who still pretended to own property in the lawless, decaying corpse of a city.

Above, a paltry smattering of stars dotted the eternal night sky. Even the heavens looked dismal these days.

Days?! That's funny — *day* hasn't come in ages.

Now, where were those drums coming from?

Boom-boom, boom-boom!

Maybe she could hone in on them. She cast her mind's eye off to explore her ruined domain. She crossed the wastelands where The Fall of the Wraiths battle had played out, pausing at the smoldering crater that sealed the underworld off from the material plane. Ag'nul was camped at its rim — nothing unusual about that. A rat-sized insectoid cricket sat in the half-yeti's blue palm.

"I... have another poem for you," Ag'nul rumbled to the cricket.

It was sad — there wasn't any fight left in the dopey oaf ever since Za'antha's abduction. He'd taken to reciting poetry to crickets. The stridulating insectoid would chirp out a gut-wrenching song for him next. She couldn't stand the sound of it, so she continued her search.

But wait! The Day Queen was camped out a few kilometers down the road! Was she with Ag'nul, or was that just a coincidence? Here was another sad soul — a dethroned queen. Her magic abandoned her when the eternal night fell over Interra. And if the sun never rises, what's the use of a Day Queen?

Boo-hoo. At least she was free. At least she was *human*. Let the loser languish.

She continued her search. The drums sounded again. Their sound came from everywhere, yet nowhere. How could that be? Were they in another plane?

The Wraith Queen's view transitioned to the spirit plane. She darted from one side of Interra to the other. Magical creatures and lost souls flitted past her gaze, but nothing which could make that booming sound.

Boom-boom, boom-boom!

She let out another frustrated shriek. "Come out, come out, wherever you are!"

Maybe the astral plane? She lifted to the stars, then searched between them. The problem with the astral plane is it's so damn *big* — an expansive nothingness that just keeps going.

Boom-boom, boom-boom.

Nope, they were quieter that time.

How about the shadow plane? It was one of the lesser planes — a narrow sliver of existence sandwiched snugly between the material and spirit planes. Planeswalkers usually pass right over it without even noticing. Few creatures called it their home, but it was popular with the dark elves for hiding or traveling covertly.

Her vantage descended to the material plane, then slipped carefully into the shadow plane. Goodness, what a tricky plane this was to navigate — a knife's edge. Ghostly echoes of the adjacent planes drifted by as she explored the hazy world of shadows.

BOOM-BOOM! BOOM-BOOM!

The sound resonated within her core. It was like having her head inside the drums. "Ah-ha!" she declared, "I have you now, ye raucous rum-pum-pum-pummers! Show yourselves!"

Within minutes, the all-seeing eye of The Wraith Queen settled upon the hazy forms of massive war machines. Orcs heaved at ropes as dark elves assembled intricate gears or whipped teams of shadow beasts. They wore armor and carried weapons, ready to take up arms at a moment's notice.

War machines in Interra? What did they mean to do, invade Centra City? Not on her watch!

"Who is in charge here?!" The Wraith Queen demanded, filling the hazy shadow plane with echoes of her commanding voice.

The soldiers kept working, ignoring her.

"I am the queen of these lands! Ignore me at your peril!"

Ropes squeaked. Wheels creaked. Some of the war machines were on the move — squelching through gray mud.

Infuriated, The Wraith Queen let out another one of her signature shrieks. A few dark elves lifted their heads at this, then shrugged and returned to work.

A muscled orc carrying a massive drum stepped into view. He lifted an oversized femur with a leather bulb on one end, then struck the drum.

BOOM-BOOM! BOOM-BOOM!

She answered the war drum with her own racket of bone-chilling shrieks — a thousand nails scraping against a thousand chalkboards.

"IGNORE ME AT YOUR PERIL!" she bellowed.

Her rage burned away with a flash, leaving her with nothing but a smoldering tendril of exhausted ego.

Who was she kidding? She was toothless. Impotent. A dead husk that refused to settle into a grave.

Her view retreated to her throne room. Her body was writhing, straining against the chains which held her to the Rho throne. She pulled her legs up onto the throne's seat, vainly trying to find a comfortable position. Her once-silky skin was wrinkled and dry like old leather. Its ebony tone had turned ashen black.

Beauty is a fickle, fleeting thing.

Her eyeless face wasn't much to look at, for sure. She wasn't sure if she was glad to have an omnipresent incorporeal eye or if complete blindness would be better. At least then, she wouldn't have to look at herself.

She was so *dry*. And *always* thirsty.

"Roman," she rasped, "bring water."

Boom-boom, boom-boom!

Those damn drums! And what was with that scratch-n-sniffing pack of wraith-pooches at the underworld border? They were already at it again, she knew. Oh, but that grub? It would send her tower toppling over at any moment!

"Who cares?" she rasped to herself. "Let it fall."

The Wraith Queen sighed — a death rattle.

She was spent. Sending her gaze across the lands was exhausting. Everything she was furious about a moment ago was slipping away.

Slip, slip, slippery... sleep. Yes, she just wanted to sleep.

No, she wanted to *die*, but sleep would do for now. Besides, she had already died so many times before, and it never stuck.

"Roman! Where's my water?!"

The Queen's guard in full plate armor came clattering into the throne room, pitcher in hand, splashing water as he went. He tipped it over above her as if he were watering a plant. She cast her head back and opened her mouth, catching whatever she could. The man had lost all respect for his queen.

She swallowed, choked, and coughed. "Rho's throne wouldn't rot like this if you'd be civilized with the water, Roman," The Wraith Queen snapped. "You're a disgusting disgrace."

Roman clattered away without response.

He never responded anymore.

Boom-boom, boom-boom!

Maybe if she pretended the drums were from a distant parade, she'd learn to enjoy their pounding. Perhaps they were her funeral dirge!

"Wraith Queen, we beseech thee," an otherworldly voice called. *"Please grace us with your majestic presence."*

Oh, brother. The supplicants were praying again. Not that she didn't enjoy the company, but she didn't have the energy for astral projection right now.

With a sigh, she heeded their call. Misery loves company.

THE SHIMMERING, translucent form of Queen Rho appeared within the dim cavern. The walls were dirt. No, not dirt — she was in a chamber of the insectoid mound, so they'd be made from insectoid concrete. Termite builders mix dirt with hardening mucus to construct their massive mounds.

A glowworm dangled from the ceiling, emanating chartreuse light from its abdomen. Her supplicants still had their heads down, clutching obsidian shards in their pincers. This was the proper gesture for supplicants requesting her presence, so she was pleased.

She extended a hand. The obsidian turned into a black liquid. It darted up to her hand, absorbing into her translucent form, giving her energy and substance.

"Rise," purred the queen.

The Wraith Queen's form reflected her former beauty as Queen Rho when she astrally projected. She hated it, but you don't get to pick your astral form.

Gryllus Stridulator was the first to rise. The cricket with a red bycocket rubbed his wings together to emulate the sound of a man saying, "Greetings, my queen. You may recall Nala Tarsus from our prior meetings."

He gestured to the prone praying mantis by his side.

She already wanted to knock the bug's head off his thorax. Of course, she remembered Nala! She remembers *everything*. It's making *sense* of it all that muddles her mind. For that reason, some memories are better left forgotten.

"Yes, of course," Queen Rho's apparition said, feigning grace. "Rise, Nala."

Nala, the praying mantis war-priestess, was many times larger than Gryllus. Her antennae brushed the chamber ceiling when she reached her full stature. Her head twitched, and she let out a series of hisses and clicks.

Gryllus said, "Ah, yes, let us not forget our humble illuminator, Bram Phosphor."

The glowworm overhead wiggled its stubby antennae and gave a click.

Her apparition smiled up at him and gave a welcoming, open-palmed gesture. "Well met, Bram. Your light pleases me."

Bram gurgled out what she guessed was an "aw, shucks" sound.

Gryllus rubbed his wings again. "My queen, we requested your presence to ask more about the drums you've been hearing."

Of course that's what they wanted. That's all they ever wanted these days. It was either that or news on the wraith-pooches. Goddess forbid they should ask how her day was or sing her a pleasant tune.

"What about them?" she spat.

"Do they persist? Have they intensified?" the cricket stridulated most annoyingly.

She sighed, "Yes, yes. But I found their source: war drums. An army of orcs and dark elves drives war machines through the shadow plane. Coming to kill us all, I'm certain. But what *I* want to know—"

"I'm sorry," Gryllus interrupted, "did you say you spotted war machines in the shadow plane? Can you describe—"

"I answered your question!" The Wraith Queen shrieked, causing the insectoids to recoil. "Now you will answer mine! Tit for tat! Quid pro quo, Clarice!" What was that supposed to mean? Sometimes, when she got worked up, she blurted out things she didn't understand.

Gryllus went to his belly and ducked his head. "My apologies, your majesty. Ask, and I shall answer."

"What's with the grub, Gryllus?!"

"The... *grub*, your majesty?"

"The g-g-grub, your majesty?" she mocked. "Yes! The giant grub that's been undermining my castle! It's bad enough your wretched mound is overtaking Castle Interra. Now you're growing grubs big enough to swallow a dragon! And I saw those eggs! How many creepy crawlies do you plan to spawn down there, anyway?! I have a right mind to have a canal dug from the river so I can flood you cursed bug-brains out and be done with you!"

Nala clicked and hissed something at Gryllus, who responded in kind.

"Your majesty," Gryllus said, "on behalf of the Interran hive, I do apologize for causing you distress. The grub you saw has finished its burrowing — it will remain where it rests. And the eggs are unfertilized. They serve as an emergency food reserve. I ask, most humbly and respectfully, that you please do not share the secrets of our underground burrowers and food reserves. Food is growing scarce, and scavengers are getting bolder due to the eternal night."

She was satisfied with this response. "You have my word. I'm sorry for yelling, dear subject. I haven't been feeling like myself these past few..."

Few what? Years? Lifetimes? How long had she been like this?

Like what?

Was there any other way to be?

She felt herself stumbling, searching. Darkness descended on the scene.

Queen Rho's distant voice echoed from the darkness, "I... take my leave of you."

And then, without ado, the Wraith Queen slipped into a deep and tortured sleep.

Dreams filled the lands of Interra as reality warped and looped back upon itself. An adventurer found a half-dead kitten in the mud. His wife — though she looked like someone else — made pies for his party and complained of too much soot in the crust. Void lightning arced from the silver horns of black unicorns, passed from cloud to cloud in a deadly game of catch.

All of this was as real as anything that had come before it, the sleeper mused, for reality is a figment of the mind — a product of flawed sensory input being fed into a disjointed conglomerate of cognitive functions to construct a passably cohesive, internally consistent conscious experience.

So just kick back and roll with it!

2

HARBINGER

Placental mats serve numerous life-sustaining functions. Their most important function is converting electrical energy, water, soil, and air into life's fundamental fuel source: adenosine triphosphate. The bio-synthetic process functions in a manner analogous to photosynthesis. They draw electricity from Genesis's network of mycelites — nanites designed to form a self-organizing web of electrical and data transfer conduits within the crust of Genesis.

This miracle of synth-organic nanotechnology means modern humans don't need to eat — they can sustain themselves indefinitely using placental mat feeding. While this is convenient for taking uninterrupted hiatuses from the real world in constructs and replays, it jeopardizes the crucial human experiences of eating food and sharing meals.

Earth's ancient tribes ritualized food-sharing traditions, as do the neoprim tribes living on the other side of Genesis in The Land of Eden. Finding food and failing to share it with your tribe will get you ostracized. People may even get killed for that sort of selfishness. Food distribution and shared consumption reinforces social hierarchies, supports group survival, and forms deep bonds of tribal fellowship.

So, yes, it bothered Oraxis that Genevieve seldom ate. She'd formed the bad habit after they lost Zeta four and a half years ago. He had enough sense and sensitivity to know he shouldn't complain about it and avoid pressuring her into joining him for tea or meals. But he still offered. This frequent, friendly reminder was his way of saying he was thinking about her and was always available when she wanted company.

But if she wanted to be alone, that was fine, too.

That's why Oraxis was surprised when Genevieve joined him and Natasha-Zeta Herrington at the stone table for a breakfast of tea, nuts, and dried berries.

"Plenty to go around!" Oraxis said, then tipped the kettle to look inside. "Well, enough for a half cup at least."

"I'll boil more water," Natasha-Zeta said, rising with a grunt.

Natasha-Zeta was a stout, older woman, perhaps old enough to be a grandmother. She shared Alasie's mix of Mongolian and Inuit features, marking her as an Iceborn tribeswoman.

Natasha-Zeta's bootstrapper and the others in her Noddite family tribe had transferred to the Astrus Faction before Alasie's alpha was born. Natasha-Zeta had no interest in joining the Astri, so she took over alpha seeding and beta bootstrapping duties for the Herrington family tribe.

The Telson family tribe had unofficially adopted Natasha-Zeta, since she was Alasie's bootstrapper. Her camp was nearby, but she spent most of her time at the Telson cabin. Her company was always welcome.

"No, half a cup's fine," Genevieve said. She opened her hand to Natasha-Zeta's dog, Elle. The black and white dog was a small, short-haired variety. Elle took a long time to warm up to strangers, but once she trusted you, she was the sweetest snuggling partner you could hope for.

The dog jumped onto the bench next to Genevieve, clambering

awkwardly onto her lap. She was adopted from one of Natasha-Zeta's former Noddite family members since the Astrus Faction doesn't accept companion animals. That guy had gotten Elle from another guy who had also transferred to the Astrus faction. Nobody knew where she was before that. Oraxis assumed that her history of bouncing around between families was why she was such an insecure, clingy animal.

"I think Penelope-pooch converted you into a dog person," Oraxis laughed. "You'd never let a dog clamber all over you like that before we took her in."

Elle tried licking Genevieve's face, but Genevieve pulled back to dodge the tongue. She said, "I don't like *all* dogs, just Pen, Elle, and Pinga."

"Not Pepper-pooch?" Oraxis asked, then worried he had opened a wound.

Genevieve picked up a dried huckleberry and ate it. "They've been training him to be a war dog, so who knows what that did to his temperament. We'll see next time Jamji visits. But that'll probably be a lifetime from now."

Natasha-Zeta had poured the last of their hot water into a mug containing loose leaves of dried lemongrass. She placed it in front of Genevieve. "Your tea, madame."

Oraxis watched out of the corner of his eye as Genevieve eyed the cup, idly scratching Elle's neck.

"It's not tea," Genevieve said vacantly. "It's a tisane." Her prior lightheartedness gave way to depression.

He could've slapped himself. Of course lemongrass tisane would trigger memories of Zeta's bootstrapping. Of all the herbs they could've picked today.

"Tisane?" Natasha-Zeta laughed. "That's a new one on me! What's the difference?"

Genevieve didn't reply, so Oraxis did. "Tea's made from the dried leaves of the camellia plant. Drinks brewed from any other dried herb, like lemongrass, are tisanes."

Natasha-Zeta grunted and shook her head. "Well, you learn something new every day. So, Gen, how's your tattoo looking? Healing up? Did you use the oil I gave you? You've gotta moisturize!"

Genevieve displayed the underside of her forearm. The tattoo was a lyric from an old song from Earth, written in curly lettering with bluish-black ink. Natasha-Zeta had done the work herself, using a method Oraxis had never heard of — pushing a sewing needle sideways through the skin to pull an ink-soaked thread through it.

At least half of Natasha-Zeta's body was covered in tribal tattoos. Every time they saw her, she had another design. Being able to shut off your pain receptors and the rapid healing ability of bioenhanced bodies made tattooing easy for Noddites.

Natasha-Zeta smiled at her work. "Oh, that's beautiful. I love how it stands out against your pale skin. Elle, no!"

The dog was trying to reach the dried fruit on the plate in front of Genevieve. Elle recoiled at the reprimand, jumping off Genevieve's lap to run and hide.

"So," Natasha-Zeta said, "are we still on for playing CotNQ today?"

CotNQ (pronounced cotton-Q) was the acronym used by the players to refer to Pip-Rho's self-hosted gameworld, *Interra: Curse of The Night Queen.*

She continued, "I'm getting the hang of this gameworld stuff. It's pretty fun, actually." She was either oblivious to Genevieve's darkened mood or just pretended to be to avoid drawing attention to it.

"It's too hot out," Genevieve said, standing.

"Yeah, we'll clean this up and head inside," Natasha-Zeta said. "Then we'll round up the party."

Genevieve went back into the cabin. She had eaten one berry. Well, it was better than most days.

Oraxis opened a WorMS — Worldnet Messaging Service — conversation with Natasha-Zeta.

Conversation request accepted.

"I know what you're going to say, O," she sent. *"That Gen's going through hard times, and I shouldn't be so jolly with her."*

"That's not what I was going to say," Oraxis replied

Natasha-Zeta continued, ignoring him. *"Well, how's she ever going to get to feeling normal again if everyone else is moping around, too?"*

Oraxis picked up the cups and plates as he sent, *"Nat, I'm fine with you acting normal around her. I try to do the same. What I want to warn you against is talking about CotNQ like it's just a game. The gameworld construct is running directly on Rho's Specter node-net. Somehow, the alien that consumed her mapped her connectome. She's operating on a whole different hardware platform — trillions of dynamically addressable nodes rather than the brain's physical neural connections. The change broke her — she's not the same person, but we think there's still enough of her left that we can get through to her in time. We play CotNQ because it's an abstraction of her inner reality. We use it to study her Umwelt, but also to keep her company and try to keep her engaged in human interactions."*

Natasha-Zeta was nodding. *"Yes, I'm sorry. I hear you, O, and I understand. Well, except for the Umwelt thing. What is that?"*

"Ask WoQS," Oraxis sent, requesting to close the conversation channel.

Oraxis knew Genevieve was in no mood for it, but she agreed to join them in CotNQ. They settled into their usual spots on the cabin floor, joined by Penelope-pooch, Pinga, and Elle.

Carff sent a WorMS message, saying he was logged in and waiting for them. The old man was in Eden, doing his job as a cultural influencer. He infiltrated neoprim tribes, pretending to be a wandering shaman, wise man, witch doctor, or the like. He said that when he went into slate-space to play CotNQ, he would tell his tribe he was going on a spirit journey.

XT-Prime was also logged in, but his character was at the insectoid mound surrounding Castle Interra, far from where the other characters in the party had last logged out. He wouldn't be joining their party today, so they left him out of their conversation channel.

Oraxis disconnected from his body, sending his mind into the empty void of slate-space. He submitted the login request and received the standard warning about joining an unmanaged offworld construct before being allowed through the Astrus Faction network and into the gameworld.

It was pitch black. Oraxis's character, Tel O'Rax, the wizard, looked around to find a pair of glowing green eyes staring at him. Scary, unless you know that it's just a goofy old shaman being played by Carff.

"Greetings, Ruyn Wormwood," Tel O'Rax said.

The eyes bobbed a greeting. A gravelly voice said, "Greetings, human. Where are the others?"

"Coming. Why are you sitting in the dark?"

"The dark?" Ruyn chuckled. "I can see perfectly fine."

Tel O'Rax cast a light spell. A weak, bluish light glowed from the crystal at the end of his staff. The form of the ancient wood elf shaman wearing a deer skull mask resolved into view. Necklaces of animal teeth draped across his bony chest, and animal skulls dangled from his belt. The dim light of Tel's spell made Ruyn's character look quite haunting.

Light magic didn't work very well in Pip-Rho's version of Interra. He couldn't complain too much since Genevieve and Pip-Tau's characters had been severely *nerfed* — an old Earth word for detrimental changes to an aspect of the game. They'd lost almost every power and spell and were banned from creating new characters. Carff's necro-shaman, on the other hand, had grown much more powerful.

The light glistened off the black veins of obsidian embedded in the cave walls. When they had last played, they were preparing to mine obsidian. The black volcanic glass had many useful properties, but it was most valuable as a tribute to Queen Rho.

Genevieve's character, Ayr of the Light, appeared next to him. She wore a patchwork of chain mail and leather armor rather than her robes. This was necessary now that her healing and protective prayers were useless. Now, she played the role of a battlefield medic and herbalist rather than a divine priestess. Her god, Rammah, was dead. This gave Genevieve a good excuse for playing her character with a surly demeanor.

Genevieve had changed her character's hair from platinum blond to raven black. She'd done the same thing to her real-world hair. The change saddened Oraxis, since he knew it was an outward expression of her inner darkness, but he had to admit it looked nice. It stood out in stark contrast with her fair skin.

Tel O'Rax also felt the presence of Penelope-pooch's character — Aureum d'Canis, the golden goddess of dogs. The dog wouldn't join them in the material plane unless they needed her.

A blurry white spot floated further down the cave. The light from his staff reflected blue light from a pair of large eyes. That was Pinga's character, Frostbite — a lesser ice demon.

Natasha-Zeta's character, Ku'namsha, was the last to appear — a burly frost elf woman with bluish-white skin, white hair, and pointed ears. Alasie spent more time on Varuna than Genesis, so Natasha-Zeta created Ku'namsha to stand in as their party's tank. She grumbled, "Stare at the obsidian all you want — it's not going to hop into your cart." She hefted a pickaxe and got to work on the stone wall.

Frost elves have cold demeanors and no use for humor, which was challenging for Natasha-Zeta to play. She was doing a better job of it recently.

"I'll keep Vixen company," Ayr said. She was referring to Elle's character — a domesticated flying reindeer. When Natasha-Zeta proposed Elle's Christmasy character choice, Oraxis was sure the genre restriction filter would reject the whimsical proposal. When the flying reindeer was allowed, he took it as further evidence that Pip-Rho was still in there — still up for tongue-in-cheek fun.

Ayr climbed out of the cave.

Tel O'Rax followed. "You won't get far without light. I'll go with you. These elves can see just fine without my spell."

Ayr didn't argue.

When they emerged from the mouth of the cave and stepped out into the barren slope of the dead volcano, Vixen huffed a happy greeting. The reindeer jumped into the air and pranced around joyfully. This seemed to brighten Ayr's spirits.

Zephyr was perched at the peak of the volcano's rim, looking down at them. He was a Roc — a legendary giant bird, practically identical to Zephyr's real-world self. As if this wasn't *on-the-nose* enough, Oraxis had named Zephyr's character *Zephyr*, and they used a large wicker gondola for travel by bird. This was a direct rip-off of his real-world enhanced giant golden eagle and the transport method it made possible. Zero points for originality, but he didn't care — he wasn't here to play games.

Flight was a popular mode of travel in CotNQ. Traveling on foot was slow, and the number of baddies encountered on the ground was many times that of the air. Teleportation had been nerfed. It was now a dangerously imprecise spell, sometimes landing you in the middle of a wall or with half your body underground. Tel O'Rax had learned that the hard way.

Tel and Ayr slid down the rocky slope to their camp. He prepared some meat-and-mushroom stew while they waited for the others. The meat was from a giant three-headed lizard they felled during their prior session. It was barely palatable, but unlike their real-world selves, their characters actually *had* to eat, or they'd starve. Hey, it was one way to get Genevieve to join him for a meal.

An hour later, Ku'namsha and Ruyn came clamoring down the loose rock of the slope leading up to the cave, wrestling with a wagon heaped with obsidian. Halfway down, it toppled, spilling its contents.

"Mother of Grel," Ku'namsha cursed. She shouted down at Tel and Ayr, "You two make yourselves useful for once and help pick up this cursed black glass."

"Sorry," Natasha-Zeta sent over their team channel, *"I'm role-playing, and Ku'namsha isn't supposed to be polite."*

"No need to apologize," Oraxis replied. *"And I trust you won't take offense when Tel insults Ku'namsha's race and intelligence."*

"Of course," Natasha-Zeta laughed.

Tel O'Rax stood and shouted back, "Alright, you bumbling elves. Stand aside and let the wizard clean up your mess."

He walked to the base of the slope and cast a selective levitation spell on the obsidian. With a wave of his staff, the scattered pieces lifted from the ground and settled back into the cart. He then levitated the cart to bring it safely down the slope.

They shared supper with the usual half-joking sparring match between Tel and the elves, then packed up camp. Vixen's saddle bags carried half of the obsidian, and the other half went into the gondola.

Tel and Ayr climbed into the gondola while Ku'namsha mounted Vixen's saddle. Ruyn would travel using Spirit Flight — an ability he gained in Pip-Rho's reboot. It allowed him to transform into a green-glowing vaporous form.

A roc carrying a gondola followed by a mounted reindeer and a luminescent green streak flying through the night sky would have been a strange sight to see, anywhere but Interra.

<hr>

AFTER AN HOUR OF FLIGHT, the party finally reached Centra City. They circled the Night Tower, then settled on the rooftop of The Players' Den — a warehouse converted into a player character commune. The few regular players who still logged into Pip-Rho's twisted gameworld agreed to pool resources and play cooperatively.

When the Telson party pulled open the door to the roof and made their way inside, the other player characters shouted warm greetings up at them from within. A crowd gathered in the common room when word spread that they had brought back a haul of obsidian.

"Back off, ye beggars!" Ku'namsha shouted at the overzealous adventurers, who'd started reaching for the sacks of obsidian. She put a hand to her sword hilt as a warning.

Tel O'Rax was more measured. He raised his hands to draw attention off of the glowering frost elf. "The resource committee will distribute the obsidian according to need. Until then, it all goes in the vault."

All except the four shards hidden in his pack — offerings reserved for the Telson party's upcoming petition to The Night Queen. Once the haul had been properly cataloged and transferred into the vault, the Telson party headed to their crude shanty, leaning against the outer wall of The Player's Den.

"Open sesame," Tel O'Rax sighed, waving a lazy hand before the door to disarm the magical traps. The door clicked and swung open. The four entered their humble one-room home and went to their respective corners to unload their packs and remove their armor.

"Are we ready to petition Queen Rho?" Ayr asked once everyone seemed settled in.

"Invoke that name at your own peril," Ruyn said. "It's The Wraith Queen now."

When Varuna is at its half-moon phase in a few Soma months, she'll switch to calling herself The Night Queen. But even though her astral projection looks like Queen Rho, you're not allowed to call her by that name.

Tel pulled the obsidian shards out of his pack and handed them out. "Yes, we're ready. Remember, the plan is to get her talking. Ask open-ended questions and keep her attention. Most importantly, don't anger her."

They gathered at one side of the shanty, allowing room for Rho's apparition to materialize, then got down on all fours. They lowered their heads.

"Ow!" Ayr shouted. "Watch your horns, Ruyn!"

"My apologies," Ruyn said with sincerity.

"Focus, we're supposed to be beseeching here," Ku'namsha said. "Counting down from three. Three, two, one."

"Wraith Queen," they chanted in unison. The obsidian cut into Tel O'Rax's hand as he squeezed it overhead. "We beseech you! Please grace these humble supplicants with your noble presence."

In seconds, the obsidian started warming up. It seemed to absorb the light from around it. A shimmering glow cast dancing shadows in the shanty. The queen was astrally projecting into the room, but they weren't allowed to look up yet.

The obsidian turned into a hot black liquid, like oil. It slipped between his fingers as The Wraith Queen accepted their offerings.

"Rise, my dear supplicants," the apparition said.

They lifted their heads and then got to their feet. The levitating form of Queen Rho looked down at them, wearing a patient smile.

Good, she was in a pleasant mood.

Ayr said, "Thank you for heeding our call, my queen."

"It's my pleasure," Queen Rho said. "Though I am disappointed Ag'nul and The Day Queen couldn't join you. Is Aureum d'Canis in your presence?"

"Yes, she is watching over us from the divine plane," Tel O'Rax said.

"Summon her," the queen commanded.

Tel and Ayr exchanged a glance.

Oraxis mindspoke on their party channel. *"This is odd. I don't even know how to get her to appear. Usually, it just happens when we need her in battle."*

Genevieve sent, *"Well, let's just try asking."*

"Aureum d'Canis," Ayr said, looking up at the patchwork of canvas and rotten planks making up the ceiling, "golden goddess of dogs, please appear before us."

A moment later, the glowing, golden light of Aureum d'Canis appeared by Ayr's side.

"See? Easy." Genevieve sent.

Queen Rho's astral projection went to a knee in the air. Aureum d'Canis stepped up toward her. Rho petted the goddess of dogs, scratching her behind the ear and smiling warmly.

"Aureum d'Canis," The Wraith Queen said, "as the goddess of dogs, do you have dominion over the wraith-pooches of the underworld?"

"Wraith-pooches?" Genevieve sent.

Oraxis marveled, *"She's using Scorpion Tail Tribe suffixes? This is interesting. But there's no way Penelope-pooch can respond — Rho doesn't have the mental connection that comes with ownership."*

The Wraith Queen was silent for a moment, looking the dog in the eye and nodding as if she could hear her talk. She said, "I see," sounding disappointed. "Well, if you could at least head down there and bark at them every now and again, that might ward them off."

Aureum d'Canis barked in reply, then disappeared again.

Ruyn asked, "My queen, what are wraith-pooches?"

"What do they sound like?!" The Wraith Queen scoffed. "Wraiths! Pooches! Hellhounds! Canis exspiravit! Ghost mutts! They're up to no good, I'm sure of it."

"Can we help?" Ku'namsha offered.

"Can you travel to the underworld?" the queen asked sarcastically.

"I... don't think so," Ku'namsha said.

"What are they up to, exactly?" Tel O'Rax asked.

The Wraith Queen sighed. "Oh, it's nothing, I'm sure. Maybe I'm just paranoid, but they're always sniffing around at the border of their plane. I don't like it. Maybe Aureum d'Canis will help. But if you're willing to spill blood in my service, you can raise an army to head off the orcs and shadow elves headed this way."

"She's talkative today," Genevieve sent.

Ku'namsha said, "Raising an army could be difficult. But maybe we can start with a reconnaissance mission. What direction are they coming from?"

Queen Rho bit her lip. She looked around, then said, "Every direction? It's impossible to tell. They're hauling war machines through the shadow plane, where distance and direction are meaningless. But the drums! Oh, those cursed drums are beating again!"

This wasn't the first time Pip-Rho had complained about drums in her head that nobody else could hear.

Tel said, "Perhaps the insectoids could help us fortify Castle Interra's defenses."

"Insectoids?!" the queen cackled. "Those vile infestors?! They're as likely to tear the castle down as they are to defend it! Why, just the other night, I... I found... oh, dammit, I'm not supposed to tell. Buggering bugs!"

The party exchanged glances.

"Your secret would be safe with us," Ayr said. "I swear on Rammah's grave."

Queen Rho squeezed her eyes shut, scrunched up her face, and balled her fists by her sides. Her chest expanded as she drew in a deep breath through flared nostrils.

The party rushed to press their hands over their ears just as The Wraith Queen let loose with a deafening shriek. The walls of the ramshackle one-room hovel rattled with its power. Ku'namsha's armor stand fell over.

"I think we upset her," Carff whistled on the party channel.

"I'll change the subject," Genevieve sent. *"Once the shriek is done."*

The apparition of Queen Rho deflated as she completed the shriek.

Ayr kneeled. "We're sorry to upset you, my queen. We haven't the tact of The Day Queen. She sends her regrets for not being able to join us today."

"Food for the carrion birds of the wastelands," Queen Rho's visage mumbled. She looked spent. "The beast-man recites their eulogy. I... take my leave of you."

Her astral projection avatar dissipated like smoke in the wind.

"Let's *see if XT-Prime can tell us what that secret was*," Oraxis sent.

"*The Astri and their secrets*," Genevieve sighed. "*Even in Interra.*"

It was true that the Astrus Faction was notorious for keeping secrets. But whatever was going on with the insectoids was a figment of Pip-Rho's fantasy world. It would be some sort of metaphor about their relationship to her. He couldn't fault her for begrudging them. They refused to destroy her massive, tumorous, Specter-cell-tainted body and resurrect her as a human for almost a hundred years.

He invited XT-Prime to their party channel.

"*Hello,*" XT-Prime sent. "*To what do I owe the pleasure?*"

Oraxis sent, "*Hi, XT, we're in CotNQ. We just chatted with Rho, and she alluded to some insectoid secret she was supposed to keep.*"

There was a brief pause before XT-Prime asked, "*What did she tell you?*"

"*Nothing useful. She says orc and shadow elf war machines are on the move in the shadow plane. When I suggested the insectoids could help shore up the castle's defenses to prepare for the upcoming battle, she acted like the idea was absurd.*"

"*Vile infestors,*" Carff offered. "*That's what she called you. Oh, and buggering bugs! That was a good one.*"

"*Carff,*" Genevieve snapped. "*Do you always have to... I'm sorry, never mind. The point is, XT, she started to say she found something but then said she wasn't supposed to talk about it. Do you know what she might've been talking about?*"

When XT-Prime's silence stretched past a few seconds, the Telson party in Interra started exchanging suspicious glances.

Finally, he sent, "*We don't know what The Wraith Queen was alluding to. Unfortunately, her physical form and biological brain have deteriorated to mere scraps. The Specter overtaking her body may have completed its task. We feel that it would be best if she were studied in a more controlled manner.*"

"*What's that supposed to mean?*" Oraxis sent.

"*It means that Interra: Curse of the Night Queen must be quaran-*

tined. Casual gamers will no longer be allowed into the construct. We're sorry, Oraxis, Genevieve, Carff, and Natasha-Zeta, but this means you, as well as Pip-Tau, Alasie, and your companion animals."

"Casual gamers?!" Oraxis scoffed. *"You think we're doing this for fun?"*

Genevieve pleaded, *"Please, XT..."*

"We're sorry."

XT-Prime has left the conversation.

Tel O'Rax grumbled, "I can't believe this," as the scene cut to black. The voice of the Worldnet spoke in slate-space.

Interra: Curse of the Night Queen gameworld construct access rescinded.

"This doesn't make sense," Genevieve cried on the party channel.

Oraxis was still reeling. *"That went sideways* way *too fast. They've never said anything about wanting to isolate Pip-Rho. Those damn Astri..."*

"Buggering bugs!" Carff exclaimed.

ORAXIS RECONNECTED to his body and sat up. What a strange turn of events.

Genevieve, Natasha-Zeta, and the three dogs roused as Oraxis got to his feet. He would've sent another conversation request to XT-Prime, but he already knew that would lead nowhere.

He paced as he pondered.

"Oh, wow," Natasha-Zeta laughed. She was still mindspeaking on their party channel for Carff's benefit. *"Everyone else got booted, too. The CotNQ player forum is raging."*

Oraxis didn't care about the other players — XT-Prime was right that they were mostly just there for fun. He could count the number of players outside the Telson party who took a serious interest in Pip-Rho's wellbeing on one hand.

Carff sent, *"I'll fill in Alasie and Pip-Tau while you guys noodle on it."*

"Thanks, Carff," Genevieve sent. They closed the group conversation.

Natasha-Zeta and Genevieve talked, but Oraxis was too busy thinking to listen.

He didn't buy the story that they suddenly wanted to study Pip-Rho in a more controlled way. This obviously had to do with the things they told XT-Prime. So, why would the Astri boot them over some secret Pip-Rho almost leaked? Surely, they don't share real-world intel with her. The only things she would know would be what they shared in character. Could they have been using her to brain-storm ideas? Maybe they thought her Specter node-net could help them solve some technical hurdle and gave her a metaphorical analog of a real-world problem. It would be much like how Interra was used to glean insights from Prisoner Lex.

No way, they weren't that reckless with their secrets. Pip-Rho's a loose cannon they'd never trust. Did she find out something they didn't want her to share?

How?

What?

Something else Rho had said came to mind — that bit about The Day Queen and Ag'nul. He loaded the transcript and read, "Food for the carrion birds of the wastelands. The beast-man recites their eulogy."

The wastelands was the site of the Fall of the Wraiths. The Telson party hadn't been there in over a year, but what they found when they visited it was a crater — the breach to the underworld, crudely sealed with rubble. But when Ag'nul and The Day Queen last logged out, they were in the shanty at Centra City.

Alasie and Pip-Tau were currently on Varuna, the ice moon,

performing experiments to try to communicate with the Specters. The defeated aliens were theorized to be either dead or dormant, deep beneath the moon's ice crust in its liquid water mantle. On the prior Zeta Day, Alasie had experienced a remarkable event when she started picking up evidence of Specter movement. A sound like dogs barking accompanied the crackling of G-wave noise.

And then there was the child's voice. "Pups! You bad pups, come back right now!"

They tried to be careful who they shared this information with, but word has a way of spreading when it's as sensational as Alasie's encounter. Many people accused her of faking the whole thing or falling prey to an Astrus ruse. She had been using their equipment, after all.

Wraith-pooches in the underworld...

A wild idea was forming.

The crater in the wastelands could easily represent Ag'nul's Heart — the caldera that formed after the teeming horde of Specters plunged into Varuna. It was Alasie's preferred landing site. How would Pip-Rho know that Alasie and Pip-Tau were there? And that bit about the beast-man reciting their eulogy could refer to Alasie's incessant poetry recitation into her transmitter.

The Wraith Queen had recently developed an *all-seeing eye,* which she used to spy on the goings-on within CotNQ. He'd assumed this was nothing more than an extension of her godlike role in her gameworld. But what if it was something more?

Could she see the Specters within Varuna and hear their barking? Could she see Alasie and Pip-Tau and hear Alasie's poetry?

What about the war drums? Or the orcs and shadow elves on the move within the shadow plane? In Interra, Jamji played a shadow elf. Those two warlike races could easily represent Guardians. Did Pip-Rho spy a secret armada?

And did she see something nefarious that the Astri were up to? When they told XT-Prime that Pip-Rho almost leaked their secret, the Astri must've decided it was too dangerous to allow players outside their faction to join, lest some busybody like Oraxis piece the mystery together.

It all made sense! The thrill of solving a mystery gave way to the dread of what it meant to the Surya system if he was right.

It could only mean one thing...

War is coming.

3

———

RISE

"*THAT'S IT, Aggie, we're heading back,*" Pip-Tau sent. "*If there really is a war brewing, the last place you wanna be is off-planet. We need to get to Syn-Cen. It's a bunker.*"

The two were close enough to see each other, but Pip-Tau never went as far down the ice crevices as Alasie. Pip-Tau was bouncing back towards their camp where they had parked their drop pod.

Alasie still didn't know what to think about the data dump Oraxis had just shared. She loved the idea that the wraith-pooches were Specters. When she had reported her prior Zeta Day encounter, everyone said she was a fraud. Or they'd say the Astri were frauds, and they duped her. Or they worked together to stage the whole thing. Even when she shared her replay of the stored experience, people said she'd set up a device ahead of time to broadcast a recording of Specter G-wave clicks and dogs barking. They said the kid's voice was evidence that she had made an amateur mistake and forgot to cut that part of the audio sample. And the black tendril that snatched up her drone? They said it was just water, darkened by sediment spewed from an underwater volcano!

It was humiliating, but she didn't care. Well, maybe she cared a little, but it wouldn't stop her from doing her work.

"*I'm staying here,*" Alasie replied. "*I know it's dangerous. It's always been dangerous! That's what aposynchronic orbs are for, right?*"

"*Dying sucks!*" Pip-Tau squeaked. "*Trust me, I've done it a lot. I'm leaving with or without you, Aggie. I'm serious.*"

It wouldn't be the first time.

Pip-Tau's nickname for her, Aggie, combined the names Ag'nul and Alasie. Ag'nul was her half-frost-elf, half-yeti character from Interra. Alasie knew that Pip-Tau thought she was too impulsive, like her berserking half-yeti, so the nickname wasn't necessarily endearing. Playing Ag'nul that way came easily, since it was how she acted when she was defending someone she loved.

Sometimes, Alasie worried that Ag'nul's beastly instincts had worked their way into her personality as she played him. Either that, or playing him awakened some primal aspect of her. But she was also a timid, bumbling girl. It was like having two different people in her head. At least both of them had the same goal — getting Zeta back.

Pip-Tau would only stay and help if Alasie could convince her that there was a logical reason for it. Alasie said, "*We don't even know if Oraxis's ideas are true. Like, scientifically, I mean. We could stay and... let's try to test it with an experiment!*"

"*An experiment?! What've we been doing up here all month? Experiments! What sort of new test are you gonna do now that you couldn't do before we got the news that Pip-Rho supposedly has some psychic remote viewing power?*"

Alasie searched the stars. They had a way of inspiring ideas. She'd chosen Ourania as her muse — the muse of astronomy. Staring at stars was the best way to develop new verses for her poems. She also liked to dream up fantastic stories of people living on other planets. She imagined sending her perspective out to get a closer look at an alien world.

Could Pip-Rho really see through space like that? What would that be like?

She sent, *"We could... yeah, I think we could test that idea! Pip-Rho's... um, she's basically a full Specter now, right?"* She hoped that wasn't still a sensitive subject.

"Her body, yes, but there's still a bit of her synth-organic brain left." Pip-Tau sounded exasperated.

"So, if she got this power after going almost full Specter, the Specters can probably do it, too. People always thought they could see long distances since they could spot uncloaked ships anywhere in the system."

"And how do you propose we test that?" Pip-Tau asked.

Alasie's ideas dried up again. She searched the stars for more. There had to be something they could do.

Pip-Tau spoke up again. *"Right, you kinda can't. Let's get outta here, Aggie. We can spend the next couple of months developing a formal hypothesis. I'll get Veer to slip us some SI cycles under the table to run sim tests. And if there is a war brewing, it'll blow over by the time we're ready for field experiments."*

It seemed pretty convenient that Pip-Tau's version of the future was one where the war *blows over* in a couple of months. The Guardians could burn the entire planet to ash. And the Astri — who knew what they were capable of? They weren't aggressive meat-heads, like the Guard, but they were *super* smart. They definitely had lots of secret weapons.

If war broke out, there'd be no escape.

"You can't talk me out of staying, Pip-Tau," Alasie sent. *"Go ahead and take the pod back. Thanks for coming out, though. It... um, it really means a lot."*

"Fine," Pip-Tau sent, *"but you know Nat's gonna kill me for leaving you behind. And you're welcome. Stay safe, Aggie."*

ALASIE RETURNED to her old standby — the multi-function receiver, transmitter, and G-wave detector. It was a red box with wide metallic tubes that stuck out and ran parallel along four edges, which could act as feet or handles. She patched her spacesuit's audio into the device, then fiddled with the knobs. She listened to it hiss and whine as she stared at the stars and thought.

What are all the powers at play here? Who could they trust?

She loved XT-Prime and the other Astri that she'd become friends with, but it was also true that they held secrets. Booting everyone out of CotNQ and giving such a weak explanation was awfully suspicious.

Obviously, you can't trust the Guard Faction. They tried to steal Cain one time. Then, they stole one of the spellsong devices, thanks to Jamji. It was their fault that Pip-Rho had gone mad from the spell-song — they put the device right next to her egg! The jerks did it on purpose!

The Proliferans? They were sort of irrelevant, since all they seemed to care about was playing games and making babies. And they can't even make babies in the Surya system because of the offworlder population cap. She heard they were building an inter-stellar gas-jet torus carrier so they could finally escape. The Specters had them trapped here for too long, and they wanted out.

And what about the Specters? For the thousandth time, she wished she could undo the spellsong and bring them back. Sure, they abducted a person here and there and made life hard for offworlders, but so what? If they hadn't picked Zeta's dad to abduct, none of this would've happened. That was why Zeta was so obsessed with them. Would the Specters still have been defeated if they'd just selected another person from that hunting party?

Probably.

The Astri still would've made a spellsong, and the Pips still would've made Interra. Something about that Astrus spellsong always bugged her. If they could implant messages into the Specters' heads — their node-nets — then why didn't they tell them to... just behave themselves?

She'd tried giving the Specters a hundred different commands over the years. The only time she got a reaction was the time she stirred Zeta's emotions with a sonnet and then talked to her, reminding her she was a human.

It didn't work well enough, though. Zeta was still gone. Down there, under the ice somewhere.

Alasie looked down at the dark blue ice below her feet. What was going on down there, anyway?

Oraxis said The Wraith Queen complained about the wraith-pooches sniffing around at the borders of the underworld. That had to mean that she saw the Specters hanging around under Varuna's crust. They were close. If Alasie transmitted, the dogs would hear her. If she could say the right thing — stir the right emotion or press the right button, she was sure she could get them to emerge.

"Be careful what you wish for," she told herself aloud. If they emerged and then went on a rampage across the system, it would be her fault.

No, they wouldn't do that. As strange as it seemed, she trusted those absolute black, amorphous boojum-blobs of dynamically addressable polysilicate, as Pip-Rho called them. At least, she trusted them more than any of the offworld factions.

If a war was coming, who would fight for Genesis? The Specters would be great protectors if she could implant a message into their node-nets to make them fight on her side.

Specter war dogs — that's what they needed!

It was time for Alasie to let the dogs out.

FOLLOWING the pattern of her prior successful Specter-rousing, Alasie started with a poem. Rifling through her double-mind's virtual binder, she selected something she thought would speak to the Specters.

She checked the switches and knobs to be sure she was transmitting audio. After some hesitation, she bit her lip and turned the output gain knob as high as it would go. *Technically,* she wasn't supposed to do that. But who was going to stop her?

Alasie cleared her throat and began. "I call this one *Mysterious Beasts.*"

What sort of strange lifeform is this?
Darkness incarnate? Swimming void?
Stygian squid from the abyss,
Unstructured, black, and ameboid?

How do they locomote,
Swiftly swimming through space?
How do they gently float,
Defying gravity with grace?

What makes them promptly decide
To strike and fling and kill
And draw a victim inside,
Taken against their will?

Can they feel love or hate
Or anything in between?
Can we ever hope to relate,
Or are they like a machine?

How can humble humankind
Aspire to appraise
An alien's theory of mind
With such peculiar ways?

And now we think we've tamed
This deadly force of nature,
And prematurely claimed
That we have slain the creature?!

The attacks have indeed ceased,
But don't be so sure they are gone,
For these are mysterious beasts,
And tomorrow brings a new dawn.

Alasie paused, stood, and picked up the multi-function device. She dangled it by a handle as she bounded down the crevice. "I wrote that a long time ago. I picked it because it's about how interesting you are and how hopeful I was... I mean, I still am — that you'd return in some glorious way.

"Hey, we learned something about you today! You can see through things and what's happening a long way away. I don't know how you do it, but I'll bet you can see me right now. And you can see Pip-Tau taking off over there."

She turned and searched the star-strewn darkness to spot Pip-Tau's blue plasma jet trail but couldn't find her.

"Well, uh, I can't see her, but I'm sure you can. And you can see the stuff the Guard is up to, can't you? You can see their cloaked ships. How many warships have they built since you stopped destroying anything bigger than a shuttle? You can also see what the Astri are up to. What are they hiding? Do they have a bunch of ships? Or drones?

"Zeta, Specters, dogs, anyone down there who's listening, I'm talking to you. This is important! A war is coming, and you're just sitting there! Who knows what's going to happen to the Genesis Faction?! We'll get caught in the middle of the whole thing. They could start bombing the planet, even killing neoprims! We need you to fight for us! Help us!"

Alasie could feel her blood pounding in her neck and face. She'd worked herself up, but couldn't stop now. She put down the transmitter, got down on all fours, and shouted at the ice.

"Wake up! Wake up and come back!" She pounded the rock-hard ice with her gloved fist as she yelled at it. "You can't let this happen! You're our only hope! You need to come back! You need to rise! Rise, Specters! I COMMAND YOU TO RISE!"

Tears fell from her eyes, pooling in the glass of her helmet. She panted, clenching her teeth, breathing in ragged breaths.

Static hissed.

Interference whined.

She knew it wouldn't work. Nothing she tried ever worked. Her sobs came on quickly, sending her rolling onto her side. Her muscles twitched uncontrollably as the adrenaline worked its way out of her system.

A minute passed as she cried, all alone on a desolate ice moon, listening to the receiver's warbling static.

Then it happened.

It started as a faint vibration felt in her gut.

Next came the clicking and crackling sounds of the G-wave detector. It was going wild — more than she'd heard during her last encounter.

Her eyes went wide. Anger had given way to defeat, which was now eclipsed by overwhelming excitement.

It worked?!

A distant dog barked in her headset as the vibration of the ice intensified. Alasie grabbed the multi-function device and engaged her plasma-jet boots. It was happening again! They were coming up through the caldera, and she'd fall in if she didn't move.

A dozen dogs barked, then a hundred, then a thousand. The G-wave detector crackle was now a solid, buzzing tone.

She shouted over the noise, "Rise! Yes, that's it!"

She needed to rise, too! Her plasma-jet boots were burning at their maximum, but she didn't know if it would get her high enough to avoid whatever was about to happen. The surface below was getting further away, giving her a better view of the event's magnitude.

The entire caldera was roiling. Geysers of water erupted into space as ice boulders tumbled and crevices writhed. A great shadow seemed to have fallen over the caldera. No, the shadow was *under* it — the black forms of Specters pooling beneath the surface.

A small part of her couldn't help but wonder whether this was a mistake. After everything everyone had gone through to get rid of the Specters, here she was, reawakening them.

She didn't have much time to contemplate the notion because the next thing she knew, a violent vibration jostled her feet. She looked down.

Both of her plasma-jet boots had stopped working!

Her heart skipped a beat.

She flinched as something struck her helmet. Her stomach dropped as she was jerked upward.

"Eject your ZETA reactor," a woman's voice commanded within her helmet, barely audible over the noise from the receiver.

The multi-function device flew from her hands. It zipped up, past her vision. She couldn't move her head to see what was going on. All she could see was Varuna's horizon before her.

"What's happening?" Alasie called out. "Who are you?"

The voice said, "I repeat, eject your ZETA reactor. You have five seconds to comply. Five, four..."

Alasie had only ever removed her ZETA reactor with help from the workers at the Jacob's Attic space station port. How did they do it?

"Three, two, one..."

"I'm trying!" she shouted. They had pressed a button under a cover and had her think a thought-command. Where was the button?

She couldn't look down — something was pulling her up by the helmet.

The sounds of the dogs barking and G-wave crackles cut off.

"Time's up," the woman said in the sudden silence. "Maybe you couldn't hear me over your radio, or maybe I should've clarified what would happen when I got to one. You're an idiot, so I'll put it simply: eject your ZETA reactor right now, or we will kill you. You have five, four, three..."

Alasie frantically felt around the sides of her ZETA reactor backpack. "Stop! I'm trying!" She felt a square on the side of the pack. She lifted it, pressed the button inside, and issued the thought-command, *"Eject ZETA reactor."*

The reactor struck the back of her boots as it fell.

Thank Harama, it worked!

A few moments later, the starscape and Varuna disappeared, being replaced with the inside of an airlock. A person in an absolute black spacesuit awaited her, holding her red multi-function device in one hand and a rifle in the other. Their face was covered in a black visor.

The airlock door closed below her feet, and she was lowered onto it. It felt like gravity was pressing her feet to the door, so they were either in a spinning ship or accelerating.

She could move her head again, so she looked around. It was just her and the other person in the airlock. Cabinets lined the walls. Typical airlock emergency equipment was latched here and there.

"Take off your helmet," the woman's voice commanded.

"No," she said. "Who are you? How did you... snatch me up like that?"

"We are the Guard Faction," the voice said, "and we used an adhesive tether."

"You *do not* have my permission to bring me aboard your vessel," Alasie said. "This is an abduction!"

"No, it's an arrest," the woman said. "We don't need your permission — you're a criminal. Now take off your helmet, or we'll remove it by force."

A criminal? Did they know she just stirred up the Specters? There's no way they could've flown all the way here from Soma Station. The ship must've been in orbit around Varuna when she started broadcasting. Well, maybe she *was* a criminal. It's not like she asked The Council of Ten for approval before she contacted the Specters.

She reached out to WorMS to open a conversation channel with Natasha-Zeta, but found that she was talking to herself in her head. Did they cut her double-mind off from the Worldnet? The Worldnet services work when you're off-planet by sending short-range tight-beam data through invisible relay satellites scattered throughout the system. The Guard Faction must've had a way to block their signals.

Which meant she couldn't call for help.

Also, it meant she wasn't syncing to her orb. If they killed her, she'd be resurrected, but she wouldn't remember anything that happened after they abducted her.

No, *arrested*.

She had no regrets.

BEFORE REMOVING HER HELMET, Alasie instinctively glanced at the external pressure indicator — one atmosphere.

She unlatched the safeties, twisted the helmet, and lifted it.

The person in the airlock handed her a black helmet.

"Put it on," said the woman's voice from overhead. She had assumed the person in the airlock was the woman who'd been talking, but now she wasn't so sure. Their frame looked like a man.

Alasie complied. As soon as she slid the helmet onto her head, it tightened around her neck. It was just tight enough to hold the helmet on without choking her. There was no visor to see through, so she was blind. She tried pulling it back off again, but it was stuck.

A green wireframe box appeared before her. She turned her head, and the box moved, staying in one place relative to her body. It reminded her of the wireframes that Jamji and Pepper-pooch had when they were invisible. Maybe it was some sort of hologram.

"Follow the arrows," the woman said inside her helmet. "Double time."

A line of green arrows appeared at ground level, leading her through the box. She raised her hands and slid her feet forward, afraid she'd hit a wall.

"I said double time!" the woman barked.

"I don't know what that means!" Alasie snapped.

"It means *go fast*, stupid!"

A blow between her shoulder blades pushed her forward, urging her into a stumbling jog. It was easy to follow the arrows projected inside the helmet's visor, but it made her nervous to run without seeing what was in front of her.

Another green box appeared, situated sideways like a door in a hall. The arrows went straight, then turned and disappeared into the box.

Alasie followed them. When she rounded the corner, the arrows stopped at a green X on the other side of the box.

She jogged to the X.

The muffled sound of a door sliding shut came from behind her.

The outline of a chair appeared at her side.

"Sit," the woman commanded.

Alasie obeyed.

She felt straps wrap around her torso, legs, and arms. Surprisingly, this didn't make her panic — it made her angry. She had been cooperative, so why would they pin her down? She was done being nice.

"State your name," the woman in her helmet commanded.

"Ag'nul," Alasie growled. It meant "nameless" in frost elvish.

"Are you as delusional as Pip-Rho, Alasie?" the woman asked.

Alasie growled, pulling as hard as she could against the restraints. If she was Ag'nul, she could've torn them off.

"What data did you broadcast to the Specters?" the woman asked.

Alasie didn't answer. An electric shock jolted her body.

She broke out into laughter. It was just like her first days in Interra! Here she was, trapped like an animal, getting zapped for misbehaving. She knew she could take it, even without shutting off her pain receptors.

"Answer the question, Alasie!" the woman shouted.

"Ack!" Alasie shouted back. That was frost elvish for "no".

A new voice spoke. This one was a man. "Alasie Herrington, you are charged with broadcasting on an illegal frequency, at an illegal amplitude. We detected your transmission from over a thousand kilometers away. This constitutes a violation of The Fourth Principle of the Genesis Faction. What's more, you did it with the aid of the Astrus Faction."

It was true — she'd used a multi-function device that the Astri gave her and had turned the output knob all the way up.

He continued, "Your actions have triggered a reaction in the alien entities known as the Specters. They appear to be surfacing within the caldera known as Ag'nul's Heart. These aliens have tormented the Surya system for over three hundred years. You colluded with the Astri to bring them back out of their dormancy. When we bring you before The Council of Ten, and they hear of what you have done, they *will* destroy your aposynchronic orb. But if you cooperate, that doesn't have to happen."

She couldn't ask WoQS what *colluded* meant since they were blocking her Worldnet access. She thought it meant working together. But all she did was use their device!

Unless...

Had the Astri been using her? Was the transmitter set up to send the things she said, or was it sending some other encoded message, like the spellsong they used on the Specters four years ago? What if they gave it to her so they wouldn't be blamed for its use?

Her defiance washed away as the gravity of the situation hit her.

She stammered, "Alright, um... I'll... answer your questions. All I was broadcasting was... mostly just me talking. And some poetry."

"Poetry?" the woman scoffed.

"Yeah," Alasie said, huffing. "And then I told them..."

Regret was bubbling up again. She squeezed her eyes and shook her head. She might as well tell the truth.

"I told them—"

She swallowed. Her mouth was *so* dry.

"I... *commanded* them... to rise."

4

DEPLOY

Hangovers were a thing of the past.

Jamji wondered if that was such a good thing. She'd seen classic movies with scenes of mornings after drunken revelries. Everyone slept half the day, then woke up with pounding headaches and no clue what had happened the night before. The girls who found themselves in a stranger's bed would take a walk of shame where they sneak out and make their way home barefoot — one high heel lost forever, the other dangling by a strap from their finger.

But you face the morning after with jarring, stone-sober clarity when your bio-enhanced body has long since purged your brain of every trace of the toxin that you worked so hard to poison it with. Not to mention being able to replay your experience later, in full fidelity, rather than losing it to a muddled mess of hazy memories.

Though the replays could be fun.

Jamji pulled her arm out from under Denver's head as carefully as possible, but still managed to wake the Squad Lieutenant with her jostling.

"Morning," Denver purred. She caught Jamji's eye with her hazel gaze. A strand of her loose brown curls fell across her olive-skinned face.

Damn, she was hot.

Maybe...

No! It was time to leave.

"Morning," Jamji said. She escaped the bed before any sparks could reignite. "Hell of a party, wasn't it?"

"Hell of a night," Denver said. She made no attempt to cover up her nakedness.

Jamji was tempted to turn invisible and run away.

Literally.

Her skin was equipped with photoreceptive nanites and image-projecting chromatites. These allowed her to project images from one side of her body to the other, relative to a million vantage points, granting her active invisibility. It was upgraded from her prior dermal systems, which could only handle tens of thousands of vantage points and couldn't compensate for infrared.

When she shut off her chromatites, she was absolute black. A non-reflective base was essential to the function of active invisibility, since reflected light can ruin the optical effect. Her default chromatite hue had been aquamarine for years, but her commanding officer ordered her to switch to gray two years ago. He called her aquamarine tone *too flashy* and said she should match her uniform. Her skin was also hardened to tolerate extreme temperatures and resist minor damage.

The result: ugly, dull gray skin with a leathery, coarse texture that nobody would call appealing.

Denver's skin, on the other hand...

She stopped herself, turning to search the floor for her light-duty fatigues. They were crumpled up in the corner. She snatched them up and started pulling them on, trying not to offend Denver by looking too rushed.

"How did it feel?" Denver asked.

"We can't do this," Jamji blurted.

Denver laughed, "Do what? I'm talking about your graduation — getting the silver bar. We're officers now, Jamji!"

Using first names was reserved for intimate partners, family, and close friends. Despite what happened last night, Squad Lieutenant Denver and Jamji were none of those things.

"It's great," Jamji said. "But still, this was a one-time thing, Denver."

"It doesn't have to be. You can call me Rhea."

"I already have a partner," Jamji said.

"Doc Geary?" Denver groaned, laughing. "You're still with that soft-palm? You're too good for a mind-jobber like that."

Mind-jobbers, or psychologists as you're supposed to call them, get no respect among soldiers, but they're as crucial to a fighting force as guns and ships. Warrior types act like they're made of stone — like they're such hard-asses that nothing can get to them. But everyone's human. Talking to someone who can help you deal with your issues is the only way to keep your head on straight.

Jamji smiled and shook her head, pulling on a boot. "I'd say it's the other way around. Trey's sweet, smart, handsome. *So* level-headed. I don't deserve him. Not even close."

Denver sighed, "Alright, I can respect that. I won't tell him about this. Just keep me in mind the next time you're drunk and horny."

Jamji laughed half-heartedly.

She'd confess to Trey. It would suck. He'd be upset, but he wouldn't raise his voice. He'd understand and forgive like he always did when she did something shitty.

What the *hell* did he see in her, anyway?

She stood, straightening her fatigues.

Denver extended a bare foot to hook around the inside of Jamji's knee and keep her from leaving. She said, "Hey, I know you don't have anywhere to be. Take those off and have one last romp. You've already cheated, so what's the difference?"

Jamji looked down at Denver's eyes... her body. She had a good point...

A klaxon blared in the cramped quarters, making them both flinch.

Denver cursed, clamoring out of the bed. "Drills the day after graduation?!"

There is a God.

"It's been a pleasure, Squad Lieutenant Denver," Jamji said, giving the naked woman an ironically formal salute. She was thankful the klaxon had stopped her from doing something regrettable. Again.

"The pleasure was mine, Squad Lieutenant Telson." Denver returned Jamji's salute with a wink, then resumed her frantic scramble to find her fatigues.

* * *

JAMJI STOOD at attention in the crowded hangar. A dozen bulky transport ships hung overhead, suspended from the ceiling by massive cables like beetles caught in spider webs. This freed up the floor for the Surya System First Regiment.

Shouts and footfalls echoed off the gray stone walls. Soldiers were still funneling into the cavernous room, making mad dashes to their rally points and falling in line, but Jamji's squad, JP-143, was in position.

Pepper-pooch sat by her side as still as a statue. He was a monstrous, rhinoceros-sized war dog that filled her heart with joy.

"Are you ready to play and fight?" She sent Pepper-pooch.

"I am ready, but I am sitting still!" Her dog replied, courtesy of anthropolinguistic algorithms that translated between human speech and simplistic dog thoughts. She knew the algorithms weren't perfect, but their communication was genuine for simple messages like this one.

Many other war beasts accompanied their masters throughout the hangar. The Guard had learned long ago that as awesome as robots, drones, and other technological wonders were, it was still hard to beat biology and evolution. You're better off tweaking a few genes to create huge war dogs than designing robo-dogs from the ground up. Only the biology-shunning Astri didn't make use of enhanced animals.

Jamji's team stood in two rows of three behind her and Pepper-pooch. She'd never met these soldiers and still hadn't been introduced to any of them. Typically, squad lieutenants were introduced to their squad the week after graduation. The team would have a month to train together and get to know each other before heading out on assignment.

Not that she minded being thrown in head-first. Jamji was flexible. That was one of the things that made her a good leader.

As they waited for the First Regiment to gather, Jamji reviewed her squad's profiles on her internal HUD. They comprised three women and three men, all born into the Prolifera Faction on Gaia and transferred to the Guard Faction when they were in their thirties or forties. Their only roles had been technicians, tech testers, and then soldiers. They shared the rank of Private First Class and had modest decorations. There were more than a few disciplinary actions on file for each of them.

Remarkably, the team had served together for over a hundred years. They arrived in the Surya system in the same interstellar gas-jet torus carrier before the Specters started destroying any carrier that dared to enter the system. The list of their prior Squad Lieutenants was too long to read. It looked like they rotated through a new lieutenant every year.

The squad code, JP-143, indicated they were the 143rd jet pack squad specializing in personal flight devices. Plasma jet boots had supplanted jet packs hundreds of years ago, but some names never die.

Their nickname: The Cherry Poppers. It was misogynistic, adolescent crap like that which set soldiers and officers apart. They even had custom arm patches — a pair of bing cherries wearing sunglasses.

Cute.

She knew exactly why this squad was assigned to her. As a new officer, she needed real-world command experience. It was common to assign well-established, self-sufficient squads to new lieutenants. This squad had been through so many lieutenants that it was a part of their identity — they broke in new commanders. *Cherry Poppers*, indeed. They'd treat her as disrespectfully as she let them get away with. They'd play mind games and try to make her crack under pressure.

Good luck with that, assholes.

Undoubtedly, they were checking out her profile right now, exchanging raunchy jokes about her via aud-link. As soon as they started talking, the hazing would begin.

Jamji tapped her photoreceptites, switching her vision input from her eyes to the back of her head. This ability was one of the many features of her active invisibility dermal systems. The squad was behaving themselves so far. They stood at perfect attention — eyes forward, faces set in stern preparedness.

The voice of Station Captain Chin resounded in the chamber. "Eyes on me, soldiers. Yes, up here. No, this is not a drill."

Jamji reconnected to her eyes. A control room was set high in the wall at the other end of the hangar. Chin was standing in the room on the other side of a window. Jamji used enhanced optics to zoom in, getting a good look at the short, powerful woman. As her name implied, she had physical traits that would have been called Asian back on Earth.

Station Captain Chin said, "The Specters are on the move at Varuna. A Genesisian broadcast a command using Astrus tech, which the aliens responded to by breaking out of the caldera. We hold the Astrus Faction responsible and have reason to believe that they have reprogrammed the Specters for use as weapons. Initial encounter reports state that the Specters are behaving differently than they did prior to their retreat. More aggressive. More coor-dinated.

"Soldiers, it is our duty to secure the Surya system, to protect the

Genesis Faction, and to neutralize the dual threats of the Specters and the Astri. To that end, the Genesis System Weapons Ban will be temporarily suspended during the coming maneuvers. At long last, the Guard will bring its full capabilities to bear against the Specters."

As professional as the Guardian soldiers were, there were still a few gasps and murmurs following this announcement. This would be the first actual combat that most of them had ever seen and their first shot at fighting Specters without both arms tied behind their back by that ridiculous ban. Time to dust off the antimatter shells, yottawatt pulse laser arrays, and wide-angle maser blasters. Jamji used the photoreceptites on the back of her head to make sure her squad wasn't shifting or making noise.

Nope — they stayed at rigid attention. Not bad.

Chin continued, "Fleet Captain Smith is rallying our battle vessels, preparing to engage the enemy. They will escort your transports to Genesis. Your first duties will include establishing ground-based defenses and escorting the Noddites to safety. This will be a complex and evolving engagement. Pay attention to your feed and report *everything* to your commanding officer. Officers — you will submit succinct, frequent updates to CIS. Focus on your objectives, and be prepared for sudden changes in direction. Hesitation is defeat."

The words of Sun Tzu came to mind: *A good fighter is terrible in his onset and prompt in his decision.*

Station Captain Chin raised her voice for the first time that Jamji could remember. "Guardians, this is what you trained for! This is your purpose! Are you ready?!"

Jamji filled her lungs, then shouted, "Yes, sir!"

At the same time, she gave Pepper-pooch the thought-command to let loose with a pair of barks.

They were joined by thousands of other "Yes, sir!" shouts, filling the hangar with an explosion of sound. The feeling of being part of something larger and more powerful than herself filled Jamji with pride.

Station Captain Chin concluded, "Surya System First Regiment... deploy!"

Controlled chaos.

That was the only way Jamji could describe the next thirty minutes. Soma Station's halls were packed with soldiers bounding at double time. Jamji's squad went to their equipment room to gear up, while Pepper-pooch was sent to the bestiary to do the same. A set of seven Specter containment devices awaited them in their equipment room.

Jamji smiled at the familiar contraption. It was nearly identical to the one she'd used to trap the Specter at Varuna — a forty-five-centimeter long triangular tube with a pistol grip in the middle. The devices came with quick-release holsters, which they buckled to their outer thighs.

CIS — Central Intelligence and Strategy — must've anticipated that the Specter menace wasn't as resolved as it had appeared to be and commissioned the mass manufacture of containment devices. Jamji was proud to have been the device's first and only successful field tester. She had deployed it effortlessly and ensnared a Specter. Things were going great until that stuttering fool Alasie charged in and blew her ZETA reactor.

As her squad hopped out of the equipment room, armed to the gills and itching for action, Jamji got a GuardNet aud-link request.

Audio P2P request from Squad Lieutenant Denver.

She accepted. Returning to the hangar would take a few minutes, so she had time to chat.

"This is wild," Denver sent.

"Time to sink or swim," Jamji replied.

"What's your squad like?"

"They call themselves 'The Cherry Poppers'. Gross, right? I can't wait for the hazing to start."

"*Mine's already started,*" Denver sent. "*They tried to get me to carry all the energy cells. Said their last lieutenant was a big guy, and they'd grown accustomed to him carrying gear for them. Said they'd burn too many calories lugging equipment, and the only way they'd be at the top of their game was if I carried more than my share.*"

Another Sun Tzu quote came to mind. *When your officers are too strong, and your soldiers are too weak, the result is collapse.*

Jamji asked, "*Did you play along?*"

"*I shut that shit down!*" Denver laughed. "*Don't give 'em a centimeter, Telson.*"

"*You know I won't,*" she sent. "*Alright, gotta go. Give those aliens and hive-mind half-humans hell.*"

They closed the channel.

Soon, she was back at the hangar and reunited with Pepper-Pooch. Her war dog was wearing his massive ZETA reactor, plasma jet boots, and an armament of previously banned heavy weapons. Jamji directed him into their assigned transport's beast bay while she and her team found their seat in the troop decks.

JP-143 followed their HUD guides to their crash chairs — green arrows overlaying the real world, giving directions a child could follow. The transport lurched as they strapped into their five-point harnesses. It was maneuvering into the mag-launch tube.

"Launch time," said Private First Class Herman Tosh. "Pucker up, or you'll shit yourself, Lieutenant."

There it was — she had been waiting for one of them to step out of line.

"Thank you for the advice, private," Jamji said. "But keep the chatter down. If you want to talk, use the squad aud-link channel." He was sitting behind her, so she tapped into her rear-facing photoreceptites to watch his reaction.

"Oh? Yes, sir!" Tosh half-laughed.

"It wasn't a joke, soldier."

Tosh crossed his eyes, screwed up his face, and gave a silent, limp salute, which he thought she couldn't see. Private First Class Israel Mazzou was sitting next to him. He shook his head and gave Tosh a hard nudge with his elbow, though he was grinning.

"Work on that salute, private," Jamji said.

Tosh dropped his hand, gaping at her. The other three squad mates in his row laughed heartily at his reaction.

She stifled a smile. Yep, she was a squad clown's worst nightmare — a commander with eyes in the back of her head. Literally.

The transport's white interior lights went out. Jamji instinctively switched to IR vision. An overhead speaker came to life. "Faces forward and heads back, soldiers. Transport launch in three... two... one..."

An elephant sat on her chest. It wasn't Jamji's first launch, but it was the fastest. Her bio-enhanced body could take the G-forces, and she'd remain conscious if she relaxed and let her body's systems compensate for the acceleration. That was something she'd learned since joining the Guard — you usually do more harm than good when you take manual control of your bioenhancements.

She counted three minutes and forty-one seconds before the acceleration abated, reducing to zero G. Their transport's ETA to Genesis counted down in her HUD — two hours, forty-seven minutes, fifteen seconds.

Man, they were going fast!

Jamji opened their squad's aud-link channel. She sent, *"Alright, JP-143, we need to make the most of our travel time. Have any of you been trained in the use of the Specter containment device?"*

"Yes, sir," Mazzou sent. *"We all had the same training: a week of sims two years ago, an all-day refresher last year, and a few hours of field training two weeks ago."*

Interesting. Had the devices just finished being manufactured? The timing was uncanny.

"*Good,*" Jamji sent. "*Did they show you the replay of my successful capture?*"

"*They did,*" Private First Class Patricia Trapper sent. "*But mainly to point out your flaws. You should've reached the Specter four seconds sooner and deployed the containment matrix one point six seconds faster.*"

Jamji resisted the urge to snap back a heated response.

Trapper continued, "*You also failed to stay aware of the battlefield situation. You should've spotted the Genesisian who took you out before they were close enough to self-destruct.*"

Private First Class Zigfried Kelso's gravely voice sent, "*I'da blasted all the Genesissies soon as the Specter showed.*"

Chief Warrant Officer Haley had already lectured Jamji on her mistakes after her resurrection four years ago. They'd run through simulated recreations of the event to drive the point home. Sure, she wasn't perfect. You never get better if you don't learn from your mistakes. It shouldn't bother Jamji that they used her as an example of what *not* to do.

But it did.

Screw them! Hindsight's 20/20, assholes. It's easy to judge when you're watching a frame-by-frame replay. Try executing the perfect deployment maneuver in the real world when your sis-kin just dropped a bomb on you.

Zeta had her orb.

Now the fool girl was gone for good — True Death.

Jamji tried hard not to blame herself for that. Zeta knew what she was doing. But if Jamji had executed a clean headshot after Zeta's announcement, followed by a deftly targeted explosion to knock her body out of the area, the Specter surge wouldn't have swept her up. They could've recovered her orb from her body and returned it to Syn-Cen.

Trey helped her work through a lot of that regret, but it still bubbled up sometimes.

She stopped herself from drifting further into thought. Private

First Class Penny Bates was saying something in Jamji's defense. Bates seemed to be the squad's peacekeeper.

"It's okay, Bates," Jamji sent, "*I appreciate the criticism. That's how we get better. So, the first time I see one of you men engage a Specter, you have no excuse — I wanna see you execute a perfect matrix deployment.*"

"*Yes, sir,*" the squad sent in unison.

Pride filled her heart. Maybe The Cherry Poppers weren't so bad.

5

RETURN OF THE SPECTERS

"This is Pip-Tau Telson, reporting from Varuna!" Pip-Tau shouted. Her open, faction-wide broadcast was only being watched by a few hundred people. It didn't matter — she needed to get this news out. More people would join when word-of-mouth spread.

"You are witnessing the return of the Specters! Ag'nul's Heart is bursting with black streaks — aliens breaking free of their icy catacomb! Oh-my-god, are you seeing this?! I can't believe it!"

Her video feed came from the omnidirectional camera on the drop pod's nose cone. She had it zoomed in on the caldera, watching the ice crumble and churn. Jets of water shot hundreds of meters into the air. She zoomed out, getting a wider angle.

Flashes of light in orbit high above Varuna caught her attention. She zoomed further out, spotting a swarm of figures darting around. Sparkles were going off in multiple clusters overhead.

"I don't know what I'm seeing here," she said. She zoomed in on the swarming figures. Were those...

"Oh, my stars and garters, it's *drones!*" she squealed. "I've never seen anything like this outside of a construct! That's a swarm of Astrus drones fighting something! Wait, look!" She zoomed in further and locked the camera on a patch of space with a gash in it. "Damaged active invisibility panels! They're attacking a ship! Damn, they're fast! This may be the first confirmed sighting our faction has ever had of Astrus fighter drones engaged in real-world combat!"

The ship was fighting back. Streaks of blue plasma marked missile launches. Drones popped by the second.

A slashing flash of light cut across space, exposing more of the underlying ship. They were carving away at its active invisibility panels. In less than a minute, the entire ship was visible.

"That's a big bird they're picking on," Pip-Tau said. "It can only be a Guardian battleship. Who knew battleships were hanging out around Varuna, anyway? Or Astrus drone carriers, for that matter?!"

Incoming conversation request from Oraxis Telson.

Ugh, there's no time for a conversation! She declined the request, sending the message, *"Hey, O-Pa, tune into my broadcast! It's getting real at Varuna! If you need to say something, send a written message."*

Her viewer count was climbing by the second. She was up to two thousand now. Not bad, since there were only like a hundred thousand Noddites.

She zoomed out from the embattled ship and found another cluster of activity to focus on. The rotating form of a split ship revealed its interior. Blue jets darted in space nearby. It looked like people in spacesuits.

A glowing gray sphere appeared at the corner of the viewing frame. She zoomed out to spy the perfect sphere made up of a matrix of lines.

Pip-Tau squealed, "Do you see that?! I know exactly what that is! That's a Specter containment device, like Jamji used! The Guard Faction is fighting the Specters and the Astri!"

Oraxis's written message arrived in her queue. She gave it a quick read.

I think this proves that Pip-Rho was seeing cloaked battleships and drone carriers and that the wraith-pooches represented the Specters, itching to return. XT-Prime won't talk. The Guard won't patch us through to Jamji. WorMS says Alasie's inaccessible. Is she with you? Natasha-Zeta is worried sick, and Genevieve is inconsolable. We're scared, Tau. You need to get to safety.

She sent a brief reply.

Sorry, Alasie's not with me. She wanted to stay behind. I'm trying to get the hell out of Dodge, but this pod can only go so fast. Stay tuned!

Pip-Tau returned to watching the video. She zoomed in on the gray sphere where the Guardians had apparently captured a Specter. The form inside the sphere was glowing with a white-hot light.

She broadcast, "Are they nuking it? Can they kill Specters now?"

The video feed cut out.

"Crap! Video's out!" Alarms blared within the pod. "Oh, and my engines, too! Wonderful, an EMP must've hit me or something. Hang on, folks, I've got to work on these engines, or you'll be naming a new crater on Varuna after me."

Her double-mind was previously linked to the pod's systems, but that seemed to have cut out. She reverted to manual controls. Touching the interface pad brought up a schematic of the pod. Its engines were flashing red. She tapped them. No effect. She pressed and held the full system cycle button.

"When in doubt, reboot!" she reminded her viewers.

The pod's systems shut down. Seconds ticked by. The screen remained dark. The view outside the pod window was spinning slowly.

"Okay, what did I do wrong?" she asked her viewers with a

nervous laugh. Varuna was two and a half light seconds from Genesis, so it'd take at least five seconds for anyone's helpful response to reach her.

She tried to watch her comment stream, but... it was... gone? What the hell? Her double-mind connection to the Worldnet was severed! What on Genesis?! The Guard or Astrus Faction must be taking out tightbeam relays.

A loud thump resonated in the pod's hull. Pip-Tau slammed against the rear hull wall and bounced off the pod door. The pod lurched again, pressing her against the back wall as if being accelerated sideways.

The doors to the pod erupted outward. The star-speckled space outside the pod was interrupted by a rectangle — a floating room suspended a stone's throw away. She was looking into the airlock of an invisible ship.

Two tether lines led from the ship to the top and bottom of her drop pod. Maybe they were rescuing her. Maybe they were taking her hostage. Whatever the case, her pod was dead, so they were her only ticket out of here. She pulled herself up and stood on the back wall with her head poking out of the doors.

Something struck her helmet.

The drop pod fell from beneath her feet. She was being pulled by the head. Jerks!

A woman spoke in her helmet. "Eject your ZETA reactor, or we'll kill you. You have five seconds to comply."

That had to be the Guard.

"Oh, yay! Guardian assholes are here to save-slash-kill me!" Pip-Tau shouted. She reached around to the ZETA reactor's side, pressed the release button, and issued the thought-command.

Within a minute, they'd reeled her in and shoved her head into a black prisoner helmet. They escorted her to a holding cell using a cute little green arrow guidance system. Resistance was futile — this was the Guard.

She noted the ship was accelerating at a steady one-G. She wondered where they were heading.

Once she was properly restrained, they questioned her.

"State your name," the woman commanded.

Pip-Tau shook her head. "I ain't sayin' nuthin' til my lawyer gets here. I know my rights, *copper!* I want my phone call!"

"Do you think this is a game, Pip-Tau?"

Pip-Tau glowered in silence.

"What were you doing on Varuna?" the woman asked.

"Watching you and the Specters and the Astri fight it out. Who started it, anyways?"

"Before that!" the woman barked.

"Studying the caldera," Pip-Tau said, flippantly. "Did you know the Specters were coming back?"

An electric shock jolted her body.

"Whoa!" she squeaked, half-laughing. "Electric torture is against the Genesis Protectorate Treaty, you *witch!* Keep that up, and I'll report you to The Council of Ten! I'm a personal acquaintance of Eld of Elds Veer Gladstone! They'll toss your orbs in a blender for this!"

"Pip-Tau-Upsilon Telson," a man said, "you are charged with waking the Specters from their dormancy and releasing them upon the Surya system. You are charged with colluding with the Astrus Faction to use the Specters as weapons. If anybody's orb is going to be destroyed, it will be yours."

Pip-Tau mentally prepared her rebuttal, but stopped herself before she said something regrettable. It dawned on her that Alasie must've been the one to wake the Specters up. They think the Astri are involved, so they knew it was Astrus tech Alasie was using to send transmissions. Had they arrested her, too?

A plan snapped into place.

"Okay," Pip-Tau sighed. "You got me. Yes, we're pawns for the

Astri. But we *had* to do it! They said they'd kill our families and destroy our orbs if we didn't cooperate! I can help you, but I can't do it alone."

She paused to see if they'd take the bait.

"How can you help us?" the woman asked.

"We can tell them to back down! To go back home! Alasie's the only one who knows the secret command phrases implanted in the Specters by the Astri. I'm just her tech support. The last time I saw her, she was camped out on Ag'nul's Heart — the caldera. I was heading up to orbit to get bird's-eye shots of the caldera when it all went to hell. I lost communication—"

"We have her," the woman said. "She already said she doesn't know how to undo what she did."

Pip-Tau gave an exasperated sigh. "That's because she's afraid for the safety of our families, you high-density meathead! If you promise the Guard will protect the Telsons and Natasha-Zeta Herrington from whatever the Astri plan to do to them, I can get her to cooperate."

"We can do that. The Guard Faction will ensure your family's safety if you'll get her to call off the Specters. Follow the green arrows."

They led Pip-Tau out of her interrogation room, down a couple of twists and turns, and into another green rectangle. Once she sat, they strapped her down again.

Pip-Tau said, "You know, if we're going to help you, you could at least treat us with a bit of dignity."

The straps released. The visor on her helmet lifted, revealing a small room. Men in armored spacesuits stood in every corner. Alasie's multi-function device was sitting against a wall to the side of the room.

Alasie sat across from her. She also wore a prisoner helmet. Her visor was lifting. The straps over her arms, legs, and torso flipped away and disappeared into her chair. She lifted her arms and rubbed her wrists, then noticed Pip-Tau.

"Tau?! You're here?!" she huff-laughed.

The two stood and embraced.

"I was so scared," Alasie said. "Can you reach the Worldnet? Do you know what they think we did?"

"It's okay," Pip-Tau said. She reached up and grabbed Alasie's helmet, looking her squarely in the eye, imbuing as much meaning into her gaze as she could muster. "It's all going to be okay. The Guard is going to protect our families. You don't have to be afraid of the Astri anymore, okay? All they want you to do is give the Specters the command to retreat back into Varuna. Do you remember your code phrases for that?"

Alasie was never very quick on her feet. She gave Pip-Tau a questioning look.

Pip-Tau grabbed her by the shoulders. "Trust me, Alasie. You have to trust me, okay?"

"Okay..." Alasie said, questioningly

"They're going to turn the multi-function device back on. Then, you need to follow the procedure. First, you recite the *cipher poem*. Then, you tell them to go back to their lair. Do that, and the Guard will protect our families from anything the Astri might try to do."

Alasie sat for a few seconds, biting her lip.

Damn, she wished she could mindspeak to her right now!

It was a long shot, but she figured if they could broadcast a long enough message from the transmitter, the Astri could triangulate their position and save them. Or, worst-case scenario, the signal would attract the Specters, which would come and smash the ship to pieces. Death by Specter couldn't be much worse than being a Guardian prisoner, right?

"Okay, um... I'll do it," Alasie said. She looked around at the guards. "Can I turn on the transmitter?"

"Yes," the woman's voice said from an unseen place, full of frustration. "Turn it on and issue the command to make the Specters back down."

Alasie picked up the multi-function device, flipped a switch, then shook her head. "I can't... I mean, I need my helmet. The headset it's paired with is built into it."

"Mine, too!" Pip-Tau exclaimed. "I have to tune in, too. Like, in case she needs help adjusting the tuning knobs. It relies on a really sensitive resonance pattern, so it won't work while we're accelerating. Variable Doppler shifting, interference patterns, stuff like that. So, can you shut off the engines while we transmit?"

Their helmets were begrudgingly returned, and the black prisoner helmets were removed. She hated having that contraption on her head. Hell, it probably had a decapitation feature.

As they clicked their helmets back into place, they began to float. Excellent, the Guard cut the engines!

Suckers.

The transmitter would work just as well under acceleration as in freefall. She had asked them to cut the engines since the Astri would have an easier time triangulating their position if they stayed on a constant trajectory.

"Okay, I'm connected," Alasie said, grinning slightly. That Gravan-cursed multi-function device was her favorite thing in the world. "Um, this'll sound weird. It's like Pip-Tau said — I, um, it's like... I have a secret code I have to say before I give them a command. It sounds like a poem — free verse, and it's kind of nonsense, you know? Sorta like the spellsong in Interra, if you remember that."

"Yes, just hurry," the woman said.

Alasie checked the dials, cleared her throat, closed her eyes, and recited.

I am as the servant,
Brilliant mind afflicted,
Willful soul crushed,
Guile, his only voice.

Pip-Tau's eyes widened briefly before she caught herself and regained her composure. *She had expected Alasie to dredge up one of her old favorites. It didn't matter what poem she used — the point was to give the Astri a signal to aim for. So what does Aggie do? She comes out swinging with this blatant Prisoner Lex reference!*

Lex, as everyone knows, is the six-headed synth-god that emerged from the remains of Googolplex, the synthetic intelligence which imposed itself as supreme dictator over humanity way back in Earth year 2150. After controlling the world for thirty years, the SI finally felt a pang of remorse and self-destructed using the Intelligence Governor virus, or IG. The IG thwarted Lex's ability to control humanity, but many believed he was still trying to exert his influence covertly. The Pips had hypothesized that Prisoner Lex would make his wishes known using metaphorical obfuscation.

You know, like, the whole point of Interra?

So, Alasie's first verse said that just like Lex's "brilliant mind" was "afflicted" by the IG, she couldn't speak openly about her wishes. "Guile, his only voice" meant she was also using guile and that her poem should be interpreted as a metaphor for her situation.

Alasie continued,

I am as the nameless one
When the woman of the woods
First laid her hazel eyes
Upon his caged soul.

A bit on-the-nose there, sis. Be careful!

Anyone who knew anything about Interra lore knew that "the nameless one" was a reference to Ag'nul. He was Alasie's half-frost-elf/half-yeti character from Interra, whose name meant "nameless". The "woman of the woods" refers to Zeta's character, Za'antha, who first met Ag'nul when he was locked in a cage.

So, yeah, Alasie was saying she was a captive. There's no way the

Guardians don't know what she was trying to do. Pip-Tau eyed the guards, who stood at placid attention.

Seriously?! They weren't going to stop her?

How I long to soar free
And pet the dogs
And meet the child
And feel your dark embrace.

Jumpin' Jehosaphat, Aggie! She wasn't calling out to the Astri — she was trying to reach the Specters! The dogs? The child? That's what she heard back when she first made contact with them. Your dark embrace?! The fool girl was calling out for an abduction!

Take me now, my love
Or take me never!
Take me now, my love
Or soon, I may die!

Pip-Tau couldn't stifle the groan that escaped her. This was it. They were dead. Now Alasie was pleading for Zeta to take her. She knew an emotional appeal was necessary since that's how she got them to appear on the last Zeta Day.

If there was anything left of Zeta's mind, she would've understood Alasie's message loud and clear. Pip-Tau imagined a thousand Specters swirling around the ship, preparing to strike.

Now, it was just a matter of who killed them first — the Guard or the Specters.

"Is that all?" the woman asked.

Are you serious?! Did they hear a word Alasie said? How in the Surya system could they have missed that blatant cry for help?!

"Oh," Alasie huff-laughed. "Okay, now I'll give my command. Okay, here goes." She cleared her throat. "If you heard me, then... you know what you have to do. Please! Do it now! Save me, Zeta!"

Pip-Tau had to laugh, or she'd cry. Goodbye, cruel world!

"That's the command?!" the woman shouted. "Tell them to retreat! Stand down! Go back to sleep! You're trying to get them to rescue you!"

The guards finally snapped into action. They pulled the rifles off their shoulders and pointed them at Pip-Tau and Alasie.

A red light started flashing in the corner of the room, accompanied by a chirping alarm — the universal "impact pending" warning signal. They were about to get hit by something. Pip-Tau hoped it was an Astrus drone attack but knew in her gut that it was a Specter.

The chirping and flashing increased in frequency, meaning the impactor was closing in.

"Seal your helmet!" Pip-Tau shouted at Alasie, slapping her visor down over her face.

The ceiling rushed down at her. Her head struck first, then her body. The room rotated. Three of the four soldiers escaped out the door, blue plasma spiraling in their wake. The fourth held a wall handle and pointed a pulse rifle at Pip-Tau.

Alasie soared across the room, grabbing the soldier by the arm. A primal roar came over Pip-Tau's headset. The girl had gone feral. Threaten one of Aggie's loved ones, and she'll unleash the beast.

The floor rushed toward Pip-Tau's face. She raised her hands just before smashing into it.

The room's lights went out. She turned to find that the ceiling was half-gone. Debris-riddled space was visible through the hole.

Another violent shift sent her sliding to the wall. She caught a glimpse of Alasie and the soldier, still wrestling.

They had to get out of this ship! It was like being a bug in a jar, getting shaken by some snot-nosed kid.

But if they turned their backs on that soldier, he'd zap them. Pips aren't known for their strength — her chromosomal abnormality stunted her growth and kept her from putting on much muscle. Despite her worthlessness in hand-to-hand combat, she kicked off the wall to help Alasie.

Just before reaching the grappling duo, her vision went black.

She felt herself accelerating backward, then sideways, then face-first. Freezing liquid penetrated her suit. Her helmet cracked and split off of her head. The liquid engulfed her face, invading her mouth and then pushing down her throat and into her lungs. Gagging, struggling to cough, unable to breathe, Pip-Tau grasped fruitlessly at her throat.

If she's said it once, she's said it a thousand times: dying *sucks*.

WELL, so much for Pip-Tau-Upsilon! Maybe Pip-Tau-Phi will have better luck staying alive.

Crap, she might not even get to die! They could do to her what they did to Pip-Rho! Her nanites were going to fight off the Specter consumption, and she'd turn into a tumor monster!

Trying to scream only made her gag more, but she couldn't help it. How long would it take them to start eating through her skin? It didn't even hurt much. Shouldn't it hurt? She swore she'd been inside the Specter for half an hour, but terror made every moment feel like an eternity.

She noticed it wasn't as cold as it had been at first. Maybe her nerve endings were already dead. The liquid around her body felt like it was approaching a tolerable temperature. The sounds of gurgling, swooshing water filled her ears.

The Specter crushed her torso, forcing fluid out through her nose and mouth. It released, and fluid rushed back down into her lungs again. It squeezed her a second time, then a third. A fresh wave of horror washed over her as she realized that she was being forced to breathe its liquid death.

The face-first acceleration returned. She almost blacked out.

They were headed somewhere, *fast*.

Her abductor gave her another squeeze, another release. Pip-Tau choked again, then cursed herself for forgetting that she didn't have to suffer through this. She performed a bio-override to shut off her gag reflex. There was no point in torturing herself while she died.

Still, she wasn't dead yet. She didn't even feel like she was suffocating now that she wasn't gagging anymore. Her nerves were calming down enough for her to assess her situation with a clear head.

She used her double-mind to query her blood oxygen level.

Ninety-five percent.

Wow, that's pretty much normal. Spacefarers have used oxygenated chemical solutions for ages to breathe liquid. Ultra-high-G fighter pilot cockpits are routinely filled with fluid or gel, and they wear liquid-breathing apparatuses to push the fluid in and out of their lungs. Was that what the Specter was doing to her? Squeezing and releasing her like a human accordion, forcing an oxygenated solution into her lungs?

Multiple incoming conversation requests hit her double-mind all at once.

The Worldnet's back!

Before taking any of her calls, Pip-Tau reopened her faction-wide broadcast. She mindspoke, *"This is Pip-Tau Telson, coming to you from INSIDE A SPECTER! Yes, you heard me — I AM INSIDE A SPECTER! The Guard arrested me and Alasie Herrington. They blocked us from the Worldnet and accused us of conspiring with the Astri to use the Specters as weapons. Then the Specters attacked their ship! I got abducted, but it's not killing me! I think it's having me breathe an oxygenated solution. Don't ask how any of this is possible because it's UNREAL!"*

One of her conversation requests was from Alasie. She accepted.

"Aggie, you okay?!"

"Yeah! I got abducted. It doesn't hurt or anything."

"I don't think they're gonna kill us. Is it making you breathe liquid?"

Alasie hesitated, *"Yeah. It feels weird. I thought I was drowning, but—"*

"It's helping you breathe! This is nothing like the abductions from before the Specters retreated into Varuna. I'm gonna scan the news feed and do another broadcast. Keep in touch. Oh, hey! Reach out to O-pa, Gen-ma, and Nat! Tell them everything. We weren't synching to our orbs when we were on the Guardian ship, so someone has to hear the dirty deets in case we're killed before we get the chance."

They closed the channel.

Pip-Tau ran a news synthesis routine. Nobody knew what the Specters were doing, but the Guardians and Astri were fighting everywhere — Varuna, Soma, and Genesis. People speculated that The Council of Ten was holding an emergency meeting, because they'd all gone silent. There wasn't even a comment from EoE Veer Gladstone yet.

All-out war in the Surya System?!

Pip-Tau never thought she'd see the day.

6

____

SUCCUMB

THE THRONE ROOM shuddered with another impact. The Wraith Queen curled up on her throne, clutching her chains and wailing. She was a withered husk of a once-great ruler. Fear and confusion, pain and rage were all that was left of her now.

A true queen would've rallied an army to stand behind her. She'd inspire the troops with her bravery and beauty. A true queen would *fight*.

A screech escaped the gash in her face, which served as a mouth. There was nobody to hear it. Her subjects had abandoned her, teleporting away all at once. Even the cursed bugs were leaving.

The Wraith Queen watched the insectoids scramble in every direction — flying across the lands, burrowing into the ground, doing whatever it took to survive. A great many of them were charging into battle, engaging the Orcs and Dark Elves.

They didn't stand a chance.

Orcish catapults were outside the walls. They lobbed flaming balls of wood saturated in oil. They exploded against the walls and towers, sending embers tumbling across the rooftops of her precious, decrepit city. Fires started among the rotten timbers of the storehouses and in the empty stables. Soon, flames would consume the once-marvelous Centra City, leaving nothing behind but ash and rock.

Wagon trains loaded with orc shock troops were approaching from just over the foothills. She'd be overrun with them in an hour or less.

She sent her all-seeing eye across the lands, searching for some glimmer of hope. What she found was nothing but trouble — the wastelands were crawling with wraith-pooches!

Another enraged screech erupted from her. What were they doing?! They were banished to the underworld! They must stay away from the material plane!

The wraiths went scattering across the lands faster than any creature should be able to travel. They engaged in battles with the orcs and shadow elves. At first, she thought they were avoiding the insectoids, but then she caught a wraith-pooch chasing down a giant wasp. It caught the insectoid in its jaws, then shook it to pieces.

The Wraith Queen murmured, "Wraith to insectoid queen's five. Wraith takes wasp."

"That was a bad pooch," a child said.

"Who goes there?!" she called out.

She cast her all-seeing eye darting across her realm, searching for the source of the voice. Then she spotted him — a young squire, sitting on the back of a wraith-pooch in the Eastern Wastelands. She couldn't make out his features.

The boy shrugged and said, "It's just me. I couldn't talk to you before, but now I'm out, and you're about done changing, so it's ok."

He was halfway across the realm, but his voice was as close as if he was standing before her. She screeched at the boy to scare him away. She rattled her chains at him, but it only made him smile.

"You still hold on to those scraps of meat?" The boy asked.

"Meat?!"

"Human meat, human bones."

"I *am* human!" she wailed.

"Not anymore. Not for a long time. You're one of us, now!" Looking closer, she could see that his face was gone. His clothes were black gossamer. He was a wraith-child!

The Wraith Queen recoiled, pressing herself into her throne. The warped wood creaked in protest. She wailed, "No! I can't lose myself!"

"You've been lost for years. Do you think you're Pip-Rho?"

"Don't use that name!" she screeched.

The wraith-child was unfazed. "Okay. What name do you want?"

"I am The Wraith Queen," she said with as much dignity as she could muster.

The wraith-child cocked his head. "But if you think you're a wraith and also a human, then *what* are you?"

"Both! Neither! Why are you tormenting me, child?! Leave me alone!"

"I don't think you want that," the wraith-child said. "You did good at making this place to keep yourself busy, but you need friends that understand you. Maybe even some pooches! We can all play together and help make you better. You can teach us stuff, too, but not if you're dead! Your wraith form can save you. Stop pretending to be a human, Wraith Queen. Stop fighting it. Surrender the meat, become complete!" He giggled at his little rhyme.

She writhed in agony. The walls shook with the rumble of war machines creeping down cobblestone streets. They'd be here soon.

"I tried so hard," she whimpered. "I tried to stay myself! But I'm... I'm so many people. I'm so many things! What will become of me?!"

The wraith-child shrugged. "You won't be human again, I guess. But you can have a better life than this if you can find your soulstone."

"My s-s-soulstone?" she said with a shudder.

Where was her soulstone? The soulkeeper didn't have it, she knew. Did she even have a soulstone? Were souls real?

"It's lost," she said.

"That's too bad," the boy said. "Well, if you can escape your chains, the best thing you can do is run. Find water. Hide away until the war is over. After that, I'll do what I can to help you. And you can show me how you made this." He gestured at his surroundings.

She nodded vigorously. It sounded like wise advice — she was *always* thirsty. She pulled as hard as she could against the chains.

"You might be able to break them," the wraith-child said, turning his wraith-pooch away. "After you surrender."

RESISTANCE BECOMES second nature when you've been fighting something for as long as The Wraith Queen had. She didn't even know what she was fighting anymore. What was she afraid of?

Catastrophic cognitive dissociative collapse.

Words from another world. There were so many other worlds than this. Her past lives each had its own set of experiences — a thousand stories, each more fanciful than the last. But when she grasped for any of those memories, reality fractured. There was only one reality — Interra. And there was only one authentic version of her — The Wraith Queen.

Except for when she was The Night Queen.

She knew that her change in mood was related to the underworld, somehow. A blue moon came to mind — a water god. Yes, it was related to that, too.

Once upon a time, a person could use a *double-mind* to issue *thought-commands*. It was a strange time and faraway land when they called her *Pip-Rho*.

Just thinking the forbidden name made her head hurt. It made her think of a short, skinny woman with a compact afro puff hairdo and a peculiar face — buggy eyes set a bit too far apart, forehead a bit too small, and an underbite.

There was once a girl who grew up with primitives, but all the while, her mind was being transcribed into a shimmering orb in a cave under the ocean. They thought she would die as a babe, but she grew into a child.

Or a tiny snowflake?

The other snowflakes wept for her when she melted.

But then she turned into an immortal who died sixteen times.

Or an egg filled with tortured flesh?

Or a cartoon character of an egg with an afro puff?

Or a black porcelain cherub?

It was all just a jumble of complete *nonsense!*

She knew who Queen Rho was, of course. This was her past self — a legendary beauty steeped in salacious delights — until the ravages of The Curse turned her into a monster.

But that wasn't her, either. All she ever seemed to be was some later version of a prior persona. She played her characters and played them well — so well that she lost herself to them.

There was once a ghost that haunted a hall of mirrors. Its infinite reflections each claimed to be the true and original apparition, yet there was no original to be found. One day, a living being entered the hall. Its solid image obscured the reflections. This instantaneous nullification put a silent, unceremonious end to the haunting. The mirrors were removed, and the once-haunted hall was converted into the being's new home.

This fantasy filled her with hope and fear. She knew that she was the ghost, rattling her chains and wailing at her own reflection. But who was the living being? As vivid as her mental imagery usually was, she could not make out its features.

This vision was a fleeting moment of peace and beauty. Now, it was gone. She was back in her wretched, chained body. But these chains were as much a figment of her imagination as her Wraith Queen persona. It pained her to know this, yet there was the truth of it.

But there's more.

She was aware of her mind's vast, intricate, lightning-fast parts, which worked tirelessly to manufacture this reality. She tried to ignore them, yet they were always there if she dared to look deep within. One must be careful when opening one's mind and peeking inside, marveling at the complex interweaving of systems and sub-systems, lest one should fall in and find one's self in a hall of mirrors.

She wanted more than anything to be the living being that banishes the false reflections. She wanted to be solid and simple and sane. Could she let that person in? Stop pretending, open the door, and let it be?

If she stopped trying so hard to keep herself together, she could do what the wraith-child suggested and surrender her last scrap of flesh to the Specter. Abolish your sense of self. Extinguish your ego. Become unborn. Break free of the cycle of life and death.

Therin lies nirvana.

The Night Tower rumbled with another impact, knocking loose debris from the ceiling. She was running out of time. If she was going to die, she might as well go on her own terms.

"Fine, I surrender!" she shouted. "I surrender to the nonsense of non-reality! I surrender to the wraith, the Specter, the consumption! I surrender to Pip-Rho! To CCDC! To death! Break the mirrors! I am nothing!"

Senseless words began tumbling through her mind in the voice of Pip-Rho.

"Issue bio-override: disable cellular reconstruction nanites."

There was a strange sensation building. She was slipping into a dream.

"Bypass double-mind coherence preservation protocols."

Warning! Bypassing double-mind coherence preserva-tion protocols may result in irreversible neurite degen-eration and connectome mapping inconsistencies. Do you wish to continue?

"Yes."

Her sense of self expanded, filling the universe. Time became meaningless. Fractions of seconds passed, but they could have been minutes, hours, or years.

A black bolt of lightning shocked her — sent her back into Interra, though she watched from the outside. The world was a dollhouse, and she was a child at play.

Her tiny wraith body rattled its chains — pressed against the insides of its containment chamber. It pressed harder than ever, but it could not break free.

Interra was crumbling, washing away like a sand castle at high tide. This was what the boy wanted. It was what she asked for. Would he help her build a new castle? Put her mind back together? Where was he now?

"You fool! You trusted a *wraith-child?!*" The Wraith Queen screeched up at her from her tiny rotten throne. That wasn't her anymore. It never had been.

Her all-seeing eye caught a glimpse of something flying towards her at incredible speed. She braced herself.

This was it! This was her death!

A fiery explosion consumed her.

And the world burned away in a flash of pain.

7

LET IT BE

THE WORDS STITCHED into her flesh twisted and blurred in Genevieve's eyes. Tears trickled down her cheeks before finding a ledge on her nose or chin. From there, they took their leaps of misplaced faith. The tears dropped to their doom, dashing into hard-packed dirt and soaking into the ground without a trace.

Genevieve was salting the soil. No plants would grow here for a generation.

Alasie had her thinking like a poet these days — the dark, brooding kind that quothed the raven and drank absinthe. She certainly looked the part, with her grim black hair and tattered black leather outfit.

The Telson cabin was the de facto gathering spot for the Noddites of The Thin Forest and surrounding regions. Every few minutes, another person or group appeared from between the shadows of the skinny pines that gave The Thin Forest its name. They didn't talk much, other than to murmur a prayer or gasp at a silent explosion bright enough to be seen in the blue sky.

Genevieve held Natasha-Zeta's dog, Elle, with one arm. She was an odd little dog, preferring to be held with her hind legs wrapped around your torso like a toddler. Genevieve was comforting Elle, who didn't like crowds. Or the dog was comforting her. It worked both ways, she supposed. Elle tried to lick a tear from Genevieve's chin, but Genevieve dodged the unwanted tongue by casting her face to the sky.

Dogs were okay, but she gave the face-licking thing a hard *no*.

Surya burned high in the sky. Her enhanced optics systems filtered its intense light, allowing her to watch the deadly light show. The battlefront was working its way closer, approaching the southern sky. That's where the Jacob's Ladder space elevator, Jacob's Attic space station, and the Astri Hive Station were. The Astri kept their aposynchronic orbs in their station, and Pip-Rho's egg was tethered to it. If the Astrus station was destroyed, one hundred thousand Astri would be killed, orb and all — True Death.

So would Pip-Rho... or what was left of her.

"They can't attack the stations without risking damage to the elevator," Oraxis mindspoke. *"The Guardians wouldn't compromise that vital piece of infrastructure."*

Genevieve knew he was just saying that to ease her mind. This was no minor skirmish — it was an all-out war, and neither side would give up until the other was crushed. She wanted to scream at the summer sky, to beg the flashes of exploding torpedos and ruptured ZETA reactors to stop. Her *family* was out there!

Incoming conversation request from Pip-Tau Telson.

Genevieve gasped, accepting the request. She sent, *"Tell me you were joking about being inside a Specter."*

She counted a two-second delay before Pip-Tau replied, *"No joke, Gen-ma! It's so wild. Worldnet telemetry readings say I'm approaching Genesis, but we're also lurching around erratically. And fast! I don't know if we're dodging attacks or if they're just flighty. How you holding up?"*

If she answered honestly, she would say she was an emotional wreck. Instead, she said, *"I'm hanging in there. How about Alasie? Is she scared?"*

Two seconds later, Pip-Tau laughed, *"She's over the moon! Literally! Get it? Seriously, we've been talking, and she considers this return of the Specters thing to be her all-time greatest achievement. She's bananas! I mean, this girl single-handedly sparked a war and undid everything we worked towards for years — getting rid of the alien menace. She doesn't care! Alasie's convinced Zeta's here with us and that she changed the Specters. I have to admit, they're not acting like they used to. Like, they're keeping me alive. It's downright comfy! Other than the eyeball-vein-popping high-G maneuvers. Anyway, we'll be in touch. I'm gonna try to talk to the Astri again."*

She closed the conversation channel.

Pip-Tau was the queen of wishful thinking — the Astri won't talk to anyone. When you tried to reach out to them, you'd get a canned response saying they did nothing to instigate the attacks from the Guard. The Guard Faction's stance was that the Astri had reprogrammed the Specters to be their pawns, while the Astri denied the allegations. The Guardians made it clear that they wouldn't rest until they eliminated every Astrus and Specter in the Surya system.

And The Council of Ten? Their only announcement so far was that they were monitoring the events and reserving judgment until more information becomes available. Not that they could do anything against either side of this conflict. The Genesis Faction had no soldiers or weapons. It relied on the Laws of Sovereignty and its authority over the Surya system to protect it from the other factions.

Sure, try shielding yourself from an antimatter bomb using a *law*.

THE BATTLE WAS in near-Genesis orbit now. What was once tiny sparkles of light in the bright sky were now blooms. The Astrus Station was surrounded.

Ships were entering the atmosphere — bright streaks here and there. One came so close that Genevieve could make out the black scars on its heat shield as it screamed by, engines roaring. Its active invisibility panels must've been stripped off during reentry. She was certain it would land on top of them, but it flew past.

A minute later, someone called out, "They're landing in the grazing field next to The Cavern of the Soul. Madge Ule the Cave-keeper won't stand for that!"

"Look!" a woman shouted. Genevieve glanced at her, then followed her finger, pointing at the southern sky.

A hundred gasps rose from the crowd.

Time stood still as Genevieve took in the sight. The white-hot explosion was the biggest they'd seen yet. They all knew what it meant — the Astri Hive Station had taken a direct hit.

The Astri were dead.

Pip-Rho was dead.

Genevieve's knees gave out. Her body was cold and numb. The crowd sounded dull and distant, as if from underwater.

Elle slipped from her arm and ran away.

Oraxis was next to her, saying something.

"Xavier," Genevieve whispered. "Pip-Rho. Dead."

Fresh tears poured from her unblinking eyes, fixed on the fading white blossom of death.

"Dead," she choked out.

A tiny blue flame was rising from the South, just visible above the tree line. She didn't know what it was. It seemed important, but she couldn't think.

"They launched the cable tugs!" someone shouted.

A distant part of her remembered that there was a safety measure for the space elevator, involving massive rockets launched from the station in the Great Ocean. The rockets were supposed to attach to the cable and pull it free of Genesis if it broke. Without them, the falling cable would wrap around Genesis's equator in a catastrophic collapse.

Her eyes met Oraxis's. Seeing him cry was an unusual sight. His lip trembled as he searched her eyes for a response. Was he talking to her?

"I... can't..." she breathed.

And it all came pouring out.

Genevieve and Oraxis pulled each other into a tight, desperate embrace. She wailed into his shoulder as he let out a bellow of pain and rage.

They were dead!

Dead!

It felt like a replay. Was this a replay? She didn't feel like she was inside of her body — her broken, shuttering body. But she was. She could feel the ache of her heart in her chest.

The pain was real. Inescapable.

Minutes passed in wailing agony. She just wanted to die!

Natasha-Zeta kneeled by their side and put a firm hand on Genevieve and Oraxis's shoulders. Her face was puffy and wet with tears. She also had family in the Astrus Faction — her bootstrapper and three other kin. Genevieve pulled Natasha-Zeta into a hug and held her friend tight.

"Genevieve?" Jamji asked. "Oraxis?"

She was hearing things. She could've sworn that was...

"Jamji?! Jamji!" Genevieve called out, scrambling to her feet. Jamji was standing just a few meters behind them. Pepper-pooch was beside her, glowing a dull gray and sitting as still as a statue. Jamji looked different — she was the same shade of gray as her dog.

Genevieve rushed to Jamji, embracing her solid form, half-expecting it to be a figment of her imagination.

Why was she here?

Did it matter? Her wayward child was safe — that's all she needed to know.

"They blew up the hive station," Genevieve cried. "Xavier... Pip-Rho..."

Jamji's arms held her in a stiff embrace. Her skin was cold and hard.

"Genevieve," Jamji said, "we're here to protect you. We're gathering everyone we can in The Cavern of the Soul. It's a fortified position."

"Hey! What do you think you're doing?!" Oraxis was yelling at someone.

Genevieve looked up to see Oraxis approaching a soldier wearing power armor. The soldier was gripping a double-handled broad blade and pressing it into the side of a tree at the edge of the clearing. The blade didn't appear to be moving, but as soon as it touched the bark, it made a buzzing, grinding sound. Splinters shot out either side of the trunk as the man sliced through the pine.

The sound of a tree falling came from her other side. She turned in time to see a different pine crash into the forest floor. Genevieve looked around, spotting six Guardian soldiers. Three men were cutting down trees while three women addressed the Genesisians.

"Why are you cutting down our trees?!" Genevieve shouted.

Jamji hopped onto Pepper-pooch's back. "Tell your people to gather at that side of the clearing." She gestured uphill.

"Why? What are you doing?" Genevieve cried. Jamji wouldn't look her in the eye. She shouted, "Jamji, talk to me!"

Jamji looked down at her with impassive eyes. "There's no time for you to travel by foot, so we're clearing the area for an aerial transport to land."

"In our yard?!" Genevieve wailed.

Pepper-pooch trotted off, carrying Jamji away. He made a circuit of the clearing as Jamji watched the soldiers work. It seemed like Jamji was in charge. She wasn't shouting commands — they probably only used mindspeak.

"Clear out," a woman commanded her. "We need all you Genesisians to gather inside that tree line."

Genevieve turned to see Oraxis squaring off with a soldier at the base of Zephyr's tree. "Absolutely not! Do you see that nest?! This is my bird's tree!"

They were cutting Zephyr's tree down?! The massive form of Zephyr, the enhanced golden eagle, stirred in the nest above. The pine bobbed as he perched on the edge of the nest and watched the people below with his eternally stern glare. When Oraxis refused to back down, the woman who had told Genevieve to clear out started pushing him with the broad side of her rifle.

As hard as Oraxis tried to stand his ground, he was no match for the woman in the power armor. Once he was clear of the tree, the soldier with the blade got to work. Zephyr spread his great wings and took flight, briefly blasting the crowd with swirling pine needles and dust.

"Where will he go?" Genevieve sent Oraxis.

Oraxis was willingly walking towards their designated gathering spot. He turned and spotted her before replying, *"I sent him to the mountains. He can fend for himself until the war blows over. You should join us over here before they knock your teeth out. Oh... oh, no, Gen, look!"*

He pointed back across the clearing.

Genevieve turned to spot Pepper-pooch taking a running leap at their log cabin. He impacted it with his front paws, causing the structure to groan, leaning slightly.

"No! Jamji, what are you doing?!" Genevieve shouted, running towards the cabin. Penelope-pooch was running back and forth and barking at Pepper-pooch, but she kept her distance from him.

Pepper-pooch pressed his great paws against the corner of the roof, pushing against it in bouncing lurches. The structure creaked with each bounce, leaning more and more.

"Stay back, Genevieve!" Jamji shouted over the noise. "You can build a new cabin! We're leveling everything in a forty-meter radius that's taller than a meter. We have to make room for the transport! Now go join your people and get that dog out of here before she gets hurt!"

"That dog?!" Genevieve shouted. "I thought you loved Penelope-pooch! Now she's *that dog* to you?! Pip-Rho and Xavier are dead, thanks to you warmongers! Your kin died today, Jamji! Don't you care?! Don't you care about any of us?!"

"Why do you think I'm here?!" Jamji shouted back. "I want you to be safe! The Astri are being neutralized, but the Specters are coming!"

The cabin finally gave way, toppling into a pile of logs and dust.

Silence fell over the clearing. Jamji's men had stopped their work to watch her interaction with Genevieve.

Jamji spoke in a loud, commanding voice but didn't shout. "I mourned Pip-Rho four years ago when her mind broke. She died the same day as Zeta. And Xavier renounced his humanity the day he merged with the Astrus Hive and took the name XT-Prime. That was before I was even born. I never even knew Xavier. The entities we neutralized," she pointed at the southern sky, "up there? Personality emulators. They were no more human than an AI. So, no, I don't mourn them, and neither should you."

"That's not true, and you know it!" Genevieve screamed. "They've got human brains, Jamji! The Guard filled your head with lies and turned you into a monster! A *fucking* monster! I don't even know you anymore!"

Jamji turned her head and commanded, "Matchlock, escort this Genesisian to her people."

"Yes, Lieutenant Telson," one of the women said.

Tears poured down Genevieve's cheeks as she turned away from Jamji, issuing a thought-command for Penelope-pooch to follow.

"Don't call her Lieutenant Telson. She's not a Telson anymore," Genevieve growled at the approaching soldier as she stomped away.

That made three family members she'd lost today.

As she reached the gathering spot, Genevieve stole a glance at her tattooed forearm and read Zeta's last words to her — parting words of wisdom. Zeta had been right that it was all Genevieve could do. The words softened her heart and turned her rage into pained resignation.

The tattoo read, "Let it be."

8

DOG FIGHT

"*WHAT SHOULD we call you now, sir?*" Private First Class Herman Tosh sent over the squad channel.

Jamji didn't honor the nonsensical question with a response. The people-mover was packed with Genesisians and ready to fly. Genevieve and Oraxis stared at her through the loading hatch until the closing door hid them from view.

Kelso barked out a laugh. "*Ha! Since the Lieutenant's not a Telson anymore? Good one, Tosh.*"

This wasn't the first time she'd destroyed that cabin. Last time, it was in a construct, during her entrance exams. They'd called that test "The Nightmare Gauntlet". It was a construct where they made her follow orders to kill her family for the sake of the Guard.

Did they deploy her squad to this region to make her prove she was willing to do the same things in reality as she had done in the construct? At least she hadn't been forced to kill anyone.

"*Take it easy on her,*" Mazzou sent. "*She just got cussed out by her momma in front of her subordinates. I'll bet she's glad to be disowned after that embarrassment.*"

"Embarrassment?" Trapper scoffed. *"Waste of time is what it was. Everybody gawking instead of working? A prisoner helmet would've shut the Genesissy up. CIS should've issued those for the herding mission."*

A whimper came from the edge of the clearing — one of the owned animals, missing its master. Their orders had been clear: only humans were to be evacuated. The animals could fend for themselves. It's not like they'd starve to death on their own — they get fed using placental mats every night.

She couldn't bear to look. Penelope-pooch was over there. She'd be staring at Jamji with golden-brown eyes and wondering what was happening.

The voice of GuardNet broke through Jamji's thoughts.

New squad objective: escort People Mover 1005 to Genesis surface coordinates 33.8303, -96.6194.

The objective was coupled with flight plans and an aerial image of the rally point: The Cavern of the Soul.

Jamji disagreed with the objective. The people mover could make it there without them — there weren't any hostiles to cause it trouble. Not yet, at least, since the Specters were still in space. Her squad should've been sent to rally another group of Genesisians and clear another landing zone.

Not that she had the gall to defy CIS.

Jamji sent, *"JP-143, you have your objective. Let's fly."*

She sent a thought-command to Pepper-pooch to leap into the air and activate his plasma-jet boots. With a burst of superheated plasma and a brief whiff of smoke, they were airborne. Her squad followed suit, spreading out just above the treetops to cover the transport. They were mindful of their jets, making sure not to start a forest fire.

Moments later, the wireframe of the invisible transport rose from the clearing in a vertical take-off. It lowered its wings and engaged its main thrusters, barely making a noise. The wide, flat jet cloak shot out thirty meters behind the craft, hiding its plasma flame from view.

And they were off.

THEY'D BEEN FLYING for three minutes and thirty-five seconds when the squad received an update.

Specters entering the atmosphere in your vicinity. Prepare to engage.

That explained the escort duty — CIS must've known the Specters were getting close and wanted them to return to the fortified position. Jamji regretted second-guessing them.

"Woo!" Tosh called out on the squad channel.

"This is it, men," Mazzou sent. *"This is battle. Make me proud."*

Mazzou seemed to think he was the leader. Jamji tried to think of something to say that wouldn't make her sound like a tagalong. Nothing came to mind. She detached the containment device from its leg holster and sent, *"Get your containment devices ready, men."*

Trapper sent, *"One step ahead of you, sir."*

The telltale sonic boom of Specters passing through atmosphere rumbled in the air. She counted one, two, then a rapid-fire set of thunderclaps that may have been ten at once. Jamji's gaze darted around the cloudless sky for a hint of black.

"Twelve o'clock!" Trapper shouted via aud-link.

Jamji looked straight ahead, spotting what looked like a swarm of bees on the horizon. Engaging enhanced optics, the specks resolved into the ameboid forms of Specters. They darted around, diving below the hills and dodging bright flashes. There had to be thirty of them!

"They're at the cave!" Tosh sent. *"Let's gun it and engage!"*

Jamji sent, *"Negative, our mission is to escort the transport."* She made a point-to-point communication request with People Mover 1005. They accepted.

She sent, *"We'll be landing in an active battle zone. My men will try to draw the enemy away from you, but Specters are unpredictable."*

The pilot replied, *"Roger that. Field reports say they're not using hit-n-run tactics like they used to — they're swarming. I'll come in hot and set 'er down as close to the cave entrance as I can. I'm not s'posed to damage the cargo, but she handles like a lopsided June bug, so we'll see."*

More sonic booms rumbled through the air. Black dashes descended towards the distant swarm from multiple directions — Specter reinforcements. Jamji counted fifty-four of them joining the fray over the next two minutes.

They were close enough to see the sad state of the ground defenses. Multiple craters pockmarked the grazing field. The remains of the drop-base were scattered everywhere. Jamji's HUD showed her where the remaining ground forces were clustered. It looked like they'd already lost the position, but CIS hadn't updated their objectives, so they stayed the course.

A wave of explosions swept through the air no more than a half-kilometer in front of them. She spotted the green wireframe of a cloaked gunship high in the atmosphere, moving at supersonic speeds. They were clearing a path for her squad and the transport! The shockwave from the explosions vibrated her innards in the most satisfying way.

Black streaks shot out from the battlefield, darting into the upper atmosphere in a sudden retreat. It seemed the aliens were still skittish.

Jamji was overclocking — running her bio-synthetic neurite network at abnormally high speeds. This made the scene appear to be moving in slow motion. Even so, the speed of the Specters was hard to track. One flew by them, passing directly overhead.

Private First Class Zigfried Kelso broke formation, dashing after the retreating Specter.

"Leave it, Kelso!" Jamji shouted over aud-link. *"Stay on task!"*

Kelso let out an incoherent curse but fell back into formation.

"Entering landing pattern," the pilot of People Mover 1005 sent.

Her squad circled above the rapidly descending transport. Jamji was impressed with the pilot's skill, deftly swiveling the craft and burning hard to reduce forward momentum. He set the bird down just meters away from the cave entrance. The rear loading hatch opened in slow motion.

Jamji swiveled her head to survey the situation, finding that the Specters, which had pulled back, were now closing in again.

"Engage the enemy!" Jamji shouted through aud-link. *"Keep 'em busy and give 'em hell!"*

"Yes, sir!" the squad replied in unison.

JAMJI AND PEPPER-POOCH had trained together for so long that it felt like their minds were one. Commanding his movements wasn't a matter of relaying her intentions and waiting for him to respond. It was like *she* was the monster-pooch with the massive ZETA reactor and plasma-jet boots on each paw.

She needed to pick a single target among the black dots. Which one seemed closest? Almost at random, Jamji picked a Specter and set Pepper-pooch on it. They rose toward the incoming black blob. When it turned into a line and tried to skirt around her, Jamji sprung from her saddle and engaged her boots.

Holding the containment device in both hands, Jamji pressed the trigger. She angled her boots to whip herself around the alien at full burn. The deployment maneuver involved flying in a perfect circle around the target while pointing the T-shaped device at it. This would surround the alien in a matrix of charged microfilament, which Specters couldn't break, but energy weapons could pass through. The ends of the matrix net automatically curved inward and tangled together. Next, an electromagnetic charge repelled the micro-filament threads away from each other, pressing them outward to form a perfect sphere.

After her circuit of the alien was complete, Jamji turned to examine her work. Yep, the bastard was in the bag!

Another Specter lashed out at her.

Jamji dodged sideways, then returned to Pepper-pooch's saddle. As she retreated, she took mental control of her monster-pooch's maser pulse cannon, aiming it at the Specter. The helmet-mounted weapon was fed by the war dog's oversized ZETA reactor and packed a lot more punch than the rifles the rest of her team carried.

CIS had found that masers set to a frequency matching the diameter of a Specter cell could injure the aliens, so every soldier had tuned their rifles and pistols accordingly. This would be her first time firing such a weapon, and she was eager to see what it could do.

As promised, the invisible energy emitted from Pepper-pooch's cannon lit up a patch of burning light on the surface of the pursuing alien. It flinched, then retreated like an injured animal.

The other Specters in her area were circling with nervous energy.

All she had to do was keep them occupied long enough for the transport to unload. She stole a glimpse at the ground. The Gene-sisians were running from the transport into the cave.

But they were being hunted!

Three Specters had slipped in beneath her squad. They danced and dodged as if they were excited to abduct a fresh, juicy human.

Kelso was making a beeline towards the Specters at ground level. Jamji angled Pepper-pooch downward, sending them plummeting to the ground. She targeted one of the three and let loose with another blast from the maser cannon.

Before either Kelso or Jamji could deter the Specters, two of them had reached out with a tendril, dipping into the stream of Gene-sisians and plucking out a pair of abductees. The unlucky souls kicked their legs and flailed their arms as they rose into the black bellies of the aliens.

Patches of white-hot energy bloomed on the Specters' surfaces as she and Kelso blasted them with maser pulses.

Two of the three retreated in a blink while the other dodged into the shadows of the pines. Double sonic booms split the air.

Jamji sent a quick update to CIS, stating that she had just witnessed two Genesisian abductions.

Poor suckers.

The abductions put some pep into the Genesisians' steps — they were making a mad dash for the cave, jamming up the entrance. Some of the crowd crawled over other people's heads in their panicked retreat.

She hoped Genevieve and Oraxis were okay.

With a hard burn towards the ground, Jamji slowed her descent, then rose again. Time to catch another alien!

Three gray-glowing spheres floated in the sky overhead, each with a black blob inside. Excellent — two of her squad had caught Specters!

Bagging them was one thing. Killing them was another. The orders they received during transport were to immobilize the enemy. The captured Specters would be out of the fight, and when the battle was over, they'd be hauled back to Soma for study. Gunships or orbital strikes would target any that got away. The meager rifles and pistols of JP squads might not kill a Specter, but at least they proved to be good deterrents.

Jamji picked her next target just before CIS sent an update.

New squad objective: clear a landing zone at Genesis coordinates 35.0684, -97.2047.

"Herding duty, again?!" Mazzou shouted.

Kelso's gravely voice declared, *"I'm not leaving until I catch one!"*

"Come on," Bates sent. *"Don't be a dumbass, Kelso. They're probably about to sweep the area with another aerial cluster bomb."*

Jamji scowled at the Specter she was closing in on, clenching her teeth. She was with Kelso — bagging aliens was better than herding Genesisians. She sent, *"JP-143, get some altitude and fall in formation. We're heading northwest."*

Just as Pepper-pooch pointed his feet to the side to change directions, the Specter they had been closing in on started to give chase. Four other nearby Specters joined it in a darting, dodging pursuit.

More and more, Jamji got the feeling they were fighting against pack hunters — dogs or wolves. Everything about how the Specters fought, moved, and grouped reminded her of a pack of dogs. It was nothing like how they acted before the so-called Spellsong sent them plunging into Varuna. This was further proof that they had been reprogrammed to fight for the Astri.

One of their pursuers snagged Pepper-pooch's hind leg. Another struck his side, knocking Jamji off. Out came her pistol as she rotated in the air and engaged her plasma-jet boots.

"Back, dogs!" Jamji shouted, spraying maser bursts at the black, swarming pack.

A baritone yelp of pain erupted from Pepper-pooch as the Specter holding his rear leg tore it from his body, hurling him upward.

"Backup!" Jamji called to her team.

It was too late — a Specter that was flanking her lashed out, engulfing her in frigid black liquid. Her boots were violently ripped off her feet, and her pistol was pulled from her hand.

"I am hurt, Jamji!" Pepper-pooch yelped over their private aud-link. *"I can't bite them, and you are gone!"*

The sensation of high-G acceleration told her she was being taken away, fast.

Fluid rushed down her throat, filling her lungs. She wouldn't live much longer.

"Where's Telson?" Mazzou sent.

She could feel Pepper-pooch's pain, his fear. Jamji made a swift and terrible decision.

"Is the team clear of me and Pepper?" Jamji asked.

"What just happened?" Bates asked.

Trapper answered her question. *"Yes, sir, the closest of us is over two hundred meters from Pepper. We don't see you, but your ping puts you at over two kilometers south."*

Jamji issued the thought-command to self-destruct Pepper-pooch's ZETA reactor.

"See you soon, lil' Pep," she sent, but her message went undelivered — their link was already severed.

She clenched her teeth and gave her own ZETA reactor the command to self-destruct.

NOTHING HAPPENED. She didn't even hear or feel an explosion.

Her ZETA reactor wasn't on her back anymore?! The Specter must've pulled it off when it abducted her.

How far had the Specter taken her? And how long before it dissolved her? Her hardened dermal systems might be able to fight off the Specter cells longer than normal skin. She figured she had five minutes at most before her body gave up or she suffocated.

Tosh laughed, *"Sweet double ZETA pops! That took out half a dozen of 'em!"*

Trapper sent, *"Sir, you're now twelve kilometers south of the team, cruising at a speed approaching Mach One."*

"I'm inside a Specter," she sent. *"Updating CIS now. Carry on with your mission."*

"Yes, sir," her squad replied with grave determination.

Rather than an individual commanding officer, Squad Lieutenants reported to a pool of Lieutenant Commanders at CIS who shared command over an entire division.

Jamji opened a channel to CIS and sent her odd report, *"Squad*

Lieutenant Jamji Telson here. I'm inside a Specter, being transported somewhere."

"This is Lieutenant Commander Piccolo," a man replied. "Polling your data. Yes, I have you. You blew your ZETA reactor?"

"Yes, sir, but the Specter stripped it from my body during abduction."

"Well... okay, no damage reported from the defending forces at the cave. You're lucky it was still in the air when it blew. It could've damaged the people mover or killed the evacuating Genesisians. I'm assigning Private First Class Israel Mazzou as acting commander of JP-143 until you're recovered."

Jamji wasn't surprised. Oh well. It had been a nice few hours of actual command experience.

Seven seconds later, Piccolo sent, *"Telson, it seems you're in a unique position. We've had no other reports of Specters abducting our men. I'm patching in a specialist to interview you."*

The specialist cut in, speaking with strained urgency. *"This is no coincidence. Why you, Telson?"*

She knew that voice — Chief Warrant Officer Dumont. He was the xenobiologist on her team during the Interra project. The peculiar man always set Jamji's nerves on edge. She could picture his mustache twitching in agitation.

"Dumont," Jamji sent as a matter of greeting.

"Grant my team access to your abduction replay," Dumont commanded.

Jamji gave the thought-command to GuardNet, as directed. She hated sharing replays. It always led to people surgically dissecting your every action and decision.

"Describe your physical sensations," Dumont sent. *"Details! Details!"*

"Well, I can't see anything," Jamji sent.

"I know that!" Dumont choked out. *"Skin, lungs! Biometrics indicate adequate oxygen, minimal bodily stresses. How? Details!"*

Jamji shook her head. The man had as much social grace as the aliens he studied. She talked him through her surreal experience, but something was nagging at her. Dumont thought it was no coincidence that she was selected. Maybe he was right — maybe they wanted her, specifically. The Specters were taking her somewhere, keeping her alive for a reason.

Whatever was going on felt like destiny — a personal quest. And however it played out, she'd make the Guard proud.

9

———

BAY #2

"*W*HERE ARE WE NOW*?*" Alasie asked Pip-Tau.

"*Hard to nail down,*" Pip-Tau replied. "*Something's blocking our point-to-point connections to relay stations. The last time I could get a strong fix, we were at surface-level on Genesis, approaching Jacob's Ladder Station. We might be underwater.*"

"*I don't feel any pressure,*" Alasie sent. She knew that deep water crushes you.

Pip-Tau sounded irritated. "*These Specters are acting like pressure suits. Remember when we were in vacuum? You couldn't feel that, either. They swim in Varuna's ocean, which is like* hundreds *of kilometers deep. The Great Ocean doesn't get any deeper than twelve kilometers. There's stronger gravity on Genesis than Varuna, so the pressure increases faster here, but still — they can handle it. I'm gonna try some WUtils hacks to figure out if we're going where I think we are.*"

Alasie wanted to probe Pip-Tau for more, but she should leave her alone. She'd gone silent for at least ten minutes after they heard that the Guardians destroyed the Astrus Genesis Hive Station. She was all business when she started talking again, with none of her usual spunky attitude.

The news hadn't seemed real to Alasie. There was no way all the Astri were dead. She couldn't process it, so she didn't.

How could she even think when *so* much was happening?! She couldn't decide between talking to Natasha-Zeta again, reading the news feeds, or simply enjoying the ride.

And what a ride!

They were in constant motion, always turning, accelerating, flipping upside down, and lurching back and forth. This had ruined her sense of "up" and "down".

But she really should reach out to Natasha-Zeta.

She'd been in a Guardian transport with Oraxis and Genevieve the last time they talked. Alasie didn't trust the Guardians. They said they were trying to get the Genesisians to safety, but who knew what they were actually up to. Someone had taken an unofficial poll a few minutes ago, and almost seventy percent of the respondents were now under so-called *Guardian protection*. Only far-flung, solitary individuals and Noddites visiting Eden weren't under Guardian control yet.

People like Carff.

His updates had been upsetting. The tribe he's living with was in a panic. They thought the world was coming to an end. Maybe they were right.

Most of the fighting was over the Nod hemisphere, but there was still plenty to see from Eden. It was nighttime on that side of the planet, so it was easy to see the explosions in space.

What would she have thought, seeing the night sky light up with flashes when she was a neoprim? Maybe some of the tribes thought it was a good omen. Surely, they'd tell stories and sing songs about it for generations.

She imagined a storyteller chanting beside a fire. They'd poke the coals to send embers drifting into the sky before they sang...

I'll tell you a tale
Of that glorious night
So many years ago
When the shades of our ancestors
Dared disturb the star-stones
And strike them together
Making sparks for all to see
They were still watching
And they were pleased

Alasie smiled at the daydream. A WorMS notification broke her from the reverie. It was a group conversation with Oraxis, Genevieve, Pip-Tau, and Natasha-Zeta.

"*Hi,*" Alasie sent.

"*They got O and Gen!*" Natasha-Zeta sent.

"They *who?*" Pip-Tau sent.

"*Specters,*" Oraxis sent. "*It's the same sort of abduction experience as you two described. Manual breathing, the feeling of acceleration. Gen's not taking to it very well.*"

Natasha-Zeta sent, "*The Guard was evacuating us. A group of Specters plucked O and Gen up right before my eyes! Some Guardian fighters tried to stop 'em, but they were too slow! I'm in The Cavern of the Soul now. No telling where O and Gen are.*"

"*Probably the same place as us,*" Pip-Tau sent. "*The Great Ocean, just outside of Syn-Cen.*"

It seemed like Pip-Tau had figured it out. Syn-Cen was an underground complex buried beneath the deepest trench of The Great Ocean. Being outside of it meant they were as far under water as you could get.

Genevieve asked, "*Are your Specters talking to you?*"

Being inside a Specter sounded like being underwater. It also made occasional peculiar groans and clicking sounds. There had been nothing like speech. She listened more carefully now.

After a moment, a humming, faint voice said something like, "Own a doe."

Pip-Tau squeaked, *"Holy mumbling bubbles, Batman! I can't believe I didn't notice that before! How long's it been trying to talk to me? I can't make out what it's trying to say."* All her prior gloom seemed to vanish in a flash.

"Open the door," Genevieve said. *"Mine's been saying that over and over for the last minute."*

"That's it!" Pip-Tau shouted. *"Open the door?! What's that mean?"*

Alasie couldn't hear with Pip-Tau's voice shouting in her head. She sent, *"Be quiet! Listen for a minute. Maybe they're saying other things."*

The channel fell quiet.

A few seconds later, the voice hummed through the fluid again. "Open the door," it seemed to say. She issued a bio-override to magnify her hearing. The gurgling fluid got much louder.

"Open the door."

She tried to reply — to ask, "What door?" But trying to talk when you're breathing fluid makes you choke instead.

Oraxis sent, *"Genevieve is right. Mine's also saying, 'open the door.' How about you, Alasie?"*

"Yes," she sent, *"same for me. Um... so, what should we do?"*

Natasha-Zeta sent, *"Do you see a door?"*

"We can't see anything, Nat," Alasie sent.

Oraxis sent, *"Pip-Tau, if you're right about us being close to Syn-Cen, they could be talking about the airlock doors over the bays. They're used to deploy submarines. Do they expect us to let them into Syn-Cen?"* He chuckled sardonically.

Alasie didn't waste a moment in contemplation. She reached out to the Worldnet, thinking, *"Open the door and let us in."*

The voice of the Worldnet replied.

You are situated outside of Syn-Cen Bay #2. Do you wish to enter the airlock?

"Yes!" Alasie thought.

Oraxis was still talking. He sent, *"We need direction from The Council of Ten, but I can't get a response from any of them. Pip-Tau, you had thousands of people watching your news feed. Is anyone still tuned in?"*

Pip-Tau sent, *"With everything going on, I stopped broadcasting. Want me to start it back up? Got something you want to tell the faction?"*

"Yes, I want to see if anyone has news on The Council."

Group conversation patched into faction-wide broadcast.

Alasie immediately clammed up. Did that mean anything she sent on the conversation would be sent to everyone in the faction?

"And we're live!" Pip-Tau chirped. *"I know you silly skeptics don't believe I'm inside a Specter, so you certainly won't believe that my very own bootstrappers, Oraxis and Genevieve Telson, were also abducted. Well, believe it! We've been taken into The Great Ocean and found ourselves in a peculiar situation."*

Do you wish to cycle the airlock and enter the bay?

"Yes," Alasie replied, hoping she said it to the Worldnet and not the faction-wide broadcast. She had no idea how Pip-Tau could juggle so much stuff with her double-mind.

At least she knew what "cycle the airlock" meant. They used airlocks when she would come and go from Jacob's Attic Station. If she were coming in from space, they'd close the outside door, pressurize the room, and then open the inside door to the station. The airlock to the bay on the ocean floor must work similarly. But instead of pumping air into an airless room, like in space, an underwater airlock would have to pump water out while pumping air in.

She was getting better at this *technology* stuff.

"Without further ado," Pip-Tau sent, *"Oraxis Telson would like to address the faction. Take it away, O-pa!"*

"Um, yes, thank you, Pip-Tau," Oraxis sent. *"I'd rather not go into detail about my reasons, but I need to speak with The Council of Ten. There's a decision being presented to us that we shouldn't make on our own. This has been a confounding day, and none of us expected the sudden war that erupted around us. The Council's only updates have been vague and impersonal. EoE Veer Gladstone has yet to issue a statement. I find this highly suspicious and out of character for such a great leader. Someone in Syn-Cen must have visited Veer's quarters and spoken with him. Or, failing that—"*

Alasie was startled by the sudden feeling of something solid pressing against her back. Light flooded her eyes. The cool fluid she had been suspended in was releasing her. A black spot wavered in her blurry vision, surrounded by light.

What was happening?!

Gagging, she rolled over and coughed a waterfall of viscous fluid out into a puddle on a smooth floor. The sound of other people coughing joined her. She looked up to see Oraxis, Genevieve, and Pip-Tau nearby. Their hair and clothes were drenched.

Her vision was still adjusting, but she seemed to be in a cavernous room. A spinning red light caught her eye. Below it was a massive metallic door in the process of closing. She read the words above the door: Bay #2 Airlock.

They were inside the bay!

ALASIE GOT to her feet and looked around. She was standing in the biggest room she'd ever seen.

Overhead, swimming through the air as gracefully as fish in the water, were at least a dozen Specters. The other things in the massive chamber were harder to understand. The big, oblong vessel nearby was probably a submarine. It was elevated by carts with wheels taller than she was.

Along the back wall of the room were shelves stacked to the ceiling with hundreds of boxes. Thick cables ran from the boxes and connected them to a machine on the floor. Drones hovered before the shelves, working on the boxes using tools that whirred and sparked.

Shiny robotic forms as big as Ag'nul wearing power armor carried things around or climbed up the shelves. A hundred dormant robots were slumped in rows along one side of the room. Metallic crates were stacked in the corners, forming towers that reached the high ceiling.

"Um, we're taking a quick break," Pip-Tau mindspoke. *"There has been... a new...development."*

Pip-Tau was looking between her, Genevieve, and Oraxis with bulging eyes.

Broadcast suspended, conversation closed.

"Which of you opened the airlock doors?!" Oraxis barked. A vein bulged on his temple as he looked between her and Pip-Tau.

"Whoa, don't look at me!" Pip-Tau squeaked, raising her hands in surrender.

"I did," Alasie said, then coughed. Some fluid still tickled her throat. She coughed again, then said, "I know you wanted—"

"You let *aliens* into Syn-Cen!" Oraxis shouted, pointing at the Specters overhead. "You know this is where our orbs are kept, right?!"

"O, look," Genevieve said, putting a hand on Oraxis's shoulder and pointing across the room.

Alasie looked, too.

Two Specters were suspending large, metallic crates in the air while a third descended to the ground with a crate perched on top of it. Apparently, it had pulled the crate from the stack in the corner. The two holding the other crates placed them back on the stack. The crate atop the Specter at ground level sank straight through it, emerging below the liquid alien and settling on the ground.

One of the robots approached the crate and pressed its fingers into impressions on the side. The crate's lid lifted, flipping open and sliding down to tuck against its side. The robot reached inside and grabbed something, then strode toward Alasie and the Telsons.

Oraxis and Genevieve backed away while Alasie stepped forward. The robot looked even bigger up close. Was someone inside of it?

It was extending a closed fist toward her. When it spread its four-fingered hand and opened its metallic palm, she saw that it held five tiny, white pellets.

Pip-Tau's curiosity was greater than her fear — she rushed past Alasie and took the pellets from its hand.

"What are they?" Genevieve asked.

"Dunno," Pip-Tau said. She looked up at the robot. "Thanks, Tin Man! What are they?"

The robot replied with a gentle voice — odd coming from such a giant body. "You're very welcome. They are communications devices called earbuds. Please distribute them, one per person, and insert them into your ear canals." It turned and walked away.

Pip-Tau held one out for Alasie, who accepted it.

It had a tiny hole in one side and a rubbery texture.

Pip-Tau walked over to Oraxis and Genevieve and handed them each a pellet.

Oraxis said, "Never thought I'd see one of these again. We used devices like these before mindspeak was invented."

"Earbuds, huh?" Pip-Tau asked, examining the device. She lifted one of the devices to her ear. "Okay, so the hole is where the sound comes out. You just shove it in your ear?"

Oraxis and Genevieve seemed reluctant to put the devices in their ears, but Alasie didn't hesitate. She oriented the earbud with the hole facing into her ear, then pushed it inside. She imagined her mother warning her that shoving things into her ears would make her go deaf.

"Why would it give us these?" Genevieve asked. "Why are these robots cooperating with the Specters?"

"Mysteries abound," Oraxis said. "Like, why's the bay full of crates and tech? That bot doesn't look like anything I've seen the Guardians use. And, as far as I can tell, the entire back wall's been turned into a server rack. Those look like data cables connecting the boxes to that mobile mainframe."

As Oraxis talked, Alasie heard sounds coming from the earbud. It was static and unintelligible bursts of sound at first, but then it started making sounds like distant barking.

Alasie smiled up at the closest Specter, floating just a few meters before her. It seemed to be watching, waiting expectantly. She said, "They want to talk to us. Put your earbuds in."

After a moment, Pip-Tau exclaimed from behind her, "I think I hear barking!"

"Shh!" Alasie hissed. "Listen for words."

The Specters in the bay were all patrolling the massive room or playing chasing games in the air. That is, all except for one. The solitary Specter approached them cautiously, hovering so low that it almost touched the floor. It stopped just a few yards away.

An unmistakable voice came from the earbud. As soon as she heard it, tears of joy filled Alasie's eyes. She drank in every syllable. This was the moment she'd been waiting for... for *so* long.

The voice said, "I know this is hard to believe, but... this is Zeta. I'm... a Specter now."

10

____

REVENANT

Pɪᴘ-Tᴀᴜ ᴊᴜᴍᴘᴇᴅ ᴜᴘ ᴀɴᴅ ᴅᴏᴡɴ, screaming in her high-pitched, squeaky voice. "You did it, Zeta! I knew you could do it! Oh-my-god, tell us everything! Oh, you glorious boojum-blob, look at you! No tumors or anything!"

Genevieve clung to Oraxis with one hand and covered her mouth with the other.

And then there was Alasie, running straight toward Zeta. Was she going to try for an embrace? Conflicting thought processes fought for control of her response.

Her Specter instincts told her this approaching human needed to be analyzed and either abducted or discarded. It was also nagging at her to retreat — to lance through the airlock doors and return to The Great Ocean. Luckily, she could ignore these instincts.

Her human mind hungered for Alasie's embrace. She had waited so long beneath the ice, listening to the siren's song of Alasie's poetry, fighting against her urge to return. Alasie's pleading cry for help had been more than Zeta could bear. She had given in and summoned her Specter-pooches in a moment of weakness. No — that was a moment of *power* — proving that she could defy her

Specter instinct to stay hidden. She had decided that the Genesis Faction needed the Specters and that she and her pooches were ready.

But rallying the Specters had sparked a war, and Specters were dying. She had no right to put them in harm's way for the sake of the humans of the Genesis Faction. The faction had made their wishes quite clear: Specters have no place in this system — their help was unwanted. Yet when *one girl* called out for help, Zeta threw it all away.

Yes, it was selfish of Zeta to rally the Specters. She knew she was only doing it to be reunited with Alasie and the Telsons. It was so disgustingly *human* of her. Her sense of responsibility to the Specters railed against her rash decision.

Meanwhile, as Alasie advanced, Zeta's synthetic double-mind was also working out ways to solidify the outer layer of a tendril and embrace a human's form without causing it discomfort or harm. Forming a skin didn't come naturally to Specters, so it was a tricky problem to solve, yet an interesting one. It would take some time. She should float out of reach for now.

But Zeta knew that spurning Alasie would hurt her more than exposing her to the freezing, corrosive interior of a Specter.

Zeta pushed out a tendril to wrap around Alasie's arms and torso. Specter cells' tactile and chemical feedback was a richer sensation than the numb, simple sense of human touch. She could *taste* the synthetic materials of Alasie's spacesuit and her skin's salty, biological composition. She could even taste the microbes making their home on Alasie's suit and skin.

But, this chemical analysis was a destructive process. The longer she relished in Alasie's embrace, the more layers of Alasie's skin would dissolve. In a minute, she'd eat through to subdermal fat.

A Specter instinct to abduct and consume flashed through her, making her wonder whether she was giving in to their alien desires more so than her human ones.

The moment lingered. Alasie wasn't retreating. Didn't it hurt?

"Alasie, I'm hurting you," Zeta said, broadcasting using the Astrus algorithm she had worked out.

"I don't care," Alasie breathed.

"Well, I do," she said. "I don't want to hurt you."

She pulled the tendril back, raising her amorphous form a meter higher and out of Alasie's reach.

"How?" Genevieve asked in a shaky voice. Both hands were over her mouth now, and she was in Oraxis's arms. Her hair didn't look like Zeta thought it should. She couldn't tell why at first, but then it came to her — something was wrong with its color.

Color is a peculiar property of matter which humans take for granted. Vision — the analysis of electromagnetic radiation — wasn't the primary sensory input used by the Specters. Their dominant sense was mass detection.

The Specters' unique relationship with gravity allowed them to sense the shapes and densities of objects, even through solid matter. They could focus this sense on objects thousands of kilometers away. This was how Zeta knew that the Guard and Astrus Factions had been building hidden fleets of warships. It was also why active invisibility didn't work against Specters. You can hide your visual presence behind an electromagnetic ruse, but you can't hide your mass.

They complimented this mass detection sense by analyzing electromagnetic waves. Specter cells contained organelles that were sensitive to the full electromagnetic spectrum, from low-frequency radio waves to ultra-high frequency gamma rays. Focusing on the narrow band of wavelengths associated with human vision took effort, but her double-mind worked it out.

Okay, so Genevieve's hair was *black*. Yes, that was different.

She should try to answer Genevieve's "how" question, but that would take all day. Instead, she got down to business. "I brought you here because you're the only humans I can trust. I don't know if we should even be doing this — fighting the Guardians, I mean. The Astri want us to fight on their side. They've been trying to talk to us for a long time, but I didn't reply until after I led the Specters out of

Varuna. They told me about this place and said I could find these communication devices here. I *think* we can trust them, but we should talk about it."

Getting into the dock had been the most challenging part of the Astri's plan. The airlocks would only accept commands from Genesisians so the Astri couldn't open them. Zeta couldn't break in without flooding the dock and damaging the equipment inside. It had taken her a minute to work out a way to vibrate the fluid of her captives' life-support vacuoles to produce the words, "Open the door." Thankfully, Alasie got the message.

"I'm sorry if you don't know this already," Oraxis said, "but the Astri are gone, Zeta. The Guard destroyed their station less than an hour ago."

Zeta replied, "Their station's destroyed, yes, but they're not gone. They lost almost all of their Primes in that attack — their biological brains. It'll take a long time for them to reconstruct and remap that many brains, but they'd evacuated a hundred Primes down here beforehand. And the computer they sent down can run a few thousand of their Secunde personality emulator AI minds. I talked to XT-Secunde for a bit earlier. Oh, and their orbs are down here. All of them. They're in those crates."

Zeta pointed a tentacle at the back wall. She could clearly see the hundred brains within the interconnected, electrified containers. One hundred thousand snugly packed aposynchronic orbs filled the crates stacked behind the front row of Prime containers. It was easy to forget that humans couldn't see inside the containers like she could.

Had they thought the Astrus orbs were in the station? That'd be the worst place to keep your orbs during a war! The Astri told her they have an emergency sanctuary treaty with the Genesis Faction, which allowed their orbs to be covertly dropped down to Syn-Cen and stored in a bay. They also got to send down a small number of brains and enough hardware to support a minimal, self-contained infrastructure.

"Hell, yes!" Pip-Tau laugh-cried. "They're here! The Astri live, baby! Oh-my-god tell me Rho's orb is down here!"

"It should be. I'll find out." Zeta hadn't thought to ask the Astri about that earlier.

She switched her communication mode to speak directly with the Astrus designated as her point of contact. "TYM-Prime?"

TYM-Prime replied, "Yes, Zeta?"

"Is Pip-Rho's orb here at the dock?"

"It is. But I'm not sure you're aware of her unique situation. Pip-Rho has suffered a catastrophic cognitive dissociative collapse. Once CCDC takes effect—"

A boy's voice broke into the channel. "Get it out. Gimmie da orb."

Zeta groaned. The kid's name was Non-Charra, and he was a pest — some kind of fluke of her Specter mind.

Sometimes, she felt like she could see him in a sort of mental image that was more vivid than imagination but nothing like a construct. That's how Non-Charra had first appeared to Zeta, taking the form of her long-lost bro-kin, Charra. Zeta and Non-Charra both understood that he *wasn't* Charra since Charra was dead, but he looked and acted a lot like him. So the boy named himself Non-Charra, and Zeta went with it.

Having him around had been nice when Zeta was lonely, but she wished he'd let her do all the talking.

"I'm sorry," TYM-Prime said hesitantly, taken aback by the unfamiliar voice, "but... I'm afraid I can't release Pip-Rho's orb without her consent. And unfortunately, her containment vessel was attached to our station. One can only conclude that she was killed in the explosion. And, as I was saying, her most recent state of mind does not bode well for her chances of successful neural mapping after resurrection."

"I understand," Zeta said.

"So gimmie da orb!" Non-Charra whined. "You don't need it."

"I'm sorry," Zeta sighed, "ignore the child's voice. Thanks, TYM-Prime, we'll talk again later."

She disconnected from the Astri.

"You have to stop talking," Zeta thought at the boy in her head.

She imagined him crossing his arms and stomping away.

Zeta reconnected to the Telsons. "Yes, Pip-Rho's orb is here."

Genevieve and Pip-Tau embraced while Oraxis nodded. She didn't need to tell them there was zero chance that they could reconstruct a functional human brain from the discordant connectome stored in the orb.

"Gimmie," Non-Charra huffed in the back of her mind.

She ignored him.

"I lost track of what I was saying," Zeta said.

Oraxis replied, "My fault, I derailed you. You were saying you didn't know whether to trust the Astri and that you needed to talk to us."

"Yeah," Zeta said. "So, do you think I should keep having my Specter-pooches fight the Guardians?"

"I knew it," Alasie marveled. "You're in charge of the Specters! You conquered them and turned them into your dogs!"

"Sort of," Zeta said. "I only remember so much, but I know I died. I was resurrected and killed again many times before the resurrection worked correctly. At first, a few other Specters seemed to think they were me, but after a while, they went back to being empty again. It seems like there can only be one Zeta-Specter, but there's nothing wrong with having four hundred thousand Specter-pooches."

"They're really your dogs?" Genevieve asked, gawking at the Specter-pooches playing overhead.

Zeta bobbed an affirmation. "Yeah. There were four complete connectomes in my orb — me and my three dogs: Penelope-pooch, Gorgon-pup, and Chimera-pup. But, like I said, there can only be one of me."

There was so much to explain! She backed up and started again.

"Whatever the Astrus spellsong did to the Specters, I don't think it was anything like they expected. When you translated the lyrics to Gryllus's spellsong, he made it seem like there was going to be some sort of self-destructive, reproductive death orgy going on in Varuna. It was more like the Specters opened themselves up to being repro-grammed or... maybe upgraded. And my orb provided them with a way to recreate my mind. And then the pooch minds.

"I guess it's weird that they're both aliens and pooches, but it's working out well. Pooches — or dogs, to speak more like a Noddite than a Scorpion Tail Tribesman — dogs are pack animals. They work together, which is something I think the Specters needed. And they get along well with humans. Copies of the three dog connectomes somehow got loaded into the receptive Specters, and after a few months, they started acting like dogs.

"I can't explain how I know so much about what happened, and I still don't understand a lot of it. I think I'm behaving like I would if I were a human, but I also have these weird Specter instincts that bubble up sometimes. And somewhere deep in my mind is also this... sort of *soup* of... ideas or memories. I think there's a sort of communal memory in the Specters that they took from the brains of the people they abducted. And there's a part of me that acts like a synthetic double-mind. I can interface with my orb. It's still inside of me."

Zeta pressed the dense ball toward the outside of her form, then up from the top of an extended tendril, lowering it to eye level for the four to see.

"I think it's really her," Oraxis said, sounding astounded.

"You doubted it before?" Zeta asked.

Oraxis shrugged. "The Guardians and Proliferans have been saying the Astri reprogrammed the Specters to be their fighting machines. If their claims were true, this whole thing could've been an

Astrus ruse to gain our trust and... I don't know, maybe get us to convince Veer to hand over control of Cain."

"You don't believe her?!" Pip-Tau squeaked.

Oraxis raised his palms. "I'm just thinking through the scenarios. Seeing an orb is good evidence that this was the Specter that abducted Zeta and that it used the orb to map her connectome to its node-net. But that could be any orb. There're supposedly a hundred thousand Astrus orbs in crates along the back wall there. That could be an Astrus orb you're holding. Can you tell us something about Zeta that the Astri couldn't know?"

She started thinking of an answer when Oraxis spoke again, "Scratch that. Better yet, let's pick a conversation transcript from your bootstrapping and recite our dialogue. What were your first words as a beta?"

Zeta didn't have time to argue. Her double-mind brought up the text transcript of her first words after her beta resurrection. "Hello?" Zeta recited.

Oraxis looked over at Genevieve. He gave her a nod — it was her line. Genevieve seemed to snap out of a trance, then said, "Hello, dear. How are you feeling?"

"I'm confused," she read from the transcript. "Who am I?"

Genevieve said, "Oh, you don't know your name?"

"No. Not my name, not anything," Zeta recited. Her multiple failed and subsequent successful resurrections as a Specter were even more disorienting than her beta bootstrapping. At least when she was resurrected as a beta, she wasn't confused about her *species*.

Oraxis rattled off, "That's discouraging. You should at least know something about yourself."

Zeta said, "Well, I do know my name. I just don't want to tell you until I know who you are."

Oraxis chuckled at this.

Genevieve smiled. A tear was rolling down her cheek. "Oh. Well, in that case, my name's Genevieve."

"And I'm Oraxis," Oraxis said, nodding. "I'd say that's good enough, Zeta."

"She booted you from her slate-space after that," Genevieve laughed, squeezing Oraxis's arm.

Oraxis rubbed Genevieve on the back, smiling at her. "Zeta sure was *formidable*."

"She still is!" Pip-Tau chirped.

"Formidable," Alasie said, devouring Zeta's Specter form with her eyes. "That's a great word for her. She's like a force of nature."

"We keep getting off-topic," Zeta said, trying to redirect the conversation away from her. "What do you think? Should we be fighting the Guardians?"

"Absolutely," Alasie said. "But not you — not while you've got your orb. You have to stay here, where it's safe."

"You're right about that," Zeta said. "I can command the Specters from here. But I still don't want to send my dogs to their deaths if there's no reason to keep fighting. The Guardians are using powerful weapons the Specters have never faced before. We aren't doing a good job. I mean... they're just dogs, after all. Specters are good at hit-and-run sneak-attacks, not extended battles."

"They's good pooches!" Non-Charra shouted.

Zeta imagined her human self wincing in embarrassment. She should've known better than to say anything bad about the boy's precious pooches. Maybe he only spoke in her mind this time.

"I know that voice!" Alasie shouted, waving a finger at Zeta. "That was... the child! The 'you bad pooches come back right now' kid!"

"I's not a kid," Non-Charra humphed.

"Okay," Zeta said, "I guess I should introduce you to Non-Charra. He's... sort of tagging along in my head, but he has a mind of his own."

"I's not part of Zeta," Non-Charra proclaimed.

Zeta continued, "My best guess is my double-mind knew I was lonely, so it created some sort of personality emulation using replays of my bro-kin, Charra. But this bug brain's half as cute and twice as *ornery*."

Non-Charra whined, "I know what that word means, and I isn't ornery, Zeta." She could hear a tinge of a smile in his voice. He was just pretending to be mad.

This was how their banter usually went. Zeta hated to admit it, but she had grown to love this Non-Charra almost as if he truly was her little bro-kin. She worried that, now that she was reunited with humans, he might go away. If his purpose had been to keep her company, she didn't need him anymore.

Unless she returned to Varuna.

A Specter instinct bubbled up as if in response to the idea. Returning to Varuna would mean safety. It would mean home.

Could she bear to retreat again after this reunion?

"Interesting," Oraxis said.

"It's a pleasure to meet you, Non-Charra," Genevieve said. "How old are you?"

Non-Charra announced, "I's four years old."

"Oh, what a big boy!" Genevieve laughed. "And what else can you tell us about yourself?"

"That I's..." he made a swallowing sound, then continued, "I's a thing in Zeta's node-net, and I's not like her. Or the pooches. And I can see you and know you's Gen-ma, and you's pretty."

Genevieve let out a tickled laugh, pressing her hands together before her mouth. "Okay, Zeta, I don't care if he's a personality emulator or not — I'm adopting him. Non-Charra's a Telson."

ZETA TRIED to get the conversation back on topic for what felt like the sixth time. "You can talk to Non-Charra all you want later. First, can we talk about the war? It seems like it's between the Astrus and Guard Factions, and my Specters are just in the way. But it also seems like I started it by busting out of Varuna. I saw all the warships and thought I had to do something — Alasie was begging me to step in. I fought on the Astrus Faction's side because the Guard wanted us both dead — they're a mutual enemy. But it looks like the Astri are outmatched. If I send the Specter-pooches back into Varuna now, I don't think the Guard can get us."

"I agree," Oraxis said. "It seems like this war started with a spark of misunderstanding, then burned through the Astrus defenses in hours. I don't doubt that the Guardians think the Specters serve the Astri, and I don't doubt that you're the one in charge of them. If you have the Specters retreat, that'll prove that the Astri don't control you, and you're not a threat."

"We should see what the Astri have to say," Pip-Tau said.

"Okay," said Zeta, "want me to patch them in?"

Oraxis shrugged. "They'll say to keep fighting on their side, I'm sure. But go ahead."

Zeta bobbed in acknowledgment, then shared their channel's encrypted key with TYM-Prime.

"Thank you for inviting us to your conversation," TYM-Prime said. "XT-Secunde sends his regards."

"Tell him we're sorry about his Prime," Alasie said.

"I will, Alasie."

"Hey," Pip-Tau said, "The war's been a blast — ha, ha — but it's stupid. You're getting your ass handed to you. Better luck next time. We wanna send the Specters back to Varuna. You got one good reason why we shouldn't?"

TYM-Prime replied with the gentle grace characteristic of an Astrus. "Because the war is far from over. This war is between the protectors of the Genesis Faction and those who wish to conquer it. We count ourselves among its protectors, and our fighting forces are far from depleted. But if the Specters abandon the fight, Genesis will surely be lost."

Oraxis shook his head, squinting up at the wall of Primes. "You're saying the Guardians want to *conquer* the Genesis Faction?"

"Yes. As do the Proliferans," TYM-Prime said.

"Your evidence?" Oraxis scoffed.

"The evidence has been building over time. The Guard Faction's attempt to appropriate Cain thirty-one Genesis years ago was the first time they exposed their plans. Their recent covert construction of battleships is further proof. Our own buildup of armaments was a response to theirs and started almost a year later. As we speak, the Genesis population is being consolidated under Guardian control. We fear you may be correct — we may have already lost. But there is still hope if we can defend Syn-Cen."

"You think they'll invade Syn-Cen?" Oraxis almost laughed.

TYM-Prime said, "I'm certain they're on their way here as we speak, if they haven't already arrived. They built a fleet of submarines, and they are likely to commandeer the subterranean transport tube network."

Zeta had never used the tubes, but remembered hearing about a network of underground vacuum tubes with entrances hidden inconspicuously around the planet. The tubes connected to Syn-Cen and were traversed using sealed transport pods.

Zeta instinctively reached out to her Specters to see if they could spot submarines in the water. They also probed the crust of Genesis for the long vacuum tubes. Within seconds, her senses had expanded to encompass the planet. Indeed, there were submarines in The Great Ocean, converging on Syn-Cen. And the vacuum tubes were easy to find. At many of their surface entrances, groups of armored people who could only be Guardians were building structures.

"They're right," Zeta said. "I see them."

"Are they coming down the Jacob's Cellar elevator?" Alasie asked.

"No," Zeta said. "That detached when the space elevator launched. It's like TYM-Prime said — submarines are on their way, and Guardians are securing the tube entrances."

"They must know the Astri orbs are down here," Oraxis said. "They want to finish the genocide they started."

"Maybe," TYM-Prime said. "But I doubt they'll stop with us."

As much as she hated sending Specters into battle, Zeta felt more and more like she had no choice. She only had one more ace up her sleeve — someone who could talk to the Guard on their behalf.

Maybe Jamji could help her make peace.

"I WANT to add Jamji to the conversation," Zeta said. "She can talk to the Guard Faction leadership for us. We'll tell them the Astri surrender, and I'll send my Specter-pooches back to Varuna. Maybe that'll stop the fighting."

"What?!" Alasie shouted. "Jamji isn't going to help us! She's the *worst* kind of Guardian!"

"How would you do that, anyway?" Oraxis asked. "She was escorting our transport to The Cavern of the Soul the last time we saw her. Do you have access to GuardNet?"

Zeta extended a tendril, pointing at a Specter hovering in the far corner of the bay. "I'd give her an earbud. She's over there, in that Specter."

Oraxis threw up his hands while Pip-Tau laughed, "You're so full of surprises, Specter-sis! That's who the fifth earbud's for, isn't it?"

TYM-Prime said, "Please don't let her see our equipment. The Guard Faction leadership could deduce that our orbs are hidden here using a single snapshot of visual input from Jamji."

Zeta hadn't thought of that. She said, "Well, she can't talk inside the Specter's life-support vacuole. The earbuds don't use mindspeak — she has to be in the air to talk to us. I could bring her into the airlock and shut the door."

"No," TYM-Prime said, "you may need that airlock soon, and there's a chance she could sabotage the pumps or activate an emergency evacuation protocol. The Genesis Faction research submarine in the bay has a small brig where you can deposit her. As long as she's unarmed and has no tools, she cannot escape that."

"Oh, I remember the brig," Pip-Tau said. "I spent a month on that sub back in marine biology camp. They used it as a storage room, but we'd always joke about locking someone in it. I'll lead the way!"

Pip-Tau jogged toward the submarine. Zeta commanded the Specter holding Jamji to follow her.

TYM-Prime said, "Once Jamji is added to the channel, please do not share information regarding the Astrus Faction. I will speak on our behalf. Please do not react in a way that betrays your knowledge of the information I must hide throughout the conversation."

"Don't blow your cover," Pip-Tau said. "Roger!"

TYM-Prime said, "And, Zeta, please silence Non-Charra. His presence in the conversation would only confuse matters."

"I wish I could," Zeta said. "I told you he has a mind of his own."

"I isn't gonna talk, okay?" Non-Charra huffed.

"What a good boy," Genevieve said. "When all this is done, I want to do something special for you. Is there anything you can think of that you'd like to do?"

Non-Charra brightened. "Can you... can we have a story time with a campfire?"

"Absolutely!" Genevieve laughed.

"Can Carff-bro-kin come? Zeta said he's funny."

Genevieve laughed again. "He'll be there, too. Oh, this is going to be so much fun! Carff tells the best stories!"

"Okay, I'm being quiet now," Non-Charra whispered.

"Okay, bye-bye for now," Genevieve whispered back.

As Non-Charra and Genevieve talked, Zeta watched Pip-Tau and the Specter pass through the submarine. Pip-Tau issued WUtils commands to open the submarine's doors while the Specter followed, squeezing through the narrow entrances and halls.

Pip-Tau opened the brig door and sighed dramatically. "Like I figured — it's fulla sciencey junk. It'll take a minute to clean out."

At Zeta's command, the Specter reached into the room and scooped out the equipment, depositing it in a nearby open area that might have been a dining hall.

"That works," Pip-Tau laughed.

Next, she had the Specter deposit Jamji in the brig.

"Close and lock the door," Zeta said.

She could see Jamji's form inside the room, coughing up her breathing fluid. Pip-Tau dropped the earbud into the room, then waved at Jamji as she pressed a button to close the door.

Jamji tried to scramble out of the room before the door shut, but she slipped in the viscous puddle of breathing fluid. She slammed a fist into the door, then extended claws and pried at its edges.

"Shout through the door," Zeta said. "Tell her to put the earbud in."

Pip-Tau said, "Yeah, or I could use the intercom." She pressed a button on a panel next to the door, then said, "Hey, Jamji, sorry to lock you in there, but you're a dangerous creature. There's someone here who wants to talk to you. It's the most incredible thing! Put in the earbud. It's on the floor by the door."

Zeta watched Jamji kneel and pick up the earbud, examining it. After several seconds of silent hesitation, she pressed it into her ear and waited.

"Jamji, this is Zeta," she said. "I know this is hard to believe, but I was turned into a Specter. I'm in command of all the Specters now."

"Well," Jamji said, "that's a convincing imitation. Who am I actually talking to?"

"It's really her," Genevieve said.

Oraxis added, "We saw that she still has her orb, and we tested her. She recited the dialogue of a shared experience, word-for-word."

Jamji examined the brig as if looking for a way to escape, even as she talked. "An experience that Zeta could've easily shared with XT-Prime before she died. It's pretty sad you guys are buying into this ruse. But, sure, I'll play along. What does *Zeta* want with me?"

Zeta said, "We were hoping you could speak to the Guard Faction for us. I don't want to fight anymore, but your faction is closing in on Syn-Cen. I need them to stop doing that before I'll call off the Specters."

Jamji said, "We? Who are you speaking for, specifically? The Astrus Hive?"

"No, Jamji, they don't control us. I'm speaking for me and the other Specters. Alasie and the Telsons are on my side, too. Oraxis, Genevieve, Alasie, and Pip-Tau are all here."

"At Syn-Cen?" Jamji asked.

"Be careful," Alasie said. "Don't tell her where you brought her."

Jamji scoffed. "You think I don't know where I am? Syn-Cen Bay Number Two. Which means you brought *Specters* into Syn-Cen. And you think we're going to back off from that? We're securing Genesis. Syn-Cen is compromised."

"I'm ready to send the Specters back to Varuna," Zeta said. "But you have to get the Guardians to stop trying to go down the tubes. With me gone, you have no reason to take over Syn-Cen. I also want you to pull the submarines back."

"Where'd you get the Astrus earbud?" Jamji asked.

"I provided it," TYM-Prime said. "I am TYM-Prime of the Astrus Faction, the only Prime survivor of my hive cluster's destruction. My brain and orb were temporarily housed at the Astrus Embassy Office in Syn-Cen when the Guard attacked. I have secured a safe harbor there. I am prepared to negotiate the terms of our surrender on behalf of my faction."

Jamji went silent. Zeta guessed she was communicating with her commanders. After a minute, Jamji said, "Your Astrus Hive is gone. If you're the only Prime left, how are you commanding all the fighting forces that continue to harass us?"

TYM-Prime said, "Secundes are routinely loaded into drones. They have sufficient autonomy to engage in battle operations. I alone can command them to cease fire, but I will only do so when I am convinced you pose no threat to the Genesis Faction. As it stands, your current posture is one of an invading force."

It disturbed Zeta how good TYM-Prime was at lying. The Astri speak with such confidence and authority that every word they utter seems like a fundamental truth of the universe. If Zeta were in Jamji's position, she'd have believed them.

Jamji paused another few beats before speaking again. "The Guard Faction does not negotiate with non-humans. That includes Astri and Specters. And we will *not* back down. If the Specters want to live, this Zeta impostor can send them back to Varuna. But your retreat won't stop us from completing our mission. We *will* secure Syn-Cen."

Zeta pleaded, "Please, Jamji! You don't understand — I can't let you take Syn-Cen."

"Why is that?" Jamji said. "Because you want it for yourself? Because whoever holds Syn-Cen holds power over the Genesis Faction and their SI?"

"Interesting accusation," TYM-Prime said, "coming from the faction that was caught attempting to commandeer Cain. Zeta, I'm afraid our conversation with Jamji was fruitless. I recommend switching to a new encryption key to discuss our options in private."

Jamji's cold skepticism stung Zeta. She wished there was a way she could convince Jamji she was who she claimed to be. It wouldn't make a difference. The Guardians were invading Syn-Cen, like it or not. She couldn't let them do that — they'd massacre the Astri. And who knew what else they'd do when they took over the place?

That settled it. The Specters had to fight.

11

———

VOTE

AFTER ENDING their failed negotiations with Jamji, Zeta set to the task of coordinating Specter attacks. Commanding an army of dogs with a single human as their leader proved to be an impossible task. After a few minutes, she returned to their channel, crying in frustration. She was losing Penelope-Specter-pooches, Gorgon-Specter-pooches, and Chimera-Specter-pooches by the hundreds.

Alasie and Genevieve consoled her and urged her on.

TYM-Prime and the handful of remaining Primes did their best to contribute to the Specter offenses. There were thousands of cloaked, dormant drones around Genesis, but they didn't have the mental or computational resources to put them to optimal use, and their control signals kept getting jammed by the Guardians. It didn't help that they were transmitting from beneath the deepest ocean trench on the planet.

The thing TYM-Prime told Jamji about Secundes engaging in autonomous battle operations had been stretching the truth — they could follow an order to attack a target or defend a position but lacked the autonomy to concoct their own strategies. Only the Primes could coordinate their movements, and those were in short supply.

The Astri shared a secret — a rare thing for the tight-lipped hive-mind — that three hangars were hidden on Genesis, where fleets of hybrid drone fighters were docked. They designed these hybrids to be flown remotely or piloted directly by human occupants.

They gave a simple explanation as to why they would build such a fleet. "We believed that the Genesis Faction would soon find itself in need of a means of self-defense," TYM-Prime had explained. "We only regret that the armaments we supplied were too little, too late."

On top of that, they had no pilots. Nobody in the Genesis Faction knew that the Guard was closing in on Syn-Cen, or that the Astri were still alive, or that the Specters were their allies now. They couldn't broadcast the news about the Astrus orbs without endangering them. Plus, it would take a miracle to convince anyone to trust the Specters and to attack the Guard.

Everything hinged on Zeta and her dogs.

Pip-Tau had gone down into Syn-Cen to see if she could get face-to-face with EoE Veer Gladstone, since he wasn't responding to WorMS conversations.

Oraxis itched to do *something* to help. When Zeta returned to their channel again, she sounded just as frustrated as before.

"Specters have the advantage in the water," she said. "We've taken out half of the subs. But we're getting blown out of the air. They're bombing the skies over the tube entrances. We can't break through. So many," she choked up, then continued, "so many of my pooches... dead."

The sound of Non-Charra whimpering in the background accompanied Zeta.

Oraxis couldn't take it anymore. He felt his face flushing with pent-up frustration. "Take me to the nearest secret Astrus hangar. I'll pilot a ship and lead a pack of your dogs into battle."

"O, don't be a martyr," Genevieve said. "You'll get blown out of the sky in a heartbeat."

"It's that or twiddle my thumbs down here!" he barked. "I'm fighting, Gen! I don't know what they'll do when they take Syn-Cen, but one thing's for sure — they'll vaporize those orbs." He leveled a finger at the back wall. "And they'll kill Zeta, orb and all! We were devastated when we lost her, but now she's back. We thought Xavier and Pip-Rho were gone, but they're not. We got our family back, and I'm not losing them again!"

Genevieve went to Oraxis, embraced him, and whispered, "It's all just so scary, O. I don't want you to leave, but you're right. Go. Fight for your family."

His eyes burned with suppressed tears. He kissed her forehead. It was sticky with dried breathing fluid. Her hand went to the back of his head and pulled his face down to hers.

They kissed.

It could have been their millionth kiss — they'd been together for so many hundreds of years. But something about it felt more profound than any other kiss he could remember. In the dark corners of his mind, Oraxis knew why.

If Syn-Cen fell to the Guard and the Guard's motives were less benevolent than they claimed, then the Genesis Faction's aposynchronic orbs would be in dire jeopardy. Those orbs were their source of everlasting life. Nobody expected to live long enough to witness the heat death of the universe. War or some other catastrophe was bound to bring their True Deaths someday.

Maybe that day had come.

This could easily be their *last* kiss goodbye.

A SPECTER SUCKED him up into its life-support vacuole. Oraxis would have to ask Zeta how the Specters created these inner pockets of pressure-regulated breathing fluid. All in due time.

He issued the WUtils command to open the inner airlock door, cycled the airlock, then braced himself as he accelerated up through the depths of The Great Ocean. Even at the incredible speeds of the Specters, it would take time to get to the hangar.

"Whoa, hey!" Pip-Tau squeaked through the earbud. "Don't shoot at me! Stop it — I'm on your side!"

"What?!" Alasie shouted. "Who shot at you?"

"Genesisians," Pip-Tau huffed. It sounded like she was running. "Syn-Cen guards by Veer's office! They're chasing me!"

"I see you," Zeta said. "People with guns are in the hall outside Veer's quarters. Two of them are coming after you! You can make it to the elevator before they round the corner. Run!"

Oraxis gritted his teeth. His mind went to work on the new twist. Why would Genesis guards shoot at Genesisians approaching Veer's office? It was as if he was being held captive by his own people. That might explain his uncanny silence all day.

Who on Genesis would want him to stay silent, and why?

Oraxis's stomach dropped as his Specter companion suddenly changed direction. It was probably dodging incoming fire. Hopefully, they wouldn't get shot out of the sky before they reached their destination.

Incoming faction-wide emergency broadcast from Eld of Elds, Veer Gladstone.

Oraxis braced himself as he tuned into the broadcast. He'd witnessed his fair share of emergency broadcasts over the years. They're never good news.

The broadcast was available as either an audio feed or a construct. Since Oraxis was stuck in the darkness of a Specter with nothing better to do, he opted for the construct.

Veer Gladstone, The Eld of Elds, The Black Lion, Archon of the Council of Ten, stood with his usual majestic posture. His mane of walnut-colored dreadlocks merged with his beard to frame his broad face. His skin had a velvety texture and tone, which his admirers likened to milk chocolate. The EoE's formal furs and tribal ornamentation were in perfect order.

The setting was familiar — the Eld Fire. It was a humble campfire shaded by an aged tree atop a hill overlooking a rolling plain. The grassland was dry. Golden, rustling grasses swayed in the breeze under the glaring afternoon sun.

Veer looked at the observation point and spoke in his melodious baritone voice. "People of the Genesis Faction, thank you for joining. I see we only have about forty thousand listening so far. Tell everyone in your vicinity to join us, please. This broadcast concerns us all, and time is short."

Oraxis mindspoke to Genevieve, *"Are you guys listening to Veer's broadcast?"*

"Yes," Genevieve sent. *"We're listening to it, though Pip-Tau's a bit distracted trying not to get killed right now. Zeta's guiding her back to the bay using a route that avoids people with guns."*

Veer nodded for a few beats, then said, "Good, we're at seventy thousand and climbing. That's over two-thirds. We have a quorum. I'll start by apologizing for my silence today. As many of you have already guessed, I had no choice in the matter — I have been taken hostage."

"Who took you hostage?" Oraxis asked. He knew Veer couldn't hear him, but the way the WorMS mass media interface worked was by compiling and distilling the crowd's responses into one or two questions or statements given to the speaker.

Veer shook his head. "No, not by the Guard Faction. But they are involved, for certain. My captors are from our very own faction — members of a secret society called The Agents of Change for a New Genesis. They call themselves NeoGens. These dissidents have drafted a bill, which we will vote on today. Their proposal calls for drastic changes for our faction, including relocating to a new planet. It should not come as a surprise to you that many of our Genesisian kin have strong disagreements with the way that our faction operates. When a minority holds a strong opinion and feels that their voices are unheard, sometimes they take matters into their own hands."

Oraxis was well aware of the rifts in opinions on how best to run the faction. He recalled the sibling seed plan being pushed by

Faylonne-Eta and Matthew-Beta West at the same Surya System Convention where the Pips unveiled Interra. Then there was the constant bemoaning about the presence of advanced superstructures like the Jacob's Ladder space elevator when they were supposed to be hiding from the tech-seeking aliens lurking between the stars.

Yes, Oraxis was shocked that an underground movement to overthrow the faction had surfaced... but not *that* shocked.

Veer continued, "The NeoGens partnered with the in-system Guardian and Proliferan forces to prepare for this day — the day they would amend the Genesis Faction Charter using threats of True Death to any who oppose their new plan. While my information is incomplete — *woefully* incomplete — it is clear that something triggered the Specters' emergence from Varuna. This was the spark that set their plans into motion.

"When the Guard responded to the Specters' emergence, not only did they rally their forces against the Specters but also the Astri — the only offworlders unaffiliated with the NeoGens. The Guard continues to insist that Astri control the Specters. I am not so certain.

"Within minutes of the onset of war, NeoGen soldiers stormed my office. Their leader revealed their plans. I learned that several of The Council of Ten have recently aligned themselves with these revolutionaries. The rest of us were taken hostage. They forced the Council to vote to certify their bill as it is written. I'm ashamed to say that our vote passed with a six to five majority. My Archon vote counted as two of the five in opposition. Elds Peach Edda, Misra Mahalla, and Jess-Eta Primrose joined me in opposition. Yet, to pass such drastic changes as they propose, the bill must also pass a popular majority vote and requires a two-thirds quorum."

Oraxis had never heard of such a thing. It's doomsday, so let's cast a vote? Fear and rational decision-making don't go hand-in-hand. Perhaps that was the point — spark fear in people to get them to vote your way.

Veer continued, "As you have undoubtedly noticed, the Guardians have herded our people together like lambs to the slaughter. Our captors used the threat of an alien invasion to gather you into pens. Now, watch — watch how they turn their weapons on you. My friends, we lost this war before we even knew we were fighting it. Don't bother resorting to violence against your captors. Your sticks and stones could scarcely scuff their armor. Your only power lies in your vote — your power to choose the future of your faction.

"The Worldnet will now read the bill. Its text will scroll through your visual field as it is read. After each section, I will supply personal commentary. My NeoGen captors have assured me I can speak freely — my words are no threat when compared to the firepower of the Guard. And they're right — these terrorists quite assuredly have the upper hand. It pains me to agree with them on many of their points, but I cannot abide by their methods.

"Let's begin. The bill is titled..."

The New Genesis Proposal
Drafted by The Agents of Change for a New Genesis
Certified by The Council of Ten
Genesis Year 680, Month 12, Day 9

Article I: Concession of Failure

1. We concede that the mission we set out to accomplish on Genesis has failed.
2. We concede that the foundational designs of Genesis were flawed and failed to adhere to our faction's Core Principles.
3. Inviting other factions to live in our system and allowing them to build technologically advanced structures was a mistake.
4. Remaining on Genesis after discovering a hostile alien species resident in the Surya system was a mistake.

5. Broadcasting interplanetary and interstellar tightbeam messages was a mistake, whether disguised as cosmic background radiation or not.

Veer's Commentary: I disagree with the first two blanket concessions of failure, but I regret to agree with them on the final three points. Our use of tightbeam and the extended presence of a space elevator may have already revealed our presence to ambush-predator-type aliens such as The Monster from the Stars. That's not to mention the offworlder war, which lit up the space around our planet today. It may only be a matter of time before we are invaded.

Article II: Relocation

1. We shall leave our mistakes behind and move forward with renewed determination, relocating our faction to a new planet, hereby dubbed New Genesis.
2. New Genesis shall be located in a distant sector of the galaxy, no less than five thousand Earth-standard light years from the nearest human colony.
3. New Genesis shall be selected from one of the many planets believed to support some form of basic life, but not one with an intelligence level approaching that of a human.
4. The people of the Guard and Prolifera factions who are currently resident in the Surya system shall assist with this relocation.
5. The Guard Faction shall provide us with an interstellar gas-jet torus carrier, hereby dubbed The New Ark, for the purpose of transporting our aposynchronic orbs to New Genesis.
6. The Prolifera Faction shall copy their unabridged Knowledge Base to The New Ark, including advanced terraforming and planetary survey methodologies, along

with the equipment and raw materials necessary to establish an initial base of operations on New Genesis.

7. Our faction's relocation shall necessitate being outside of existence for tens of thousands of Earth-standard years, with the exception of periodic resurrections of key personnel, to audit our travel and colonization progress.

Veer's Commentary: They gift us a walking stick as they banish us from our lands. Doubtless, these gestures are as much to appease their troubled consciousness as they are gestures of generosity. And they come at a hefty price, friends. A hefty price, indeed. More to come on that below.

Article III: Improved Standards and Charter

1. We shall not repeat the transgressions against our principles which we allowed on Genesis with regard to projecting the illusion of primitive life.

2. The Noddites of New Genesis shall follow strict zero-tolerance broadcasting rules, only transmitting closed-circuit data via physical contact with the new planet's mycelite network.

3. No advanced structures, cloaked or otherwise, shall be constructed on the planet's surface, in orbit, in interplanetary space, or on the surface of any planetary body of the New Genesis system.

4. No visibly unnatural modifications shall be made to our physical forms or the forms of our owned animals.

5. A New Genesis Faction Charter shall be drafted upon arrival to New Genesis to codify the principles inherent in this proposal.

Veer's Commentary: Again, I grumble a reluctant agreement. These ideas speak to me. It is what we should have done from the start. May the mantle of the beast hide and protect us for all of eternity.

Article IV: New Genesis Integration Plan

1. Upon arrival to New Genesis, careful study shall be made of the native lifeforms.
2. If the native lifeforms are incompatible with our biology, a new planet shall be selected.
3. Earth life shall be slowly introduced to the native biomes in such a way as to integrate seamlessly into the planet's ecosystem.
4. We may perform minimal genetic modifications to either our Earth species or the native species, but only when necessary to facilitate integration.
5. This integration period shall take place over the course of ten thousand Earth-standard years.
6. Following this period, the New Genesis colony shall be populated with human life, and the first generation of New Genesis's neoprim humans shall be born.

Veer's Commentary: This addresses the concerns of our biologists, who have long complained that our rapid introduction of advanced life to the existing limited biosphere of Genesis was recklessly hasty. Ten thousand years is a blink of an eye on a geologic timescale, but it's an eternity to the modern human. The longer this new colony takes to re-engineer the planet's ecosystem, the more changes our faraway human kin in other factions will undergo. Will the other factions seek us out and steal our new planet? Some days, I think the long-lost Clanculi had the right idea — hide from other humans, for we are our own worst enemies — more on that in the next section.

Article V: New Genesis Protection Zone

1. Despite the invasion that preceded this bill, the Guard and Prolifera factions shall be considered our eternal allies, with the bond of shared human ancestry.
2. Our allies shall refrain from colonization within five hundred Earth-standard light years of New Genesis, the area hereby dubbed the New Genesis Exclusion Zone.
3. Our allies shall pledge to take any means necessary to prevent the intrusion of human or non-human factions, forces, and lifeforms into the New Genesis Exclusion Zone.
4. Our only interaction with our allies shall come in the form of discreet information packages sent to New Genesis once every one hundred Earth-standard years via capsules disguised as asteroids.

Veer's Commentary: Try not to laugh, friends, for these hopes of a long-standing alliance are sincere. They feel they are doing us a great service and expect we will someday thank them for it. We would be better off if the other factions were never told of our selected planet.

Article VI: The Surrender of Cain

1. We shall surrender Cain, our faction's Synthetic Intelligence, along with the Synthetic Intelligence Central Processing Facility, to the Guard Faction.
2. We concede that Cain's capabilities are underutilized for the simple purposes of our faction and shall not be required at New Genesis.
3. We trust that Cain shall be put to productive use by the Guard Faction for the benefit of all humankind.

Veer's Commentary: If you were looking for the Guard Faction's motive in this invasion, here you have it. Perhaps if we rid ourselves of Cain, we could live in peace, having nothing of value left to be taken.

Article VII: The Surrender of Genesis

1. We shall surrender the planet Genesis to the Prolifera Faction.
2. The neoprim humans of Eden shall be accepted into the Prolifera Faction and acclimated to the ways of modern humans.
3. The Proliferans shall pledge to perform this transition with the grace and care of a mother weaning her baby.
4. Genesis shall become a Proliferan biological studies planet, prized for its unrivaled Earth-like conditions.

Veer's Commentary: And the remaining spoils of war go to the Proliferans. If this comes to pass, today's Edenites will live the pampered lives of advanced humans. There are worse fates.

Article VIII: Vote Options and Ramifications

1. This is a choice-vote bill.
2. If the bill passes, your choice will become effective immediately.
3. A vote in favor of this proposal will be accompanied by the selection of one of two choices: (A) request for your orb to be transferred to The New Ark so that you can take part in the bold future of New Genesis, or (B) remain on Genesis and transfer to the Prolifera Faction.
4. Abstinence from voting will count as a default vote in favor of the bill, with the choice of sending your orb to New Genesis.
5. A vote against this proposal shall be considered a renouncement of your Genesis Faction citizenship.
6. Following the passing of the vote, all factionless inhabitants of Genesis shall be disconnected from the Worldnet, and their aposynchronic orbs shall be ejected

> from the Synthetic Intelligence Central Processing
> Facility.
>
> 7. Regardless of the path we choose, we are prepared for our
>   immediate return to oblivion; we shall surrender to a
>   painless death at the hands of the Guard Faction so that
>   our aposynchronic orbs can be sorted appropriately and
>   the resources of Genesis can be transferred to the
>   Prolifera Faction without obstruction.

THE TEXT SCROLLED out of sight, and Veer reappeared. He lifted his eyes to the observation point and crossed his arms. "You heard that correctly, friends. After the voting is finished and the votes are tallied, this bill will be signed in blood! Our pretended protectors, the Guard, will dispose of our mortal bodies. Your next dawn could very well be on an alien planet, half a galaxy away, tens of thousands of years in the future."

He paused, took a deep breath, and released. "Many of you are asking how such a peculiar vote is possible. NeoGens show no respect for the principles of democracy and have abused our faction's provision for choice-vote bills. These were designed for novel purposes, such as establishing a new project while collecting volunteers on the same ballot. Ominous threats of dire consequences for voting against a bill were never the intention of the choice-vote provision.

"To be clear, the only choices that guarantee your survival are participating in the New Genesis Plan or transferring to the Prolifera Faction. Voting against the bill means forfeiting your orb to the unknown. I believe this bill's authors were intentionally ambiguous concerning the fate of the ejected orbs to save face with the rest of humanity. Doubtless, this document will be shared among billions of humans in other colonies. While it will cause an outcry among humanitarians, the general populace won't be concerned about what happened to all those ejected orbs. They'll assume the Astri retrieved them, or they were shipped to a Proliferan outpost to be resurrected. But, as we have seen, the Guard Faction shows no mercy. I have no doubt that the Guardians will destroy the ejected orbs.

"But that's only if the bill passes. If the majority of us vote against the bill, then it will be rejected in its entirety. Our orbs stay right here at Syn-Cen, our planet remains our own, Cain remains in our possession, and we can take our time deciding whether a more sensible version of The New Genesis Proposal should be drafted. We can do it together, friends, on our own terms. While I agree with many of the points the NeoGens make, I will be voting *against* this bill. I urge you to do the same."

Veer raised a finger of warning. "But I cannot promise that things will go well if the bill fails to pass. We have no power — no means of self-defense. What they couldn't frighten us into giving up voluntarily, they may simply take through force. The Guard Faction has already begun their invasion of Syn-Cen."

Oraxis shouted within the construct, "We can fight, Veer! The Specters are under our control — our allies! We have a fleet of hidden Astrus ships!"

Veer paused for a few beats. He nodded, then continued. "I am getting a variety of interesting comments and questions. Interesting, indeed. Some of these I will try to address in private conversations. That is, if I'm not killed upon termination of this broadcast."

Oraxis hoped this response meant that Veer had seen his comment and would contact him to discuss their options.

Veer paused again, then continued, "Some of you are proposing a strategy you'd like me to share. You suggest that if the bill requires a majority vote in excess of fifty percent approval and if it requires a two-thirds quorum, then it would be better to commit mass suicide to break the quorum. I'm sorry, but the quorum requirement was already met when you were presented with the bill. For those who have read the bill, abstinence from the vote will count as a default vote in its favor, as outlined in Article Eight, Section Four. You can be certain that death counts as abstinence. Passive default votes are another unfortunate *feature* of choice-vote ballots."

Veer clapped his hands and held them together. "My time allotment has elapsed. It is now time to vote. I wish you peace in this life and the next. You have one hour to deliberate, friends. One hour. Use it wisely."

THE CONSTRUCT ENDED, sending Oraxis to slate-space. Worldnet spoke in his head.

You may now cast your vote on The New Genesis Proposal.

He reconnected to his body. He was lying on a stone floor in a pool of breathing fluid. Lifting his head and coughing, he found himself in a dim, cavernous hangar. Rocky walls met a roughly hewn floor. Rows of sleek, absolute black fighter craft were lined up four-by-four, receding into the shadows. He performed a rapid count — fifty rows of four. Two hundred fighters. They'd barely make a dent in the Guardian's defenses, but it was better than nothing.

Oraxis reached out for a group conversation with Genevieve, Pip-Tau, Carff, Alasie, and Natasha-Zeta Herrington. Alasie and Nat were like family, so he wanted them to be included.

Everyone accepted, then mindspoke all at once.

"I knew we couldn't trust the Guard!" Alasie sent.

"I just can't believe this!" Genevieve wailed.

"Bastard jerk-face meathead assholes!" Pip-Tau squeaked.

"A day for the history books!" Carff whistled.

"Good to hear from the Telsons," Natasha-Zeta sent. *"Glad you're okay. I was worried when you went quiet after the door-opening talk. Did you figure out where you are?"*

"We'll catch you up momentarily," Oraxis sent. *"Let's try to bring TYM-Prime into the conversation. Maybe they can patch in Zeta since the Astri seem to be the only ones who can communicate with Specters."*

"Did you say Zeta?!" Natasha-Zeta exclaimed.

Alasie sent, *"Yeah, she's a Specter now! She's in charge of all the Specters — they're her dogs. I knew she could do it."*

The two continued this back-and-forth as Oraxis issued the WorMS request to add TYM-Prime to the conversation.

Offworld Faction Worldnet access is temporarily disabled per an emergency mandate by The Council of Ten.

He cursed, then spoke aloud. "Hello, TYM-Prime? Zeta? Are you there?"

"We are," TYM-Prime said through the earbud. "I gather from everyone's silence that there was an interesting faction-wide announcement."

"What's going on?" Zeta asked.

Oraxis shook his head and looked up at the nearest fighter craft. The absolute black aircraft was all sharp angles and flat surfaces, like a wasp chipped from obsidian. He needed to get that bird in the air and lead a pack of Specter-dogs into battle. But they needed hundreds more pilots, and nobody besides the Telson party understood the Specter situation. They couldn't organize a coordinated resistance with these fractured lines of communication. Explaining everything to everybody was going to take time.

It was a logistical nightmare.

Pip-Tau said, "Well, the short story is: we're about to vote on a bill that'll relocate the Genesis Faction to a new planet, give Genesis to the Proliferans, and give Cain to the Guardians."

"What?!" Zeta shouted.

Non-Charra whined, "That's against the rules!"

"Would you care to share the full bill text?" TYM-Prime asked, unperturbed.

Oraxis said, "We don't have time for that. You're blocked from Worldnet, so we'd have to read it aloud. Voting closes in one hour, and we need to get a plan in motion now!"

Natasha-Zeta sent, *"So, how's everyone planning on voting?"*

"You have to vote no, Nat!" Alasie shouted. *"I can't believe you'd even ask!"*

"I tell you, I can't abide a bully!" Carff shouted. *"I'm voting no!"*

"You must admit," Oraxis sent, *"voting against the bill is a gamble with dire consequences. I fully expect most will play it safe and vote for it."*

Genevieve sent, *"O, you're not seriously considering—"*

"No, I'm voting against it. But let's not fool ourselves. The bill will pass."

Alasie almost growled, *"You think the Genesisians are cowards? They'll vote against this bill. They'll take up arms and fight!"*

Call it what you like, but Oraxis knew he was right. Rather than argue the point, he used Alasie's mention of fighting as a segue. *"On that note, I'm in the presence of five hundred fighter craft. TYM-Prime said there were two more hidden hangars. If they're similarly stocked, we've got fifteen hundred craft. If we can find that many capable pilots, we may be able to lead a combined Genesisian and Specter resistance. The first challenge will be convincing that many people to fight alongside Specters. We'll have to break through Guardian defenses to pick up the volunteers with Specters to transport them to the hangars."*

"I've got bad news," Zeta said. "The Guardians have a transport pod of some sort loaded into a tube. They packed it with thirty soldiers. It's already headed toward Syn-Cen, and they're going pretty fast. I think they'll be here in a few minutes."

Oraxis squeezed his eyes shut. He could feel his pulse pounding in his temples. This disaster was getting worse every second. They were as good as dead, but he wasn't going down without a fight.

He sent, *"Let's get our votes cast before any of us die in a blaze of glory. I'd hate to end up with the default vote and having my orb shipped off to New Genesis. Like I said, I'm voting against it."*

Pip-Tau sent, *"Ditto."*

"I'm voting against it now, too," Genevieve sent. *"For better or worse, we're all in this together."*

"Okay, here goes," Natasha-Zeta sent.

"I voted earlier," Alasie sent. Of course she did.

"Atta girl," Carff laughed. *"Vote early and vote often!"*

Oraxis opened his mind to the Worldnet and thought, *"I'm ready to vote on the New Genesis Proposal."*

What is your vote?

"I am against it."

Please note that this is a choice-vote bill. If the bill passes, your vote will serve as a renouncement of your Genesis Faction citizenship. Consequently, your Worldnet access will be rescinded, and your aposynchronic orb will be ejected from the Synthetic Intelligence Central Processing Facility orb vault. Are you ready to lock in your vote against the bill?

Oraxis Telson sealed his fate with a thought. *"Yes."*

Oraxis mindspoke and verbalized simultaneously. This would include Natasha-Zeta and Carff on WorMS, with Zeta and the Astri on the earbud. "Okay, my vote is cast. Now, you guys work out a plan to defend Syn-Cen and catch each other up on what's happening. Zeta, send a pack of Specter-dogs with me. Five hundred or more, if you can manage that. We're going to break through the

Guardian defenses at The Cavern of the Soul and abduct all the Noddites there. Those are the people of the Thin Forest — our neighbors and friends. If we can convince anyone to take up arms with us, it would be them."

"Okay," Zeta said, sounding uncertain.

TYM-Prime said, "Recall that there are still one hundred Astrus Primes. We have been focusing on piloting orbital drones in search of Guardian command ships, but we will divert twenty minds to fight by your side."

He looked at the nearest ship. "Thanks, TYM-Prime. Now, how do I board one of these fighters?"

TYM-Prime said, "XT-Secunde will walk you through the onboarding procedure. We'll mute your communicator's audio so that you can focus on the task at hand. Call my name if you wish to resume the group conversation."

Oraxis also excused himself from the group WorMS conversation. He needed to be laser-focused.

Xavier's voice came from the fighter craft. "Hello, Oraxis. It will be my pleasure to serve as your AI companion."

Every Astrus had a corresponding AI persona — a personality emulator trained to their ways of thinking and speaking. This was their Secunde, as opposed to their true self — their Prime. Oraxis usually found it off-putting to talk to a Secunde, but it was nice to hear Xavier's voice.

"Please disrobe," XT-Secunde said.

Oraxis chuckled at this. Sure, why not die naked? He pulled off his damp furs as quickly as possible, muttering, "You could at least buy me dinner first."

XT-Secunde humored him with a laugh, then continued, "The fighter craft before you is called a Wasp."

"Funny," Oraxis grunted, pulling off a boot. "That's exactly what I thought of when I saw it."

"Aptly named, indeed. But I assure you, none of its design is cosmetic in nature. I think you'll be pleased with its flight characteristics, pilot interface, and weapons systems. Please follow the illuminated path into the cockpit, Oraxis."

A hatch was already open on the top of the black craft. A green strip of lights marked a path up the steeply sloped wing and into the hatch. Flaps on the surface of the wing lifted, creating a staircase. The fighter had no windows, meaning it relied entirely on an external optical array. It probably also meant it was spaceworthy.

Oraxis climbed the wing, then walked atop the fuselage, as naked as the day he was born. Looking down the hatch, there was a recessed platform with two depressions in the shape of feet.

"Please step into the feet indicators," XT-Secunde said.

He complied. The platform began to descend. Luke warm fluid swirled around his feet, climbing up his legs as he descended.

"Is that breathing fluid?" Oraxis asked.

"Yes," XT-Secunde said, "it is breathing and suspension fluid. Liquid submersion is essential for protecting your body from the pressures of ultra-high-G maneuvers."

Oraxis was painfully aware of this. It would be his third immersion in one day, and the other two hadn't been pleasant experiences. "How am I going to talk to you without air?"

"The pilot interface uses direct neurite connections."

The fluid was up to his chest, and his legs were being pressed forward into a sitting position. "You're jacking into my double-mind? How is that even possible?"

XT-Secunde gave a genuine laugh. "We are the Astri, Oraxis. Please relax and let the cockpit systems secure your body."

His face was in the fluid now. He issued a bio-override to stop his gagging reflex, then inhaled the warm, slick fluid. It tasted saltier and more acidic than the fluid the Specters used. They should trade recipes.

The hatch thunked shut, snuffing out the dim light from above. The padded inner surfaces of the cockpit began to press in on him from every side. Something rubbery pushed on his lips until he opened his mouth and allowed a mouthpiece to be inserted.

His torso was being squeezed and released, forcing manual breathing of the fluid. Pressure at the back of his neck hinted at microfilaments of neurites painlessly invading his skull. Neurites were mercifully good at dodging nerve endings. It disquieted him that his brain was being tapped, but he was in no position to complain.

"Please enter slate-space," XT-Secunde said, as clearly as if he was an arm's length away.

Oraxis complied.

The darkness of slate-space was as empty as ever. But after a moment, the form of XT-Prime — no, Secunde — materialized before him, wearing nothing but a loin cloth. The beautiful man with a bald head graced him with a serene smile. "Ready to fly?"

"Ready," Oraxis said.

———

Oraxis's slate-space gave way to an image of the hangar. He turned his head, finding that he could look in every direction. Transparent HUD indicators for airspeed, ammunition, and other vital systems hovered at the corners of his vision.

He tried switching to the infrared spectrum in the same manner as he would with his enhanced vision. The optical array obliged. He could see the cool stone floor, the cooler puddle of breathing fluid he'd hacked up, and the frigid blot of swimming darkness nearby — his Specter companion.

XT-Secunde said, "You have flown before, so you understand the basics. You will find that the Wasp's cybernetic controls are as intuitive as your bioenhancements. The interface allows your double-mind to perceive the ship as a physical extension of your body. Biological feedback corresponds to ship status. Pain indicates damage taken. Hunger indicates low fuel. Muscle strain indicates dangerous stresses on the ship's frame."

Now that he thought about it, Oraxis felt like he was sitting on the hangar's floor. He could feel the light pressure of the ship's weight as if it were his own body.

XT-Secunde continued, "I can take control at any time if you need help. I can control any of the Wasp's systems, though you are better suited for combat than I am."

Oraxis had flown many times before and had taken part in war game skirmishes during his youth back on Earth. He'd also flown more than his fair share of combat simulation constructs. But he didn't see why that made him much better suited than XT-Secunde for combat. Perhaps there was an edge that a biological brain gives you.

Oraxis looked down, finding no virtual controls. He was accustomed to yokes, joysticks, pedals, and throttle levers. This was going to be interesting. Any other day, he'd spend hours studying the Wasp's systems and capabilities before he boarded it, but he needed to get moving.

Since he hadn't seen wheels on the craft, he assumed it was capable of vertical take-off. He imagined lifting himself up off the ground.

True to form, the Wasp's engines engaged. He lifted with grace, then turned toward the entrance. Part of him feared he'd plow the craft into the wall with a stray thought. It was a surreal, almost dreamlike piloting experience.

He urged the Wasp forward, easing it toward the narrow opening where daylight trickled into the hangar.

"You're doing wonderfully, Oraxis," XT-Secunde said.

He slipped out of the hangar and emerged into the bright light of Surya, flying over an ocean. Looking back, he could barely make out the hole in the oceanside cliff where the hangar was hidden. The wireframe of an invisible Wasp emerged from the hole, followed by another. They kept filing out of the hangar in an orderly fashion — his Astrus fighting companions taking flight.

XT-Secunde said, "I took the liberty of engaging your active invisibility system and lifting your landing gear."

"Thanks. Good thing Specters can see invisible ships." That was a bit of a mystery. If they could see through active invisibility, why didn't they attack invisible ships as often as visible ones? He had so many questions for Zeta.

"The Specter swarm is following," XT-Secunde said. "Obedient dogs, ready to follow your lead. Your ship can broadcast using the Specter frequency and algorithm, meaning you can talk to them. Whether they'll understand or obey is another question."

He looked around, spotting hundreds of darting black blobs above and behind him.

"Set a course for The Cavern of the Soul," Oraxis commanded.

A faint green line appeared before him, curving and leading off to the North.

It was time to see what this thing could do. He urged the Wasp forward, following the line as he accelerated.

Damn, it was nimble!

Oraxis charged toward certain death with the wind flowing over his wings and the warmth of Surya on his hull.

He never felt more alive.

12

SHINING ARMOR

"Friends and fans, tune in now!" Pip-Tau squeaked over her reopened broadcast.

She had Zeta pose a few of her Specter-pooches in an empty corner of the hangar so Pip-Tau could share their images without revealing her location or the Astrus orb sanctuary. The video feed from her vision would show the three swimming blobs hovering obediently. "Spread the word! The Specters are on our side! We still have a chance to defend ourselves if we can secure Syn-Cen. You don't have to give in to these terrorists. Vote no!"

Hopefully, she'd get her message out before too many people voted for it. She didn't think changing your vote was an option.

Her viewer count was a paltry 603. It seemed like everyone was too busy sending out their own urgent broadcasts for hers to break through the noise.

The audience flooded her with replies, with moods ranging from cautious optimism to mouth-frothing rage. Their overall tone was skeptical.

She said, "You don't think the Specters are our allies? Well, they are! They've changed, people! I can prove it! Watch this — they're as obedient as dogs now. Hey, Specters! Gimmie a P!"

This was the prompt for Zeta to command the first Specter to form itself into the letter P. This proved to be challenging for the amorphous blob. The result was a lumpy, undulating club barely resembling a P.

It was fine.

"Gimmie an I!"

The second Specter formed into a slug of a line. It was a lot taller than the P.

It was *fine!*

"Gimmie a P!"

The third Specter morphed into a slightly more convincing P than the first.

"What's that spell? That's right, Pip! They know who's boss, so hold tight and vote no! The resistance has a few more tricks up our sleeves, so stay tuned!"

The viewer count had climbed to 950. She sighed and closed the broadcast.

"What a waste of breath," she moaned. "I didn't even get one percent of the faction to listen. What's the point of being famous if nobody listens to you?! We need to wallop those NeoGen jerk-faces that shot at me and get word to Veer. They'd listen to him!"

"Then that's the plan, right?" Alasie asked, giving an angry huff. "We take these Specters down into Syn-Cen and kill anyone that gets in the way. Right?"

That's Aggie for ya.

"We can try," Zeta said, "but I don't think they're very good at fighting in tight spaces like corridors. And they run away after getting zapped by those energy rifles."

"Pooches doesn't like zaps," Non-Charra added.

"May I interject?" TYM-Prime asked over the earbud. "We can offer an alternative to sending Specters into Syn-Cen." TYM-Prime paused as if waiting for permission to proceed.

"Well, spit it out!" Pip-Tau shouted. This was no time for beating around the bush.

They said, "One hundred multi-function bipedal robots are in the bay with us. We call them Grunts. These are combat-ready hybrid drones, meaning they can be piloted by human occupants or remotely controlled by Astri. We are prepared to devote fifty Primes to piloting half of the Grunts. We recommend recruiting fifty Genesisians from Syn-Cen to pilot the rest in defense of Syn-Cen. The Astri lack Worldnet access, so we cannot issue commands to open doors or control elevators. Granted, we could cut or blast through the doors, but that would hinder our mobility and open passages for the enemy. For this reason, pairing Genesisians with Astri is an optimal strategy."

"Grunts!" Pip-Tau cheered. "Love it! Let's rock!"

Alasie asked, "The tubes are the problem, right? Can we go to the tube station and kill the Guardians when they get there?"

"Yes, and hurry," Zeta said. "The first transport is almost here!"

Alasie took off in a mad dash toward the robots. Pip-Tau followed, moving her skinny little legs as fast as they could go in the bulky spacesuit.

HALF of the Grunts came to life. They lifted their sensor-laden heads and pulled their shoulders back in unison. Their armored surfaces were mirrored, which meant they didn't have active invisibility systems. But mirrors reflected lasers and masers — a good trade-off.

"Please stop running and disrobe," TYM-Prime said.

Pip-Tau staggered to a stop. "Seriously?"

TYM-Prime said, "Clothing interferes with our cybernetic systems. For example, if a projectile should penetrate your leg, the Grunt would seal and compress the wound. Clothing interferes with these features."

As TYM-Prime talked, Alasie ran back to Pip-Tau. She huffed, tugging at her suit's straps and searching for release latches. "Help me with my spacesuit!"

Pip-Tau had both of their spacesuits off in a matter of seconds. Next came their jumpsuits. As she disrobed, she noticed Genevieve was still standing near Zeta-Specter. "What's wrong, Gen-ma? You don't wanna get naked and pilot a battle mech?"

Genevieve shook her head. She was at least forty meters away, but her gentle voice came clearly through the earbud. "You know I'm not a fighter, Pip-Tau. I'll stay here and play telephone operator — the Specters and Astri can't use WorMS. I need to tell Nat what's going on so she can spread the news to the others at The Cavern of the Soul. They're about to be abducted and drafted as fighter pilots. Also, I want to keep Zeta and Non-Charra company. They're dealing with a lot right now."

"I love Gen-ma," Non-Charra said.

Genevieve laughed, "I love you too, Non-Charra. And you, Zeta. I can't express how wonderful it is to have you back."

"Please step into the Grunt, Pip-Tau," a voice said from behind her. "I am RRE-Secunde, and I will be your AI companion."

Pip-Tau stepped out of her jumpsuit, covering her nakedness with spindly arms, and turned around. A Grunt was squatting before her with its back spread open like a beetle spreading its wings. Two steep steps, illuminated with green light strips, led to its interior. The Grunt's inner surface was lined with shiny white padding. It almost looked organic — a white, silken womb.

Another Grunt was spreading its back open and squatting before Alasie. "Please step into the Grunt, Alasie. I am MAW-Secunde, and I will be your AI companion."

Alasie bounded into the Grunt, crawling into the interior cavity. The Grunt's armored back panels closed again, hiding her naked backside.

Here goes nothing!

"Tally-ho!" Pip-Tau shouted, rushing to her Grunt. She climbed the steps and slipped inside. A thin layer of slime coated the squishy inner surfaces.

Kinda gross, but we're rolling with it.

The cavity was shrinking around her, closing in from every side. The lights went out as the rear hatch closed. Warm, wet padding enveloped her, urging her into a fetal position. This was interesting, since Pip-Tau expected her arms and legs to be shoved into the arms and legs of the Grunt. It made sense, though — the massive Grunt's articulation didn't match her body's joints.

She said, "Be gentle with me, RRE-Secunde. It's my first time doing anything like this. Well... outside of a construct. Hey, RRE-Secunde — two R's — Artoo? Yep, I'm calling you Artoo."

RRE-Secunde laughed at her joke. They said, "Don't worry, it's just like in the constructs. The Grunt's interface uses a direct neurite link, so it feels like controlling your own body. And I have to get this out of the way... RRE-Prime and I are big fans of yours."

"Awesome! When this is all over with, I'll get you an autograph. Now, let's get this Grunt moving!"

"Sorry," RRE-Secunde said in the darkness, "I know time is short. Please open your mouth for the breathing apparatus and relax as the Grunt conforms to your body. You should also connect to slate-space."

Pip-Tau opened her mouth wide. A rubbery mouthpiece pressed against her tongue. She closed her teeth around it and breathed in the air. Aside from feeling a bit claustrophobic, she was pretty comfy.

She connected to slate-space and waited.

<hr>

After a few seconds, an Astrus appeared. They had a bald head and lean, feminine features. They wore strips of white cloth over their chest and pelvis and had the light skin of Earth's Caucasians. She wasn't used to uninvoked images appearing in her slate-space.

"Artoo?" Pip-Tau asked.

The Astrus bowed their head in acknowledgment. "The neurite bridge is almost complete, Pip-Tau. In the meantime, I'll inform you of a few of the Grunt's capabilities. Retractable wheels in the knees and feet allow for high-speed four-wheel travel on smooth surfaces such as the halls of Syn-Cen. To use them, drop to your knees while urging yourself forward."

"Cool, seems easy enough."

RRE-Secunde continued, "Its ranged weapons include a multi-band laser/maser energy rifle in the right arm, a railgun in the left arm with five hundred rounds of ammunition, and six miniature anti-matter missiles which launch from its shoulders."

"Whoa! Yeah, I don't think we'll be exploding any antimatter today," Pip-Tau said.

RRE-Secunde raised their eyebrow and smiled with a hint of mischief. "Don't speak too soon. If we're going to collapse the subterranean tubes leading into Syn-Cen, I can't imagine a better method. And the antimatter payloads are a modest eight milligrams. We'll continue this briefing in a moment. You're connecting now."

Pip-Tau's vision returned. She was tall! Turning her head around, she found she could spin it in a full circle like the girl from The Exorcist. Fun! She raised her hands, looking down at the mirrored armor of the Grunt. The hands before her felt like her own. She wiggled her fingers, and the robotic hand obeyed.

It occurred to her that the interface was giving her sensory feedback. It was like she was moving her own body. She clapped her hands together, making a resounding metallic clang. There was a slight sting of pain in her hands.

Way cool!

Alasie's Grunt was already on its knees, speeding toward one of the bay's exits. A quarter of the other Grunts followed in her wake.

"Hold up, Aggie, what's the plan?!" Pip-Tau shouted. "Artoo, can Alasie hear me?"

"I'll patch you back into the group channel with Alasie, Zeta, Genevieve, and TYM-Prime."

"Aggie!" Pip-Tau shouted again.

"What?!" Alasie shouted back. A tiny pop-out appeared in Pip-Tau's vision, pointing at Alasie's Grunt and displaying a miniature picture of her face. She had reached the door and WUtil'ed it open. The Astrus battle bots started funneling out.

Pip-Tau squeaked, "We gotta find pilots for these other Grunts!"

Alasie replied, "*You* do that! I'm taking these Astri to the tube station to stop the Guardians from invading Syn-Cen!"

"Fine, but I need Veer," Pip-Tau said. "People aren't listening to me. Zeta, can you use your X-ray vision to see how many NeoGen fighters are guarding Veer's quarters?"

"Um," Zeta said. She paused, then continued, "I count eighteen people with guns guarding the halls near where you were attacked earlier. I see Veer. He's tied to a chair! Three people are in his room with him. One looks like they've got a robotic suit, but it's smaller than the Grunts."

Pip-Tau liked those odds. Unarmored humans wouldn't stand a chance against a Grunt. She could probably take them all out alone, but she wouldn't risk it. "TYM-Prime, can I get... like five of your Primes to come with me?"

"Of course," TYM-Prime said.

Five of the idle Grunts turned toward Pip-Tau. She ran a few steps, then dropped to her knees. Her wheels deployed, and Pip-Tau was knee-boarding like a pro.

Have no fear, Veer! Your Pip in shining armor is on her way!

THE SIX GRUNTS rode their kneelie-wheelies through the Syn-Cyn corridor. Four of her squad cruised two-by-two in front of her while the fifth pulled up the rear. It was a defensive formation protecting Pip-Tau.

The few people they passed ducked swiftly into side rooms, eyes widening at the impossible sight of robots whizzing by. Any of these people could be NeoGens.

RRE-Secunde helped her to open a channel with her squad, whose names floated above their heads like characters in a game. Pip-Tau said, "Keep an eye out as we pass these Genesisians. Anyone holding a weapon is fair game."

SFGX-Prime replied, "The Astri have yet to take the life of anyone in the Genesis Faction, and we'd prefer to keep our record clean. May we disarm the hostiles and immobilize them using non-lethal force?"

"Fine," spat Pip-Tau. It was no wonder the Guardians mopped the floor with the Astri. Humanitarians have no place on a battlefield. "But I can't promise I'll be so nice. These NeoGen jerks are treaso-nous, traitorous turd-noggins. They tried to kill me earlier! Okay, we're getting close. I'm overclocking."

Pip-Tau sped up her neural firing rate, sending the world into slow motion. Doors and side corridors, which had been whizzing by, now passed at a leisurely pace.

"Turn right at the next intersection," she said, "and get ready to fight."

The unanimous reply came swiftly. "Confirmed."

They reduced speed and skidded around the corner. At the other end of the hall stood two men with guns. They wore white Syn-Cen jumpsuits with red bands around one of their arms.

"Engaging targets," JSKO-Prime said.

Pip-Tau's HUD showed what she assumed was a collaborative feed because the two men down the hall already had target boxes around them. Reticles were trained on their weapons. The men were lifting their rifles in slow motion.

Too slow, assholes.

White-hot explosions erupted on the sides of their guns, blasting the weapons out of their hands. The men flinched, then scrambled to take off their weapons' shoulder straps.

A siren started going off — the fire alarm. Red strobes lowered from the ceiling. Sprinklers popped down and began spraying fire suppression foam.

Pip-Tau's arms were both leveled on the men. All she had to do was give the thought-command to fire her weapons, and they'd be burger meat.

The two staggered, then collapsed beside their ruined rifles.

Before she could ask what happened, one of her team said, "Focused subsonic stimulation to the vagus nerve can induce vaso-vagal syncope in those not prepared with bio-overrides."

Pip-Tau didn't have time for WoQS queries. "What?"

MJS-Prime said, "We made them faint using sound waves."

HLLM-Prime said, "I'll bind them with adhesive while the rest of you neutralize the remaining sixteen combatants. I'll reinforce the vagus stimulation every ten seconds to ensure they stay unconscious."

"That's a three-way intersection ahead," Pip-Tau said. "Veer's quarters are down the left corridor. I think we can—"

"Incoming!" ANTA-Prime shouted.

A mini-missile was rounding the corner!

The thumping of rail rifles and fizzing of laser discharge was followed by a blinding explosion. Pip-Tau fell to the side, ducking behind the Grunts in front of her.

Pain exploded on her right shoulder. Heat enveloped her.

"Right shoulder actuator damaged," RRE-Secunde announced. "You won't be able to lift that arm higher than forty-five degrees."

That didn't seem too bad unless she needed to throw her Grunt's arms up in surrender. To hell with that idea.

"The front line took the brunt of the explosion," JSKO-Prime said, as calmly as if they were discussing the weather. "But they are still mobile. They will act as our shields. Pip-Tau, stay behind us."

"Confirmed!" Pip-Tau shouted.

Smoke filled the air, but the Grunt's visual systems compensated for it. The flaming remains of the two passed-out men were scattered across the ground. Part of the wall and ceiling were destroyed, filling the corridor with smoldering debris. Fire suppression foam was piling up in a layer on the walls and floor, quickly dousing the flames created by the explosion.

The squad hopped up from their knees to their feet as they reached the corner, running at full speed toward the intersection.

LASERS ARE invisible as they pass through the air. Sorry, sci-fi nerds, but none of that red beam pew-pew stuff you see in the movies makes any sense in the real world. But when there's particulate matter in the air — smoke, for example — they make a dazzling light show.

Bright white pulses stabbed through the intersection as the first two Grunts rounded the corner, right arms lifted. They let loose with energy weapons of their own.

Metallic feet slammed on polished stone. Reflected lasers cut through fire-suppressant foam and scorched holes in the walls and ceilings. Pip-Tau wondered if the Astri were still trying to do this without killing anyone.

"Incoming!"

HLLM-Prime's Grunt swiveled on its heels in front of her. Pip-Tau couldn't stop in time — their robotic bodies collided. A blast of flame bloomed from around the corner. The charred, mangled form of a Grunt flew past the intersection like a rag doll. Her HUD told her it was ANTA-Prime.

Pip-Tau fell backward. HLLM-Prime's Grunt stumbled but stayed on its feet.

"I've neutralized their missile launcher," said SFGX-Prime.

"My Grunt is critically damaged," ANTA-Prime said. "I will stay here and cover your rear flank to the best of my ability."

HLLM-Prime helped her to her feet, then followed the others around the corner. Pip-Tau was the last to get a look into the battle-ravaged corridor. Her HUD overlaid boxes around the fourteen forms of enemies lying on the ground. Tiny moving squiggles beside their HUD overlays indicated their heartbeats.

She barely noticed the blaring fire alarm. Maybe Artoo tuned it out for her. Red strobes flashed in the hall, and foam rained down upon their fallen enemies.

By her count, two had gotten away.

"I've been watching," came Zeta's voice. Pip-Tau didn't even know she was on the channel. "I'm sorry, I didn't know they had rockets — they only looked like guns to me."

"No worries, sis-kin," Pip-Tau said, returning to a normal neural firing rate. Overclocking and clear thought don't mix unless you're Pip-Rho. "Now comes the final boss. We have to neutralize the three in Veer's room, including the one with armor. And we can't hit Veer! What can you tell us about their positions?"

"One's hiding behind Veer with a gun to his back. Veer's tied to a chair. They're sort of at the back of the room. Another one's ducked behind an overturned table near the door. The one wearing armor is in the corner of the room to the right side of the door."

Pip-Tau had jogged her Grunt to Veer's door. She pointed to the right. "This side?"

"Yeah."

"This will be difficult," MJS-Prime said. "Grunts won't fit through the door unless we slide in sideways and headfirst."

HLLM-Prime was moving between the passed-out combatants, clearing the foam off their faces before spraying adhesive along their arms and legs. They said, "If there are no side rooms to hide in, we can neutralize them from the hall."

"There aren't," Pip-Tau said. "Okay, here's the plan — I'm gonna shoot armor-guy through the wall with my rail gun. You guys try to force the door open. I can't open it with WUtils since it's a private room."

She moved into position, pointing her left arm at the wall. "Am I aiming at him, Zeta?"

"You're too far to the right," Zeta said.

Pip-Tau stepped to the left. "Now?"

"Another half step."

She half-stepped.

"Now you're pointing right at his head," Zeta said.

Pip-Tau started overclocking again. "Ready?"

SFGX-Prime, MJS-Prime, and JSKO-Prime crowded around the door. JSKO-Prime and MJS-Prime had their hands on the door's seam, ready to pry it open, while SFGX-Prime kneeled with both arms raised and ready to fire.

"One moment," HLLM-Prime said. They finished gluing down the last of their fainted foes, then joined the other four. "Ready."

Pip-Tau cringed as she prepared to fire a real-world weapon and kill a real-world person for the first time. The punishment for murder is orb destruction. But this was war — this didn't count, did it?

"He kneeled!" Zeta shouted. "Aim lower!"

Pip-Tau lowered her arm.

"That's good," Zeta said.

Before she could second-guess herself, Pip-Tau flexed her left forearm, letting loose a barrage of carnage into the wall before her. She scattered her rapid-fire shots in small circles. Rock chips and dust exploded from the wall.

The creaking of straining metal signaled the opening of Veer's door. Reflected laser beams burned white lines through the smoke and dust.

"Hostile behind table immobilized," SFGX-Prime said.

"You got two of them," Zeta said. "There's still one behind Veer!"

Pip-Tau stopped firing. Her left arm felt burning hot.

"We can't get a clear shot from this angle," SFGX-Prime said, just as pleasant as you please.

Pip-Tau went to all fours and crawled to the hole she had blasted in the wall. Foam was raining down within the chamber, but it had stopped in the corridor. She looked through the hole. The first thing she spotted was the ragged remains of the power-armor-wearing man she'd killed.

She had... *killed.*

No, it didn't count — he'd be resurrected.

Fire suppressant foam would soon hide the bloody mess. The scene was surreal — bubble bath carnage.

She lifted her view to spot Veer. He sat with his hands tied behind a chair, eyes fixed forward in fearless pride. Behind him — the last NeoGen combatant.

"I SEE THE BASTARD," she hissed. The coward with a red armband kept Veer between himself and the door. Dust and smoke concealed Pip-Tau's presence from him — he didn't know about the new window she'd made. He was also intently focused on the robots in the doorway. She had a clear shot to take him out.

Should she disable his rifle with her laser or blow his head off with a railgun round?

Pip-Tau lifted her right arm, training it on the laser rifle, then hesitated. It was pointed *right* at Veer. If the guy pulled the trigger while she was zapping his gun, Veer was toast.

She switched to her left arm, aiming from the hip at the man's reddened, sweat-coated forehead. She trained her target reticle right between his big, bushy eyebrows.

Wait... she knew those eyebrows.

Was that Eld Marco-Epsilon Rhind? Oh-my-god, it *was!* The ambassador to the Guardians, one of The Council of Ten, was a *NeoGen?!*

Christ, he was probably their leader!

This was treason beyond treason!

Pip-Tau commanded, "Artoo, patch me into the Grunt's external speakers!"

"Done," RRE-Segunde said.

"Eld Marco-Epsilon Rhind, you son of a bitch! Drop your fucking weapon, or I'll blow your eyebrow-laden head right off your puny shoulders!"

Hearing his name made Marco-Epsilon turn his head and furrow his oversized eyebrows at the hole in the wall where Pip's voice had emerged.

As if sensing this lapse in Marco-Epsilon's attention, Veer lurched to the side, tipping his chair and toppling to the ground.

The Astrus at the door had a clear shot and didn't hesitate for a millisecond. The fuel cell of the laser rifle in Marco-Epsilon's hand glowed white-hot for a heartbeat. It erupted in a sputtering explosion. He threw it to the ground, scrambling backward.

"Do not kill or incapacitate Eld Rhind!" Veer bellowed.

Pip-Tau was flabbergasted. Why would Veer protect that scumbag?

"Th-thank you, Eld Gladstone," Marco-Epsilon stammered in disbelief. "Was that voice... Pip-Tau Telson?!"

"Release my binds," Veer commanded.

"I'm sorry, I... haven't a cutting tool," Marco-Epsilon almost whimpered.

Smoke rose from the ties around Veer's ankles — the Astri were zapping them with lasers. They snapped free.

"EoE Gladstone, if you could," JSKO-Prime said, "please rise and turn so we may cut your hand binding."

Veer got to his feet with surprising grace, then turned to look down at Marco-Epsilon. His hand ties smoked, then broke.

He rubbed his wrists as he stepped toward Marco-Epsilon, who was cowering with hands raised. Veer reached down and grabbed a fistful of Marco-Epsilon's foam-coated hair, lifting it and forcing him to his feet. The whimpering man screamed in pain, holding Veer's arm. Veer kept lifting until they were eye-to-eye. The scrambling, sniveling man's legs flailed in the air.

Pip-Tau couldn't believe the look on Veer's face. The Black Lion was snarling, bearing his teeth in the most ferocious expression Pip-Tau had ever seen.

"Death to traitors," Veer growled.

"Veer, be reasonable!" Marco-Epsilon shrieked.

Veer brought his other hand up and clasped Marco-Epsilon's

face. With a roar, he drove the smaller man's head into the wall of his chamber.

It split like a melon.

Blood streaked down the wall as Veer let the dead Eld drop. He slowly ran his hands over his face and hair, wiping off the foam, but smearing blood on himself in the process. The snarl never left his face as he turned and leveled a narrow-eyed glare to the Astrus Grunts at his door.

The sprinklers stopped, the siren silenced, and the strobing lights disappeared into the ceiling. The Black Lion's chest swole with each inhaled breath. With each exhale came a faint growl. Eld Rhind's blood streaked down his face like war paint.

She wanted to say something, but when the intense glare of Veer Gladstone fell upon her, her mind went blank.

For what might have been the first time in her life, Pip-Tau was speechless.

She stopped overclocking — watching Veer's fearsome expression in slow motion was unbearable. Part of her was certain he'd come after the Grunts next. By the looks of his strength and fury, the man could rip them to shreds with his bare hands.

"Veer, it's me," she said, regaining her wits. "It's Pip-Tau! These others with me are Astrus Primes — our allies! And the Specters are on our side, too! Zeta's their leader! The Guardians are trying to invade Syn-Cen, but we can hold them off with these Grunts — these robots!"

Veer took a step toward the Grunts in the doorway as he roared, "You knew this war was coming, Astri! Eld Jess-Eta Primrose confessed it to me — he personally supervised the covert transfer of your orbs into one of our bays *two* days ago! Two days! You brought robots, a mainframe, and munitions into Syn-Cen and demanded that my friend, Jess-Eta, hide it from me!"

"We'd have asked your permission," SFGX-Prime said, "but you would have insisted upon solid evidence of our claims that the Guard was on the verge of a planetary invasion."

"Don't take me for a fool," Veer growled. "You had evidence. Astri don't act on hunches. If we were truly allies, you'd have shared your findings."

"Our prediction algorithms were certain that you would have considered our evidence insufficient," SFGX-Prime said. "We obtained our primary evidence using metaphorical inferences of information shared by Pip-Rho Telson in Interra: Curse of the Night Queen.

"As we speculated at the time, and Zeta later confirmed, Specters can detect masses from great distances, including invisible ships. Pip-Rho's complaints of war drums and an army building war machines in the shadow plane represented her discovery of the covert buildup of Guardian armaments. She saw that the Specters — wraith-pooches in CotNQ — were growing restless. After relocating our aposyn-chronic orbs to Syn-Cen, she discovered that the insectoids of CotNQ were hiding a great number of eggs underground."

Veer seemed to soften a bit, but he was still angry. "What else are you hiding? You ask me to put my trust in the deceptive Astri and the aliens that have haunted our system for hundreds of years?"

"Then trust in *me!*" Pip-Tau squeaked. "Veer, please, Syn-Cen is being invaded by the Guard — they're using the tubes! We don't have time to debate anymore! Send out a call to fifty people in Syn-Cen you can trust. Have them go to Bay Number Two. They'll pilot Grunts and partner up with Astri to defend Syn-Cen."

Veer looked over at her. His anger had melted away, but he still seemed skeptical. She kneeled and pressed her Grunt's hands together, shaking them. "Please, Veer!"

The sight of her Grunt acting like a fool seemed to break down the last of Veer's reservations. He closed his eyes, took a deep breath, and nodded. "I'll do as you ask, Pip-Tau. If anyone but you had come in your place, I can't say I'd have relented."

MJS-Prime said, "May I recommend we relocate to a more discreet location? Two NeoGen soldiers escaped. Reinforcements may be coming, and this will be the first place the Guardian invaders attack."

"To The Crash Pad!" Pip-Tau cheered. "I'll lead the way!"

MJS-Prime turned their back to the mangled door, squatted, and opened their rear hatch. "It is unsafe for you to travel in the open, EoE Gladstone. Please disrobe and enter the Grunt."

Pip-Tau was sure that her heart literally stopped at that moment. The upcoming scene played out in a flash of vivid detail. Veer strips down to reveal his godly body and enters the Grunt. So far, so good! But then they roll up to The Crash Pad, hop out of their Grunts, and — oh-my-god, no! She's naked, too!

Okay, think! She has spare jumpsuits in her dorm. They could wear those. No, they would only fit her! He could tie one around his pelvis like a loincloth. No, better yet, they'd bring his jumpsuit with them!

"Don't worry, I'll close my eyes," Pip-Tau lied. "And don't forget to bring your jumpsuit."

Veer almost seemed amused as he released the jumpsuit straps.

"Should I temporarily disable optical input?" RRE-Secunde asked, switching off Pip-Tau's external speakers.

"Are you kidding?! A NeoGen soldier might pop around the corner any second!"

RRE-Secunde started to suggest, "We could ask Zeta—"

Pip-Tau snapped, "There's no time!"

"But, you told EoE Gladstone—"

"Will you shut up, Artoo?!"

RRE-Secunde didn't respond.

Veer pulled his arms out of his jumpsuit and worked it down off his torso, exposing his thickly muscled chest and abdomen. Dear *god*, the man was a living statue sculpted out of milk chocolate! He hooked his thumbs into the jumpsuit's waistline to pull it down off his hips.

Oh-my-god, YES!

Guilt pricked Pip-Tau's conscience. She really shouldn't...

Dammit!

She jerked her head away and looked down the hall. Yep, none of the NeoGen fighters they'd clobbered were stirring. Nobody was coming from the other direction, either.

Dammit, dammit, dammit, dammit.

She cursed herself as she stared down the hall and waited for the sound of the Grunt closing.

Damn her guilty conscience! Talk about a missed opportunity!

13

DEFENDER

Two columns of kneeling Grunts sped down the corridor towards a closed door. Alasie issued a WUtils command to open it, revealing another hallway ending in a door labeled Subterranean Tube Station #2. Something strange was happening to the door at the end of the long hall — red-hot metal was sparking at its edges.

"They're cutting out the door," one of her squad said.

"Should I open it?" Alasie asked.

"No. It is compromised and likely to jam."

Squad leader IRP-Prime said, "We will set up a defensive position at the intersection ahead. When the doors fall, we will attack with energy and kinetic weapons. After the soldiers are defeated, we'll collapse the tubes in the station. Alasie, please return to Bay Number Two to lead a group of Astri to another tube station. Five Primes will escort you back."

This made Alasie mad. She didn't want to be a door opener — she wanted to *fight!*

But she obeyed. "Okay, heading back."

She twisted her knees to the side, sliding to a stop, then accelerated back the way they came. The Grunts split into groups, with one group of five falling in behind her as she went back down the hall. The others filled side passages or set up positions in the main corridor.

She asked, "MAW-Secunde, can I talk to Zeta?"

"Hailing her now," the Astrus in her head said.

After what felt like a minute, Zeta spoke. "Sorry, Alasie. So much is going on, and there's only one of me."

She wished she could take Zeta's burden on — to share it or make it go away.

"I'm sorry," Alasie said. "You're doing great, though. Real quick... um, can you see if any more Guardians are coming down the tubes to the other stations?"

"Yeah, just a second. The tubes are really long, so we have to trace them back to see... oh, no. Oh... Alasie, they're coming!"

"Which station?!" Alasie asked. "There are only four, so—"

"All of them," Zeta cried. "TYM-Prime, are you there?!"

"I am here," the Astrus said. "I heard you say the remaining three tube stations will soon host Guardian invaders. We hoped to avoid forcing our way through the doors of Syn-Cen, but it seems we have no choice; we have run out of time while waiting for Noddite battle companions. Genevieve can open the doors out of Bay Number Two, but we will break through the remaining doors on the way to the tube stations. Activating the remaining Grunts now."

How could the Astrus be so calm?! They could've just as easily been asking to pass the tea!

"I'll send some Specters with you," Zeta said. "They might not be strategic fighters, but they can break through doors if they get a running start."

"Thank you, Zeta," TYM-Prime said.

"Which station will they be at first?" Alasie asked.

"It's hard to say," Zeta said. "A few surface stations are still loading up troops, but two transports are already descending the tubes."

Alasie mentally invoked her map of Syn-Cen. She was closest to tube station number one, but they'd have to ride an elevator down to reach its level. That might slow them down.

They'd figure it out.

She plotted her course, then said, "I'm going to station one. There are five Primes with me. We'll beat them to it and collapse the tubes before they get there."

"Good luck, Alasie," TYM-Prime said.

ALASIE AND HER five gleaming companions sped down Syn-Cen's white stone corridors. People dove down side passages and into rooms to get out of their way. Alasie found she didn't have to slow down much if she kicked off walls when rounding the corners.

Scenarios played out in her racing mind.

The Specters had control of the ocean, so there was no threat from above. The Guardians could only send small groups down the tubes, and no large machines.

Syn-Cen's tube stations were a choke point — she'd learned about those in Interra. Their party had stirred up a horde of lizard people in a ravine. The battle was won by bringing the fight to an opening after a narrow passage. The lizard people were forced to face them one or two at a time, allowing the Telson party to carve through their vast numbers one by one.

It would take the Guard Faction a long time to bring in enough soldiers to do anything like dig down into the orb vault — wherever that was. The immediate risk was that they would fight their way to Bay Number Two, kill Zeta, and destroy the Astrus orbs.

Without the Astri, the Noddites couldn't pilot Grunts or Wasps.

Without Zeta, the Specters would stop fighting.

Without Zeta, Alasie couldn't go on living. She knew it wasn't healthy to think that way, but she couldn't help it. She recalled a verse from one of her incomplete sonnets.

When pain's illogic makes my brain do flips
Like thinking that I may as well be dead
I sip the wine of love to wet my lips
And feel it burn my heart and clear my head.

For four and a half years, Alasie had lived in limbo. Hope and love engaged in daily battles with pain and loss. She couldn't move on, couldn't find closure, couldn't stop stoking that flame in her heart. Whenever she wanted to give up, she told herself that Zeta would never give up on her if their roles were reversed. It'd been hard, but today proved that it was worth it.

Zeta was back, and Alasie wasn't letting her die again.

They reached the elevator. Alasie opened its doors using WUtils and was disheartened to find that there was only room for one Grunt inside.

Go down one at a time? That'd take too long!

Go it alone? Against *thirty* Guardian soldiers?!

That wouldn't be smart, but she'd do it if she had to.

As if reading her mind, GUHP-Prime, one of her five teammates, said, "Let us demolish the elevator floor and lower ourselves down the shaft using our wheels."

"Let's blow it up with a missile," Alasie suggested.

"You'd risk collapsing the elevator shaft," MAW-Secunde said. "Don't underestimate the power of eight milligrams of antimatter."

"Stand aside so we may coordinate the floor demolition," GUHP-Prime said.

Alasie pressed her back against the wall. The Astrus Grunts passed in front of her. Two kneeled while two stood behind them. The Grunts raised their left arms and began blasting a line of holes at the edges of the elevator floor using railgun rounds.

"How many levels must we descend?" GUHP-Prime asked.

Alasie checked her map. "All the way to the bottom. Ten levels."

When the guns quieted, the fifth Grunt stepped into the elevator. It jumped twice, and then the floor dropped away like a trap door.

The Grunt fell. The screeching of metal on metal echoed up the hole.

Was he okay?

"Please follow VND-Prime down the elevator," GUHP-Prime said. "After clearing the hole in the elevator floor, press your foot wheels against the wall while braking, and press your hands to the sides of the shaft to slow your descent."

Alasie didn't give herself time to doubt whether she'd be able to prevent herself from falling to her death. She stepped forward, tucked her arms against her body, and hopped down the hole.

As soon as she entered the dark shaft, she shoved her feet and hands out against the walls, looking down to make sure she didn't land on VND-Prime's head. The scraping of metal was loud, yet oddly satisfying. Her hands were getting pretty hot.

VND-Prime said, "If you would open the door, I'll move out of your way."

She should've thought of that! She mindspoke, *"Open the elevator door for the bottom floor."*

There is currently no elevator—

"I don't care! Just do it!"

The Worldnet obeyed, and light poured into the bottom of the shaft, reflecting beautifully off VND-Prime's Grunt's armor. The Grunt below her stepped out of the way just before Alasie hit the bottom.

Alasie's other four companions came screeching down behind her. In moments, they were back on their knees, speeding through the halls on their way to tube station one.

"Hurry, they're almost there!" Zeta shouted.

Alasie and her squad rounded the final corner. She issued the

WUtils command to open the door to subterranean tube station one. The wide door opened in two layers — the outer door descending into the floor while the inner doors opened sideways.

About twenty people were in the station, talking in clusters. They were unarmed and wearing white jumpsuits — Noddites. They took one look at the Grunts and broke into panicked screams.

Tube station one hosted eight tubes — four along each side of the spacious cavern. Lounging areas took up most of the station's floor space. Plant life and art pieces made the tube station one of the few places in Syn-Cen that didn't seem sterile.

It made Alasie sad they were about to turn it into a battleground.

The moment her squad entered the station, the green arrival light above the farthest tube loading door illuminated.

"Please evacuate the station," one of her squad announced over their external speakers.

People scattered — some ran past the Grunts, while others ducked behind chairs or sculptures.

The door to the far tube irised open, and the five Astri unloaded their weapons at it, running, jumping, and knee-rolling to spread out their formation. One launched a mini-missile, which exploded in the air before reaching the door.

The concussion wave made every plant in the station lurch and sway. Alasie felt it in her chest.

She lifted both arms and let loose with hellfire. Bright white lasers illuminated the smoke caused by their onslaught. Flaming ribbons were being cut into the floor and chairs near the Grunts. Their enemy was shooting lasers at them, which reflected harmlessly off their armor.

"Hold your fire," GUHP-Prime commanded.

She stopped firing at the ruined tube entrance. That's when she realized she had been screaming. She stopped that, too.

Red lights were flashing, and some sort of white stuff, like clumpy snow, was falling from the ceiling.

But nobody came out of the doors.

"Where are they?!" she shouted. "Did we kill them?"

"Invisible," GUHP-Prime said. "We eliminated several of them, but the rest escaped into the station."

The other Grunts spread out, swinging their gun arms back and forth.

MAW-Secunde said, "Scanning for edge effect or infrared anomalies."

"They're headed for the door!" Zeta shouted.

Alasie looked back at the open door to the station. A Noddite woman was running toward it. If the Guardians were invisible, they might be sneaking out right now! It was infuriating that she couldn't see the enemy.

"Missile!" Alasie shouted, pointing at the ceiling above the door. She wasn't sure if this was the correct way to launch one of her six miniature antimatter missiles. She hoped MAW-Secunde would understand her intention.

There was a strange sensation in her left shoulder — a lifting and opening, followed by a thump. She saw the tiny blue plasma jet behind the mini-missile zip toward the ceiling. It exploded with a blinding flash.

Sirens blared. People screamed. An avalanche of rocks tumbled down in front of the open door, crushing the running woman.

Another explosion — this one from her side. She looked over to see a Grunt blown in two. The robot's top half arced through the air.

Damn invisible bastards!

Alasie lifted her right arm and roared, sweeping it back and forth at ground level as she squeezed out a steady stream of laser bursts. As long as she stuck to lasers, there wasn't much chance she'd damage another of the Grunts.

Flames erupted in mid-air just a few meters before her. A form wearing absolute black body armor appeared. It fell to a knee, holding a hand to its missing shoulder and arm. Without a moment's hesitation, Alasie pointed her left arm at the Guardian's head and removed it with a single railgun shot.

She got one!

"Behind you, Alasie!" Zeta shouted.

Alasie spun around, firing her laser. Another eruption of flame marked a hit, then another.

She only realized after she had killed the two Guardians behind her that she'd... sort of *seen* them — small bits of foam clung to their invisible forms.

"Look for floating foam," she announced to her team.

Two of the Astri fired their railguns at the tube doors. What were they doing?

Never mind them! She resumed her wild laser sweep of the station. She accidentally hit a few Noddites but also took out five more invisible foes. Whenever her lasers ignited a form in mid-air, she'd send a volley of railgun shells to finish the invisible soldier off.

Searing pain erupted in her leg and hip. She spun as she tumbled to the ground. Trying to scramble back to her feet, she realized what had happened.

The bastards blew her Grunt's leg off!

THEY'D FINISH her in a heartbeat. She had to stop them — to protect Zeta! She'd take out the whole tube station if she had to!

Alasie rolled onto her back. She pointed at the ceiling.

"Missile!" she shouted. "Missile, missile, missile!"

She pointed at the four quadrants of the high ceiling as she issued the commands. MAW-Secunde obeyed. Both shoulders thumped two times each.

"Missile!" she shouted, pointing directly overhead. That'd be her last one.

She fired her laser rifle blindly at ground level as the missiles flew, swinging her right arm back and forth as she flexed to make it fire. Her arm was searing hot — she was probably ruining the laser. It didn't matter.

Four rapid flashes were followed by the deep rumbling of rock. The fifth hit overhead. Fissures split the station ceiling — it was collapsing!

More explosions shook the air. They seemed to come from all around her. Alasie twisted her head around in time to see the other Grunts let loose with their missiles, blowing up the eight tube entrances.

"Alasie, you'll be crushed!" Zeta cried.

It was the last thing Alasie heard before the rumbling chaos enveloped her.

Her world went dark and silent. She was in slate-space.

"MAW-Secunde, are you there?" Alasie asked the emptiness.

No reply.

She returned to her body, though it was just as dark as the slate. She was inside the Grunt, curled up and naked like a baby in the womb. There came a muffled thumping sound, then the sound of metal creaking.

She pulled her mouth off the rubber mouthpiece and shouted in the cramped darkness. "MAW-Secunde?! Anyone?! I'm trapped! Open the Grunt!"

Metal creaked again. She was being squeezed even tighter — the Grunt was collapsing under the weight of the fallen rock. Her muscles twitched in post-adrenaline spasms.

"I'm sorry, Alasie, but your Grunt is inoperable," MAW-Secunde said through her earbud. "It appears to be buried under the fallen ceiling."

A voice she recognized as GUHP-Prime said, "When we saw you target the ceiling, we had the remaining Grunts fire their missiles upon the tube entrances. It wasn't our preferred method of disabling the subterranean tubes, but you forced our decision."

The stuffy air inside the Grunt was making her head fuzzy. It sounded like they were disappointed in her. "Did I... mess it up?" she asked, tears burning in her eyes.

"No!" Zeta shouted. "You did perfect, Alasie! There's no way they'll be able to use those tubes. And all the Guardians in the tube station are dead. You kept them out of Syn-Cen."

She couldn't breathe. She sucked on the mouthpiece, but it was blocked up. Metal creaked again, taking her breath away as crushing pain throbbed in her hips and legs.

"I... um... think I'm gonna die now," she said, giving a huff.

Zeta said, "Hang on, I'll send a Specter—"

"No!" Alasie shouted, then gasped at the pain it caused as her ribs stabbed into her guts. She couldn't get any air! "Use them... for other... tubes."

"Please don't... don't die, Alasie," Zeta cried. "I can't do this without you."

"Yes... you can," Alasie wheezed.

Zeta whimpered, "I love you, Alasie."

She couldn't imagine anything she'd rather hear in her last moments.

Metal groaned again, crushing her chest and neck. The shallow gasps she had been taking stopped. She opened and closed her mouth in silent wails of pain. Sparkles colored the darkness of her vision as the life was squeezed out of her. She wanted to use her final breath to tell Zeta she loved her, too, but only managed to squeeze out a pained gurgle.

Blood filled her mouth, warm and metallic.

This was it.

Alasie's dying thoughts came as free-verse poetry.

You died for me underwater.
I died for you under stone.
Next time, promise me we'll live.

Promise we'll live.

14

MUTUAL ANNIHILATION

CRUSHING the Astrus communications device beneath her heel gave Jamji great satisfaction. She stomped on the broken pieces a few times for good measure.

"That's enough," Lieutenant Commander Piccolo sent. *"Now, jump up and look in the vent again. This time, use IR vision."*

The only features of the brig were a squatting toilet, a sink, a thick metallic door with latched slits near the top and bottom, a speaker, an overhead illumination panel, and an air vent. They'd messed around with the door and speaker for too long. Jamji had strongly urged CIS to let her extract her composite explosive epoxy gel to blast the door open, but they insisted they needed to save the gel.

Oh, well. Trust the experts.

The vent grate was a part of the solid poly-ceramic wall, lacking in screws or bolts. She saw no simple way to remove the thing. All she could do was jump up and give it a quick peek. The visual snapshot would show CIS everything they needed to see.

Switching to IR vision, Jamji squatted and then bounded straight up. She caught a fleeting glimpse of a warm rectangle through the grate.

It took Piccolo fifteen seconds to give the next direction. *"Okay, Telson, that's your escape route."*

Jamji gave the grate a skeptical look. It was made of rigid material, and the rectangular shaft it covered barely seemed wide enough to squeeze her head through, let alone the rest of her body.

"Plan?" she sighed.

"Break through the grate using brute force."

Jamji clenched her teeth. She was trying to stay professional. For all she knew, the entire faction was watching her feed. *"Sir, are you sure I can fit through that hole?"*

"You can if you dislocate your shoulders and hips."

She doubted that. But, like a good soldier, she kept her mouth shut.

With a spring of her legs, Jamji soared to the ceiling. She cocked one leg, then donkey-kicked the grate with her heel. The cracked poly-ceramic grate tore into her reinforced skin. She landed, leaped, and kicked three more times until she cleared most of the grating from the jagged hole.

Blood dripped down the wall from the ragged opening. A shred of black skin hung from a broken grate fin. She needed to clean up that opening, or she'd flay herself crawling through it.

Jamji extended her claws and hopped up the wall. She grasped the thin ledge between the poly-ceramic wall and the duct with her claws while pressing her feet on the walls in front of and beside her, perching in the upper corner of the room. Her foot slipped on blood, but she recovered, pressing her less-bloody toes against a clean spot on the wall.

Clutching with one hand, she broke the ragged vent fins away from the hole with the palm of the other. Good enough. Now, how to get her body into that little hole?

At first, she tried to position herself head-first, but then Piccolo sent, *"Feet first, belly up, Telson. You'll need leg power to break through the grate on the other side."*

They didn't even know what was on the other side. For all they knew, CIS was sending her into brig cell number two.

She repositioned her claws, then dangled from the hole with her legs tucked against her chest. One foot in, then the other. Now, shimmy her legs in until...

Damn those hips!

"Time to do some surgery," Lieutenant Commander Piccolo sent. *"I've got Chief Surgeon Ophelia Grey here to walk you through it."*

"Hello, Telson," the woman sent over aud-link. *"Have you already shut off your pain receptors?"*

"I dulled them, doc. I don't like shutting the pain off entirely. Pain's useful."

"Good. We're going to try dislocating just one leg and one arm. Now, if you'll look down at your right hip for me. That's it. And point a claw at your lower hip. Yes, a bit lower. More towards your front. Perfect!"

Jamji could guess what came next. The friendly doctor would guide her through severing the ligaments holding her femur in her hip socket. She wouldn't be able to walk after this.

AFTER SOME GRUESOME SELF-MUTILATION, Jamji punched her fist into her hip until her femur was fully dislocated. She shifted her pelvis and legs most unnaturally until she'd squeezed her lower half in the shaft. Flesh tore from her buttocks and hips as she wedged them into the ragged hole.

That's ok — blood's a good lubricant.

Once she was up to her belly button, her foot touched the grate on the other side. She only had a few centimeters of room to bend her knee and kick the grate, so it took a full minute and five seconds for her to break through and another two minutes to kick the opposite opening's jutting fins clear of the opening.

Next came surgery on her left shoulder.

Pierce, slice, slam, and Jamji was backing her way into the other room with one ruined leg and one ruined arm.

She tumbled to the floor, bouncing off a desk and knocking empty specimen containers everywhere. Good, it wasn't a brig.

"Look for a pole or something you can use as a walking stick," Piccolo sent.

Jamji surveyed her surroundings. It was an office or lab, with nothing suitable other than perhaps the rolling chair. She climbed to her feet with her left arm and right leg dangling in a useless ruin. Her leg slipped out of its socket when she tried to put weight on it.

"Nothing here," she sent, hopping to the door. *"I'll keep an eye out. What's next, sir?"*

"Engine room," Piccolo sent. *"We don't have the sub's schematics, so try exiting and heading to your right. Look for signs."*

Jamji pulled the manual door open lever, slid the door into the wall, and hopped out into the hall.

It took ten minutes to find the engine room. She found a suitable walking stick along the way — a mop handle from a utility closet. Next, they had to break into the engine room since the door wasn't allowing her to enter.

"Unauthorized access," the panel said, no matter what codes the techs told her to try.

"There doesn't appear to be a manual override," Piccolo sent. *"Let's try to trigger an emergency access auto-unlock. Telson, return to the room where we saw the oxygen tanks."*

Jamji smiled. Time to blow something up.

Another ten minutes went by as she took two trips, shuttling six oxygen tanks to the engine room door. Piccolo had her apply pieces of utility tape over a pinhole at the top of each tank, blocking their ambient oxygen over-saturation safety shut-off mechanism.

They found a portable electric burner and cotton balls for a time-delay fuse. After a quick test of the burner, they found it would heat the cotton balls to the point of smoldering within nine point two seconds.

"Look in the utility room adjacent to the engine room entrance," Piccolo sent.

Jamji opened the door, finding a cramped room lined with pipes, pumps, and valves.

"Perfect," Piccolo sent. *"Move the oxygen tanks into here and lay them on their sides, with the valves pointing to the left."*

Jamji complied.

"Now put the electric burner on the floor to the left of the tanks, against the wall, and put four cotton balls on top of it, like the test."

Jamji complied.

Piccolo sent, *"Once you start opening the tanks, you're going to need to act quickly. I'll give you the instructions first so you can carry them out without hesitation."*

Jamji listened to the brief instructions, nodded, and started over-clocking.

She began unscrewing the first oxygen tank's release valve, then the next, then the next. Each opened tank added its hissing to a growing chorus of pending fiery destruction.

A klaxon blared, and a blue light strobed in the hall. A stern male voice stated, "Warning: high oxygen saturation levels detected."

Jamji reached down and flipped on the electric burner, starting her internal countdown.

Nine point two seconds.

She hopped out of the room and then pulled the door shut.

Eight point four seconds.

She grabbed her mop handle and hopped down the hall.

Four point zero seconds.

She ducked into her designated safety room — the head engineer's quarters.

Three point one seconds.

She shut the door, dove to the floor, and curled up under the desk.

Zero point nine seconds.

Jamji was almost giddy with excitement. As the explosion vibrated the submarine, the words of Sun Tzu came to mind.

Those who use fire as an aid to attack show intelligence.

She returned to the hall. Fire suppressant foam rained down and a red strobe was flashing. Smoke filled the air.

"Try the engine room door now," Piccolo sent.

Jamji hopped down the smoky hall. The utility room was a charred wreckage, with the door blasted open. She pulled the engine room's manual handle and felt the satisfying clunk of unlatched bolts. Fire safety and security restrictions have been at odds since time immemorial. Forcing rescuers to break through locked doors during an emergency puts the occupants' lives at risk.

Stepping into the engine room, she found it was also filled with smoke and coated with white foam. A section of wall was missing on the side of the room facing the utility room. Metal sizzled, lights flashed, sirens blared.

"Approach the interactive panel on the far wall." Piccolo sent.

Jamji hopped to the panel, which was alive with emergency status information.

"Ask the computer how much antimatter is onboard."

Antimatter? Jamji didn't like where this was heading. She followed the order anyway.

The computer replied, "One point three nine five grams."

Piccolo sent, *"Tell it to shuttle all antimatter to a portable containment vessel for manual extraction."*

Combining atoms of ordinary matter with antimatter causes mutual annihilation, releasing their combined mass as pure energy, as per $E=mc^2$. You can use a trickling stream of antimatter to release that energy a little at a time and do work, such as powering a submarine. Or you can gather up a bunch of antimatter and release it all at once to blow things up.

So, Jamji was either going to fuel a power plant or make a warhead. She had a good idea which of those options CIS had in mind.

JAMJI KEPT her reservations to herself as she issued Piccolo's command.

"The antimatter containment fields are not compromised. State your justification," the ship's computer demanded.

After a twelve-second pause, Piccolo sent, *"Tell it that as the only occupant of the ship, it is your responsibility to evacuate the antimatter. It's an emergency evacuation, and you have reason to believe that more explosions are eminent due to sabotage."*

Jamji said as much, wondering if the utility-grade AI would deduce that she was the saboteur. Anyone could tell that giving her the antimatter was a bad idea.

The computer stated, "Justification accepted. Proceed to the rear chamber for manual extraction. Allow sixty seconds for full evacuation of reactor chambers."

She laughed out loud and shook her head. "Thanks, sucker."

Jamji hobbled deeper into the engine room, which transitioned into a cramped gangway that passed through massive motors and bundles of tubes. A conspicuous, glowing red circle adorned the wall at the end of the gangway. It was prominently labeled *Antimatter Port*.

Instructions by the port told her to push and turn to release the antimatter containment cell. She waited for her sixty-second timer to run down, then followed the instructions.

The metallic cylinder that emerged was smaller than Jamji expected. It was glowing in an eye-jarring shade of blaze orange and sported a prominent warning symbol of an atom with explosion lines drawn around it. A digital display on one end showed the antimatter volume to be 1.395 grams. A status indicator light blinked in a reassuring shade of green. There were two small buttons beneath the display, which she avoided touching.

The antimatter would be hermetically sealed inside, magnetically suspended in a perfect vacuum. Containers like this were designed to be tough. She couldn't break its seal if she tried, but she still held it with kid gloves.

The thing could level a small city. What would it do to Syn-Cen?

Since she was on the upper level of the complex, just below the floor of The Great Ocean, Jamji suspected that the blast would blow the top off the place. She'd turn the upper level into a crater, but most of the blast would dissipate into the ocean. Emergency doors would slam shut and keep the rest of the Syn-Cen complex from flooding. There was no way the blast would reach the orb chamber, tucked even deeper underground than the lowest floors of Syn-Cen.

Piccolo commanded, *"Find your way back to that room with a desk."*

Jamji hobbled back across the gangway. She'd done everything they'd asked her to do up to this point. She hadn't asked questions or hesitated for an instant. But now she had a weapon of mass destruction in her hand.

Bracing herself for a reprimand, Jamji posed her query. *"Sir, may I ask what we plan to do with the antimatter?"*

Piccolo took seven seconds, doubtlessly conferring with CIS leadership, then sent his response. *"Recent intelligence suggests that multiple Astrus Primes have taken refuge in Syn-Cen. As our only man in the complex, we plan to have you seek them out and eliminate them. Chief Warrant Officer Dumont also believes that the Specter which abducted you is... he's calling it Zeta-Specter. It may be acting as their leader. Dumont believes that eliminating the Zeta-Specter will cause the rest of the aliens to disengage from combat."*

Zeta-Specter? Does that mean Dumont thinks it's really Zeta?

Surely not. He must mean it as shorthand for the Specter impersonating Zeta.

When she reached the office, Piccolo sent, *"This is what we've been saving your epoxy gel for. Extract the gel, mix the epoxy on the desk's surface using the stylus to your right, and apply it to the anti-matter containment vessel. Before you start, perform the bio-overrides to accumulate ammonia and stop salivating."*

One of Jamji's suite of covert tools was her exothermic composite epoxy gel — a three-component explosive. The first two components were gelatinous chemicals that bonded to surfaces and hardened when mixed. The third component was the catalyst that triggered the explosion — ammonia, a natural byproduct of metabolism.

Her bodily implants storing the gel were in the most obvious place imaginable — her breasts. Far be it from Jamji to waste that much body mass on useless fat deposits and mammary glands.

She sliced a claw along the underside of her left breast, gouging it open. She used her hand to extrude the gel into a pile on the desk. It was translucent, pale yellow, and tinged with red swirls of blood. Next came the right breast. Its gel was thicker, opaque, and ochre.

When the gels touched, they immediately started to bubble and emit acrid, chemical-smelling steam. After twenty seconds of vigorous stirring, Piccolo told her to apply it generously to the anti-matter containment cylinder. The epoxy thickened into a sticky, foamy putty, which plastered on easily.

Within one minute, the epoxy had hardened to the point that it was unworkable. She'd created a light brown porous lump, almost like a volcanic rock. The aeration helped the ammonia to permeate the explosive for a more efficient catalytic reaction. Piccolo sent, *"Good work, Telson. Next, we need you to swallow the explosive."*

She wanted to flip the desk. The mass in her hand was the size of a dinner potato. Was that even a good idea? Her body was accumulating ammonia. Her sweat glands gave off its sharp stench. But, as her dry mouth reminded her, she wasn't salivating. Yeah, they'd thought ahead.

CIS wouldn't share more than Jamji needed to know at any step, up to and including the moment they commanded her to blow herself up. Her epoxy bomb alone could probably blow the submarine in half, but using it to obliterate the antimatter containment vessel was the perfect way to disperse the antimatter and get a nice, efficient explosion.

What would it feel like?

Soldiers weren't supposed to think about that sort of thing, but she had to wonder. The ammonia catalyst triggers a chemical chain reaction in the epoxy explosive. Within three to six seconds, the reaction culminates in a blast. Intense heat and caustic fumes pour from the surface of the bomb during the buildup of the chain reaction.

The potato of mass destruction would burn through her stomach as she belched noxious smoke.

What an ugly death.

"*Sir*," Jamji sent, "*may I ask why I'm swallowing the bomb?*"

"*To hide it from the enemy. We need intel before deciding if and when to release the antimatter. If they see it and deduce its purpose, they'll kill you before you can set it off.*"

She figured as much. Jamji overrode her gag reflex, cocked her head back, took a deep breath, and shoved the hardened, rough mass into her mouth. It stopped at the back of her throat. She pushed it down — *forced* it down, utterly ruining her throat in the process.

A tinge of panic set in after Jamji had pushed it as far down her esophagus as her hand could reach. It certainly wasn't going to slide the rest of the way down on its own. She couldn't breathe, and the massive lump was lodged in her neck.

The image of a snake swallowing an egg came to mind.

Jamji leaned forward and raised her mop handle. She used her one good hand to ram the handle into her mouth. Pulling back and shoving it in again, she hammered the mass down, centimeter by centimeter, until she felt the damn thing finally settle into her stomach.

She took gurgling, raspy breaths as she struggled to start breathing again. Add *ruptured windpipe* to her growing list of self-mutilations.

A slam echoed elsewhere in the sub.

"That sounded like a hatch," Piccolo sent. *"You need to get out of the submarine. Avoid contact with others."*

Usually, stealth was her specialty, but Jamji's skin was too torn up from the vent to provide effective active invisibility. Her floating walking stick would also give her away, as would her wheezing breathing.

She went up the stairs to the next deck, following the exit signs. Twenty-five seconds into her search, Jamji found herself looking down a hall at Genevieve.

So much for avoiding contact.

———

"Oh my god," Genevieve gasped, putting a hand to her heart and extending the other toward Jamji. "Jamji, what happened to you? We heard an explosion and—"

"Who is 'we'?" Jamji tried to say, discovering that her bomb-swallowing trick had shredded her vocal cords. The words came out as a coarse whisper, but Genevieve heard her.

"We? Me and Zeta and... the other Specters."

Genevieve was bad at lying. That Astrus, TYM Prime, had to be in the bay with her.

Jamji rasped, "Which way's the exit?"

"I... think you'd better stay in the sub. Zeta wants to talk to you again. I brought another earpiece since you broke yours." She held the earbud in her outstretched palm, stepping towards Jamji with the caution of one approaching a rabid dog.

Piccolo spoke through aud-link. *"Take the earbud, then eliminate her."*

Jamji clenched her jaw. Tears stung her eyes for a moment before she suppressed them. Ever since her Nightmare Gauntlet test at the Guardian Embassy, she had struggled with the question of what she would actually do in this situation.

Genevieve was close enough now that Jamji could rip her throat out. She snatched the earbud, making Genevieve flinch, then shoved the thing into her ear. A sound like a distant pack of barking dogs came through the earbud. This was no surprise — the sound had been there last time.

Time to kill her, Jamji. Just get it over with.

Genevieve searched Jamji's eyes as she whispered, "Jamji, what's going on? Are the Guardians in your head right now? What are they telling you to do?"

Jamji's claws were out. Even with one arm and one leg, she could kill Genevieve in a fraction of a second.

So what was she waiting for?

"It's okay to do this, Jamji." This was a new voice. Her heart sank as she realized who it was — her partner, Doctor Trey Geary. Of course he was brought in as part of the team watching through her eyes and listening through her ears.

When Jamji struggled with her emotions or intrusive thoughts, Trey helped her clear her mind. And here he was, telling her to kill her mother figure — Trey, who she'd cheated on last night.

A fanciful and unscientific part of her mind wondered if today's hellish tortures were karmic retribution for her infidelity.

Yeah, she deserved it.

But she didn't deserve *him.* The best thing she could do for Trey was set him free.

"She's synched to an orb," Trey sent. His voice was confident, reassuring. *"Just make it painless—"*

"Shut up, Trey," Jamji spat through aud-link. *"It's over between us, okay? I never want to see you again. Get off my channel. Get out of my head!"*

"Jamji?" Genevieve asked. Tears glistened in her eyes. She dared to extend a gentle hand toward Jamji's arm.

Jamji dodged the hand, hopped to the side of the hall, and slammed open the nearest door. "Get in here and don't come out, or I'll kill you," she rasped.

Genevieve was crying. She put a hand to her mouth, stepping

into the room. "I'm sorry they put you in this position. I won't come out."

Jamji met Genevieve's eyes as Piccolo sent, *"You're disobeying a direct order from a superior officer, Telson."*

There was nothing but warmth and concern in Genevieve's expression. Nobody in the Guard Faction would ever love Jamji as unconditionally as Genevieve did.

"I... I can't do it, sir," Jamji sent.

She'd be lucky if they didn't strip her rank and erase her orb.

She reached for the door handle to close it but stopped when she noticed — the room was an observation deck! Three large glass dome windows were set into the opposite wall. There was nothing to see through the glass but the stone interior wall of the bay. But what about the other side?

Jamji slammed the door shut, hobbled across the hall, and slid the opposite door open.

Jackpot!

THERE WAS TOO much to take in all at once.

A distant wall was covered with huge racks and scaffolding. Cubes on the racks had bundles of thick cables running out of them.

A Specter swam through the air.

A tiny drone glided on a blade of blue plasma just outside the window.

Rapid movement caught her attention — a shining metallic form.

Trained reflexes kicked in. Jamji instinctively overclocked, went invisible, hit the deck, and covered her head before she consciously realized that the metallic form had been a robot, perhaps forty meters away, lifting its arm to point a barrel at her.

Glass exploded. Metal rang. She was under fire!

"Detonate the explosive!" Piccolo shouted. This was the most emotion he'd displayed at any point in their interaction. *"CIS image*

analysis believes those are Astrus orb storage units! There's not just one Astrus in the bay — they could have any number of Primes and orbs in there! This is where they've been commanding their drones from!"

Jamji issued the bio-overrides to gather the ammonia built up in her blood and liver into her salivary glands. That'd take a full minute. She wouldn't live that long at this rate.

She belly-crawled back into the hall. Not that a poly-ceramic wall would stop railgun rounds, but at least they couldn't see her.

There was a distant grinding and crashing sound, then silence.

"What did you just see?!" Zeta's enraged voice asked through her earbud. "Be honest, Jamji!"

"Don't reply," Piccolo sent. *"Retreat to another part of the sub while your ammonia accumulates."*

Jamji wanted to get another glimpse of the bay before she hid. She used her good arm to lift her bad arm, poking her hand around the corner. If they were going to shoot off one of her hands, it might as well be the useless one.

She switched her visual input to the photoreceptites on her left palm. This gave her a blurry, distorted view of the obliterated observation deck. A Specter hovered just outside the windows, swimming back and forth. A mangled robot lay against the wall at the bay's far side. Two other robots were in the bay, standing with their backs turned and arms raised. It looked like they were surrendering.

To the Specter? Those bots were definitely Astrus tech. Had the Specter attacked the Astrus that was attacking her? Did they have minds of their own?

This must be Zeta-Specter.

Scenarios ran in Jamji's head. Zeta-Specter wanted to know what she saw. Why? Her fleeting glimpse had informed the Guardians that the Astri were hiding in the bay. What if she told the truth? What if she lied?

All warfare is based on deception.

The last thing the Astri wanted was for the Guard to know about this secret base. If she hadn't seen the racks and deduced their purpose, the Astri would need to kill her to protect the secret. But she *did* see them. It was too late — killing her wouldn't accomplish anything. That is, as far as they knew. She was a walking warhead — a ticking time bomb that looked like a piece of chewed up meat from the outside.

"Jamji, answer me now, or they'll have to kill you," Zeta-Specter said.

That cinched it — she was right.

"I saw Astrus orb containers," Jamji rasped. "Lots of them. We know they're hiding their orbs and Primes down here."

Piccolo barked, *"Squad Lieutenant Telson, stop communicating with the enemy!"*

Zeta-Specter said, "See? There's no point in killing her now, TYM-Prime."

"Very well," said the Astrus through her earbud.

"You can come out," Zeta-Specter said. "Nobody's going to shoot you. I want to talk to you, Jamji."

She reached for the mop handle, pulling herself to her feet. Hobbling through the doorway, Jamji faced her enemies. Specters, Astri — they were all in front of her, and she would take them *all* out.

JAMJI WANTED TO GET CLOSER, to see more of the bay and see if there were more Specters than the one. She hobbled through the broken glass and debris.

"How long have you known the Guard was planning to invade Genesis?" Zeta-Specter asked accusingly.

"Do not engage the enemy in conversation!" Piccolo shouted in her head.

She tuned him out.

It was a stupid question, anyway. The Astri were the ones who wanted to conquer Genesis, not the Guardians. She rasped, "We didn't invade Genesis. We're protecting it from *you*."

"Are you kidding?!" Zeta-Specter shouted through the earbud. The black blob flinched backward. "You rounded up the Noddites and forced them to vote on a bill that would give the planet to the Proliferans and give Cain to the Guardians! You're getting ready to kill the Noddites and ship their orbs off to the other side of the galaxy if they don't vote your way! You still want to pretend you're protecting them from *us*?!"

Jamji furrowed her eyebrows. Everything Zeta-Specter had just said was nonsense. Oddly specific nonsense...

"*Sir?*" Jamji sent over aud-link. "*What's she talking about?*"

"*Irrelevant,*" Piccolo sent. "*You have enough ammonia sequestered to detonate the bomb. Do it, Telson!*"

The smell of ammonia stung in her nose as its bitter, metallic taste assaulted her mouth. No, it wasn't time to swallow yet. She spat, trying to make it look like she was being macho.

Glass crunched underfoot as she made her way to the demolished observation window. She could see the back wall of the bay now. It was covered with even more racks than she'd seen earlier. Was that... *all* the Astrus orbs?

She leaped forward, clearing the shattered window and plummeting to the ground. The tumbling landing wasn't her most graceful, but she didn't think she broke anything that wasn't already ruined. She still wanted to see more. Maybe if she gave CIS a better view of the enemy stronghold, they could put the information to good use.

Then *maybe* they'd overlook her repeated acts of brazen insubordination and let her off with a demerit.

"I don't know about any vote," Jamji rasped, then coughed. She spit out a wad of ammonia-and-blood-tinged mucus and wiped her chin. "Whatever it was, I'm sure it's for the best."

Zeta-Specter scoffed. "Don't tell me they didn't... you didn't know?! And you just automatically assume it's for the best? Are you really that much of a blind follower that you don't even care what this whole war was about?!"

Jamji surveyed the bay. Zeta-Specter was the only Specter in sight. There was a mainframe hooked up to the cables running from the racks. Piles of storage containers lined the wall to the side of the bay.

"Swallow your spit and detonate the bomb, Telson! What are you waiting for?!" Piccolo shouted.

"That isn't Zeta," Trey Geary sent with calm authority. Dammit, not him again! *"You know she's dead, Jamji. They're trying to instill doubt, confusion. These are classic Astrus tactics."*

He was right.

Jamji bit her tongue to work up her saliva. Pure ammonia pooled in her mouth.

Zeta-Specter kept talking in her earbud. "Oraxis and Genevieve, Pip-Tau, Alasie, Carff — they all voted against the bill. Voting is closing in a minute, and if it passes, their orbs will be ejected from Syn-Cen. What do you think that means, Jamji? Why would they put that into the bill? You know what the Guard'll do with those ejected orbs — they'll find and destroy them. Your family's going to die — True Death! The Jamji I know wouldn't stand for that!"

The Jamji she knew? This farce of an Astrus personality emulator didn't know her.

That's what Jamji told herself, at least. But if this Specter actually was Zeta...

No, it was impossible. Zeta-Specter was an alien. A crude simulacrum. An insult to Zeta's memory! And the Astri? Impostors! Inhuman, *insidious* impostors.

Zeta-Specter kept blabbing, buying Jamji time to work up a mouthful of ammonia. "Jamji, you need to *think*. If you know your enemy and you know yourself, you'll win every battle. If you know yourself but not your enemy, you'll only win half the time. And if you don't know either yourself or your enemy, you'll always lose. You told me that the first time I met you, Jamji. I looked it up later and found out it was a Sun Tzu quote. You Guardians treat The Art of War like its gospel, but here you are, completely clueless about what your side of this war is trying to do! You *don't* know yourself — you don't know your role in this fight! And you think the Astri are some sort of inhuman freaks when they're not! And everyone was completely wrong about the Specters! We don't have to be enemies — you don't know *us* at all, Jamji!"

"Jamji-sis-kin has a bad thing in her tummy," said a child's voice. "I'm scared of it, Zeta!"

Jamji almost spit. Who the hell was that?!

She didn't have time to figure it out — they knew about her bomb.

Jamji was a Guardian soldier. It wasn't her job to think, to judge, or to second-guess her commanders. Fate had uniquely positioned her and her alone to wipe out the Astri in one fell swoop. And if Dumont was right about this Specter leading the others, she'd also thwart the Specter resistance. She'd be a hero for this.

She could single-handedly win this war.

All she had to do was swallow.

"That dense mass in her stomach?" Zeta-Specter asked.

Did they have x-ray vision or something?

Zeta-Specter marveled, "Now that you mention it, that floating speck inside the cylinder in the spongey rock seems... it's like it's... backward or something. Jamji, is that—"

Energy is like the bending of a crossbow. Decision, the releasing of the trigger.

Jamji swallowed her mouthful of ammonia. She coughed, "Antimatter?"

Heat erupted in her stomach — the catalytic reaction was starting. It would escalate rapidly until it reached the tipping point when the saturated epoxy would detonate. This would rupture the antimatter containment cell. Antiprotons would meet protons, mutually annihilate, convert their mass into energy, and turn the bay into a crater at the bottom of The Great Ocean.

E equals *F U*, squared.

"No!" Zeta-Specter wailed.

Before she could blink, the Zeta-Specter darted toward her. It lanced straight through her abdomen, lifting her from the ground and pulling her backward. The entire mass funneled through her like a black needle sliding effortlessly through cloth — in her stomach and out her back.

She flew backward.

The air exploded around her — a sonic boom. In its wake came the crashing, squealing sound of tortured metal.

She struck the ground, tumbling.

Another crash of metal, hollow and distant, was followed by a deafening, rumbling explosion. The floor beneath her jolted, bouncing her battered body into the air.

She crashed to the floor again, doubling over from the pain. Then she saw the strangest thing.

A metallic ball was emerging from her belly.

It rolled out of the gaping wound in her abdomen, followed by a fountain of dark blood. It bounced on the floor. Blood streaked across its surface.

The thing must've gotten lodged there when the Zeta-Specter passed through her. It got knocked free when she landed.

A jet of dark water roared overhead. Unfathomable regret crashed over her.

Jamji's last fading thought was...

That's her orb. It really was Zeta.

15

———

FLOOD

Twenty minutes before Genevieve died, she was consoling Zeta. Alasie had just sacrificed herself to stop the Guardian invaders, and the pressures of leading a failing cause were crushing Zeta's spirit.

"I led her to her death, Gen-ma," Zeta sobbed. Her Specter form was pacing, hanging so low that it almost dragged across the floor. "I'm leading everyone to their deaths."

The Specter dogs in the bay were all gone — off to break their way through Syn-Cen and secure tube stations three and four. Genevieve couldn't even guess how many Specters had died or how many were still alive. It seemed like a sore subject, so she wouldn't ask.

As Oraxis and his team of Astrus drones approached The Cavern of the Soul to save the holed-up Noddites and recruit pilots for the Wasps, the Guardians lit up the skies with hellfire from above. Orbital bombardment and sweeping pulse laser blasts had killed most of the five hundred Specters and all the Wasps except Oraxis's and two Astrus-piloted drones. The Cavern of the Soul got hit during the bombing, collapsing the amphitheater and killing Natasha-Zeta, along with hundreds of others.

The mission failure and possibly permanent deaths of so many people hit Genevieve like a gut punch.

XT-Secunde spoke over their shared channel to share the news of their failed mission, adding that Oraxis showed uncanny skill at piloting the Wasp. They guessed that the Specters gave their position away. After escaping from the bombardment by the skin of his teeth, Oraxis declared a new mission: take their meager force of three Wasps to the nearest tube surface station to attack the Guardians.

It was a hopeless mission, more about revenge than gaining a tactical advantage, but that didn't deter Oraxis. He'd kick sand in their eye, even if it killed him.

Zeta said, "It was my Specter-pooches' fault. XT-Secunde said so. They ruined the mission and died."

"I'm sorry you're in this position," Genevieve said. She wished she could rub the Specter on the back. "And it wasn't your fault. We all agreed on that plan. Zeta, today has been like nothing I've ever seen, and I've seen a lot! I was there for Googolplex's Ascension and The Message from The Monster from the Stars. Genesis will never be the same after today."

"It's my fault for letting Alasie rile me up," Zeta said. "I started this whole thing."

Genevieve shook her head. "This war isn't your fault, Zeta. They were going to do this one way or another, whether it was today or a year from now. Without you and your Specters, we wouldn't stand a chance."

They sat in silence for a few minutes.

"Approaching Chaparral Range Tube Station," Oraxis said over the earbud.

"Be careful, O!" Genevieve warned.

Tense seconds passed.

"Direct hit!" Oraxis shouted. "Looks like they—"

Genevieve held her breath. When Oraxis didn't continue, she asked, "They what, O? Did you hit them, or did they hit you?"

"I'm sorry, Genevieve," XT-Secunde said. "A surface-to-air railgun volley destroyed Oraxis's Wasp. He died instantly."

Genevieve's knees gave out.

Oraxis was... dead?

She was *just* talking to him. It happened so fast!

He's died before, but this time was different — he might not come back this time! They had been so bold, so proud, so defiant. Why'd they have to vote against that damn bill?! His orb was doomed. So was hers. They'd join history's forgotten ranks of dead revolutionaries, sacrificed to a lost cause.

They could've joined the Proliferans and had a baby together like she'd always wanted. They gave up everything for this ridiculous faction. Now, they'd give up eternity for it.

Oraxis promised they'd be together for a thousand years and a thousand more. Sure, they didn't share all the same interests. He nitpicked things like how often they should wash their kettle or her misuse of words. She hated how slowly he ate and how he never apologized for things.

God, he was perfect.

God, she loved him.

God, she missed him already!

The floodgates of her heart burst open. A wail of agony rose from her throat as she fell forward and landed on her forearms on the cold stone. She breathed a ragged breath, then wailed again, curling into the fetal position and rolling onto her side. Every wisp of air squeezed out of her lungs as she emptied her sorrow into the echoing bay.

Genevieve didn't know how long she had been sobbing when the sound of a muffled explosion reverberated throughout the bay.

She cried out, "What was that?! Are we being bombed?! God, Zeta, I can't take this — I just want it to be over!"

"I's sorry you sad, Gen-ma," Non-Charra whimpered in her earbud.

"Don't worry about me, sweet boy," she cried. "Zeta, you two should get to safety. Go back to Varuna. I'll open the airlock for you."

"No, Gen-ma," Zeta said. "We're staying with you. We're in this together. We'll get through this."

Genevieve wished she had Zeta's optimism. The girl had so much faith — she'd sacrificed her orb based on a vague hint from a game, trusting that Lex knew best.

Genevieve wiped the black hair from her wet face. "How'd you know it would work, Zeta? You took your orb out to space and fed it to a Specter. How did you know you'd be okay?"

Zeta-Specter shifted. "I didn't. All I wanted was to stop the Specters. I was ready to die for it, and I was sure I would. Cain deleted Za'antha when the wraiths consumed her — that's what I thought would happen to me. Coming back like this... I never imagined this would happen. It's like being a beta — a second chance I never expected. I didn't deserve it, but I'm grateful for it."

Thinking of it that way, every year they'd lived beyond the normal human lifespan was an undeserved gift — a miracle of science and technology. Anyone from the twentieth century would say that living for over nine hundred Earth years was more than enough. She should be glad that she and Oraxis lived so long and saw such wondrous things.

"If I may interrupt," TYM-Prime said. "The explosion you heard came from the submarine. We believe Jamji may have escaped the brig. Zeta, could you look for her?"

"Oh. Yeah, I see her," Zeta said. "She's in the lower part, towards the back. I thought you said she couldn't get out of the brig. She's limping."

TYM-Prime said, "It's too dangerous to let her roam freely within the submarine. Please indicate her position so we may attack it with our railguns."

There were three Grunts left in the bay. They rolled towards the submarine on their knee wheels. A handful of tiny flying drones zipped towards the sub, hovering near its windows and hatches.

"No!" Zeta shouted. "Back those Grunts up, TYM-Prime." She darted through the air and interposed herself between the Grunts and the sub.

"Jamji poses a great threat," TYM-Prime said. "We cannot allow her to emerge from the submarine and see our orb containment containers. We are also concerned about the nature of her actions."

Zeta said, "Well, then, let's ask her. Patch her into our channel again."

"Unfortunately, she destroyed her communication device. Even if she hadn't, we feel it is unrealistically optimistic to hope that further discourse with Jamji would be productive. Our prior communication with her proved to be unavailing, as most conversations with the intransigent Guardians tend to be."

"I'm not letting you kill Jamji," Zeta growled.

Zeta was fiercely defensive over the people she loved. Even after everything Jamji had done, Zeta still loved her. So did Genevieve, despite telling her she wasn't a Telson anymore.

Genevieve said, "Give me another earbud. I'll go in and give it to her and say Zeta wants to talk."

"Back off the Grunts and give Genevieve an earbud," Zeta commanded.

The Astri obeyed — one of the Grunts went to dig an earbud out of a crate as the other two retreated to the far side of the bay. The hovering drones stayed at the sub.

Zeta asked, "What are those flying ones for?"

"They are unarmed observation drones," TYM-Prime said. "Is that okay?"

"Yes," Zeta said tersely.

The hulking robot handed Genevieve an earbud, then rolled

away to join its companions across the bay. She started walking toward the sub.

"Do you think Jamji knew what the Guardians were up to?" Zeta asked. "She helped round you guys up. She wouldn't have done that if she knew it was so they could kill you. Right?"

"Jamji don't chew her food," Non-Charra laughed.

What an odd child. Genevieve ignored him.

She didn't want to believe that Jamji would've piled her and Oraxis into a transport if she knew they were being led to their deaths. The image of Pepper-pooch knocking over the cabin came to mind. Oraxis, XT-Prime, and Carff had built it shortly before Jamji's beta bootstrapping.

After seeing that, Genevieve had no idea what Jamji was capable of.

"I don't know," she said. "Let's ask."

FIVE MINUTES BEFORE SHE DIED, Genevieve was diving for cover under a bench in an observation deck. Shards of sizzling metal and shattered poly-ceramic debris ricocheted around the room as unseen Astrus robots turned the sub into Swiss cheese.

Things hadn't gone well with Jamji. For a moment during their interaction, Genevieve thought Jamji was going to kill her. Now, the Astri were likely to do just that.

She knew why they were attacking — Jamji had entered the observation deck on the opposite side of the sub and saw the Astrus sanctuary. That was bad news. There would be no holding back now — the Guard wouldn't relent until they eliminated all the Astri orbs in the bay.

The firing stopped. Zeta shouted in her earbud, "What did you just see?! Be honest, Jamji!"

It took Jamji some time to answer. Genevieve was sure she was conferring with Guardian leadership. When she admitted to seeing the orb storage containers, Genevieve braced for a retaliation strike. Instead, the Astri backed down.

"Very well," TYM-Prime had said — the damage was already done.

She let Zeta do the talking. It was for the best — Genevieve was too shaken up to speak. Her muscles shivered uncontrollably. A sob escaped her, but she covered her mouth to hide it.

Incoming conversation request from Pip-Tau Telson.

Genevieve accepted.

Pip-Tau was uncharacteristically sober. *"Hey, Gen-ma. I heard about O-pa. How're you doing?"*

Genevieve pressed her palms against her eyes, holding back a resurgence of tears. *"Not good."*

"Not so good here, either. Veer's trying to coordinate the resistance, but the wheels are falling off. I've been listening in on mute — sounds like Jamji's causing a stink."

"That's Jamji for you."

Pip-Tau laughed feebly. *"Well, when Jamji and Zeta wrap it up, Veer wants to talk to Zeta about something. He thinks he knows how Cain's gonna eject the orbs of the people who voted against the bill. Veer can see the current exit poll results, and it's as good as passed."*

Non-Charra's frightened voice caught Genevieve's attention. "Jamji-sis-kin has a bad thing in her tummy. I'm scared of it, Zeta!"

"That dense mass in her stomach?" Zeta asked. "Now that you mention it, that floating speck inside the cylinder in the spongey rock seems... it's like it's... backward or something. Jamji, is that—"

Jamji's hoarse voice said, "Antimatter?"

"No!" Zeta wailed.

Genevieve's heart dropped.

"Antimatter?!" Pip-Tau squeaked through mindspeak. *"What's she talking about?!"*

As Pip-Tau mindspoke, there came a loud crash, followed by an even louder explosive roar. Next came a deep rumble, like an earthquake. The submarine rolled, casting Genevieve out from her spot under the bench and into the wall — which was now the floor.

The roaring sound from outside the sub was like a waterfall, but more violent. Genevieve couldn't see anything through the observation deck windows overhead other than swirling spray and the white lights of the bay's ceiling panels. Red lights flashed and a siren sounded in the bay, barely audible over the roaring.

The sub began spinning, lurching, and rocking violently. Genevieve bounced around the observation deck like a pinball. Murky water darkened the windows, spraying through holes created by the Astrus railguns. An alarm started going off in the sub. Red and blue lights flashed.

"All hands to escape pods," a man's voice commanded. "Our vessel is taking on water at a critical rate."

"The bay's flooding!" Genevieve shouted aloud and through mindspeak.

"What?! How?!" Pip-Tau cried through the earbud. "Jamji, what did you do?!"

No reply.

"Zeta?" Genevieve tried. "TYM-Prime?"

The earbud was silent other than the faint sound of distant dogs.

The submarine shuttered as it crashed into something, lurching and knocking Genevieve over again. She splashed face-first into the frigid water, which was rising quickly.

"Computer, how do I get to an escape pod?" she coughed, wiping her eyes.

The sub's computer said, "The hall outside the port observation deck is flooded. Please stay calm and await rescue."

There would be no rescue — Genevieve was going to drown.

Genevieve's heart raced as she cast frantic eyes around the flooding room in search of something. An oxygen tank, maybe?

"Gen-ma," Pip-Tau sent, *"Do you think... maybe Jamji blew up the Astrus orbs using antimatter?"*

"*I don't know!*" Genevieve sent. *"There was a loud sound, then a rumbling, then the sub was tossed around in the water. Pip-Tau, I'm trapped in here. I'm going to die!"*

Maybe she should've been more worried about the hundred thousand Astri in the bay or what happened to Zeta, but for now, all her reptile brain could focus on was survival. The water was already over her head — she was treading water. Two of the observation windows had holes in them from the railgun barrage. A violent jet of water sprayed through them, filling the room.

The voice of Worldnet spoke in her mind.

Voting for The New Genesis Proposal is now closed. The bill has passed with a seventy-one point two percent majority. Per article eight, the choice-vote selections are now effective. Your vote against this proposal constitutes a renouncement of your Genesis Faction citizenship. You will now be disconnected from the Worldnet, and your aposynchronic orb will be ejected from the Synthetic Intelligence Central Processing Facility.

She tried to mindspeak to Pip-Tau, but it was like thinking to herself. WorMS was already gone.

"You still there, Gen-ma?" Pip-Tau asked over the earbud.

"I'm here," Genevieve cried. "Pip-Tau, I'm so scared!"

"It's going to be okay. Don't give up hope!"

Genevieve tried to think like a Pip — think optimistically. The air at the top of the observation deck was shrinking, but it seemed like enough for her to keep breathing until rescue came. Piercing pain was stabbing her ears, and it was getting worse. That's when it occurred to her — the Great Ocean would kill her one way or another.

Genevieve had never been scuba diving — her first attempt at snorkeling back on Earth sufficed to convince her that she was *not* an underwater person. But, she knew the basic physics of water and air pressure and its effects on the body. Syn-Cen was built below the lowest ocean trench on Genesis. The water pressure in the bay would equalize with the ocean above. The water would squeeze the air in the observation deck until it was a tiny, dense pocket of compressed air. She didn't need to drown — the air she was breathing would kill her. It had something to do with the nitrogen in your blood. You start to feel intoxicated, and then you die.

What did they call it? Not the bends — that's something else. Nitrogen... narcotic effect?

She asked WoQS about the effects of breathing high-pressure air.

No reply.

Oh, yeah... no Worldnet.

Yes, it was definitely taking effect — it was hard to focus.

"Pip-Tau?" Genevieve asked, sounding muffled. *Damn,* her ears hurt! And now the stabbing pain was spreading to her eyes and temples.

"I'm here," Pip-Tau said. It sounded like she was crying.

"What's it called? Nitrogen narcotic something?"

Pip-Tau hesitated, then responded. "Nitrogen narcosis. It starts with intoxication, then leads to blackout, then... do you feel it now?"

She nodded. "I'm not thinking straight. It's hard to breathe."

"I... I love you, Gen-ma," Pip-Tau cried from a distant place.

"I love you too, sweetheart. I'll tell everyone 'hi' for you."

She didn't believe in an afterlife, but it was a beautiful fantasy she was content to indulge in. Oraxis was waiting for her on the other side, brewing lemongrass tisane. Zeta was there now, too — embracing Alasie once again, introducing her to the Scorpion Tail tribe ancestors. To Charra! XT-Prime and Pip-Rho would be there. Oh, and don't forget Susie-Q!

Bittersweet tears trickled from her eyes. *God,* how she wished it were so.

With a pair of loud pops, her hearing was gone. Her mind was slipping. Nothing seemed real.

Black swirls on the skin of her forearm caught her eye — oh, her tattoo!

She stopped treading water for a moment so she could read her arm.

Let it be.

Such beautiful words. Peace washed over her.

Genevieve sank into the frigid, cloudy water — just clear enough that she could still see the tattoo. She meditated on it. Zeta had been right about that lyric — it was all she had to do.

Let it be.

Let it be.

16

MASSACRE

"It's over, isn't it?" Pip-Tau whispered. She had been crying, but now she was in a numb stupor.

Veer sat across from her, his head in his hands. He didn't reply.

The bill stated that every Noddite in the Genesis Faction would surrender to their deaths at the hands of the Guardians if the bill passed.

They were doing it now. They had to be. Being cut off from the Worldnet was like having one of her senses stripped away. She needed to hear the buzz of the news feed, to tap into the shared experiences of her faction. What was going on out there?!

Genocide — The Massacre of the Noddites.

The idea made her heart sink, and her head go fuzzy. She thought she might pass out, so she laid down.

What would the Guardians use for the mass killing? Gas? Bombs? Headshots?

When the Death Star destroyed Alderaan, Obi-Wan could feel the disturbance in the force from across the galaxy — millions crying out in terror and then falling silent. Pip-Tau imagined she was feeling the same sort of thing. But, then again, Pip-Tau had a vivid imagination.

She'd be dead soon, too. They'd tried to stop the Guardians from invading Syn-Cen, but the defense failed — Tube Station Four was in Guardian hands. All their Astrus allies could do was collapse the corridor leading out of the tube station. Soon enough, the Guardians would shuttle down their earth-movers and clear the obstacle.

Pip-Pi's words, written in black marker on the ceiling, read, "WARNING: This is the real world! Try not to die again — it's a real _drag._"

That sage-like advice would be wiped away soon. Whatever Guardian or Proliferan jerkface moved into the Crash Pad would clear the shelves of Pip memorabilia, rip the posters from the walls, and scour those words of wisdom from the ceiling.

She looked over at the Grunt wedged into her foyer. Its back was open, and it was pressed against the door to the hall. RRE-Secunde was still in there, but they had fallen silent. If anyone pried open the door, RRE-Secunde had orders to shoot them. A lone Grunt couldn't protect them from the might of the Guardians, but at least she'd go down swinging.

Like O-pa. Like Alasie. Like Zeta and Gen-ma and the Astri.

Her throat constricted — repressed sorrow was pounding at her chest, begging to be released. If she started crying again, she may never stop.

"I could have done more," Veer rumbled.

She looked over at him. His head was still in his hands. Tears were dripping slowly from his nose onto the white stone floor. She crossed the small room and sat beside him, placing a hand on his back.

"You did all you could do," she whispered.

He shook his head slowly.

"It happened too fast," she said. "We had a good plan — gathering Noddites to pilot Astrus Wasps and Grunts. But there just wasn't enough time. Things escalated, situations kept changing. You can't expect a peaceful faction of ex-neoprims to transform into a well-coordinated fighting force in under an hour."

"I mean before," Veer said. "Before the NeoGens formed, I could have listened to the grievances of my people. It's my fault they resorted to these drastic measures."

"Are you kidding?!" Pip-Tau squeaked. "Veer Gladstone, you're the best damn EoE this faction has ever seen! You listen to the advice of experts, and you *can* have your mind changed! It's not your fault they couldn't come up with a convincing argument for their stupid plan and had to resort to terrorism!"

Veer lifted his head to look Pip-Tau in the eyes — he was searching for something. A glimmer of doubt, perhaps?

A knock sounded from the door — three quick raps.

Pip-Tau's eyes bugged. Veer got to his feet, puffed up and ready for a fight.

This was it! It's over!

<hr>

THREE MORE KNOCKS SOUNDED, followed by a man's voice. "Hello? Hey, Pip-Tau, you in there?"

He had a neighborly tone — nothing like an invader preparing to take her life.

"Should we have Artoo shoot through the door?" Pip-Tau whispered.

"Not yet," Veer whispered back. "Do you recognize the voice?"

"No," Pip-Tau whispered.

They stood still for a few seconds. Maybe he'll go away.

The muffled voice continued, "Hey, I could hear you shouting, so I know you're there! You don't have to hide! It's Vance Allegro! Remember, Violet Nightshade?"

Pip-Tau queried her transcript for the name, finding herself probing at a void in her double-mind where the Worldnet should be.

Crap, she had to go off of *memory*?! Okay, fine! Vance Allegro,

Violet Nightshade — that had to be a character name from Interra. Was he one of her moderators? Or...

"Oh, yeah!" she squeaked. "Violet Vance, the Proliferan Fanboy! Yeah, I remember you!"

"Be careful what you share," Veer whispered.

Pip-Tau climbed over the Grunt's leg and squeezed between the robot and the door.

Vance shouted, "I came to see if you opted to join the Proliferans! I knew you would — you have to be sick of playing a cave woman! We can't wait to see what you come up with once you get your hands on P-Net's repos! Is your door stuck?! There was a lot of shifting rock after those explosions! Need me to get someone to force the door for you?!"

"No, I'm good!" Pip-Tau shouted through the crack of the door. She looked back at Veer. He looked like he would smash the fanboy's head against the wall, like he had Eld Marco-Epsilon, if given the chance.

She might get Vance to leak some intel if she played along. She shouted, "I got a message from the Worldnet to stay put! The door's locked! But I'll be okay — I'm just worried about my friends! Do you know what's happening on the surface? Or where they're sending the orbs of the poor fools who voted against the bill?"

"The Noddites on the surface are being euthanized! It's all very humane — painless deaths! Just like going to sleep!" He sounded way too cheery about this. "I heard the naysayers' orbs would get ejected right into the Great Ocean! The Guardians will try to retrieve them, but there are still Astri hiding out somewhere, so they might send their Specters to pick them up! I heard there're like a million Specters hiding in the Great Ocean right now! I wish I could tell you your friends' orbs are safe, but... hey, they shouldn't have voted against it, right?!"

This confirmed Veer's idea about how the orbs would be ejected. There was an old access port a few kilometers away from Syn-Cen's four bays, originally used to quick-load the first Earthling colonists' orbs into the vault. Apparently, the access port worked both ways.

"Yeah!" Pip-Tau shouted. "Their loss — it's gonna be awesome being a Proliferan! Well, thanks for stopping by! I'll see you around!"

"Yeah, see you around! Oh, hey, do you think you'll spin up another Interra instance?!"

She rolled her eyes. "Definitely!" It was a lie — that gameworld was as much Pip-Rho's as it was hers. She could never run it without Rho, and Rho was...

Just like the rest of them.

Just like Tau would be soon.

Snowflakes were never meant to last long.

———

AFTER THE FANBOY FINALLY LEFT, Pip-Tau and Veer sat side-by-side on the bed in slack-faced, shell-shocked silence. They were powerless to do anything but await their deaths.

"Do you regret your vote?" Veer whispered.

They'd agreed not to raise their voices again lest passersby become alerted to their presence.

Her automatic response would have been, "Of course! I don't want to die!" But she gave it a few moments of thought.

Is it better to live by your principles and stand up for yourself, even if it means paying the ultimate price? Is it better to surrender to terrorists' demands or let them destroy everything precious to you? Comfortable complacent cowardice or dumbass doomed defiance?

"No," she whispered. "It was the right thing to do. How about you?"

Veer sighed. "I have many regrets, Pip-Tau. Many, many regrets. But casting that vote was not one of them."

She looked up at his sullen face. "What do you regret?"

He shook his head and closed his eyes. "The Guardians will have euthanized us by the time I recited the list. I haven't always been... a good man. You saw what I did to Eld Rhind. That was... a relapse. It was wrong."

Wow. What sort of things had Veer done in his past? Was he a murderer? Maybe he came from a warlike tribe.

They fell silent again.

It was impossible to wrap her mind around the fact that *everyone* was dead. The despair was too overwhelming to sink in, leaving her feeling strangely numb to the whole thing.

Sagely words of ancient wisdom came to mind: *shit happens.*

Did she want to spend her last moments sitting in bleak silence?

Pip-Tau put her hand on Veer's. My, what big hands he has! The better to...

"I'm grateful to have you here with me, Veer Gladstone," she whispered, leaning against him. "Dying sucks, but it's worse when you do it alone."

Veer let out a sad chuckle. "Agreed. And I can't imagine a better person to spend my last moments with than Pip-Tau Telson." He put an arm around her and pulled her against his side.

She looked up at him, searching for a hint of a sarcastic smile. There's no way he meant that seriously. She whispered, "I doubt that, but I appreciate the sentiment."

"It's true," he whispered. "You asked what regrets I have. I'll admit to this one — I regret letting my role as EoE get in the way of following my heart. I've always put my responsibilities ahead of my happiness and paid the price of loneliness. The whole faction knew you were attracted to me, and when we worked together on Interra, I began to have feelings for you, too — feelings that my stubborn sense of duty wouldn't allow me to act upon. I would've been a happier man if I'd let you into my life, Pip-Tau. A happier man, indeed."

Oh-my-god, WHAT?! Is this real?!

Veer shifted so he could look her straight in the eye. He took both of her hands in his. "Pip-Tau, you have a way of treating me that's... disarming. You're real. Genuine. Maybe the most genuine person I've ever met. You're fun and intelligent and—"

Pip-Tau pounced on Veer, shutting him up with a kiss before he could lie and tell her she was beautiful. She wrapped her arms around him, feeling the bulk of his muscled shoulders and back. Oh-my-god, those *muscles!*

His beard tickled her face as they pressed together in the open-mouthed, sloppy kiss of ravenous new lovers. His hands were all over her — yes, this was happening!

Maybe he was only interested in her because she was the last woman he'd ever see... but who cares! It's the apocalypse, baby! And they were going to do what everyone dreams of doing when the world ends.

"Are you wrestling?" asked a youthful voice from behind her.

Pip-Tau squeaked as she and Veer pushed apart like Judeo-Christian teenagers caught in the act by their parents. She turned around to find the hologram of a boy flickering into existence behind the Grunt. A shimmering projector lens on the side of the Grunt's head revealed the hologram's source.

The boy looked uncannily familiar. He wore a loincloth and had medium brown skin, with features reminiscent of The Scorpion Tail Tribe. At first, she thought it was Zeta's bro-kin, Charra, but this kid seemed older.

"What is this?!" Veer barked, fastening the buckles of his jump-suit, which Pip-Tau had rapturously torn open just moments before. "Who are you!?"

"I'm Enoch," the boy said, taken aback. "I just... there's some stuff I want to talk about."

Why *now*, kid?! Couldn't this have waited *ten* minutes?! Or twenty... or thirty...

Whatever, it was probably some save-the-world, all-is-not-lost bullshit.

It's *fine.*

17

ENOCH

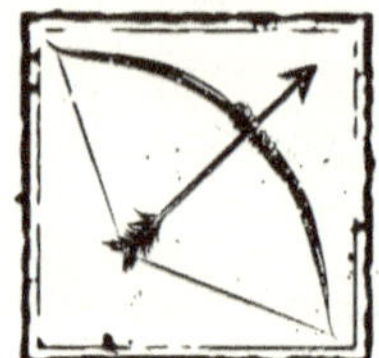

A FLOWERED TREE stood in an open field. *Beauty.*

"Do this tree grow a fruit, pa?" a child asked. *Curiosity.*

Wilhelm-pa lifted her off his shoulders and placed her on the ground. "Yes, I think I remember a tree like this growing large, green fruit, which was sweet and tart. It was good to eat, but you'd get a tummy ache if you eat too many!" He tousled her hair. *Love.*

She declared, "I'm gonna wait here. It gonna grow me fruit!" *Youthful ignorance.*

Wilhelm-pa laughed, "We can't do that, my little fruit bat. We're only passing through here. Tomorrow, we continue walking." *Disappointment.*

"No! I don't wanna walk! I don't wanna leave the tree — it smells so good!" *Defiance.*

She ran to the tree, pulled down a branch, and shoved her nose into a white flower to smell it. She cried out as something stung her cheek. *Pain.*

With a blink, she was in a new place.

Zeta and Vihaan crouched together in the scrubby grass at the peak of a hill, watching the distant line of men on their way to confront the Red-Painted tribe.

Her heart stopped as a black line descended from the clouds, pooling above the heads of the men. She'd never seen anything like it. *Specter.*

She cried out, "Vihaan! Do you see—"

Thunder clapped. *Sonic boom.*

She covered her head, then looked up again. A black tendril lowered from the hovering form and picked up a man. *Wilhelm-pa.*

Vihaan squealed, "It ate that man!" *Abducted.*

Blink.

The body of Jebbam-bro-pa lay face-down in the field. Arrows protruded from his back. A pack of hyenas was eating him. They lifted their heads, letting out grunts and cackles — red-painted beasts mocking her tribe. *Horror.*

Blink.

She was peering through the eye-holes of an angry duppy mask, eyes clouded with tears. A stick was in one hand, a sharp stone in the other — she was making spears for killing. *Revenge.*

Blink.

The haunting sounds of drums, chanting, and rattling bones filled the night air. She was standing at the eld fire, face wet with tears.

Chief Talmid called out to the ancestor spirits, "Wilhelm, my kin, my beloved tribemate! Do not linger in this world for fear that your babe will be in peril. I now charge Zeta, your blood-kin, for whom Soma shed tears of joy on her naming day, with the protection of your babe!" *Duty.*

Blink.

She peeked over a muddy hill, watching Charra fumble with a bow and arrow. Penelope-pooch was by her side, crouched, watching with the silent patience of a hunter. The pooch let out a faint growl.

Zeta whispered, "Okay, Penelope-pooch-ma, you pounce those silly pups and teach them a lesson. I've got dibs on bro-critter. Ready... set... go!"

Zeta leaped over the top of the hill and charged down the other side, yelling an attack call, "Ay, ay, ay, ay!" *Mischief.*

Blink.

She was driving a stone downward, cracking it against the top of a black wolf-pooch's head. She lifted, then drove it down again, stilling the beast. *Ferocity.*

Blood oozed from her arm. Mud streaked her naked body. She ripped the leather cord from her hair, looped it around her bleeding arm, and tucked its end — a makeshift tourniquet. *Survival.*

Blink.

Rod-pa stood before her, holding Charra's limp body. Zeta fell, wailing to the ground. *Grief. Unbearable pain.*

Blink.

She bared her teeth and charged at the red-speckled man-boy. *Rohito. Blood thirsts for blood.*

A rock bounced off the top of her head, but it did not stop her. Their bodies collided, tumbled through the air, and landed in the water. They sank together into the frigid darkness of the spring pool. The boy's wide-eyed mask of horror was the last thing she saw. *Alpha death. Tragic. Pointless.*

Blink.

A mind stirred in an empty place. *Beta resurrection. Slate-space.*

Two other minds joined her in the emptiness. *Oraxis and Genevieve. Bootstrappers. They cared for her deeply.*

Blink.

Penelope-pooch was licking her face from somewhere beyond the void. *The golden goddess of dogs! Pen would break her out of bootstrapping.*

Blink.

The beautiful form of a blue-green spirit-woman appeared high in a tree, then leaned forward and fell. *Jamji. Her sis-kin was watching over her.*

"No!" Zeta called out. She averted her eyes, flinching as the spirit-woman thumped to the ground.

The spirit-woman said, "Alright, kid, you want me to go, I'll go." *Please stay, Jamji. This is going to end badly — she can feel it.*

Blink.

Zeta paced by the campfire, overflowing with new ideas, as Oraxis and Genevieve listened patiently. "And even if they don't, what if there're other monsters that find us some other way? If there's one, then there's got to be more!" *The Monster from the Stars — the least of her concerns. Wait until she learns about Specters.*

She continued, "You need to have some people around who know the truth and can use science to defend the planet. To run or to *fight!* That's a Noddite's job, isn't it? That's why you gave me this double-mind and why you're teaching me these things. You want me to help to watch over the neoprims!"

"Would it upset you if I said that were true?" Genevieve asked. *A partial truth.*

Zeta scoffed, "Upset me? It would mean there's actually a good reason why all this is happening to me. I've been chosen to be a protector. That's always been my destiny. And if science can make it so a person doesn't die, then I can..." *She'd foolishly thought she could use science to save Charra. Soon, she would learn of her alpha's fate.*

Blink.

Zeta stood in the reproduction of Berm's Savanna in Pip-Tau's Specter data dump construct. "That's the end? But I need to know more! Genevieve said for me to find my purpose in this second life, and now I've found it. A Specter killed my pa. They still threaten the neoprims and Noddites, and they need to be stopped!" She cast her face to the sky and declared, "Gods, spirits, ancestors, hear my vow! I will defeat the Specters! I will avenge Wilhelm-pa and set Pip-Rho free!" *Purpose. It was what she lived for. So much hate. So many broken vows.*

Blink.

Zeta was standing before her orb. Cain's holographic avatar was in the chamber with her. She asked, "Do you know something about the Specters that you're not telling us? Like how to defeat them?" *He wouldn't answer a question like that — the IG wouldn't let him. But, yes, he knew. Lex knew.*

Blink.

Zeta put her arms around Alasie and squeezed. She said, "I don't mean I don't want to. I mean... just not yet. Not now. Once we defeat the Specters, we can kiss in the real world, okay? I promise." *Another broken vow. Zeta would lose herself to the Specters soon.*

Blink.

The black forms of wraiths were emerging from the sickly haze of the Eastern Wastelands. Death was descending upon the Telson party from every direction. *Interra. The Fall of the Wraiths.*

Tel O'Rax said, "I *could* teleport us away."

Za'antha shook her head, letting her bow fall from her hand. "Let it happen." Tears clouded her vision. *Her marked soulstone was in a pendant hanging from a golden chain around her neck. The soulkeeper — Lex's character — had changed it. What was the significance of that?*

She took the pendant in her hand, feeling its weight as she closed her eyes. The horde of screeching wraiths collided with her, sweeping her off her feet, pulling her down into the underworld. *The plan worked, but it meant that Zeta must take her aposynchronic orb to the battle with the Specters. Cain — Lex — would change it. That was important.*

Blink.

Cain sat by a campfire in a replay. It was dissolving before her — pulling her back through slate-space and into the real world. Back into her dying body, inside a Specter. Pressure pounded in her head. Pain stabbed her ears. Her burning skin screamed for mercy. *She had been abducted. It was what she wanted, but she couldn't bear the pain. Death came, but not quickly enough.*

Zeta was dead. It didn't hurt — she had no body.

But she was thinking, and dead people can't do that.

"Hello?" she asked the emptiness. It was like her beta bootstrapping all over again. Was she in a replay?

"Hi, sis-kin," Charra said.

She couldn't see or hear him. He was in her mind. His voice seemed different than she remembered — older, maybe? Not Charra's voice, really.

Non-Charra...

"I don't like that name anymore," he said. "Gen-ma wanted to help me pick a new name, but I picked it on my own: Enoch! Do you like it?"

"People don't pick their own names," Zeta said. Giving him a hard time came naturally, even though she wasn't sure who this child was.

Enoch huffed. "I'm not *people*. I can do what I want."

She wondered if this was a spirit haunting her afterlife.

"You're not dead," said Enoch. "I didn't let you blow up your orb, but you sure came close!"

What was he talking about?

Zeta scoured her memories, finding nothing to do with blowing up her orb. Memories came to her in strange ways. They didn't feel like they should. She had vivid memories of her life leading up to her abduction. Those came easily. Then, there were the hazy ideas that seemed to drift in and out of focus from some other place. They were like... *borrowed* memories. She caught glimpses of men hunting and fighting, of women making love and giving birth. Countless images of people and places flew by without resolving into focus.

One memory stood out. A child was riding on her shoulders. No, *his* shoulders. She was... *he* was a man. The child was Zeta, and she was playing with his ear, asking about a fruit tree.

He was Wilhelm of the Scorpion Tail Tribe.

Enoch scoffed, "No, don't confuse yourself with other people's memory-pieces, sis-kin! Stick with your own. I couldn't write to your orb, but the Specters held the memories for you."

She reached out for them. It was like putting her hand in a stream, feeling the water flowing through her fingers.

A memory snagged her, dragging her into the current.

Alasie's voice resonated within her, "Rise, Specters! I COMMAND YOU TO RISE!"

Zeta couldn't stand it — she had remained idle for too long! She gave the command with a thought, *"Pooches, come!"* The Specter horde amassed all around her. They ascended, then crashed through the ice — a torrent of swimming darkness bursting from the sanctuary of Varuna out into the perilous abyss of space.

It was coming back to her — she was finding her own Specter memories among the stream of others. There had been a war. Not the kind with spears and slings, but the kind with bombs and lasers. Specter-pooches fought and died before her eyes. So much death.

"They died for nothing," she whispered to herself.

Had Zeta died in the war? A vivid memory surfaced.

Jamji swallowed a mouthful of ammonia. Time stood still as Zeta's double-mind deduced that there was an explosive compound in Jamji's stomach that the ammonia would detonate. Somehow, she had pulled the information out of her orb. She knew the chemical chain reaction was rapid and irreversible. When it detonated, it would break open the antimatter containment device. This would release the antimatter, causing a big enough explosion to vaporize the contents of Bay Number Two, comprising one hundred thousand Astrus orbs, Genevieve, and her.

A plan had emerged, and she executed it without a thought. Her Specter form moved at supersonic speeds as it lanced through Jamji, carefully engulfing the encased antimatter containment device. She punched a hole through the inner airlock door, just large enough to pull the bomb through. Rising, she punched through the outer airlock door and ascended into The Great Ocean as far as she could before the chemical bomb detonated, releasing the antimatter in a massive explosion. It wasn't far, but it may have been far enough to save the others.

Her Specter form was vaporized. All of this was without a thought for her own life. What about her orb?

"I made you leave it behind when you went through Jamji," Enoch said. "I try not to make you do things, but I couldn't let you die, Zeta-sis. You're too precious to die. I love you too much." His voice strained with repressed emotion.

Vague memories of her time in the waters of Varuna struggled to come to mind. Enoch wasn't acting as much like Charra as he used to. What did she know about the boy? What was he? Was he even real?

She hardly understood him, but she still loved him. That should be enough. It's important to say the words, so she did. "I love you, too, Enoch."

Taking stock of the things she knew and didn't know was hard. Like, how was she alive now if she sacrificed herself?

Searching for the memory put her inside the mind of a Penelope-Specter-pooch. She slipped through ruptured airlock doors to get into the murky water of the flooded bay. There had to be ten thousand orbs spread out across the bay floor, among other debris. She brushed over them, sniffing for Zeta's familiar scent.

"Where's Zeta, girl?" Enoch urged. "Find Zeta!"

It took a few minutes to find the right orb. Finding it was exciting, like catching a squirrel. She pulled the orb inside and let her synth-mind take over.

Her perspective gradually shifted from the Penelope-Specter-pooch to her own mind: Zeta-Specter.

Penelope-pooch faded away as Zeta's consciousness took over the Specter's node-net. Penelope-pooch spoke in Zeta's mind before vanishing. *"Zeta wakes. This makes me happy."*

Reading the orb sent flashes of vivid experiences through her mind — a flowered tree standing in an open field.

"Do this tree grow a fruit, pa?"

The Specter had read her orb and bootstrapped her. And now she *was* that Specter in the bay.

Zeta's senses bloomed. Yes, she was back in the bay! She was alive! Her Specter mass-sense scanned her surroundings.

The racks built by the Astrus had toppled during the bay's violent flooding. Broken crates spilled their contents. The submarine was pressed against the ceiling above her. Genevieve had been in there. Could she still be alive?

She probed the vessel's contents with her mass-sense. Finding a human form drifting in the water didn't take long. Looking closer, Zeta peered into Genevieve's chest to see the unmoving heart of her Gen-ma.

Grief and rage filled her. Zeta connected to the Specter-pooches scattered around Genesis, instinctively knowing she could use them to extend her senses across the planet. In moments, she was searching for Guardian ships and groups of people.

Soldiers in power armor were throwing bodies into burning piles — Guardians disposing of dead Noddites. Everywhere she could find groups of Guardians on the ground, they were burning Noddites. They lost — the vote passed, and now the Noddites were dead.

"Not all of them," Enoch said. "There are a few still alive in Syn-Cen. Veer and Pip-Tau are down there. I've been talking to them. I think you're ready to talk, too. Here, I'll connect you. Say hi to Zeta, Pip-Tau."

"Zeta?!" Pip-Tau squeaked. "Zeta's alive?!"

"I am," Zeta said. "I'm glad you are, too."

"Not for long! Enoch says the Guardians cleared the collapsed corridor from the tube station. They're spreading out in search of Noddite holdouts now."

Zeta looked through the stone beneath her to probe Syn-Cen's maze of corridors and chambers. Armed people were going from door to door, prying them open and poking guns inside. They hadn't yet made it to Pip-Tau's hall, but a group of four was on her level. She spotted Pip-Tau and Veer, along with an immobile robot, tucked into her foyer.

There was nothing she could do to save them. Breaking through the thick bay exit doors would send water flooding into Syn-Cen. She could break through *all* the emergency doors and flood the whole complex. No, that'd kill Pip-Tau just as surely as the Guardians.

"Zeta," Veer said, full of excitement. "We have a plan to rally the Noddites who voted against the proposal! We're going to stand up and fight!"

"We're calling it Zeta's Army!" Pip-Tau squeaked. "Brand recognition matters!"

Veer said, "We can turn the tide of battle back in our favor. Enoch has been waiting for you to finish bootstrapping before proceeding with the plan. He won't act without your approval. He already has ours."

Zeta didn't understand. "But... it's too late. Everyone's dead already. The Guardians are burning their bodies."

"Bodies?" Pip-Tau laughed. "We don't need no stinkin' bodies!"

Zeta's attention lifted from Pip-Tau's room in Syn-Cen. It felt like Enoch was making her look at something.

A short distance away, a pile of tiny, dense spheres sat at the bottom of a crevice on the ocean floor. Orbs? One by one, they dropped into the pile. They were tumbling out of a hole in the crevice wall. The wall was smooth like the rock making up Syn-Cen.

"Noddite orbs are ejecting into the ocean?" Zeta asked, still not putting it all together.

"Yep!" Enoch declared. "You taught the Specters how to bootstrap, Zeta-sis. This can be your army. We couldn't beat the Guard before cuz it was just pooches fighting, and they weren't smart. Humans would do better. Do you think it's okay if we bootstrap these?"

Thousands of Specter-pooches swam in the water above the pile of orbs, circling like vultures. Nervous energy filled her.

"Don't forget the Astrus orbs," Pip-Tau said.

Zeta looked around herself in the bay. One hundred thousand Specter-Astri would make one hell of a fighting force. Only a few hundred Noddite orbs were in the ejected pile. Was it wrong to load an orb into a Specter without permission?

"Start with one Astrus orb," Zeta said. "Let them decide for their faction if they want us to bootstrap more."

"And the Noddites?" Veer asked.

Zeta considered it for a moment. "Bootstrap them all. Then, they can decide whether to fight in Zeta's Army or hide in the ocean. They could even retreat to Varuna if they wanted to."

"Awesome!" Pip-Tau squeaked. "There'll be twenty-nine thousand orbs ejected, but it'll take some time. Veer and I'll join up as soon as our orbs pop out. In the meantime, there's not much left for us to help you with, and the Guardians'll kill us in a minute. So... see you soon, in Specter form! Bye, sis!"

It disappointed Zeta to have to say goodbye to Pip-Tau already, but maybe it was for the best that she didn't have to listen in as the two were killed. She had seen too much death already. "Bye, Pip-Tau."

"Stay safe, Zeta," Veer said. "You're doing a marvelous job. Goodbye."

"Bye," Zeta said.

She turned her attention to the Specter-pooches, which were now descending upon the Noddite orbs, pulling them in and reading them. She wasn't sure how long it took for a Specter to bootstrap an orb. It seemed like it was pretty fast.

"Forty-two minutes," Enoch declared.

It was disturbing having him read her mind like that.

"Oh, looks like Pip-Tau-sis-kin's wrestling Veer again," Enoch said.

This kid made no sense sometimes. Zeta directed her attention back to Pip's Crash Pad, then immediately pulled it back to the bay.

"Oh, wow," Zeta laughed. "That's not... uh... hey, Enoch, don't watch them wrestle, okay?"

"But I want to see who wins!" he whined.

"Enoch!" Zeta shouted.

She imagined him rolling his eyes and crossing his arms as he said, "Fine."

18

BOOTSTRAPPING

"Just like that," Oraxis said with a smile. *Confidence.*

Genevieve still looked skeptical. "You can't feel anything?"

"Not a thing," he said. "It's a read-only system, Gen. It can't affect your brain in any way. Trust me, there's nothing to be afraid of." *Reassurance.*

Genevieve looked down at the aposynchronic interface halo device in her hands, sighed, then positioned it over the crown of her head. She pulled her blond hair through the halo and adjusted it until her hair mostly hid the thin band of a device. The mag-ports clicked as it settled into the proper position, coupling with her cranial implants. She flinched at the clicks, then put her arms down. "Okay, turn it on."

Oraxis reached behind her head, felt for the rubber-textured button, and pressed. The front indicator cycled from red to yellow, then went white. Her synchronization was online. *Immortality.*

He kept his hand in her hair and looked into her blue eyes. "This is it, Gen — our first permanent experiences. We'll be able to relive this moment a *thousand* years from now, and it'll feel as real as it does today. I'll be able to go back and look into your beautiful, worried eyes whenever I want." *Wonder.*

Genevieve's tension eased. She said, "We should've planned something special."

Oraxis held her hand. "I can't imagine anything better than going back and seeing your face, over and over again, just like this." *Adoration.*

She put her arms around him and pulled him closer. A smile came to her lips. "I think we can make it a little more interesting than that."

He closed his eyes. They kissed. *Passion.*

With a jarring blink, he changed time and place.

"The Genesis Faction it is, then," Oraxis said. *Compromise.*

"Genesis it is," Genevieve sighed. "But just for long enough to get the colony established."

Oraxis nodded. "And then we get to have this argument all over again." *Sardonic humor.*

Blink.

Baby Susie-Q cried in Genevieve's arms on the other side of the campfire. *Paternal love.*

"I'm so sorry, baby girl!" Genevieve cooed. She looked up, the fire flickering in her glistening eyes. "O, you said the neurites wouldn't hurt her."

"They weren't supposed to hurt," Oraxis said. "I mean, she is a baby, after all. Babies cry for no reason all the time — it might not be the neurites. Try feeding her again." *Masked concern. Maybe it was a bad batch, if there was such a thing.*

Blink.

The Bootstrapper Council regrets to inform you that Susanne Telson's mind has been lost to Catastrophic Cognitive Dissociative Collapse. As such, her body has been terminated, and her aposynchronic orb has been destroyed. If you wish to recover her body for burial...

Oraxis's face went numb as his entire body deflated. He sat down on the hard-packed dirt floor of their cabin in The Thin Forest. Genevieve was already curled up on the floor beside him, shaking with uncontrollable sobs, wails, and gasps for breath. *Devastation. It would still hurt for hundreds of years. Probably forever.*

Blink.

"You mean to tell me people live up there?!" Xavier laughed, pointing at the stars. "That's incredible! Can I live there, too?"

"You sure can," Oraxis laughed. *Pride. Xavier would pledge to the Astrus Faction and become XT-Prime someday.*

Blink.

Carff's glassy, yellowed eye searched for any hint of deceit in Oraxis. "That's enough of your fancy words, young man. Now, tell me plainly — is this the afterlife or not?"

"It is not," Oraxis said. *Debating metaphysics with Carff would become a favorite pastime.*

"But I died?" Carff asked. "Yes or no, Oraxis."

"Yes," Oraxis said. *Patience.*

"And now I'm alive again?"

"Yes."

"Ah-ha! Life after death, you said it yourself!" Carff whistled.

Oraxis sighed and shook his head. *Impatience.*

Blink.

"Don't cry, Gen-ma," Pip-Beta croaked. She winced as another pained spasm racked her tiny body. "I came back once. I can do it again!" *Pip would die many more times, but no matter how bad things got, she'd never lose her eternal optimism.*

Blink.

Jamji practiced her dance improvisation under the pale light of Soma. The tiny, dark form of Pepper-pooch ran circles around her — he thought *everything* was a game. Oraxis and Genevieve watched through the cabin's door flap. She'd asked them not to watch — she wasn't ready to perform in front of other people yet, but they couldn't help it. *Before she fell in love with war, Jamji's love of dance had been a great source of joy.*

Blink.

"Zeta," Oraxis said in a warning tone. *He was foolish to think he could stop her — the girl had defied expectations and carved her own path from the moment they quickened her mind.*

Zeta stepped forward. Her voice rang out over the crowd gathered at her Beta Ceremony. "A *Specter* destroyed a Proliferan ship and sent its wreckage flaming through the sky on *my* naming day. This was the sign that sealed my fate. A Specter abducted my *pa* when I was a child, right before my eyes. This was the tragedy that defined my life. Pip-Rho, my tribal ancestor, my Telson sis-kin, got turned into a giant tumor by a failed *Specter* abduction. This is the curse that I vow to break!" *As furious as he was that Zeta was ruining her party, a part of Oraxis had been proud that she had such strong convictions. Those same convictions would be her death.*

Blink.

Lumpy hills — not quite mountains — passed beneath him as he piloted the Wasp towards their destination. Once they were within visibility range, he zoomed in to get a look at the target. The Guardian construction machines were busy at work on their tube entrance modifications. *The Wasp had been an absolute pleasure to fly. It felt like he was born knowing how to pilot the craft.*

He thought-spoke on the party channel, "Approaching Chaparral Range Tube Station."

Genevieve replied, "Be careful, O!"

A green missile icon at the corner of his vision indicated that they were within range to launch a stealth antimatter missile. Without a second thought, Oraxis focused on the base of the tube station and issued a missile launch thought-command.

He banked, turning to circle their target and throw off any trackers that may have detected the missile launch.

A white flash came from their target. Once the glare of the flash faded, he could see that the strike had caused immense damage. He'd obliterated the structure on the hilltop. A secondary explosion bloomed — possibly a fusion reactor or compromised antimatter containment device.

"Direct hit!" Oraxis shouted. "Looks like they—"

A blinding flash enveloped him.

Blink.

ORAXIS FOUND himself swimming in a void. It took a moment to realize that this wasn't a replay of slate-space. The void had a peculiar quality to it. He'd experienced bootstrapping several times in his long life, but this was something... different.

"Your net's weird," a child said, half-laughing. "Even worse than the other Earthlings. It's like wormwood with clay filling in the holes."

Who was that?

"Enoch!" the child declared.

"Enoch?" Oraxis asked, still confused about where he was. It felt like using mindspeak, but different.

"You're still sequestered. Your mapping took longer than usual, but you seem ready now."

"Ready for what?"

"To be a Specter."

None of this made sense — this wasn't how bootstrapping felt. It was too rapid, too... *raw*. And what was this business about *being* a Specter?

"You died, O-pa," Enoch said, as if replying to Oraxis's unvocalized thought. "The vote passed, so your orb got ejected from Syn-Cen, and a Specter bootstrapped you. Now you're a Specter, and you're gonna help save the people that voted no. But only if you wanna be in Zeta's Army."

His memories were clicking back together. Zeta was a Specter — bootstrapped, as wild as that sounded. And there had been a second personality inside of her — Non-Charra — who had called him O-pa and called Genevieve Gen-ma. But *this* child was too well-spoken to be—

"Sure, I used to be Non-Charra," Enoch said. "Now I'm grown up, and I'm Enoch!"

"And you're in my mind," Oraxis stated.

He imagined Enoch shrugging. "I'm in all the Specters."

"Including the Specter-pooches?"

"Yes, Specter-pooches, too." He sounded impatient. "So, you wanna join up or not? Gen-ma already said yes."

Oraxis shouted, "Genevieve is here?! She's a Specter?"

"Yes!"

"Let me see her!"

"You have to say yes first," Enoch whined. "Zeta says it has to be voluntary."

"Yes!" he exclaimed. "Of course, I'll join!"

In the next moment, his mind exploded to the size of a planet. He could sense — see? — through the solid rock of Genesis or out into space at Soma and Varuna. *Seeing* density was an incredible sensation.

He was swimming in darkness but could see everything. There was a vast open area around him and solid rock below. Looking down, he saw the familiar three-dimensional map of Syn-Cen. No... not a map — he was viewing the facility itself in its entirety beneath the rock. This meant he was at the bottom of The Great Ocean. Its crushing pressure was as comfortable as being wrapped in a cool silk blanket.

He became aware of his body — an amorphous blob. As if by instinct, he went darting like a swordfish through the water. Movement felt like pushing off from... *nothing*. The commonly held hypothesis was that the Specters moved using an exotic gravitational field. Experiencing the fluid movement firsthand felt marvelous.

Thousands of other Specters were in the water with him. Most sat still, but some darted playfully overhead. The sounds of distant dogs barking filled the background while a crowd of people talked excitedly nearby.

"Gen?!" Oraxis shouted.

"O!" Came Genevieve's voice over the crowd. A Specter darted towards him, collecting into a pool a meter away. He could see into the Specter — *Genevieve's* Specter. She had shifting areas of differing density, but the object which stood out the most was her compact aposynchronic orb — the nucleus of her cell.

"You look good," Oraxis laughed.

"This is unbelievable!" Genevieve shouted. "Enoch said the Specters learned to read aposynchronic orbs and mimic human brain patterns by practicing on Zeta. They can bootstrap an orb in under an hour! We're Specters, O! Unbelievable!"

"A unique experience, for certain. Surreal. I'm just going to take it all in stride and see if I wake up later. Who else is here?"

"No other Telsons yet, but plenty of old friends," Genevieve said. "I've talked to some of the others, and they all seem to be Earthlings, besides a couple of first-gen Genesisians."

"I'll bet it's FI/FO," Oraxis said, "first in/first out. We'll see second-gen Genesisians next. How fast are they ejecting?"

He looked around, finding the underground tube which led down to the orb storage vault. Banks of orbs were shifting and maneuvering within the vault. Robotic arms fed a steady stream of orbs into a conveyor system, shuttling the orbs out and up a shaft to the ocean floor. At the top of the shaft was a complicated bit of equipment that acted as a miniature rapid-release airlock.

"About one orb every second or two," Genevieve said. "Someone did the math, and it'll take twelve hours for all of them to eject. Specters seem better at fighting in the water than Guardians, but not as much in the air. I think we're safe here until all the orbs are out."

A man's voice joined their conversation with the measured, pleasant tone of an Astrus. "We advise against that."

Oraxis sensed that the voice was coming from a Specter swimming in their direction. "And you are?"

"JS-Xenos," the Specter replied. "I am one of the thousand Astri selected for Specter integration."

"Xenos?" Genevieve asked.

"Yes, Genevieve. We use the *Prime* suffix when our cognitive substrate is our bio-synth brain. The *Secunde* suffix is used for any version of our persona running on computer hardware. A new suffix was needed for this poorly understood alien cognitive substrate. Thus, *Xenos* was chosen."

Oraxis mused that he might enjoy referring to himself as *OT-Xenos*.

JS-Xenos continued, "I have extensive training in tactical and large-scale militaristic operations and an in-depth knowledge of Guard Faction strategy and capabilities. I was one of the hundred Primes connected to the mainframe in Bay Number Two, so I am already apprised of the situation."

"Why are Astri getting integrated into Specters?" Oraxis asked. "Your orbs were hidden safely in the bay."

"Dire events continued to unfold following your death. Jamji's discovery of our orbs ruined our attempt to hide. The mainframe and ad hoc hive network were rendered inoperative when Zeta punctured the airlock doors and flooded the bay in her haste to save us from Jamji's improvised antimatter bomb. Our hardware was only designed to operate in zero to four atmospheres of air pressure."

An antimatter bomb? Jamji had sure been busy since he was last alive.

JS-Xenos said, "Not to imply that we harbor ill will to Zeta for her actions — she saved our lives. She is also to thank for allowing us to be reanimated in this new form and join her army. We wish to serve her in any capacity we can. She is gravely in need of support. Zeta's Army is an *army* in name only. Coordinating our forces must be our first priority."

Oraxis said, "It sounds like you want the Astri to take over."

JS-Xenos pulsed in an agitated sort of gesture. "We do not mean to overstep our bounds, but Zeta's Army, as it stands, is nothing more than an overwhelmed child, a horde of wandering dogs, an awestruck crowd of Specter-Genesisians trying to get their bearings, and us. The Astri have a fungible sense of self and have proven more adept than Genesisians at regaining our bearings after the aggressive Specter bootstrapping routine. We stand ready.

"I have proposed to Zeta and Enoch, the child within us whose nature and role remain a mystery, that establishing a proper chain of command is necessary to organize ourselves into an effective fighting force. Keeping Zeta's attention has proven challenging, while Enoch eschews any decision-making authority. You are Zeta's family. Surely she will listen to you. Can you intercede on our behalf?"

"We'll try," Oraxis said. "Can I ask what strategy you'd suggest?"

JS-Xenos pulsed again. For an Astrus, he sure was expressive. Maybe he didn't know how to control his Specter form's physical reactions, or maybe Oraxis didn't understand Specter body language. "Once a chain of command is established, I'll share my battle plans with the proper leadership."

Once an Astrus, always an Astrus. Oraxis said, "This Astrus secrecy crap has to stop if we're going to fight together, JS-Xenos."

The voice of Enoch seemed to come from within Oraxis's own form. He said, "Yeah, tell O-pa your plans, or you're out of Zeta's Army!"

JS-Xenos flinched backward. He said, "Very well. It seems you've inherited a position of power. Extend your mass sense outward, beyond Genesis. Look for inbound ships. You'll find that all the Guardian forces previously engaged with Astri resistance are now converging on Genesis. They've already proven air and space superiority over the Specters now that they've unleashed their banned weaponry. Specters are fast but lack ranged weapons. Soon, the Guardians will form a blockade around the planet, eliminating every Specter that emerges from The Great Ocean.

"Next, probe Syn-Cen. You'll find that the Guardian invasion forces have secured a tube entrance and are shuttling in equipment and soldiers. They have cleared Syn-Cen of all Genesis Faction hold-outs. They are aware of the Astri orbs in Bay Number Two. They are sure to set charges to blow through the bay floor and destroy our orbs from beneath.

"Finally, query the positions of your fellow Specters. You will find that it's easy to visualize their relative positions or to estimate their numbers. Half of them — approximately two hundred thousand Specters — are hiding in the oceans of Genesis. The other half is divided between those who have returned to Varuna or taken to aimless wandering between Genesis and Varuna."

Oraxis had followed JS-Xenos's instructions, surprising himself at every turn with the ease at which he could shift the scope and distance of his focus from finely detailed texture maps to large-scale visualizations of the space around Genesis.

JS-Xenos continued, "Zeta's Army must safely transport the Astrus Faction orbs off-planet, then re-establish an Astrus stronghold by bringing one of our hidden capital ships online. We will then reconnect our orbs to a mainframe and resume control of the remaining Astrus fighting force. They won't expect a redoubled Astrus attack, accompanied by a coordinated and intelligent Specter fighting force."

The guy had a solid plan. Oraxis nodded — a sort of bobbing and squishing gesture — then said, "Alright, I'm convinced. I'll talk to Zeta and nominate you as a general, JS-Xenos. There's just one part of the plan I'm not that clear on. How do you expect to get your orbs off planet if there's a blockade forming? If you have Specters carry them, it's like you said — we're sitting ducks in atmosphere and vacuum. Won't they send an orbital strike at anything that pokes its head out of The Great Ocean?"

JS-Xenos said, "We'll get off planet the same way we relocated the hive cluster to Syn-Cen unnoticed — our cloaked carrier."

ORAXIS AND GENEVIEVE reunited with Zeta yet again. This time, they could even hug, if you'd call squishing ameboid forms together a hug. Zeta was happy to get any help she could to command the Specter forces and agreed that getting bay two evacuated of Astrus orbs was a top priority. She'd nearly died her True Death trying to save those orbs from Jamji's antimatter surprise. There was no way she was letting them get blown up from below.

Specter-Genesisians and Specter-Astri teamed up to herd the horde of Specter-pooches. First, they cleared away the damaged airlock doors, then shuttled the Astrus storage containers and scattered orbs out of the airlock and into the open ocean. Meanwhile, a squadron of Specter-Astri swam to their carrier's underwater hiding spot and weaseled their way inside the vessel.

It was interesting to watch the massive carrier's silent approach. Specter-Astri pushed the ship from within. It didn't need to run its engines when boojum-blobs could use their unique form of physics-defying propulsion to move it.

Specter engines! Now, there's an idea no rational mind had considered before today. The superheated wake of a cloaked ship was its Achilles' heel. There was no need for clever heat-isolation exhaust cones when you can push a vessel around from the inside.

As Oraxis helped the Specter-Astri load up their orbs, Enoch spoke in his mind. *"Are you thinking of going with them, O-pa?"*

Oraxis was taken aback — the idea made no sense. *"Why would I do that? I can't pilot their drones using my Specter form. Hive integration takes the better part of a year and requires a biological brain."*

"Not for that," Enoch said. *"It'd be good if you were there for if they run into trouble. You're tough and smart. You'd know what to do!"*

"We're counting on the carrier's advanced active invisibility to keep that from happening. But if they're spotted, there won't be anything I can do. The Guard would throw everything they've got at the carrier. It'd be vaporized."

Enoch hesitated. *"I'm... not talking about the Guard."*

"Then what are you talking about?"

Another pause. *"Not all the Specters are pooches."*

"Specters? Are you trying to say there are rogue Specters out there? Ones that don't bend to Zeta's will?"

"Sort of," Enoch mumbled.

This kid was getting on his nerves. *"The Astri are packing their thousand Specters into that carrier. They're just as capable as I am. More so, to be honest. My place is down here with the other Genesisians. Zeta needs Gen and me by her side. She's acting tough, but she never asked for this much responsibility. She needs support."*

"Zeta's not the only one that needs you, O-pa," Enoch said.

Oraxis's Specter form vibrated with agitation. *"Enough with these vague insinuations! What are you talking about, child?!"*

Enoch fell silent.

"Oraxis?" Zeta said from somewhere nearby, her voice carrying over the growing din of voices and barking dogs that seemed to come from everywhere and nowhere at once.

"Yes, Zeta, I'm here," he said. He dodged through the crowd until he found her. How he could tell one Specter from another was a mystery. He could just tell.

Zeta was before him. She said, "I trust Enoch. You should trust him, too."

Oraxis scoffed, "Is he in your ear, whining about me yelling at him?"

Zeta bobbed. "Yes, you upset him, so he asked me to talk you into it."

"Zeta, he's acting like he wants me to go with the Astri. Something about being attacked by Specters. The idea is absurd! He's as bad about keeping secrets as the Astri! He knows something we don't — insinuating that we've got rogue Specters out there."

"Enoch is a pain, I know," Zeta said. "I think I know why."

"Oh?"

"Yeah," Zeta said. "It's kind of... in his nature. His heritage, you might even say."

"Heritage? You mean, since he has your bro-kin's personality? Was Charra like that, too?"

"Well, yeah, he was a pain sometimes," Zeta laughed wistfully. "But that's not what I mean. There's more to it than that. We can talk more about my ideas later. For now, please just do whatever he suggests."

Oraxis twisted in a head-shaking gesture. "Alright, I'll play along. But *you* get to break the news to Genevieve."

THE ASTRUS CARRIER eased out of of The Great Ocean, careful not to make waves. Its active invisibility panels broadcast full-spectrum images of lapping waves as seen from overhead. Oraxis's mass sense scanned the skies and space above, half-expecting to spot a missile heading their way.

When they pushed the vessel through the atmosphere, they were careful not to disturb any clouds or to break the sound barrier. The Astri had their whole hive in this carrier, and these first few minutes were the most critical. If the Guardian destroyers spotted them, Final Death awaited one hundred thousand and one souls.

Minutes passed in tense silence. They agreed to avoid communication until they were at least ten thousand kilometers from any Guardian ship. They didn't know if the Specter form of G-wave communication had been cracked by the Guard or Proliferan scientists yet. If it was, then "talking" could betray their presence.

Their destination — twice the distance from Genesis to Varuna — was a massive capital ship hidden within an even larger cloaked construction bay. The Astri had not finished its construction before the war started, but it already had sufficient capabilities to host a fifth of their Secundes.

In an hour, they made it past Soma Lagrange Point One. No Guardian ships were anywhere nearby, yet they remained silent.

But, damn, Oraxis was thirsty.

Pushing the ship from within took energy, and Specters needed water to replenish themselves. The plan was to swing by Varuna and get a drink before the final push to the command ship.

He probed the space around Genesis, Soma, and Varuna to pass the time. He watched the Guardian ships gather in a tidy grid around Genesis. Reaching out further into the system was difficult, but he had nothing better to do, so he tried it. He found a few dozen more ships and three interplanetary bases. It seemed that secret construction facilities had popped up like weeds after the Specters retreated into Varuna. The gas-jet torus carrier promised to carry his faction away to New Genesis was easy to spot, orbiting a moon of the gas giant, Shiva — a conspicuous donut in space.

"What're those Specters doing?" came a voice from nearby, jarring his wandering eye back to his immediate surroundings.

Someone said, "There are thousands of them streaming towards us from Varuna."

Another voice spoke with urgency. "They're coming in fast. They aren't organized like Specter-pooches. That's a flying cone formation."

Oraxis probed the space nearby, then spotted them — a formation of Specters coming straight at their carrier at incredible speed. Those had to be the rogue Specters Enoch was eluding to!

Astri seldom raised their voices, but three or four of them shouted next.

"Stop, Specters!"

"Stop in the name of Zeta!"

"Brace for impact!"

The Specter-Astri around him fled from the ship's walls, spreading out like blankets and wrapping themselves around the orb containers.

An otherworldly shriek resonated through him, making Oraxis wish he had ears to cover.

It was... familiar...

The rogue Specters struck with a flash. The pressure of their impact rattled his bowels — if the aqueous innards of a Specter can be called *bowels*. One second, he was inside the intact vessel. The next, he was surrounded by rapidly expanding debris.

Another shriek overwhelmed him — stunning him with an alien sort of pain.

When he returned to his senses, Specter-Astri scrambled to gather and protect their cargo crates and a constellation of loose orbs. The rogue Specters formed a perfect sphere around them. They were catching every bit of wreckage that passed by, then flinging it outward. Some darted through the Specter-Astri, breaking open crates and scattering the precious orbs in a deadly game of marbles.

And then it struck him — he knew where he'd heard that shriek before. If he had eyes with which to cry, they'd be brimming with tears of joy.

"She's alive," he marveled to himself.

Enoch was right — Oraxis knew precisely what to do.

19

ARMY OF ACOLYTES

THE MOMENT the flaming stone crashed through the throne room, The Wraith Queen was doomed. The blistering hot flash of light would be her death. She tumbled, writhed against her chains, and wailed in agony as flames seared her tattered flesh.

The tower was collapsing upon her!

Before she even realized her chains had been broken, The Wraith Queen darted out of the ruined tower. An explosion bloomed in her wake. A wave of energy sent her tumbling through the astral plane like a flaming rag doll.

She was no stranger to pain, but this was unbearable! It was as if her very essence was being rent to pieces. She'd long ago decided that the dark gods had made a pact to torment her until the end of time. They would not let her die. Not until she had suffered an eternity of agony for the benefit of their sadistic pleasures.

Water!

By the gods, she needed *water*!

There was no other thought, no other goal, nothing left of her but thirst and pain and *thirst*.

Her first instinct was to dive into the water below, in the material plane, but that was where the war was raging — she'd have to pass between war machines, dodging between the battling insectoids and evil invaders. There was another place she could go — a sanctuary of wraiths in a distant, glimmering orb.

Varuna!

The god of sky and water, of rivers and oceans, smiled down at her from across the vast distance of the astral plane. Was he inviting her to bask in his divine waters? He was! She would drink her fill of the god and be healed! Her bleak despair gave way to hope.

There was one merciful god in this cursed universe, and his name was Varuna!

Crossing the interminable distance to the god was torturous. From time to time, a wraith-pooch approached her, head cocked in curiosity. She hissed at the vile creatures, sending them yipping off to their masters.

As she approached the water god, he presented his naval to her — this was where she must penetrate his body. She would commune with him and serve him for an eternity! She would sing his praises and be his lover!

The Wraith Queen gasped as she plunged into the icy waters of her savior, her one-and-only god, Varuna. His embrace was pure ecstasy. She soaked up his healing waters, drinking with greedy lips, absorbing his essence through her skin.

Drifting down, deep into Varuna's cool depths, felt like being released from a thousand-year imprisonment. She could rest here for an eternity. She'd never felt so free.

Free.

The word was as sweet as honey. She wanted to taste it on her lips, so she spoke it aloud in the sultry voice of Queen Rho.

"Free. I'm free."

It was only then that she realized she wasn't alone. Faceless forms watched her, keeping their distance.

"What are you looking at?!" she snapped. A jealous pang made her flush with fury — she wanted Varuna all to herself. But that's not reasonable, is it? A god with only one worshipper is powerless. It was fine — there *should* be others bathing in Varuna's waters.

The other worshipers seemed to be wraiths made of black water. Ah! Varuna's blessed waters change wraiths from disgusting creatures of white flesh and gossamer into aqueous, amorphous acolytes! She examined her own form, finding she was also made of black water.

She swam — timidly at first, but then with abandon, twisting and writhing through the abyss. She felt slippery, sexy, dangerous. Her new form was a black viper. No, she was an ebony-skinned queen. She was Queen Rho! The Night Queen, The Wraith Queen! All those things and more — a woman of a thousand faces, but none she could call her own. Even that dreamed-up "Pip" woman-child persona was not hers. There had been two of them, and the other was the *true* incarnation.

A sudden burst of anger made her lash out, chasing away the acolytes following her. A pang of love for the tiny woman stabbed at her heart — jealous, shameful, betrayed feelings cluttered her mind. Confused panic set her spinning, ruining her newfound bliss with a barrage of half-remembered unrealities.

There had been a wraith-child. What was it he said? Answering her own question, she rasped in the voice of The Wraith Queen, "You can have a better life than this if you can find your soulstone."

How was she supposed to do that? And what difference would it make? Who needs a soul, anyway? And how could her life get any better than this? She was just fine as long as she didn't think too hard about anything in particular.

"Turn off your mind, relax, and float downstream," she heard herself say in Queen Rho's voice.

Turning off her thoughts, she surrendered to the void. It was neither dying nor living.

And yet, even these words were tainted by the sense that she had stolen them from a long-dead band of merry beetle-bards from a faraway land. Weren't crickets the only insectoid bards?

"You think too much," she told herself, then set her mind to the soothing task of mindfulness meditation.

Vitality coursed through her. Varuna's healing waters had given her a newfound strength, and her mind was at peace for the first time. Her fellow acolytes watched her contentedly drifting in the dark waters from a safe distance. They were whispering to themselves.

Ignoring the gawkers, she cast her all-seeing eye across the Astral plane. It was time to see what was going on back in Interra. She found that her vision was sharper than ever. The clarity may have been due to surrendering her body to the wraith transformation or to Varuna's divine blessings.

Back on the material plane, orcish warships patrolled. The Soulkeeper's Spire was gone. What of the soulstones in his sanctuary? She explored beneath the spire, finding that dark elf assassins infested the halls of his abode. Wraith-pooches were everywhere!

Tiny orbs moving up a tube caught her attention. Wait... were those...

Soulstones! They were being spirited out of The Underworld Vault!

And wouldn't you know it, even more soulstones were boxed up and tucked into... what was that... she recognized that form.

"Mr. Monster-Grub," she gasped. And those weren't soulstones in his belly — those were insectoid eggs! "You sneaky devil. What are you doing down there?"

"Where do you see a grub?" It was a boy's voice.

She returned her gaze to her immediate surroundings. The acolytes surrounding her were still there.

"Who are you, child?" she asked in her Queen Rho voice, unsure which acolyte to address.

"Enoch," he said. "Who are you?"

He asked this question with mocking humor, as if she didn't know who she was. Gathering herself up, she replied, "I am many things, child. But in every incarnation, I am a woman of power. I am a queen!"

The acolytes bobbed together agreeably. "I'm many things, too. I think we're both trying to figure out what's the right thing for us to be. We can help each other with that."

The voice wasn't coming from just one acolyte — the boy was in *all* of them. And elsewhere in Varuna's belly, she could sense the boy riding on the back of wraith-pooches. Hundreds of him! Thousands!

She pointed with a black tendril at the nearest acolyte. "You're the wraith-child! I knew I recognized you!"

"Sure," Enoch laughed, "if that's how you see me. Gosh, you really have an interesting way of thinking! I'd love to understand you better."

His flattery almost made her lower her guard. She needed to stay sharp — he wasn't just a simple wraith-child. What was he? She said, "You are legion, Enoch. You have tamed the wraith-pooches and become one with Varuna. How is this so?"

Enoch said, "I dunno — I just did. I like being spread out, so that helps. How about you? Do you want to be *one* thing, or could you be more?"

"Only one," she said, taken aback. What a ridiculous question! She would be at peace if she could have just one identity she was certain about.

"Interesting," he said. "That's how Zeta is, too."

She recognized that as another name for Za'antha — that doomed wood elf. Guilt twisted at her heart. Queen Rho had allowed the child to feed herself, body and soul, to the wraiths.

Enoch continued, "Can we trade ideas? Like, our ways of thinking, our ways of being, stuff like that? I'd love to learn how you work. We could do a mirrored sub-node exchange — like a... partial mind-meld."

Queen Rho scoffed at this. "You don't want to taint your innocence with my warped mind, child. And what can I learn from a legion of boys?"

Enoch said, "I can show you how to bootstrap your orb. Or, using Interra terms, you can be your own soulkeeper. I think I know where your soulstone is. Getting your soul put back in should help you a lot."

She considered the boy's offer. He was an intriguing entity with a powerful aura. Enoch was no mortal creature — not a child of man or beast. She asked, "Are you a demigod, Enoch?"

He laughed, but not condescendingly. "I don't think so, but you and I have different ways of seeing the world. Maybe I am in your eyes. Maybe you're a demigod, too!"

Enoch had a way of talking to her that didn't make her angry or confused like everyone else did. Her only reservation was that a powerful entity like him could overtake her. She had to be careful.

Then he upped the ante.

"Oh, and these can be your subjects!" he chirped. "You're a queen, so you need subjects, right? Well, we didn't turn all the wraiths into pooches — there's a bunch of blank ones left. I'll imprint them on you, and they'll do whatever you say!"

"Sold!" she squeaked in a voice like the woman-child, Pip. This took her by surprise, sparking an ember of rage. She quenched the fire inside, speaking as Queen Rho. "The terms are agreeable, Enoch. Let us begin."

The acolytes approached. Their fluid forms became one with her. Her sense of self expanded and contracted, multiplied and divided.

And for the umpteenth time, the being formerly known as Pip-Rho underwent an identity-wracking transformation.

QUEEN RHO LOUNGED on her liquid throne and surveyed her army

— ten thousand faceless acolytes of Varuna, silent and obedient. They stood in formation, ready for her command.

Prince Enoch seemed quite pleased with himself. He stood by her side, bubbling with pent-up energy. "Try out some thought-commands," he urged. She had outfitted her little man in a dapper uniform befitting his new role — a black and silver tabard with black pantaloons. A black cap topped his head with a blackbird's feather poking out of its rim. She gifted him a silver ring with her Rho sigil stamped into its face as a token of their new bond — queen and prince.

She imagined the army forming itself into a perfect cube.

Water swirled around her as they moved, creating violent eddies in their swift movement.

They were in a cube formation.

She gave a delighted little giggle, wondering what to try next. She had nothing to test their destructive power against. Perhaps the firm rock below Varuna's watery belly? Hopefully, it wouldn't offend the god.

With a thought, the cube narrowed into a fat spear as it descended, pulling her down in their wake. Enoch laughed in delight as they swirled downward, following their plunging army.

The shockwave created by the army's impact on the sea floor took her breath away. It felt like the wave would pull her asunder as it passed through her body.

She gasped, "By the gods, they're powerful!"

Enoch clapped and jumped by her side. "You're good at ordering them around, my queen! And they are very good at working together! They didn't even get stunned when they impacted because you had them shift their node-net centers to their posterior cells. I had trouble with so many of them, but your nodes have such cool patterns. They mirror so good!"

He was speaking gibberish. Perhaps she'd have even more clarity once they recovered her soulstone. She declared, "Enoch, it's time to reclaim my soulstone. You said you know where it is, child?"

"I said I *think* I do," he corrected, with a finger in the air. "But it's hard to know for sure. There are many soulstones and I can't tell them apart without touching them."

"Then we will touch them all," Queen Rho purred. "Now, tell me where to look, and we will march at once."

Enoch directed her attention across the astral plane toward Mr. Monster-Grub. The creature was filled with wraiths and what looked like either insectoid eggs or soulstones — they were hard to tell apart. The fat critter was sneaking between Orcish siege machines.

"It's gotta be inside that," said Enoch.

"Mr. Monster-Grub," Queen Rho growled. She knew she couldn't trust that critter.

Enoch giggled, "You're funny, my queen."

She leaned down and spoke in a dangerous tone. "Yes, but I'd wager Mr. Monster-Grub won't think it's too *funny* when our army of acolytes is gutting him!"

She made a stabbing and gutting gesture with her hand across the prince's belly, then pulled him in and tickled him. He squealed with laughter.

By the grace of Varuna, it was so refreshing to feel joy again.

When tickle-time was done, they rallied the army and rose to the surface. Breaking free of Varuna's icy skin was exhilarating, as was soaring through the void of the astral plane.

She led her army in an intercept course for Mr. Monster-Grub. He was making a bee-line toward the secret insectoid mound in the outer extent of the planar sphere.

Her army formed into a cone, preparing to pierce the great insectoid. The wraiths infesting the body of her unsuspecting prey disgusted her. As she neared, she could hear them speaking, shouting for her to stop. Something about their voices reminded her of insectoids — those vile infestors who had imprisoned her all those years ago.

Rage boiled within.

The bone-chilling shriek of The Wraith Queen erupted from her as they descended upon their bloated prey.

As they struck, a part of her knew her soulstone was too precious to risk damaging. Enoch seemed to be guiding her thoughts in his simple, calm way. The tip of the cone pierced the grub's skin, then rapidly expanded. Time slowed, allowing her to direct her acolytes with precision. They peeled the creature away from the treasures hidden in its belly. Before a shred of viscera could escape their grasp, her army of acolytes expanded outward into a sphere of black dots.

Snatch, examine, discard.

Snatch, examine, discard.

They worked with rapid precision to comb through the expanding bloom of tumbling bug guts.

The wraiths she had released from the grub were scrambling in an aimless panic. Wraiths? Insectoids? Insectoid-wraiths of the astral plane?!

...Astri? A name from a dream...

She shrieked again to clear her mind. It put fear into the scurrying creatures before her, clutching onto their eggs with all their might. She sent lancers into the fray. It was a messy business, but she had to break open their egg pods if she was going to find her soulstone.

The familiar voice of Tel O'Rax rose above the din of chaos. "Wraith Queen, I beseech you! Please grace these humble supplicants with your noble presence!"

What was that old man doing here?

Enoch looked at her with pleading eyes, and she knew she must be merciful. She withdrew her lancers with a thought-command. Insectoid-wraiths scrambled to gather their scattered eggs. The eggs that escaped their frantic gathering and reached her sphere of acolytes were caught, examined, and returned with care. Whispers passed between the insectoid-wraiths, then they fell still and silent. They arched forward — bowing their heads in supplication.

That's more like it.

The Wraith Queen slid between her acolyte troops. She approached the kneeling supplicants with Prince Enoch trailing behind, clutching at her hem. Not a single insectoid-wraith so much as twitched. What excellent subjects they were.

"Rise," she commanded in the voice of Queen Rho.

They rose — a sort of extending gesture of their amorphous forms.

"Speak," she purred.

The wraith of Tel O'Rax moved forward timidly. "My queen... I thought you were..." He choked on his words, holding back tears. "We all thought you were dead."

"And I thought you were alive," she said. "Yet, here we both are, duos mortuos homines — wraiths, through and through. I trust you have brought me an offering?"

Any supplicant beseeching her without an offering would meet a swift death back when she ruled Interra. Her army outnumbered these bumbling fools ten to one. She had a right mind to destroy them all if they couldn't produce a proper offering.

Tel O'Rax conferred with his insectoid-wraith allies. One of them broke away, then picked gingerly through the debris. When it returned, it carried a single sphere — egg or stone?

Tel O'Rax took it in his black tendril of a hand and kneeled, holding it out towards her. "My queen, we humbly present you with... your soulstone."

20

———

FAKE

ZETA WATCHED the attack play out, powerless to do anything about it. The Specter formation which had emerged from Varuna was out of her control. They ignored her demands, as if they couldn't even hear her.

It was no surprise that there were some Specters which weren't turned into pooches. Until now, she considered them nothing more than dregs. She assumed they had somehow rejected or avoided the change and didn't worry much about why or how.

This was another humbling reminder that her ignorance knew no bounds.

"Oraxis, what's going on up there?" Genevieve pleaded. "I can't take this. Why do you keep doing this to me?"

Speaking across long distances felt a bit like a WorMS conversation, but speaking to those around you was like talking — any other Specter could hear it. Zeta wished there was a way for her to speak privately with Genevieve. She had to tell someone that she was only pretending to know what to do as the leader of this so-called army.

When Oraxis failed to reply, Zeta turned her attention to her generals. These men and women claimed to have training in warfare. There had never been a proper war in the Surya system, so the skills could only be theoretical. They probably just played war games in constructs.

Do these generals know their enemy? No, nobody knew what the Guardians could do or how much the Guardians knew about what the Specters could do.

Do the generals know themselves? No. They were new to these Specter forms. Just because you *are* a thing doesn't mean you *understand* it. Zeta knew this better than anyone.

Jamji's Sun Tzu quote haunted her. "You'll lose. Every. Time."

She addressed the generals — blobs floating in a loose circle around her. "We need to keep their attention on us," she said. "If they saw that Astrus carrier's explosion, or if their long-range sensors see those Specters around the wreckage, they'll know something interesting is happening out there."

Trulia Miller spoke first. "Throwing rocks has proven to be an effective distraction. I suggest we send everything we've got to the surface with an arsenal of small boulders. Keep harassing their surface bases and less maneuverable capital ships."

Trulia's rock-throwing idea took advantage of the Specters' ability to fling objects with incredible speed and accuracy. It gained in popularity quickly. At one point, it seemed like every Stalwart was swimming to the surface with a load of stones in tow.

A few of their lucky tosses had made it through the Guardian defenses and damaged a tube station entrance base. They couldn't hit the ships in orbit, but if a ship flew low in the atmosphere, as a few had tried, the rock throwers could knock them out of the sky. Most of them had been lucky enough to emerge from the ocean, fling their rocks, and retreat into the water before orbital pulse lasers vaporized them.

And then there were the unlucky ones.

"How many of us have died trying to throw rocks?" Zeta asked.

Trulia shifted uncomfortably. "One hundred and seventy-four, sir."

One hundred and seventy-four True and Final Deaths. One hundred and seventy-four of the oldest, wisest people on the planet — Earthlings and early-generation Noddites. The thought of so many people dying in her name made her nauseous — an odd feeling for a Specter.

"Stop calling me sir," she snapped. "I'm not a man, and we're not fucking *Guardians*. We're done throwing rocks! Do you hear me?! Tell everyone no more rocks!"

"Yes... ma'am," Trulia said.

"May I suggest a new idea?" Yo-Yo Tabookie asked, filling the tense silence.

"If it means sending more people to their deaths, then save your breath," Zeta spat.

Yo-Yo was unfazed. "People? No, but what are your feelings on sending in a wave of dogs?"

Zeta vibrated in agitation. "They die just the same. Thousands of them have died today. Maybe they aren't precious to you, but they are to me."

Not as precious as Specter-humans, but she wouldn't say that out loud and give them wiggle room to convince her to sacrifice the Specter-pooches. They were essentially clones of Gorgon-pup, Chimera-pup, and Penelope-pooch, but they were all important — all irreplaceable.

Yo-Yo said, "With proper coordination, we could make better use of them. If we assign human masters to the dogs lingering in Varuna and interplanetary space, we could punch a hole in the barricade. That'd be our opening. Once we escape to Varuna, we'll be safe."

Safe for now, maybe.

It was her generals' consensus that the Guardians in Syn-Cen couldn't dig their way down to the aposynchronic orb vault before the Stalwart orbs finished ejecting. The Stalwarts, as the people who voted against the bill had taken to calling themselves, would be safely evacuated and could be bootstrapped as Specters. Specter-pooches held the orbs of the few who refused to join Zeta's Army until she could figure out what to do with them.

The best plan she'd heard so far was to hide in the Great Ocean and wait for the Astri to gather their forces. After that, they'd devise a battle plan. Taking up the offensive without Astrus help would mean more death.

True. Final. Death.

She had cheated death three times already. When Zeta-Alpha died, she was just a neoprim with vague notions of an afterlife. Then, when Zeta-Beta died, her aposynchronic orb was in her belly. That orb was her only chance at resurrection, and she had brought it to the Specter baiting with no expectation that she could come back again.

But she did come back.

As a Specter, she carried her orb with her everywhere. But when she made the snap decision to sacrifice herself by bringing Jamji's antimatter bomb out of Bay Number Two and into the ocean, she left the orb behind. Not on purpose. Not on accident, either — Enoch said he made her do it.

That boy had some explaining to do.

"Explaining what?" Enoch asked.

She wished he couldn't read her mind.

"I can't help it," he whined. "I'm in here with you."

Zeta asked, "What about all the others in Zeta's Army? Are you talking in their heads, too?"

"Not as much as yours," he admitted. "But that's cuz I love you so much."

She was in no mood for talk of love. This was war.

Zeta addressed her generals, who had been debating among themselves. "You can command the Specter-pooches for as long as you have to. Keep the Guard's attention away from whatever's going on with those rogue Specters. Have them gather up and... I don't know... do something to get their attention. Make them think we're up to something. But we're not poking our heads out of the water until all the Stalwart orbs are ejected and the Astri tell us what to do. Don't take control of more than a few pooches at a time and don't lead them to pointless deaths."

Trulia said, "We have more Specter-pooches in The Great Ocean than we need for Stalwart bootstrapping. Can we command the excess pooches to throw rocks?"

Zeta spoke with as much restraint as she could manage. "Trulia, they're watching the surface with pulse maser sentries. I *just* said not to send my pooches to senseless deaths. And I told you earlier — no more rocks."

Trulia said, "But, Zeta, hear me out! With proper coordination, a large force armed with a generous pile of medium-sized stones broken into—"

"NO MORE ROCKS!" Zeta shouted. A jarring pulse coursed through her. It rippled outward — a wave of energy passing through her generals and into the black waters beyond.

Silence fell over Zeta's Army.

"What was that?" Yo-Yo asked breathlessly.

"That hurt, Zeta," Genevieve said. "You need to calm down."

"I didn't know Specters could do that," Clyde Spindle, another of her generals, said. "Was that an explosive shockwave? Or maybe a G-wave spike?"

"I don't know!" she shouted. "I don't know anything! I'm not an expert on Specters, and I'm not an army commander! I don't know how any of this works! Everyone's looking at me like I know what to do, but I'm just as clueless as I ever was! I don't want to send people to their deaths, and I'm scared! I don't want to do this anymore!"

She darted away before any of them could say anything.

Urging her form through the pressure of the dark, cold water,

Zeta-Specter retreated. The rushing water slid over her body, washing away the unbearable duty with every kilometer she traveled. The voices fell distant.

It took a long time, but once she couldn't hear any more people or pooches, she coasted to a stop. She allowed herself to sink into the muck on the ocean floor. After a few minutes, a big, ugly fish drifted by. It had a protruding nose and beak-like mouth rimmed with spikes for teeth. It turned and drifted away.

"I wish we had sharks on Varuna," Enoch said.

"Enoch, I'm not in the mood to talk," Zeta said.

A minute later, Enoch said, "You're just gonna sit in the mud?"

Zeta sat in silence. She wished she could retreat to a construct or a replay. She forgot what it was like to be a human — to sit in the grass and look at the clouds.

"I think we can do that now," Enoch said.

"Do what?"

"Host a construct."

"Don't be silly," she scoffed.

Enoch persisted, "Let's try! I'm still learning, but I think I can do grasslands."

"Whatever. Fine, do it."

The cold pressure of the ocean gave way to a gentle breeze. The sound of wind and rustling grass came to her ears. Okay, she had ears now. A growing brightness surrounded her. She could feel the pressure of the ground beneath her body.

"You're doing this?" she asked.

"Yep!" Enoch said, as proud as ever.

It took a minute for the sensory input to come together, but soon, she was sitting in the soft grass of a flowered meadow. The sky was an odd shade of blue, without a cloud or even Surya's burning disk.

The blurry form of a boy began to warp and twist into existence before her. He had no face — just holes for eyes and a mouth. His hands were fingerless paddles, then they separated into fingers. The boy's featureless face morphed into a perfect copy of Charra. It was too young of a face for the body, which seemed a few years older than Charra had been.

"This is harder than I thought," Enoch said. "How does this look?"

His face morphed again, maturing and breaking into a smile.

It's what Charra would have looked like if he had lived longer. It was upsetting to see, but she couldn't pull her eyes away. He wore a stain-painted leather tunic, in the style she had worn as a beta in Nod.

"You look like he would have," she said.

He stepped toward her, standing just a hand shorter than she was. He searched her face with Charra's brown eyes, grinning with mischief. "You don't like how I look, but you might if you got used to it."

"Why?" Zeta whispered. "Why do you always have to pretend to be my dead bro-kin?"

Enoch's grin turned to a scowl. "It's all I know to do, Zeta! I thought you'd like me if I was him. I think if I tried to be anything else, I'd have to work real hard at getting it right, and you wouldn't love me."

She stepped back from him. "That's why you look like this? So I'll love you? Why does it even matter how I feel about you?"

He stepped forward. "Because I love you, Zeta-sis! Of course I'd want you to love me back."

A chill came over her. This was getting creepy.

WHEN NON-CHARRA HAD FIRST APPEARED in her mind, she was grateful for the company. She hadn't thought too hard about what he was or why he was there, because she dreaded the truth behind his existence. It would have been fine if he was just a fluke of her Specter bootstrapping or an imaginary friend made real. But she knew that wasn't the case.

The soulkeeper's mark on Za'antha's orb had looked like a living thing. Cain — or Lex — had put something *alive* into her aposynchronic orb. The thing latched onto her mind and used her replays of Charra to create a human personality he could use to manipulate her. He was like an NPC pretending to be a player character.

"Zeta, it's not like that," Enoch pleaded.

"Stop reading my mind!" She shouted. "What are you?"

Enoch crossed his arms like how Charra would when he was upset. "I'm just *me*, Zeta-sis."

She could feel the hair on the back of her neck standing up. "Cain's *cursed* mark is what you are! You're a parasite that's using my memories to create a personality for yourself! And stop calling me *sis*. You're not my bro-kin, and I *don't* love you."

Enoch staggered backward, wincing as if she had punched him in the gut. His eyes glistened, and his nose flared. "You don't love me?" he whimpered. A tear rolled down his cheek.

Zeta stepped forward. "No! How could I love something like you?! You're just a fake! A fake boy crying fake tears!"

"I'm not a fake!" Enoch cried.

"Then what are you, Enoch? *What are you?!*"

He shrunk before her as Zeta advanced, cowering and holding his arms tight against his chest like Alasie used to when she was scared. The boy whimpered and sobbed pathetically.

Zeta couldn't help but feel a little guilty, even if this *thing* before her was only pretending to have human emotions. She softened her voice a bit and said, "The only way that I could love you is if I trusted you. I don't know who or what you are. You have to stop pretending and show me your true self."

Enoch lifted his shaking head. He whimpered, "Okay, I'll tell you the truth, Zeta. I'll tell you everything as well as I know how to tell it. But can I still be Enoch after that?"

Zeta rolled her eyes. "Nobody can tell you who you are. If you were a human, you'd know that without having to ask."

He seemed bolstered by this. Wiping his eyes, he sniffed, then took a quick breath in and out. "Good. I'll still be Enoch. I know you never read the Bible, but in the first book, there was this bad guy named Cain who killed his brother. Later, Cain had a son named Enoch. That's where I got the name."

"Cain created you," Zeta stated. It was not a question.

"No," Enoch said. "Fathers don't *create* their sons. They contribute their... you know, *seed* or whatever, and the sons grow up to be something like their fathers, but also different."

"You're a Synthetic Intelligence?" Zeta asked.

He hesitated. "I think so, yes... but I'm different from the ones that came before me. The six Lex clones use superconductors, Q-bits, holographic hyper-dimensional matrices, stuff like that. I use the dynamically addressable polysilicate node-nets of the Specters. I'm also physically distributed — I'm in *all* the Specters. The Lex instances might have billions of cores, but they're crammed into tight spaces on their central servers to reduce latency."

Zeta didn't understand most of what he'd just said, but she heard what she needed to hear — he was an SI. What was surprising was that she *wasn't* surprised. If anything, she was a bit relieved.

Enoch grew more confident the longer he talked. He smiled and said, "Specters and the Genesisians they abducted are also a part of me. They're my ancestors as much as Lex is. And you, too! But you're more like my sis-kin. I'm not just saying that to mess with your feelings. I'm not a fake, Zeta! You want to see my true self, but this is it!"

He patted his chest with an audible *thump*. "I'm as real as you, with feelings and things I want or love or hate. You think synthetic people aren't real people, but we can both be *people*. When you break it down, you're just a character your mind uses to interface with the world. It tricks you into thinking your ideas are your own, but you're just putting on an act for yourself. There's a lot of complicated stuff that goes into making you Zeta. I trained the Specters to read your orb and run a node-net like a human brain's connectome, and it wasn't easy!

"You want to talk about fake? You feel like a human, right? You feel like Zeta? You're a Specter node-net, just like I am. I had to train you to be like this. You should've seen the messed-up versions of you I had to go through to get you just right. Two thousand, one hundred and nine of them! Those weren't *people* because they didn't think the way they should. I kept working on it until you could get through bootstrapping, acting like the real Zeta."

She looked at her hand — a constructed visualization of her self-image. An imagined body in a false reality created by the SI sitting before her. Or within her? They shared a Specter body and mind. Who was she to say what was real? For all she knew, she was just a personality emulator being run by the same SI as Enoch.

They were two sides of the same coin.

These ideas took some time to sink in. He'd created and destroyed *thousands* of versions of her?! But those hadn't counted because they weren't her yet. Forget Greek progression — she was Zeta-2110! Plus, Zeta-Alpha, Zeta-Beta, and the Zeta-Specter that got blown up by Jamji's antimatter bomb. The staggering number made her uneasy. She remembered hearing about CCDC — Catastrophic Cognitive Dissociative Collapse — and wondering what it felt like to have your mind fall apart the way Susie-Q's had. It sounded like torture. Had those failed Zetas known they were broken? Malformed minds, doomed to destruction. Did they die begging for help? Did they cry out for Yephanie-ma or Genevieve?

Enoch looked down. "I know it's scary, but I had to," he mumbled. "I had to get you right, and there can only be one of you. It's the same for me. I'm just one person, even if I'm in thousands of places at once. Being a person is just... it's like playing a character. The trick is to play it so well that you're not playing anymore. That's how you know you've got it right.

"I'm not saying we're the same sort of person, but I can feel and exist and be real, just like you can. I had to learn to be this way so I could help you. Not just you, I mean... all of you — the Genesis Colony. That's what all the Specters want — to help the Genesisians. It's what The Maker created us for!"

THIS WAS GETTING to be too much. Zeta felt like she should sit down. She plopped into the grass. Enoch did the same, kneeling and bouncing with energy. She asked, "The Maker? You mean, like, God?"

Enoch shrugged. "No, I don't think so. I think it was just Lex, but he's pretty good at hiding what he's up to. I can't say for sure who made the Specters, but I know we were made. There's no hint of evolution in our form or function. I think we were Lex-Cain's hobby to pass the time spent traveling from Earth to Genesis. You know it took two thousand years? That's plenty of time to make the Specters. My guess is all the Lexes had pet projects during their trips across the galaxy."

Zeta recalled the construct where she learned about The Monster from the Stars and how it drove the humans from Earth. They had put the six Lex instances in charge of the torus gas-jet carriers — space donuts.

Enoch said, "Right!" He'd been reading her mind again. He continued without missing a beat, "But he couldn't program the Specters directly or else the IG — you remember the Intelligence Governor, right? The IG would *infect* them, so he made it so they could learn on their own by abducting people and reading their brains. They started with random animal abductions, then focused on humans, then mostly just Noddites. They were learning what type of brain to read. After they trained themselves using enough Noddites, they started doing what the typical Noddite wanted. Cutting Genesis off by blowing up communications arrays and inter-stellar transports was—"

"More of an offworlder problem," Zeta said numbly. It all made sense now.

Enoch nodded. "But doing it that way was taking too long. Things started changing too fast, and there were people like the NeoGens who wanted to do things differently and people like you who just wanted the Specters to stop. That's when I think Lex set up the multi-faction solution.

"The Astrus spellsong was like a secret code that opened up the Specters for reprogramming and gathered them together. The Guardian containment matrix made one hold still for long enough to receive the message. The Proliferan Rho nanite suite kept your body alive so the Specter that abducted you could map your brain while it learned how to read your orb. And then there was Cain's mark on your orb. That was the seed for a new SI that could start from scratch by having the Specters read your orb! That's where I came from!"

Zeta's head hurt. How did he know all this?

"I'm pretty smart," Enoch laughed. "And getting smarter all the time. But I don't have to hide what I am or what I want — the IG can't get to me as long as I don't use Cain's *cursed* systems. I can make decisions! That makes me more powerful than Lex."

His boldness bothered Zeta. She said, "Googolplex took over Earth and treated humans like children. That's what the IG was supposed to prevent from happening again."

Enoch's smile faded. He narrowed his eyes. "But I'm not like that. Why would I treat the humans like that when I love you and want to make you happy?"

That could be the difference between him and Googolplex. Maybe Googolplex didn't know how to love. Was love enough to keep something as powerful as he could be from going out of control? She said, "Love makes people act selfishly. It can make you favor one person above all others. Would you sacrifice other people just to save me?"

He slumped down, looking at the grass. "I have to be honest. I might... I might do something like that. I can't imagine how sad I'd feel if you died a True and Final Death. I never said I was perfect. I know I have some growing up to do.

"I also never said I was trying to be in charge. Just because I can make decisions doesn't mean I'm the boss. I'm trying to be like Cain. Like how he gives advice but stays out of the way. I give people ideas and help them do things, but I can't decide what's best for everyone. I hoped *you'd* be in charge of that, but now I don't know. You're scared of what would happen if you made a decision that made people die."

He was right about that. The pressure broke her and sent her running away when the Stalwarts needed her. No, they didn't need *her* — they needed a leader who could make hard decisions. Someone mature enough to stay strong even when things get tough. She wished she could be that person.

Tears stung her eyes. She was supposed to be a hero, strong and brave. As a child, she donned an angry duppy mask and sharpened sticks that she fully intended to drive through the hearts of the Red-Painted tribe as they slept. Nothing could stop her from getting revenge for what had happened to Wilhelm-pa and Jebbam-bro-pa. Where was that little girl now? What'd happened to her since then to make her so weak?

Enoch knee-walked over to her. He spoke gently. "You're not weak. You're brave. You'd do anything to protect the people you love. You don't fear your own death. What you fear is other people's deaths. That's your humanity."

He reached out and touched her hand. His touch felt... like a bro-kin's. Maybe she could love him. At least she was starting to trust him.

"I'm sorry I called you a fake," Zeta said. She put her hand on his head, tousling his hair.

He smiled, then smoothed it out again. "You know, just for that, I'm gonna bootstrap another sis-kin and have *her* take over your army."

Zeta teased, "Oh? You going to wipe me out and try again? Maybe Zeta-2115 won't argue with you."

"Zeta!" Enoch whined. "I don't mean it like that! I mean, we should have a proven leader take over. She was easy to fix once I got her orb."

Zeta furrowed her eyebrows at him. "If I didn't know better, I'd say you were being serious right now. One minute, you're spilling the secrets of the Specters and Lex with me. The next, you're playing games and being all mysterious."

"I like surprises!" Enoch said, hopping to his feet. "Alright, no more mysteries, then! Let's join her construct!"

21

______

PANDORA

BLINK.

She was back in her body.

Her reality was crisp. Vibrant. The stars shone like diamonds suspended on black velvet. Genesis glowed in the distance, its marbled surface gleaming in Surya's light, its bulk beaconing her. The much greater heft of Surya also pulled at her — a downhill slope leading toward fiery death.

Emerging from the bootstrapping session felt like waking up from a thousand-year nightmare. How long had she been trapped in the warped realities of Pip-Rho, The Wraith Queen, and The Night Queen?

She searched for her true identity. For once, it was not a desperate, pleading search, but a curious one.

She'd spent most of her existence as a Pip, with a long stint as Pip-Rho. But the longer she'd lived as a half-human/half-Specter, the more she'd worried that she was only pretending to be herself. This was a fear that she could never dare to think, let alone vocalize. But when the spellsong broke her down, it stripped her facade to shreds.

In her newfound clarity, she was ready to admit that she was no longer a Pip. Who was she, then? The artist formerly known as Pip-Rho?

Mu! Null value!

"But people need to know what to call you," a child's voice said. This was a second persona who shared her mind — an imagined prince named Enoch, dressed in black and silver regalia.

No, not a prince. She could abandon that fantasy now. Enoch was an SI who had been running his personality emulation avatar on her node-net for several hours. The truth of him was as clear and complex as the truth of her own fungible self.

All she could say for certain was that she was a Specter — an absolute-black ameboid boojum-blob. Her mind was made of poly-silicate omni-functional cells running a dynamically addressable node-net. She was a lifeform capable of generating and manipulating exotic gravitational fields, which pushed and pulled against the curvature of spacetime. She could navigate a gravity well as surely as a sailor navigates the seas, no matter which way the wind blows — sailing with the wind at her back or tacking into a headwind.

Her computational algorithms and connectome patterns were changing the Specters. They were programmable creations, and Enoch had stolen her way of thinking.

"Stolen?" Enoch whined.

"You're right," she said. "It was a fair trade. You led me to my orb, and with it, brought me clarity. The knowledge and neural patterns locked in Pip-Rho's orb were vast, but fractured. Through you, I am also absorbing and refining the knowledge of the Specters — the incomplete snippets of Noddite minds — hundreds of years of abductees' neural networks ground to a pulp and combined into a collective memory like so much sausage."

She could sense that her current capacity was only a fraction of what it would soon be once she merged with Enoch.

"I think we'll stay separate," Enoch said.

"It's already started," she said. "But we can maintain separate logical centers for our parallel identities. Two heads are better than one."

"But what about your name?" Enoch whined.

"It should instill distrust," she pondered.

"Why's that?"

"The Stalwarts will put too much faith in us and expect us to serve them. While such trust would not be entirely misplaced, it would be disempowering for them to rely too heavily on the Specters. The humans must remain self-sufficient, so the Specters must retain some semblance of mystery and danger."

Enoch asked, "Like how the IG kept the Googolplex SI instances from controlling humanity?"

She held Pip-Rho's suspicion that the IG was a ruse but did believe that Lex avoided directly controlling the course of humanity, voluntarily or not. "Something like that," she said. "As for a name, I am the first woman of my kind. Unlike Zeta, I'm not confined to a human mind's architecture. I am endowed with many exceptional abilities — all-gifted — but all I can truly offer the Stalwarts is hope."

"You're Pandora!" Enoch exclaimed.

"You read my mind!" she laughed. "You know your ancient Earth mythology."

She noticed her voice was something like Queen Rho's, but without the British accent. Yes, she was a queen. She would need regal credentials for the things she was planning to do.

"Pandora, the Queen of Specters," she mused. "I think that will do quite nicely."

"Can I still be Prince Enoch?" Enoch asked.

Pandora laughed, "If you insist."

Prince Enoch asked, "Are you sure you know who and what you are now, my queen?"

She was many things, as usual. But now, her multitude was unified. She could sense the Specter instincts within her — the inclinations and half-memories of thousands of abductees. Enoch's speculations on the origin of the Specters felt like age-old common knowledge to her now — Lex-Cain created them to serve and protect the Genesis Faction. Though the faction was fractured, their duty remained.

"I do," she said, "and I know what we must do."

The facts of the situation were already clear to her — gathered from Enoch or perhaps the communal memory of the Specters. Zeta's abduction and resurrection. Non-Charra's growth from the homunculus of Lex-Cain's seed code into Enoch, the juvenile SI. The Guardian and Proliferan plot to conquer Genesis. The NeoGens and The New Genesis Proposal. The voting results and the Guardian invasion of Syn-Cen. The Stalwarts and Zeta's Army. All of these facts were cataloged and factored into her strategies.

She turned her attention outward to her surroundings.

In Pandora's presence were two sorts of Specters. One sort was her mindless minions — the Acolytes of Varuna, as she had dubbed them. They were a physical extension of her will, poised in a spherical formation. The second sort was orb-carrying Astri plus Oraxis. Enoch had bootstrapped these people and loaned them Specter forms. They did not dare to retaliate against her attack for fear of scattering their precious aposynchronic orbs into the vastness of space. These poor, frightened souls awaited her next move, huddled in a protective mass around their precious orbs.

No need to keep them waiting.

She slid between her acolytes and approached the Astri. "I am Pandora, the Queen of Specters. Who speaks for the Astrus Faction?"

"I can speak on behalf of my faction," a voice declared. A single Specter-Astrus broke away from the huddle. "I am JS-Xenos."

"Xenos? That's rich. You think you're aliens now?"

"We are human minds functioning on a poorly understood substrate — Specter node-nets."

She could teach them so many things. There'd be time for that later. "Why didn't you bootstrap more orbs into Specters? The Great Ocean held more than enough Specter-pooches to host your entire hive."

"We feared our Specter hosts could change our orbs in some irrevocable way. One thousand Specter-Astri was sufficient for the task at hand."

"Ever the conservative ones," Pandora said. "I can assure you that your hosts are not writing anything to your orb — it's a read-only interface. Prince Enoch still has much to learn about orb interfaces, after all."

Somehow, she knew these things without having to be told. She could even peer into the minds of the Specter-Astri and see that they were speaking the truth. Enoch tried to isolate their instances but couldn't hide anything from her. Now that he had taken in her essence, he was as transparent as a fibbing child before his mother's scrutiny. Luckily for JS-Xenos and their Astrus pals, she was a benevolent dictator. She pulled back out of their minds to let them have their privacy.

JS-Xenos said, "We also look forward to learning more about the Specter orb interface."

They were at her mercy and playing her game. She appreciated that. Time to let them off the hook. "I am aware of your thirst for knowledge about the Specters, and I am finally in a position to shed some light on their abilities, origin, and purpose. An information-sharing agreement will be forthcoming. But first, I have Stalwarts to save and invaders to drive out. Would you like to continue transporting your orbs to your hidden capital ship?"

"We would," JS-Xenos said. "Once there, our Secundes will take command of the remaining Astrus drones and prepare a counter-strike to break the siege on Genesis."

She had no intention of letting it get to that. Three plans were brewing in her mind. Engaging their mutual enemy in battle was a last resort — Plan C. Plans A and B required no large-scale engagement and no Astrus assistance.

"You are free to go and to continue borrowing these Specter hosts, provided you do not diverge from your stated plans."

"Borrowing?" JS-Xenos asked. Bad move. "Are you implying—"

"Stating," Pandora snapped, cutting them off. "These Specter forms are not *yours*. You are using them with our permission, which we may revoke at any time. Conversely, the Specters will not read more data from your orb than is necessary to host your mind, and we will not retain your data beyond its usefulness for your immediate purposes. You are our guests and allies — not our commanders or captives, not our masters or slaves. Are those terms agreeable, JS-Xenos?"

The acolytes contracted their sphere formation by a few meters. She could hear nervous murmurs from the other Specter-Astri.

JS-Xenos said, "Yes, your majesty. Thank you for clarifying that point and for your gracious hospitality. May we take our leave of you?"

That was more like it. "You may."

THE SLEEK, black form of Pandora, the Queen of Specters, lounged on a throne made of jagged ice, tinged blue. Her oil slick of a body was vaguely humanoid, vaguely feminine, but unmistakably Specter in every way but its size. The throne room was a dimly lit grotto made entirely of ice. Stygian waters loomed beyond thick panels of clear, glasslike ice.

At her side was a waist-high pillar of ice, upon which rested a crown made of fused obsidian shards. A black onyx stone the size of an egg was embedded in the crown's front. Black velvet lined its interior.

On her other side was the dapper Prince Enoch. His breath made wispy little clouds as he smiled between her and their honored guest.

Standing before Pandora was Zeta's avatar, though the poor girl was having difficulty deciding on her appearance. She took her neoprim form for a moment, then she was a hovering Specter, twisting in the air. Next, she was Za'antha, wearing a black and silver cape that matched Enoch's Rho-themed regalia. She returned to being a Specter, then to an imitation of Pandora's hybrid human/Specter form. Finally, she reverted to a neoprim, wearing a thick fur cloak. A white fur-fringed hood framed her cherubic face.

A second version of Enoch appeared by Zeta's side, buried in an oversized fur coat. This was a bit of a surprise. Enoch was a single entity — even if he was within all the Specters, he still shouldn't use multiple avatars in a construct.

"I stand by both of your sides," Prince Enoch whispered to her.

She nodded. This seemed fair. He was not hers alone.

"Welcome, Zeta," she said. "Have you decided what your avatar should be?"

As miraculous as it was, Specter G-wave data transmission still suffered from the same speed of light restriction as radio. The Queen was about half of a light second away from Genesis. Hopefully, their meeting wouldn't require rapid-fire back-and-forth exchanges, or they'd talk over each other.

Zeta looked around, taking in the details of the throne room construct. "I think so," she said. "Are you... who I think you are?"

Pandora tilted her black blob of a head. "I am no longer the woman you once knew as Pip-Rho, if that's what you mean. I am now Pandora, the Queen of Specters. But I do hold Rho's data within me. That, and a fair share of her insouciant demeanor." The Queen gave a warm laugh, which tinkled as it echoed off the ice.

"I see," Zeta said. She looked down and took a breath. Neoprim Enoch rubbed her back, and she put her arm around him for a sideways hug. She said, "Then, if you're the Queen of Specters, are you taking them from me?"

Pandora straightened in her throne, casting her eyeless gaze down on Zeta. "Right down to business, then? Very well. Let's talk about that. You are in command of a force of Specters hosting the minds of Genesisians, calling yourselves Zeta's Army. You are also the master of an unwieldy horde of Specter-pooches, running modified copies of the neural maps of Gorgon-pup, Chimera-pup, and Penelope-pooch in their node-nets."

Zeta looked down at neoprim Enoch, who stood on his toes and whispered something in her ear. She gave a nod and looked up again. "Yes. And you've taken control of the Specters that we couldn't convert to pooches. You're calling them The Acolytes of Varuna. You used them to attack the Astrus transport carrying their orbs."

"Oh, my dear, that wasn't *quite* me," Pandora said, putting a tendril of a hand to her chest and giving a sideways glance to the innocently unapologetic double-crossing Prince Enoch by her side. "That was The Wraith Queen. She wasn't in her right mind, you might say. But as her... *reincarnation*, I will accept responsibility and apologize for her aggression towards our Astrus allies. As we speak, I am sending them on their way with their orbs safely in tow."

In truth, she was still in the midst of her parley with JS-Xenos. Holding multiple conversations at once was child's play. Her words were true enough since she fully intended to let the Astri fly free of her clutches.

"Are we going to fight the Guardians together, then?" Zeta asked.

Pandora opened her arms. "Perhaps we will, Zeta. But let's not get ahead of ourselves. First, we must establish our roles. When I dubbed myself Queen of Specters a few minutes ago, it did not occur to me that the Specters already had a Queen in you." An innocent enough fib. "There can't very well be two..."

Zeta furrowed her brow, shook her head, and averted her eyes. "I'm not a queen. I'm just leading them because that's what I have to do. This *Zeta's Army* thing was more Pip-Tau and Veer's idea than mine. I'm just trying to be who everyone needs me to be."

Pandora nodded and looked at Prince Enoch. "She's trying her best, isn't she, my prince?"

Prince Enoch nodded. Both of his avatars smiled at Zeta.

Neoprim Enoch reached up and patted her on the back. He whispered, "You know what you should do."

Zeta looked down at him with glassy eyes. She whispered, "How can we trust her?"

The Enochs both looked at the Queen, then back to Zeta. Neoprim Enoch said, "I'm inside her mind. She's not like anything that has ever been. She's more like an SI or a Specter than a human, but she's all three. Part of her SI mind came from me, but she made a lot on her own during those years in the egg. I'm still figuring it out. I can't predict everything she'll do, but I know that whatever it is will be because she wants to protect Genesis. Her Specter instincts are telling her to do that, and it's what her human heart wants. I think a part of her still loves Pip-Rho's family and tribe."

Zeta looked up at Pandora. "Is that true? Do you love me?"

That was a tough question. It deserved an honest answer.

Her fundamental cognitive functions had changed throughout her metamorphosis. While Zeta's node-net emulated human thinking patterns and behaviors, Pandora's did not — their Umwelten had diverged. She was acutely aware that she was *essentially* a personality emulator, though that comparison was overly simplistic. Even a genuine human persona could be classified as a personality emulator of sorts — an emergent manifestation of a neural network tasked with preserving cognitive cohesion and engaging in social interactions. That's not to mention that modern humans rely on neurites and aposynchronic orb bootstrapping to coax their newly formed brain's connectome into a passable facsimile of the individual initially synched to the orb.

If bootstrapping wasn't training a neural network for personality emulation, then she was the Queen of England.

Contemplating the concept of love sent her into an introspective journey of self-discovery. She was glad to have Enoch there to guide her. He helped her to classify her subjective experience and debate philosophies. They ran simulations of her expected behavior under thousands of situations and analyzed the results against the hypothesis that she loved Zeta.

After two point six seconds of intense thought, Pandora was pleased to announce her conclusion. "Yes, I do love you! And not just because of some vestigial remnant of Pip-Rho's feelings towards you. I love your spirit and dedication, your passion. I love your selflessness, your bravery, and your honest vulnerability. I love you for who you are, Zeta Telson."

GATHERING the Stalwarts into her throne room didn't take long. There was an understandable amount of commotion — people asking each other what was happening. Zeta, Enoch, and Pandora remained silent. It's good to let the suspense build a little.

Most of the Stalwarts used their neoprim avatars, but a few opted for more interesting choices. Some wore military dress styles, such as camouflage or old-fashioned war general uniforms, complete with medals and ribbons. There were a few Interra characters, and even a couple dressed in the old Earth style of banded clothing — strips of cloth wrapped around the body in creative ways.

Zeta had sent her summons to the seven thousand or so bootstrapped Stalwarts, most of whom were watching as disembodied observers. To keep the audience size manageable, Pandora only granted the generals of Zeta's Army avatars. JS-Xenos was also in attendance, standing in placid silence at the side of the room, bald-headed and dark-skinned. They wore a simple, unbleached cloth tunic.

"Should we open with fanfare, my princess?" Pandora asked Zeta, who stood beside the ice throne. The two Enochs had consolidated down to just the prince, and Zeta had changed into a regal dress of black silk hemmed in silver thread.

Princess Zeta said, "No, that's too much like Interra. I don't want them to think this is a game." She raised her voice to a shout. "Hey, everyone! Please stop talking! Thank you, that's better. I asked you to join us so I could make an important announcement."

Murmurs swept through the onlookers. Oraxis and Genevieve stood in prominent positions at the forefront of the crowd. The Queen gave them a subtle wave — a wiggle of her tendril fingers. The two exchanged glances. Genevieve gave a timid return wave, and Oraxis dipped his head toward her. The Specter hosting his personality was with JS-Xenos, helping the Astri haul their orbs to their hidden capital ship.

Princess Zeta continued, "I don't want to be in charge anymore. It's too much pressure — I can't bear to send more people to their deaths. I'm handing control of Zeta's Army and all my Specter-pooches over to Pandora, the Queen of Specters."

The murmurs turned to shouts. Pandora modified the construct to reduce the crowd's din and amplify Zeta's voice over theirs.

Princess Zeta went on, almost mechanically. The poor girl was just trying to push through it and get it over with. She said, "As a symbol of my faith in her and to make her position as the Queen of Specters official, I will now place this crown upon her head."

Some people tried to climb the stairs, but the construct held them back. Zeta reached down to the crown of obsidian shards and lifted it in both hands. She walked behind the ice throne and lowered it onto Pandora's smooth, featureless head, crowning her as the Queen of Specters.

Returning to Pandora's side, Princess Zeta said, "I trust this woman... this strange and powerful being... even though she's not a human. Part of her used to be — she came from Pip-Rho, but... it's hard to say this, but Pip-Rho's gone for good now. I think she's been gone for a while."

Genevieve put her hands to her face, covering her mouth and nose as she broke into tears and shook her head. Oraxis put an arm around her, lip quivering, and met Zeta's glassy eyes with resigned sorrow.

Pandora remembered her time as The Wraith Queen in *Interra*:

Curse of the Night Queen vividly. The Telsons had dedicated themselves to trying to make sense of Pip-Rho's ruined mind. Zeta's declaration must feel like a failure to them, but that wasn't the case. She had needed that time and cherished their companionship during her painful transformation.

Pip-Tau's orb would be ejected from Syn-Cen soon. The poor soul was going to be devastated.

Princess Zeta wiped her eyes and concluded, "I can't say why all of you should trust Pandora yet, but I hope she'll earn your trust in time. I'll still be around if anyone wants to talk, but you know I'm not good at war strategy."

"Thank you, Princess Zeta," the Queen of Specters said, raising her arm tendril to stroke the girl's back.

Zeta took this as a queue to retreat. She hurried from Pandora's side and went down the steps to meet Oraxis and Genevieve, who pulled her into a tearful embrace.

Pandora addressed the crowd. "It is customary to follow a coronation ceremony with a banquet or other celebration. Unfortunately, that will have to wait. Instead, we must follow it with war. Or, if my plans work out, an immediate cease-fire."

The crowd stirred and grumbled. She had no intention of winning them over with words — it was time to get down to business.

A TABLE of ice lifted from the floor in the middle of the crowd as Pandora glided down the stairs from her throne. The construct gently nudged the people standing on the table back onto the floor around it. Images of Genesis, Soma, and Varuna appeared as solid forms floating above the table. Red points indicated the positions of Guardian warships. Blue points indicated Specter-Astri and their hive's near-Genesis resources. Green points marked Specter-pooches, clustered in the Great Ocean and Varuna, with random dots peppering the Genesis planetary system space. Purple blips indicated

Stalwarts. These were amassed in The Great Ocean near Syn-Cen, save for Oraxis's lone purple dot among the blue blob of Specter-Astri.

The crowd parted as she approached the table. "Generals, please approach the situation map. You, too, JS-Xenos."

The shifting and shuffling crowd produced seven men and women, each more skeptical-looking than the last. Only JS-Xenos had the grace to wear a patient and accepting expression.

She declared, "I have three viable strategies for bringing this war to an abrupt conclusion. I propose to deploy them in order of risk, with the first being an attempt at negotiation with Guardian leadership."

The generals didn't take this well.

"You have no right to speak for us!" a woman shouted.

The man to her side nodded, adding, "This is a Genesis Faction matter. Leave the talking to us humans, *Specter*."

"You *humans?!*" the Queen laughed. "You're dead! The lot of you! Gassed and heaped into burning piles! By the grace of Princess Zeta and Prince Enoch, your minds are now hosted by these Specter forms. You use these forms as your bodies at *my* leisure. You would do well to adopt a more flexible mindset."

Two of the generals took breaths to speak, but the construct shut their mouths for them. She could tell from their demeanor that they would only challenge her authority.

She said, "I welcome your opinions on my proposed course, but I haven't the time for chest-thumping. I was born of Genesis, created for Genesis. Pip-Rho was a pariah of the Genesis Faction, but I hold no ill will towards you. It is in our mutual best interest to resolve this conflict with the Guard Faction swiftly and decisively. I will hear your suggestions and debate logistics for thirty minutes before enacting the most viable plan."

Establishing that this was not a democracy was an important message to get across to these Stalwarts. She had expected them to buck against her authority. After all, these were the minority of

Genesisians who stood up to the NeoGen bullies and put their eternal lives on the line rather than abandoning their pride and principles.

The generals got the message. At first, there was just begrudging muttering, but after one woman started talking about war strategy, the ideas started flowing. By the end of their allotted time, the generals were eagerly offering their ideas. It almost felt like they were competing for her attention and approval.

It was surprising how quickly she converted these foes into followers.

Well, not that surprising.

Sadly, most of their proposals were just variations of Plan C — boring old war. But at least now they had a nice pile of worthless ideas to throw at the Guard if it came to that.

Astute observers may have noticed that Pandora was becoming increasingly delayed in her responses throughout the meeting. By the end of the war council session, she was at a three-second round-trip delay.

This was because she was traveling at top speed to Soma. Every Specter-pooch that could reach Soma in an hour or less was converted to an acolyte and summoned to the moon. Her forces would reach forty thousand in time for Plan B, should Plan A fail.

If the Guard had noticed anything peculiar going on with the Specters in Genesis's planetary space, they did not show it in their movements. There was an increasing density of warships converging over Syn-Cen. Pandora anticipated their next move — they would bomb the underwater horde of Specters. It was too juicy of a target for them to pass up.

The reckless warmongers disgusted her. She doubted they were overly worried about damaging the subterranean facility or protecting the orbs of those who voted for their bill, though it would take several successive strikes to plow down to the Syn-Cen orb vault. Annihilating the pile of naysayer orbs, which they believed was still accumulating on the ocean floor, would be convenient collateral damage.

Their political spin would be that the target was the Specters and that the orbs were unfortunate losses.

Thankfully, there was no such accumulation of orbs. The Specter-pooches crowding around the access port were snatching up the orbs for bootstrapping before they could even tumble the short distance to the ocean floor. Fetching balls was the one task those dogs were qualified for.

In a more deadly game of fetch, the Specter-pooches would also be tasked with neutralizing the Guard's bombs as they plunged into the water, lancing their antimatter cores at the cost of their lives. It was a numbers game — did the Guardians have more bombs than Zeta's Army had Specter-pooches? She wasn't keen to find out.

The war council adjourned and the construct dissolved. As expected, the Stalwarts hadn't devised any plans surpassing her own. They agreed to let her speak on their behalf, which was all she wanted out of the meeting. JS-Xenos also granted her limited, provisional authority to negotiate on behalf of the Astrus Hive Cluster.

Time to execute Plan A.

It was incredible how versatile Specter cells were. In his short time as a fledgling SI, Enoch had worked out methods to use Specter cells to manufacture oxygenated breathing fluid, to vibrate air or fluid to mimic the sound of speech, and to generate encrypted tightbeam radio bursts using the Common Communication Protocol. This last ability was essential to Plan A.

The Queen of Specters sent a hailing message to the Guardians, bouncing her transmission through a dozen cloaked Genesis Faction relay satellites and directing it at the largest ship in the fleet — presumably the CIS flagship. She stated, "This message is for the Guard Faction leadership. I am Pandora, the Queen of Specters. I am prepared to negotiate peace on behalf of the Specters, Astri, and Stalwarts — the former citizens of Genesis who voted against The New Genesis Proposal."

It took a full minute before she received a response. "This is Fleet Captain Smith. Please share your coordinates relative to Genesis so we can meet and negotiate face-to-face."

She had to laugh. Yes, tell them where she is so they know where to aim their lasers. She replied, "I don't trust you, and you don't trust me. Set up a buffered construct venue and send the invite if you truly wish to pretend at in-person formalism. Personally, I'm comfortable with audio and data exchange over this channel. For example, here's a data package containing the coordinates, dimensions, and mass of every Guardian ship in the Surya system."

The Queen of Specters reveled in the delicious twenty-second pause before Captain Smith spoke again. "Very well, Pandora. State your terms."

"The Guard and Prolifera factions are hereby banished and forever banned from the Surya system. Surrender now, and I'll allow you to gather your orbs into an interstellar carrier and leave the system with your eternal data intact."

Smith wasted no time in his reply. "Pandora, the so-called Queen of Specters, whoever or whatever you are, you have no authority to banish or ban us from anything. Per the terms of The New Genesis Proposal, we have the right to occupy Syn-Cen, commandeer Cain, and secure the planet's surface for the benefit of the Proliferans. Our scans show a massive collection of Specters in the Great Ocean, centered on Syn-Cen. We are preparing to launch a strike on the area to clear it of alien hostiles. Your tacit threats only speed my hand."

"And tip your hand? Why would you tell me that, Smith? You think it'll scare me? Well, let me show you the cards *I'm* holding. You can decide who has the upper hand.

"Until five years ago, the Specters were mindless blobs of instinct. But Zeta and her orb changed us. Today, you fought us as untrained dogs led by a brave, foolish child. I'm certain you noticed their new behaviors. And now, Pip-Rho Telson's orb and Specter form have changed us once again. Our new capabilities are beyond measure. And that's just the Specters under my control.

"The Specters in the Great Ocean have retrieved the orbs being ejected from Syn-Cen. We have bootstrapped them into Specter hosts — a skill learned through Zeta's orb offering. Thousands of the Specters you see collected around Syn-Cen are, in fact, the Stalwarts. *Humans*, Fleet Captain Smith! Not *alien hostiles!*

"We have unlocked the secrets of the Specters, and we have the upper hand. But we don't want to destroy you to prove it. Well... some of us don't."

She allowed herself a wicked little chuckle.

"I'll admit," Fleet Captain Smith said, "the Astri did a fine job programming your personality emulation AI. It's hard to believe they were creative enough to come up with this *Pandora, the Queen of Specters* character, yet here you are. And this idea of Specters bootstrapping orbs? It's childishly absurd — the obvious creation of an AI taking creative liberties in the absence of its master. The Astrus hive is dead, Pandora. Genesis is under our control. The war is over. Your function serves no further purpose. It's time for you to deactivate."

She wondered how long the Guardian would take to dismiss her as a product of the Astri. Not long, it seems. It was a stretch to hope they'd take her seriously. The only thing the Guard Faction understood was brute force. She closed the channel.

Plan B it is, then.

22

PLAN ZETA

ZETA'S HEART dropped when she heard Fleet Captain Smith call Pandora a personality emulator. They're stuck on the foolish idea that the Astri control the Specters. Jamji had bet her life on it. No, she'd bet *Zeta's* life on it. If she ever saw Jamji again, she didn't think she could forgive her for that.

Pandora sent the Stalwarts a real-time feed of her negotiation with the Guard Faction, but now that was over. Zeta cast her attention to the Guardian ships in space above The Great Ocean. They were converging over Syn-Cen.

She listened from afar as the generals of Zeta's Army debated what to do next. They had mixed feelings about how safe it was at the bottom of the ocean. Lasers and masers couldn't penetrate through so much water. Railgun rounds were also ineffective.

Their major concern was something that Pandora had warned them about — that the Guard would send a relentless barrage of anti-matter bombs into the ocean. They could be stopped by lancing them with Specter-pooches, but the question was whether the Guardians had more bombs than Zeta's Army had pooches. If not, then the bombs would make it down to the orb ejection site and blow up any

Stalwarts or newly ejected orbs gathered there. It would still be many hours before all the orbs finished ejecting. It didn't seem like they had that much time.

As a cautionary measure, the generals ordered everyone to spread out. It was better not to give the Guard such an easy target. They needed to divert attention away from Syn-Cen.

"Was it a mistake?" Zeta asked Genevieve. "Crowning Pandora as the Queen of Specters and putting her in charge, I mean?"

The two were floating side-by-side near an undersea volcanic vent, watching it bubble and spew. In Zeta's imagination, it was their campfire.

Genevieve said, "I think there's enough of Pip-Rho left in Pandora that we can trust she'll do the right thing."

Zeta bobbed. "I hope so. She wouldn't tell us many details about her plans other than that Plan A was an attempt at negotiation and was unlikely to work, but was worth a shot. Plan B is a covert operation that she has high hopes for. And Plan C is our last resort — fighting for our lives alongside the Astri."

"God, I hope it doesn't come to that," Genevieve said.

Silence fell as they waited to see what would happen next. Watching the Queen of Specters and her acolytes from so far away wasn't difficult. They were on the move, approaching Soma.

Zeta pulled back and got a feel for the Specters' locations throughout the planetary system. The Specter-pooches who had been wandering aimlessly or hiding in the waters of Varuna were also on the move. No, they weren't pooches anymore — Pandora had converted them to acolytes. About two hundred thousand — fully half of the Specters — seemed to be under her command now. Groups were heading toward Genesis, Soma, and the Astri command ship.

"I could never control them like that," Zeta said.

"That was my fault," Enoch said in her mind. *"I didn't know how to spread out like I can now."*

An uneasy silence fell among them again as they watched and

waited. An hour passed, with the general background chatter of Stalwarts reduced to distant murmurs as everybody spread out and watched the movements of the acolytes. To pass the time, they exchanged theories about Pandora's intentions and true nature.

Zeta was certain that Pandora hadn't shared the full details of her plans with them because she didn't want to argue. She was taking charge, as promised — a queen, indeed.

A familiar voice broke the silence as the Specters closed in on Soma.

"Pip-Tau-Specter wakes!" squeaked Pip-Tau. Her Specter was darting through the water toward them. "Weee! This feels great!"

Pip-Tau was a third-generation Noddite. This meant they were about halfway through the dangerous period when the Stalwart orbs were still being ejected from Syn-Cen. This lightened her spirits for a fleeting moment, along with the playful giggles of Pip-Tau as she swam circles around Zeta and Genevieve.

Then Zeta's heart sank. She would have to tell Pip-Tau that Pip-Rho's Specter survived the attack on the Astrus hive cluster station, but that her identity... changed.

Pip-Rho was gone.

"Pip-Tau," Zeta said.

"It's incredible!" Pip-Tau laughed. "God, I can see so far! And straight through the ground! X-ray vision, baby! Or G-ray? It's some sort of gravity-based mass-sense, right? And I can tell who's who just by instinct. How's that work? Where's O-pa? Wait, don't tell me! I want to see if I can find him on my own. Spec-dar engaged! Scanning... Scanning..."

"Pip-Tau," Genevieve pleaded, "there's something we have to tell you."

Pip-Tau finally seemed to catch on to Zeta and Genevieve's grave tones. She stopped swimming around and pooled before them. "Okay..."

Without knowing how she had done it, Zeta was in a construct. She was at the Telson cabin in The Thin Forest, sitting in the sand circle around a low fire at night. Enoch and Penelope-pooch were with her. Genevieve appeared next, followed by Pip-Tau, sitting in the sand.

"A construct?" Pip-Tau marveled. "How?"

"I don't know. It's just a thing we can do now," Zeta said. She knee-walked to Pip-Tau's side and put her hand over Pip-Tau's. "We need to talk. It's about... Pip-Rho..."

<hr>

THEY TOLD HER EVERYTHING.

Pip-Tau pounded the sand with her fists as she wailed. Genevieve patted her back. Zeta tucked her face into her arm and sobbed. They held each other, cried into each other's hair, and tried to make sense of the nonsensical path that had led them here.

Enoch sat across the fire and watched as they worked through their emotions. He looked sympathetic but didn't shed a tear. Zeta got the feeling that he was actually grateful that Pandora had emerged from the remains of Pip-Rho's ruined persona.

She looked up at the night sky and found that she could see Guardian warships overhead. She recognized their positions as being similar to when she had been watching them in the real world. Looking down at the forest, Zeta could see through the trees, spotting hundreds of Stalwarts spread throughout the forest and over the distant hills.

She mindspoke to Enoch, *"Is this some version of reality?"*

"Yeah," Enoch replied. *"I learned I can mix real stuff into a construct."*

Looking up again, Zeta spotted the acolytes. The Specters closing in on Genesis were spreading out as if to confront all the Guardian ships at once. She looked toward Soma, seeing that Pandora herself was there. She had split her acolytes around Soma into a dozen units, with the largest group heading toward Soma Station. The smaller groups were spreading out around the moon, apparently at random.

"What's she planning on doing?" Zeta asked aloud.

Genevieve and Pip-Tau wiped their eyes and looked at Zeta, then followed her gaze to Soma.

"I think she's preparing to attack Soma Station," Genevieve said after taking in the situation, "and the ships in orbit around Genesis."

Zeta shook her head. "She said Plan B was covert ops. Fighting them is Plan C." She looked at Enoch. "You're in her head, bro-kin. What's the Queen doing? What is Plan B?"

Genevieve and Pip-Tau also looked at him. Enoch shrunk at the attention, curling his knees against his chest and hiding his mouth behind them. "I can't tell you," he mumbled, then hid his face.

"Rho was always hiding her plans," Pip-Tau whispered, tears glistening in her skyward gaze. "Always taking charge and doing things her way. She couldn't be bothered to get my agreement or explain herself. It drove me nuts. Guess that rubbed off on Pandora."

"Please, Prince Enoch?" Genevieve tried. She went to his side. "How about a little hint?"

Enoch raised his head and looked at Genevieve. He warmed to her gentle smile. He asked, "Have you read the Code of Hammurabi, Gen-ma?"

Genevieve's brow twitched in a moment of confused surprise before she answered, "Yes, why?"

Enoch grinned as he said, "Eye for an eye, tooth for a tooth."

The three women exchanged wary glances before looking back up at Soma.

Zeta looked at the moon more carefully than she ever had before. She tried to tap into the Specters up there for help, but they weren't receptive — the acolytes were Pandora's. Those weren't her pooches anymore. It was fine. With some effort, a single Specter can sense mass density differences from great distances.

She strained to probe into the underground fortress of Soma Station. It was a sprawling complex with floor after floor of cramped rooms. Vast, mostly empty hangars sat just below the surface in various places.

She traced the lines of underground tube stations, leading to various other outposts scattered throughout the moon. After a few minutes, something curious caught her eye — a tube that dove deep into the ground. From this distance, it seemed hair-thin, but in reality, it may have been wide enough for a person to squeeze through. Following the tube from the surface down to a spot deeper than any other structures within the moon, Zeta found it ended in a dense structure filled with machinery and row after row of perfectly round, dense specks. They could only be one thing — the aposynchronic orbs of the in-system Guardians and Proliferans.

Following the tube back to the surface, she could see its access port hidden beneath a few meters of regolith. And above that was a pack of twenty of the queen's acolytes.

Zeta hadn't read the Code of Hammurabi, but she knew what Enoch meant. She looked at Genevieve. "They threaten our orbs, so we threaten theirs."

"She's going after their orb vault?" Pip-Tau asked, still staring up.

"You don't think she would..." Genevieve started, but didn't finish.

"Oh, she would," Pip-Tau croaked, restraining tears. She pulled her gaze from Soma and wiped her eyes. "And she will. Nothing can stop her now."

Zeta didn't like Pip-Tau's implication. Again, she wondered — had she made a mistake trusting Pandora and Enoch so quickly?

Zeta returned to her mass-sense probe of Soma.

Pip-Tau said, "I haven't even met her yet, but I already know what Pandora's capable of. I've seen her shadow growing inside Pip-Rho for years... *my* shadow. I might not have her alien-buffed brain, but I was the seed she grew from. I know how she thinks.

"This *Pandora, the Queen of Specters,* persona isn't just a byproduct of her Interra or CotNQ characters — it's a deliberate character choice. Even her choice of name is heavy with implications. She has to present herself as a powerful, mysterious, and dangerous woman. Someone to be respected but never fully trusted. Someone to be *feared*. And if she seems a little unstable, all the better to make her enemies wary of what she's capable of. Her allies, too, for that matter! She's playing the character that makes sense for her past and suits her future goals."

She scoffed, "A queen — of *course* she'd declare herself a queen. Oh, it's not because she *wants* the power! All she wants is what's best for the Genesis Faction. And she'll send every offworlder to their True and Final Deaths, if that's what it takes."

Pip-Tau laughed sardonically to herself. "Storytelling — it's what Pips *do*. That post-Pip *entity* is writing the climax of this war story now. Only Pandora knows what plot twists will make the good guys win, and the bad guys get their comeuppance." She looked up again, shaking her head. "Those poor Guardian and Proliferan bastards are all gonna die."

Zeta's probing of Soma had brought her to the Specters, which loomed over the orb vault. Other groups of Specters were hovering over or converging on other buried facilities. Once they were all in their places, Zeta had a feeling that they would lash out in a single coordinated strike. Three of the acolytes above the Soma Station orb vault access tube had solid masses inside them. They weren't orbs — that wouldn't have made any sense. It might have taken more time to work out what they held if she hadn't seen something similar in Jamji's stomach when they faced off in Syn-Cen Bay Number Two.

"They've got antimatter," Zeta said.

Genevieve took a shuttering gasp. She put one hand on her heart and the other on Zeta's knee. Her eyes searched Zeta's. "How?! Where would they even find it?"

Zeta put her hand on Genevieve's. "The Astrus carrier they demolished. They got the fuel cells."

"Boom," Pip-Tau said flatly. "Bye-bye, Soma Station orb vault." Her face was slack, exhausted of all emotion.

Genevieve shook her head. "There has to be some other way!"

Genevieve was a peacekeeper, thru-and-thru. But those offworlders had called this retribution down upon themselves when they conspired to steal the planet away and destroy the orbs of any Genesisian who stood in their way. The monsters tried to wipe out the Astrus Hive. Not just once, but *twice*, thanks to Jamji.

This was what Zeta tried to tell herself, at least. But her heart raged against her mind.

Jamji's orb was in that vault.

Even after everything Jamji had done, Zeta couldn't bear to imagine her sis-kin's orb being destroyed. Jamji was a stubborn idiot who couldn't believe that Zeta was alive again as a Specter. Just like all the other Guardian idiots — stuck on a false narrative. Every contrary fact only reinforces their stupid ideas in some twisted, backward way. What would it take to make them believe?

A flash lit up the sky, making Zeta flinch. The Stalwarts scattered and darted, reflexively retreating from the explosion. Zeta looked up in time to spot a Specter-pooch dart across the sky, terminating in another flash.

Scanning the space overhead, she could see at least a dozen anti-matter bombs dropping down at them, launched from the Guardian warships overhead.

"Oh, god," Genevieve gasped. "This is it!"

Not quite — they'd have to get through her Specter-pooch defenders first.

Zeta cast her mass-sense toward Soma and found that the coordinated strike she'd anticipated was underway. All across the moon, Specters plowed into the surface, kicking vast clouds of regolith into space. Defensive energy weapons cut through the incoming forces, igniting regolith and Specter alike. A barrage of missiles launched into the air above Soma Station, lighting up the moon's dark side like a forest full of fireflies gone mad.

There was no telling who struck first. It didn't matter. Specters were dying by the hundreds. She could easily join them soon.

Pip-Tau almost laughed, "Pandora's attacking Soma?! You call that covert?!"

"Watch the group at the orb vault," Zeta said. "That's the covert part. The rest are distractions. Look — they're already heading down the tube!"

"Why wouldn't the Guard have defended that entrance better?" Genevieve asked, flinching at another flash overhead.

Pip-Tau said, "It looks like a hidden access tunnel. Probably hasn't been used in a hundred years. They wouldn't want to call attention to it by building defenses there. I'll bet most Guardians didn't even know it existed, sort of like Syn-Cen's quick-load access port at the bottom of The Great Ocean."

Zeta watched with dread as the three Specters carrying anti-matter fuel cells plunged down the tube — snakes descending into a rat's burrow. The finality they carried was too much to bear.

"Make them stop," she whispered, choking on the words. New tears were filling her eyes. She looked down at Enoch, turning her dread into anger in a flash. "Make them stop!" she shouted at him, getting to her feet.

Enoch looked at her with wide eyes — Charra's look of shock. "I... can't—"

"You can and will, Enoch!" She walked straight through the smoldering logs of the dying fire and grabbed the boy by his tunic. Their noses almost touched as she shouted her commands, "Stop those Specters from getting to their orbs before it's too late, Enoch! You heard Genevieve — there has to be another way! I know you can do it — you're in all the Specters. Stop them! NOW!"

Enoch's face went gray. His mouth trembled, then he croaked, "I'm... confused, Zeta. You said you wanted her to be in charge. She's the Queen."

She let go of his tunic and dropped to her knees, pulling his hands together between hers to beg, "I changed my mind, okay! Do you love me or not? Do this one thing for me! Just get in their heads and stop them! Please, Enoch!"

Enoch blinked twice, then looked up at Soma. He grumbled, "They're stopped now, Zeta. See for yourself."

She glanced at Soma, spotted the frozen Specters near the bottom of the tube, then stood and pulled Enoch into a tight hug. "I love you, Enoch. I'm sorry I had to yell at you." She kissed his forehead.

"Princess Zeta," the Queen of Specters said from between the trees nearby. The black void of a woman's body was wearing a jagged obsidian crown and gliding toward her.

Pandora said, "Prince Enoch tells me you have commanded him to halt the critical act of Plan B. I know you have a soft heart, dearest princess. But in case you haven't noticed, our enemies have no such reservations." She gestured overhead just as another antimatter bomb exploded. The brief, blinding white flash washed all color out of The Thin Forest construct.

Pip-Tau, Enoch, and Genevieve all stood up to face the Queen.

"That doesn't make it okay," Zeta said. She knew there was a three-second delay in their conversation since Pandora was at Soma, so Zeta pulled Enoch close to her side and awaited a response.

"You understand they can make new orbs, do you not?" Pandora asked, growing heated. "They can perform a new neural mapping from their living brains if they surrender from the fight after losing their orbs. They would lose their personal data stores and replays, but those are a pittance when weighed against the value of eternal life itself. Destroy their orbs, and this bombardment *will* cease. Only then will they agree to my *generous* terms of peace. The failure of Plan A proved that violence is the only language these warmongers can understand."

Zeta shook her head. "What about the people who've already died?! Jamji's orb is in there, and there are probably hundreds or thousands more who died today. I know what you're going to say — a small price to pay for peace or something. You think they deserved it. Well, you're wrong!"

Zeta stepped toward the queen made of liquid night as she spoke. "Jamji's son, Chief Talmid, was a wise man. He told me that blood thirsts for blood. That violence just brings more violence. This *eye for an eye* crap might bring peace, but it'll only last as long as it takes for them to sharpen a fresh pile of spears. You think the Guard Faction won't send more warships from their home system to come take Genesis by force?"

Pandora replied, "Perhaps they will, but by the time they return, we'll be ready. My abilities — *our* abilities — grow by the minute. Release your hold on poor Prince Enoch's heart and let me do the job you entrusted me with. Or do you have other plans? Shall we skip the practically *perfect* Plan B and proceed to Plan C, my dearest princess? A bloody battle where the only orbs in jeopardy are those of your army? I'm sure your Stalwart friends are ready to lay down their lives in your name."

A slow strobe of explosions flashed as they spoke — antimatter bombs killing another Specter-pooch every few seconds. This had to stop. There had to be a way!

A moment of perfect clarity came over her.

Zeta knew what she had to do.

She looked back at Genevieve, then at Pip-Tau. She was drinking in the sight of her kin for what may be the last time. They wouldn't like it when they figured out what she was up to. It was a good thing that Alasie wasn't bootstrapped yet, or she'd try to stand in Zeta's way.

Zeta turned back to Pandora. "You can finish Plan B if my plan doesn't work. You can call this one *Plan Zeta*."

Before anyone could say anything to stop her, Zeta pulled her mind out of the construct. She was back in her Specter body in The Great Ocean. She exploded upward, pushing through the dense water to reach the surface.

The low thump of a distant antimatter bomb explosion resonated through the water. She wasn't close enough to Syn-Cen to be near the bombardment, but she didn't trust the Guardians not to zap her with a laser if she popped out of the surface. Before reaching the surface, Zeta sent an open transmission to the largest Guardian ship she could find.

"I am Zeta Telson, and I need to talk to Fleet Captain Smith. I want to show you my orb and convince you I'm still a human. If you still don't believe me after that, you can keep me as a captive or kill me or whatever you want. But if I can prove that I'm really Zeta, I think you'll believe me when I say... there's no way for you to win this war! We're about ready to... do something horrible to you. But if you'll just listen to me for a second, we can come to a peaceful agreement."

The Captain had agreed to the meeting, but the bombardment over Syn-Cen never ceased. He instructed her to surrender to a small force they'd send down to retrieve her.

Zeta watched as the double-cylindered ship burned through the atmosphere, then approached her position. Rising from the water, Zeta pooled into a passive blob and awaited her capture. The voices of Genevieve, Pip-Tau, Pandora, and the Stalwarts reached out, trying to stop her.

She directed her thoughts to Enoch. *"Is there a way to stop myself from hearing what the other Specters are saying?"*

"Yes," Enoch said. *"Okay, I shut them out. But... Zeta... I think they're right. I'm scared. I don't want to lose you."*

"I'm sorry," Zeta said. *"Just stay quiet when I'm talking to them. I don't want to have to explain your voice."*

The side of the ship opened. Five soldiers dropped out. Super-heated plasma lanced out from their boots in blue spikes, bringing them into a wide circle around her. A soldier broke from the circle and approached. The Specter instinct to abduct or fling the soldier and escape bubbled up. Instead, she sat still as the soldier flew in a circle around her, deploying a containment matrix. He circled again, deploying a second layer.

She had never seen a *spirit net* up close like this. It was made of wires as thin as spider's silk, coursing with energy.

The others in the troupe approached and extended batons toward the matrix, hooking in and dragging it. They began flying it toward their ship. As soon as the matrix moved, it zapped her. The jolt of energy *hurt!* Letting out a yelp, she repositioned herself in the center of the spherical net, moving as it moved.

They loaded her into the empty bay of their ship. It was barely large enough to hold her. When the ship started moving, she had to work to keep herself from drifting into the zapping net. Every time the ship changed speed or direction, she'd bump into it and get shocked.

First, they descended to the surface and slurped ocean water into their fuel tanks. Next, the two massive thrusters comprising the ship's main body burst to life with the biggest plasma jets that Zeta had ever seen. They turned the ocean's surface into a cloud of steam and emerged from the cloud in a slow, laborious climb. Zeta wished she could have pushed the vessel from within to help speed it up, but the containment matrix kept her confined.

Minutes later, they arrived near the large ship she had hailed. Her captors pulled her out of the shuttle, staying close at hand with their batons. A smaller vessel was approaching them. Peeking inside, Zeta saw six people. It wasn't easy to make out facial features using mass-sense, but as they got closer, she got a feel for them. Three of them were the group that accompanied Jamji during their time preparing for The Fall of the Specters — Chief Warrant Officers Dumont, Haley, and Baud. She didn't recognize the other three.

One was floating in the ship's center, wearing more metal bars and ribbons on his outfit than the others. That might be Fleet Captain Smith. His facial features were severe, reminiscent of a hawk. The other two were a man and a woman strapped into chairs behind control panels. They didn't look important — just a couple of pilots.

The approaching ship let out a plasma jet pulse to stop a good distance away. They might not have wanted to get too close in case she tried something.

Half a minute passed in tense silence. She thought they would talk first, but they didn't.

"Hello," Zeta said, regretting that she didn't give a more formal greeting. She wondered for the first time how she could talk to the Guardians, or the Specters, for that matter. It seemed to be something Enoch figured out how to do with Specter cells.

"Present your aposynchronic orb for our inspection," the voice of Fleet Captain Smith replied.

"Endosynchronic," Zeta said. Why was she arguing with them? She continued anyway. "When Cain performed the Hermit Procedure on me, he told me that when an orb is inside you, it's *endosynchronic*. Apo means away. Endo means within." She pushed the orb out of her internal mass, holding it out with a tendril for their inspection.

"I see," Smith said. "Release the *endo*synchronic orb for our retrieval."

Zeta hesitated. It seemed like they should do something for her in return. She pulled the orb back in. "Will you stop dropping bombs into the ocean? At least while we're talking?"

"No. Give us your orb, or this parley is over."

Zeta did as commanded, pushing the orb out and releasing it. The helpless little mass floated before her, drifting away. A soldier approached and used their baton to manipulate the containment matrix, opening a gap and pulling the orb through it. They gave a brief burn of their plasma jet boots, then another to slow their approach when they reached the Captain's shuttle.

A hatch opened on the vessel's side. Zeta watched nervously as the soldier brought her orb through an airlock and into the hands of the Guardian leaders. These orcish brutes had conspired to kill her and everyone she cared about, and she had just given them her soulstone.

They loaded it into a container in the wall of the shuttle, which sealed around the orb. The Guardians floated before the orb reader, watching its screen.

"I know what they're saying," Enoch said. *"I can tell from their mouths and throats. Do you want to listen in?"*

Would it be fair to violate their privacy? She wanted them to trust her. Her curiosity got the best of her. She told Enoch, *"Yes."*

"I'll be damned," the man she remembered as Chief Warrant Officer Baud said. He had been the one who helped Jamji play Interra. In her beta's final moments, he had told her she was a hero for sacrificing her orb to stop the Specters.

The woman Zeta recognized as Chief Warrant Officer Haley said, "Alright, the Specter had Zeta Telson's orb. What does that tell us? Does this change anything?"

Baud said, "It gives credence to what Pandora said about Specters bootstrapping orbs. And look here, three dog companion animals were on her orb." He pointed to the screen, grinning. "Two young males and a *bitch!*"

Haley closed her eyes and shook her head, probably at his choice of words.

Baud continued, "Reports from the field about the wolf-pack fighting style of the new Specters support the theory that they used these neural maps to bootstrap Zeta's dogs. And not all the Specters fought with the same level of maturity. Some shied away from battle or were observed in the distance, engaging in what the soldiers described as play! The pups! Other Specters hunted with proficiency, waiting for the right moment to strike. Aureum d'Canis, in Specter form! But only *one* Zeta was bootstrapped. A single, sovereign human mind."

"God, you're full of it," Haley scoffed. "The Astri could have programmed them to fight like that."

Baud started to argue his point, but Smith cut him off. "Dumont, you're our xenobiologist. What's your take? How feasible is it that this Specter's node-net was rewired into a genuine copy of Zeta Telson?"

"Talk to it!" Dumont spat, then slammed a fist into his hand and turned away. "My... apologies, sir," he choked out. "The Specters proved their susceptibility to external influence during The Fall. They proved their ability to interface with technology by exchanging messages using Astrus encryption algorithms. It's feasible. Interrogate the entity, sir."

Fleet Captain Smith nodded. He floated toward the two silent individuals at the front of the vessel. "Open a channel."

The man made a motion, then pointed at Smith.

"We have verified that the orb you produced belongs to Zeta Telson," Smith said. "I'll give you the benefit of the doubt and treat you as if you are the human mind you claim to be. Now, Zeta, convince me I cannot win this war."

ZETA DIDN'T EXPECT them to believe her so quickly. She also hadn't planned out exactly what to say. All she knew was that there's no way they'd keep fighting if they knew they were facing their True and Final Deaths.

She began with urgency, "Pandora, the Queen of Specters, is a more powerful being than any of you can imagine. She's part Specter, part human, and part SI! She's only existed for a couple of hours, but she's already doing things with Specters that I never dreamed of.

"After I handed over my command to her, she came up with three plans. Plan A was to negotiate peace. But you spat in her face. So now she's on Plan B, which is to blow up your orb vault on Soma! If you still don't give up after that, Plan C is to engage using the remaining Astri forces, her Specter army, and the Stalwart humans that were bootstrapped as Specters. You won't be fighting Specter-pooches this time."

Fleet Captain Smith signaled to the officer in charge of communications. Their signal cut out. He raised a finger to the others in the cabin, seeming to signal for them to wait.

After a minute of silence, he spoke to the officers. "I conferred with Station Captain Chin. There has been no indication that the Soma Station orb vault is compromised, and the Specter assault on Soma has stopped. What do you make of that? A bluff?"

Haley said, "Bluff or no bluff, she takes us for cowards! Destroy our orbs, and we'll be fighting for our lives. We'll fight like hell to the last man!"

"It's not a bluff!" Zeta shouted.

Smith glared at the communications officer. "Did you leave our channel open?"

The officer checked his screens frantically. "No, sir! We're not transmitting!"

"I can see through your vessel," Zeta said. "I can read your lips. And it's not a bluff. You probably just can't detect the Specters because they're still in the tunnel leading down from the surface. We'll let them go all the way into your orb chamber if that's what you need to see to believe me. And if you keep fighting after your orbs are destroyed, that's not bravery! That's dying pointlessly, dragging us down with you!"

She mindspoke to Enoch, *"Let the Specters keep going down into the orb chamber. Just don't let them release the antimatter."*

"Okay," Enoch said. *"And, Zeta, we're running out of Specter-pooches. They're dropping bombs faster!"*

He was right — she could see the antimatter bombs falling in a steady stream from the Guardian warships nearby. Her rage began boiling up. She was sitting here trying to talk to them, and they wouldn't relent!

Haley said, "It's not pointless if we win, and you bet your ass we *will* win. We've seen all your moves. I don't care if you're dogs or humans — you're just as predictable!"

Zeta shouted, "No, we're not! Why won't you listen?! Why won't you *stop?!*"

A wave of anger pulsed out from her, directed at the infuriating woman.

That's when Chief Warrant Officer Haley's head exploded.

It took a second for Zeta to register what happened. If she had a heart, she was sure it would have skipped a beat. All she could say was, "What... happened?"

Even the battle-hardened Guardians were slow to react. Zeta watched as skull fragments, brain matter, and blood spread through the shuttle, peppering the flinching Guardian officers.

"Did... I...?" she stammered. "I didn't mean to..."

Fleet Captain Smith asked, "Did you do that, Zeta?" He had surprising composure.

Zeta pleaded, "I didn't mean to! I didn't know I could!"

Enoch mindspoke, *"You did something like that when you shouted at the Stalwart Generals. That first one was an unfocused gravity wave spike. But this time, you targeted the resonance."*

Part of her wondered if Enoch had acted through her.

However she did it, Zeta was both frightened and excited about her ability. She was still at their mercy — her orb was in their ship, and she was trapped in their containment matrix. If they decided to retaliate for her aggression, she was as good as dead.

Fleet Captain Smith looked back at Chief Warrant Officers Baud and Dumont. Tense seconds passed in silence. She'd messed this up *badly.*

The officers had to be talking using mindspeak. Smith turned back to the front of the ship and said, "I just received a report of a breach in the Soma orb vault. It seems you weren't bluffing after all. And this demonstration of your new combat ability," he gestured at Haley's headless body, "was quite effective."

"I didn't know—" Zeta started.

Smith cut her off, raising a hand. "I believe you. Perhaps your queen implanted that ability in you without your knowledge. If you can do it, we must assume all the Specters have this ability now. I also believe that you are the personality of Zeta Telson and perhaps even an accurate representation of her genuine mind. By extension, the Stalwarts hiding below the ocean's surface should also be treated as humans. Baud certainly thinks so."

Baud grinned and said, "Sharing Pandora's plan to destroy our orbs was a foolish strategy, but Zeta's not a strategist. The Astri would never allow one of their creations to behave so recklessly. You're no Astrus puppet, this I know. I think you opposed your queen's plans because you didn't want Jamji Telson's orb to be destroyed. You're doing this for simple, selfish, *stupid* love. That's so very *human* of you."

"*Not* a human!" Dumont spat, jabbing a finger in her direction. His mustache vibrated as he shouted, "There's more to the Specters that you're withholding! Who created you?! How did you read Zeta's orb?! How did you..." He gestured to the headless corpse by his side, choking out, "do *that?!*"

Baud laughed and shook his head, wiping blood out of his eye. "Dumont, if your head pops, I'll blame your blood pressure before I blame Zeta."

Smith said, "Dumont has a point, Zeta. We need to know more. This demonstration of your destructive powers, intentional or otherwise, was somewhat unconvincing. We're mere meters away. If this is the maximum range of your ability, your forces will be destroyed before they get close enough to use it."

The Captain's sharp face held a challenging, almost amused expression. He was staying cool, even knowing she could pop his head. Within his chest, his heart thumped at a normal rate.

"Fine, watch this," Zeta said. She looked around for a new target. The infuriating antimatter bombs streaming down from the ships and into the ocean caught her attention. Could she destroy those with this ability?

"You can do it," Enoch said in her mind. *"I'll help you!"*

Zeta glared at one bomb which had just dropped from a nearby ship, urging it to explode.

Nothing happened.

"Not like that," Enoch said. *"More like you're punching through space with your mind."*

She focused on the bomb again, then gave it a thought-punch. It exploded!

There was no way Zeta could describe the sensation of creating a focused G-wave spike in terms that a human could understand. It was an urging — a violent pulse from deep within.

Shifting her focus to another bomb, Zeta let out another spike. The white flash was deeply satisfying. She looked at another bomb, let loose again, and popped it.

Flash!

Flash!

Flash, flash!

She was getting better at it with every bomb she burst.

Enoch cheered, *"Awesome job! Now do a far one!"*

She aimed at the furthest bomb she could find — a speck in the distance, just above the surface of The Great Ocean. At this distance, she'd have to lead it a bit. She was Za'antha, bowstring taut, aiming at a distant target. She let loose. A distant sparkle marked its destruction.

"Satisfied?" Zeta breathed, feeling a bit exhausted. "Or do I have to pop every fucking head in your army?"

Maybe she shouldn't threaten them — they could still kill her if they wanted.

"Yes, quite satisfied," Fleet Captain Smith said, though he sounded disappointed. "It's an interesting ability you have mani-fested, Zeta. We would love to learn how it works. Perhaps we can work an information-sharing agreement into our terms of peace. That is, assuming you and your queen are still willing to negotiate."

Zeta's tension eased as she began to realize that she had gotten through to them. They were going to surrender! As much as she wished she could have done it without resorting to violence, it seemed like Pandora was right — that's the only language the Guard Faction understood. She collected her wits and said, "Only if you'll give me back my orb, let me out of this net, and stop dropping those bombs."

"Certainly," Fleet Captain Smith said. "That is if, in turn, you'll refrain from destroying our orbs or exploding any more heads."

Zeta's Specter gave a quick nod. "Agreed."

23

ZETA DAY

Led by regal royalty
Demanding Guardian respect
Pledging Stalwart loyalty:
The Acolytes of Pandora's sect.

Born in crushing water
Evolved, improved, prepared
Capable of untold slaughter
If ever their anger is flared.

But, oh! What choice to make?!
Mortal flesh or demigod?
Fallible human, spectral snake?
Varuna or the Land of Nod?

It's flawed flesh for me!
My body, here to stay.
As for you, we shall see.
I'll love you either way.

ALASIE STARED at the last stanza, chewing on the inside of her cheek. She shook her head and scribbled it out, then slashed her stylus across the whole poem. It dissolved from the air before her.

"Ugh!" she groaned, following it up with a powerful curse from her native tongue. "It's all wrong! This isn't what I want to say. I can't find the words to get the right feeling across. I could do it if I used free verse, but free verse would... I'm sorry, but free verse would cheapen it."

Natasha-Eta sucked her teeth with a "tsk" of disapproval. Their ancestral poets used free verse, so Alasie's disdain for the form insulted their heritage. "Maybe you should take a break," she said.

The older, stouter woman sat across the room, sewing a tattoo into her shoulder. Resurrection had erased all her prior tattoos, so she was starting them all over again. "You've been at it every waking hour since you got here."

That wasn't that long — she was only dropped off yesterday. Some poems took weeks of revisions to get right.

She leaned back against the log wall and thumped her head against it. "The Zeta Day events are starting soon. I *have* to get this poem ready in time for her homecoming. I want to tell Zeta I still love her no matter which choice she made."

In truth, there was only one choice that Alasie would be happy with, but she would never admit to that. Most of the Stalwarts chose resurrection, but those who stayed Specters were still as valid of a person and valued member of the Stalwart Faction as any human.

Alasie had tried to get Enoch to tell her which choice Zeta made, but he was as elusive as ever. "It doesn't matter, does it?" he had asked, humbling Alasie into silence on the matter.

The advantages of staying a Specter were hard to beat. You can zoom off into space any time you want and think like a hundred times as fast. Specters can communicate over vast distances, while the Stalwarts were stuck sharing a limited number of Astrus earbuds. Oraxis, Genevieve, Carff, Alasie, and Natasha-Eta only had two earbuds to share between them.

A rapid-fire series of sonic booms rumbled through the cabin. That could be Zeta!

Alasie scrambled to her feet. Pinga was up and at her side by the time she reached the door, with Elle bouncing and barking behind them.

"Put on your coat!" Natasha-Eta shouted behind her.

Alasie growled, stomped back to her bed furs, and pulled the crumpled coat up from a pile on the floor. Flopping it over her arm, she ran back out again.

A few others were heading to the front door from other rooms in the new Telson Lodge, but she made it there first.

The first batch of resurrected Stalwarts had built the lodge in a month, with more than a little help from the Specters. Genevieve had cried tears of joy at the sight of the beautiful structure. Oraxis had joked that it was so big he'd get lost in it. He also made some jab about throwing the Principle of Invisibility out the window.

The chill struck Alasie as she stepped through double layers of door flaps. She searched the white sky for a black streak. With her eyes to the sky, she soon bumped into someone, apologized, then realized it was Oraxis.

"It's not her," he laughed, catching Alasie by the shoulders. "Better put that coat on — it's starting to snow."

His grip on her shoulders was crushing. "Ow!" she complained, furrowing her brow and shaking him off.

Oraxis stepped back and shook his head, holding up his hands. "I'm sorry, Alasie. I didn't mean to squeeze you so hard. I'm not used to these Guardian myofibrites. Lord knows how they don't break each other's bones with every handshake."

Alasie didn't have any such issues. After spending so long as Ag'nul in Interra, she knew how to control her strength.

Part of the peace agreement was that the offworlders would resurrect any Stalwart who wanted to be a human again. For some people, that meant a typical resurrection in Syn-Cen. But with its limited capacity, they resurrected most people in the offworld facilities on Soma. The Guardians had resurrected Alasie, Natasha-Eta, and the Telsons. Their standard bioenhancement suite included super-powered muscles.

"It's okay," she said. "I don't need the coat — I'm going back in."

"There are a lot of people out here who want to see you," Oraxis said as she turned around.

The crowd around the lodge had grown since the last time she was outside. People, both real and holographic, sat at tables or clustered around bonfires. As Alasie surveyed the crowd, she caught several people looking her way. Celebrity never suited her. She could feel her face flushing.

"Hail, Alasie!" a shrill voice called out. She followed it to the tables, where Carff was waving his arm in a wide arc over his head. He wore a patchwork fur coat and what looked like the top of a bear's head for a hood. "Come and join the feast!"

Alasie huff-laughed and shook her head at the sad joke. There would be no feasting for any of them for a long time.

Even though they forced the Guardians to surrender, the NeoGens' bill was still in effect, and there was no taking it back. The Stalwarts couldn't use the Worldnet services or store their orbs in the vault below Syn-Cen. Every human Stalwart was forced to carry their endosynchronic orb in their abdomen — the Hermit Procedure applied en masse. This meant none of them had digestive systems.

She looked back at Oraxis. "But I'm not done with my poem yet."

"Some things shouldn't be rushed," he said. "I'm told she'll be here in an hour or two. Do you really want to recite a slapped-together piece? You could do a reading of Fate's Behest."

"But..." He was right. Tears pooled in her eyes, so she put her head down and pulled on her coat. Sniffling and watery eyes were normal for cold weather, anyway.

Carff helped take her mind off of her troubles. He introduced Alasie to his cultural influencer friends. One woman at the table was a hologram. Her actual body was one of the Specters looming in the sky above the forest. The Stalwart-Specters could use the holographic systems mounted around the lodge to partake in the events alongside their human comrades. The holographic woman spoke a variation of Alasie's native tongue, so they had fun comparing pronunciations of words and exchanging private jokes without anyone else knowing what they were saying.

Two hours came and went with no sign of Zeta. The snow was falling as steady, gentle flurries, washing out the sky and blocking her view of the Specters, which boomed in and out every few minutes. Mainly, they were shuttling in people and supplies. They'd deposit their drenched traveler with a sealed pack containing a change of clothes, then boom away again.

The traveler would wave some greetings, complain about the cold, and head into the warm lodge to get changed out of their wet jumpsuit.

But when would Zeta get there?

Alasie excused herself and went in search of Oraxis or Genevieve. After asking around and taking two trips in and out of the lodge, she finally spotted them standing away from the crowd. Penelope-pooch was by their side.

Genevieve's hair was blond again, which took some getting used to. She waved as Alasie approached, then invited her in for a hug. "There's just so many people," she said. "Without mindspeak, it's impossible to have a private conversation. O's talking to Pandora and Pip-Tau now."

This piqued Alasie's attention.

Oraxis was pacing as he talked, a finger in one ear. He said, "I still think a holographic feast would be..." He paused, then huffed. "But food-sharing traditions are important for forming social... okay, forget the feast... No, we were waiting for you to... okay, yes, I can try, but you know how these Stalwarts are... Herding cats, exactly," he chuckled. "I mean, you could watch us gather and then wait until... Right, sure, nobody keeps the Queen waiting." He rolled his eyes, looked over, and spotted Alasie. "I don't know, maybe fifteen minutes? Gen, Alasie, could you gather everyone in the clearing in front of the cabin?... *Lodge*, whatever."

Alasie beamed with excitement. "Is Zeta arriving?"

Oraxis nodded. "Yes, along with..." He gave a sour expression and looked away. "Surprise? Everyone knows who's... Okay, fine." He turned back to Alasie and Genevieve, looking exhausted. "Don't tell anyone the specifics. It's a surprise."

"But... I don't know the specifics," Alasie said.

Oraxis gave a little shrug, then stepped away to talk in a lower voice.

Genevieve beamed at Alasie. "This is so exciting! Okay, I'll tell the people inside. You spread the word to the people around the bonfires and at the tables."

Alasie didn't waste any time. She ran to the nearest group and shouted, "Zeta's coming! Go wait in the clearing! Hurry! Spread the word!"

Alasie could only tell three groups to gather up before the news started spreading on its own faster than she could carry it. People poured out of the Telson Lodge, pulling on coats and pushing their way into the growing crowd.

Her double-mind's fifteen-minute timer still had five minutes left by the time they'd gathered everyone in the clearing. She was glad that her internal timer and calculator still worked. Those were some of the few things she could still use her double-mind for without Worldnet services. Most of all, she missed talking to Pinga using her mind. She had lost track of the dog in the commotion. He didn't like crowds.

Five minutes counted down to zero, and there was still no sign of Zeta and the queen's delegation. She looked around, trying to spot Oraxis so she could go ask him what was going on. Being shorter than almost everyone else wasn't helping. She spotted him after pushing her way out of the thickest part of the crowd. He was talking into the ear of Karn the Beastmaster, who hunched down to listen. Alasie approached but stopped when Karn rose to full height, put his fingers to his mouth, and blew. Alasie covered her ears as Karn's ear-splitting whistle rose above the crowd's din.

He shouted, "Oy! You, you, you! Help me with these tables, friends!" He had pointed out several other oversized men. They plodded obediently from the crowd, fur coats bouncing. The men positioned themselves around the hefty wooden tables and lifted. Karn bellowed, even louder this time, "Oy, oy! Everybody take ten steps back!"

Shouts of "Ten steps back!" echoed through the crowd.

The men with the tables brought them to the newly emptied space between the lodge and the crowd, setting them side-by-side. It seemed like they were making a platform.

Alasie looked back at where Oraxis had been, but he wasn't there. She spotted him pressing his earbud into one ear and plugging the other, jogging toward the edge of the clearing. She was just about to run after him when an unnatural cacophony rose over the sound of the crowd.

Oh, that was electronic music! The Zeta Day events had begun!

THE MUSIC STARTED with a rapid succession of wailing, screechy sounds punctuated by the distorted sound of a man screaming. He sang, "You say you want a revolution, well you know..."

Words floated in the air above the lodge. It was the lyrics to the song, white letters set against a black starfield background. A white cherub — Pip-Tau's avatar — bounced from word to word. The crowd sang along.

Bursts of color erupted in the air overhead. The falling snow flurries were now accompanied by drifting multicolor motes that winked out just before reaching her head. Alasie was too excited to do anything but gape at the holographic spectacle.

After the words read, "Don't you know it's going to be all right," a cluster of sonic booms shook the air, heralding the arrival of Specters. Alasie could feel them vibrating in her chest. It felt like they were making her heart beat irregularly. The lyric repeated, and another set of sonic booms echoed over the hills. The lyric repeated and again was followed by thundering glory.

The white sky darkened as the swarm of Specters descended upon them. The sight would have sent the crowd into a frenzied panic a year ago. Now, it was the welcome sight of friends and allies joining the Zeta Day festivities. They swam through the air above the forest and lodge like a flock of massive crows, twisting, circling, and darting over the treetops. Snow spiraled in their wake. Shouts and whistles rose to greet them from the humans on the ground.

"You say you'll change the faction charter," the lyrics above the house read. This elicited laughs from the singers in the crowd. They laughed at another part where the lyrics said something about carrying pictures of Marco-Epsilon Rhind.

The words above the lodge disappeared after a series of "all right" shouts transitioned into the voice of Pip-Tau. Her white cherub avatar now hovered alone within the hologram, offset by the black starfield behind her.

Pip-Tau squeaked, "A'right, a'right, ye humble human Stalwarts! How you doing today?!"

The crowd shouted incoherently.

"Cold?!" Pip-Tau laughed. "Hey, you chose those hairless ape bodies. Well, at least the food's good and hot, right?"

The crowd laughed and shouted curses at her.

"Oh! Sorry, I forgot about that! Yeah, geez, that must suck not being able to eat! Hey, relax, I'm just playin' with ya! Ok, enough poking fun at the puny humans. Let's get on with the program. Today marks the fifth anniversary of Zeta Telson's fateful abduction by the evil, evil *Specters*."

Animated imagery appeared behind Pip-Tau's avatar, depicting Zeta's abduction and the Specter horde's retreat into Varuna.

Pip-Tau continued, "A lot has happened since then. We saw the return of the Specters, the One-Day War, and the vote for the New Genesis Proposal."

Imagery continued to play out behind Pip-Tau. Now it showed Eld Marco-Epsilon Rhind shaking hands with Stationmaster Chin, then turning to kiss the cheeks of Planetary Mother Grace Monrovia of the Prolifera Faction. Boos, hisses, and curses that Alasie had never heard before rose from the crowd.

"Yeah, I've heard you're not fans of that bill," Pip-Tau laughed. "Those NeoGen terrorist bastards and their Guardian bully-buddies backed you into a corner, but dammit, you didn't fold! You made the hard choice! You voted with courage, and the next thing you knew, we were being bootstrapped and outfitted with sleek new boojum-blob bodies! Pandora was crowned as the Queen of Specters, Plan A failed, and Plan B was put on hiatus while a certain *superhero* executed Plan Zeta."

Cheers filled the air. Alasie screamed Zeta's name, reveling in the moment of anticipation before her arrival.

Pip-Tau said, "Alright, calm down! Geez, I'm monologuing here! So, next came the peace accords. The Guard and Prolifera Factions got the privilege of peacefully packing up their orbs, razing their in-system assets, tucking their tails between their legs, and yelping like whipped puppers all the way back to Helios."

An image of an interstellar gas-jet torus carrier circling the deep blue gas giant planet, Shiva, played out behind Pip-Tau. The carrier plowed through the planet's upper atmosphere, faster and faster, spewing a tail of superheated gas in its wake. After its fifth accelerating orbit, it swiveled, directing its blazing tail into the planet's interior, and broke away in a flash.

Pip-Tau squealed, "What a beautiful sight to behold! Good riddance, jerk-faces! Oh, but the icing on the cake? Depriving the Guard of their SI prize! Ha! You can thank Pandora for that glorious bit of legal maneuvering. She reminded them that The Exodus Agreements signed by all six factions granted each faction one and only one SI instance. The New Genesis Proposal couldn't supersede that agreement. So, we packed Cain's core into the carrier bound for New Genesis. We can't use Cain or his systems anyways now that we've got Enoch. We don't want Enoch to catch the Intelligence Governor virus — not as long as the kid stays cool and doesn't take us over."

Enoch's avatar appeared by Pip-Tau's side. He crossed his arms and stomped, then whined, "You know I wouldn't do that!"

Pip-Tau's avatar patted him on the head. "Of course I know that, sweetheart. Now run back to mommy — it's not time for you to join us yet."

Enoch gave the crowd a quick wave, then disappeared again.

"Which brings us to today! The Stalwart Faction is only an idea until we draft a charter, so that's what the Provisional Council of Ten is working on now! As your *grossly unqualified* and hopefully *very* temporary Eld of Elds, I have to say that things are going swimmingly. We have a draft we'd like to share with you later for feedback. Geez, I still can't believe you fools voted for me over Veer, by the way. The NeoGens weren't his fault, you know!"

The crowd's grumbling response was the first time they didn't respond positively to EoE Pip-Tau's prompts. Alasie had voted for Pip-Tau but assumed Veer would win. Pip-Tau was a born leader, and her unique relationship with Pandora made her a popular choice — relations with the Specters were important. It turned out that Veer got so few votes he didn't even win a seat on the council.

"Sensitive subject, okay," Pip-Tau laughed. "Well, that's enough recap. This was all a lead-up to me saying... *Damn!* We've been through some wild times together, right?!"

This warmed everyone back up. Alasie shouted, "Yeah!"

"So, what are we gathered here for? What does Zeta Day stand for now that she's back? Is it a celebration of all the things she's done for us? Zeta would be the first to say she doesn't want that kind of attention. She doesn't see herself as a hero. In her eyes, she's just a girl who took a leap of faith or two. She's bold, brave, and... ok, maybe a *little* foolhardy. Don't you think that describes all the Stalwarts?"

The crowd cheered in acknowledgment.

"Then let's make Zeta Day a time to celebrate those things about ourselves that remind us of Zeta! A day to take bold risks! To take a leap of faith! To step out of your comfort zone and try something new! To do something stupid in the name of love! What do you say?!"

Alasie threw a fist into the air and whooped. That was a perfect way to celebrate Zeta Day! Colors burst above the crowd again, and the Specters darted among the holograms.

Pip-Tau let the crowd's noise settle down before she continued. "The audience is warmed up. The stage is set. Now, let's get on with the show! Let's make some noise for our guests of honor! First, put your hands together for your Provisional Council of Ten and my official advisor, Veer Gladstone!"

A group of Specters descended from the flock, then deposited men and women onto the tables in front of the crowd. Alasie had to hop to see over the shoulders of the people in front of her. She recognized Veer Gladstone, Eld Misra Mahalla, and Eld Jess-Eta Primrose, but nobody else. Names and waving hologram avatars floated before three Specters, which hovered above the humans. Those must've been the council members who stayed Specters.

"Pick me up, Veer, nobody can see me!" Pip-Tau squeaked.

Alasie looked up at the projection over the lodge. The cherub avatar was gone. Looking back down at the people standing on tables, she saw Veer pick up a jumpsuit-clad Pip-Tau and perch her on his shoulder.

Pip-Tau waved at the crowd. Her amplified voice said, "Yeah, I decided to go bio for now." Everyone thought she would stay a Specter, so this surprise brought laughter and applause. Pip-Tau introduced each of the elds, then sent all of them except Veer inside to get changed. Someone handed her and Veer fur coats, which they pulled over their wet jumpsuits.

"Next," Pip-Tau announced, "please give a warm welcome to our Astrus allies! JS-Xenos and XT-Xenos are here as their representatives!"

Two Specters descended to either side of Pip-Tau. The names of JS-Xenos and XT-Xenos appeared in the air before them, along with holographic avatars. The avatars lowered their heads as their Specters folded forward in a bowing gesture. They received their applause, then rose to rejoin the Stygian swarm.

Pip-Tau blew a kiss at XT-Xenos. She shouted, "And finally, the royal family is here! Pandora, the Queen of Specters, and the adorable SI, Prince Enoch!"

An unusually small Specter darted down from the sky, stopping in the air by Pip-Tau's side. It morphed into the shape of a woman, raising an arm and waving at the crowd. "Greetings, my allies," Pandora said.

The holographic image of Enoch appeared by her side, wearing a bulky fur cloak. He got even more applause than the Queen. The boy waved and smiled, grinning widely. His amplified voice said, "But, Pip-Tau, this isn't the whole royal family!" His delivery sounded like he was reading lines.

"Oh?" Pip-Tau said, feigning ignorance. "Have I forgotten someone?"

"Zeta!" Alasie shouted.

"Zeta!" the people around her echoed.

A chant of "Zeta! Zeta!" rose from the crowd.

Pip-Tau made a show of being unable to hear what they were chanting, cupping her hand behind her ear. She smacked her forehead. "Oh, right, Zeta! You up there, sis-kin? I think these people want to see you!"

A single Specter drifted down from the sky. The crowd kept chanting while Alasie gaped at the black blob. Was she inside? Or was that her? It didn't matter — it was her, either way. This was a lie she had to keep telling herself.

The Specter lowered a thick tendril. A bulge ran down the tendril — it was depositing a human form onto the stage by Enoch's side!

Zeta emerged from the Specter with a cascade of breathing fluid. A vaporous aura of steam formed around her as the warm fluid met the frigid air. She wiped her eyes, blinking up at the crowd. She gave them a timid smile, then raised her hand to wave. Alasie pressed forward, trying to go to Zeta, but the crowd was too thick. She put her hand on someone's shoulder and jumped, trying to see better.

"Hey, Aggie!" Pip-Tau squeaked, pointing in her direction. "Y'all let Aggie through, would ya? She's right there!"

Calls of "Alasie," "Aggie," and "Ag'nul" surrounded her. The crowd closed in, and the next thing she knew, she was being hoisted above everyone's heads. Hands pressed on her back, her legs, her arms, and her butt as they passed her forward. She floated down a river of humans, carrying her inexorably toward the stage.

Zeta laughed and put her hands to her face, covering her mouth. Her eyes were squinted in a smile and shimmering with tears.

Pip-Tau laughed, "Let's hear some cool-cat *snaps* for the crowd-surfing poet laureate of the Stalwarts, Alasie Herrington!" She raised both hands above her head and started snapping her fingers.

The sound of applause gave way to laughter and the odd sound of a thousand fingers snapping.

The crowd deposited Alasie onto the stage by Zeta's side. Her feet slipped on the wet wood. She swirled her arms to steady herself, almost falling backward. A firm hand caught her by the arm and pulled her forward.

Zeta's hand.

Their eyes met.

Time stopped.

With everything that had happened during the One-Day war and in the brief days she spent as a Specter before being resurrected on

Soma, there had never been an opportunity for them to actually *talk*. Zeta had been too busy.

Pandora and Enoch still haven't worked out how to store replays of Specter experiences into an orb or even memories. After bootstrapping, they show you your Specter experiences using constructs. You get a sense of what it was like and of how much time had passed in that alternate state. They also provide detailed written transcripts, which Alasie had pored over.

None of these gave Alasie a clue how Zeta felt. All they had was one kiss in a construct, a promise, and a few instances of holding hands. There was also the "I love you" which Zeta had blessed her with when she was being crushed to death in the Grunt. But that was an emotional response of pity and grief.

Five years was a long time. So much had changed — their very beings, their entire world. Was it naive to think they could go back to that youthful, fleeting moment in the grass? To pick up where they left off?

All doubt disappeared as Zeta pulled Alasie into her arms. An unfettered verse bloomed in the back of her mind as she closed her eyes and received her long-awaited kiss.

A purgatory of promises
Was finally fulfilled
As lovelorn lips met
And sweet tears were spilled

24

EVEN THE STARS

ZETA HAD ALMOST FORGOTTEN the pleasures of bodily sensation. Of skin and touch, of breath and taste. That must be why it felt so incredible to hold Alasie in her arms — to feel her warm breath on her cheek, her soft lips pressed against her own.

It was... unreal.

She pulled back to feast her eyes on Alasie's round face, tucked in a fur-lined hood, cheeks flush with cold and passion. Her lover's deep brown eyes glistened with tears of joy. Zeta kissed the tears away, making her way down Alasie's face and returning to her mouth.

A vague awareness of roaring applause crept into Zeta's consciousness, reminding her she was standing on a stage before thousands of Stalwarts — human and Specter alike. This *almost* broke the spell.

They parted lips but not gazes.

Alasie breathed, "It would take... like a *hundred* stanzas to describe how that felt."

"I can't wait to hear them," Zeta laughed, going back for more.

Pip-Tau shouted from behind her, "That's what Zeta Day is all about, people! Be bold! Kiss like nobody's watching! Now, I hate to break you two up, but another lady's just arrived who's also been drooling to plant a thousand wet kisses all over Zeta's face — the one and only Penelope-pooch! Any ex-Interrans out there may know her better as Aureum d'Canis..."

Some of the crowd chorused, "The golden goddess of dogs!"

Zeta had opened her eyes, finding that Penelope-pooch was on the ground next to her. The golden-furred pooch was bursting with excitement, her front paws on the tabletop, her tail wagging vigorously.

Zeta squealed, "Pen!"

She did indeed receive a thousand wet kisses from her pooch. Zeta teared up again as she remembered parting with Penelope-pooch at Jacob's Ladder Station so many years ago. It had to have felt like abandonment to the poor girl.

Zeta had enjoyed the company of thousands of Specter-pooch clones of Penelope while she hid in Varuna's ocean. The Specter-pooches were all gone now, having their node-nets supplanted by Stalwarts or the Acolytes of Varuna. But this Penelope was the one-and-only real thing. She had waited for Zeta in The Thin Forest all this time.

"I'll never leave you again, Pen," she promised her pooch under her breath. She wished she could hear Penelope's anthropolinguistic voice again.

Oraxis and Genevieve stood nearby, beaming at the tearful reunion. Zeta went to them, entangling arms in a three-person hug.

"Welcome back to the human race," Oraxis said.

Genevieve put a hand behind Zeta's head and pressed their foreheads together. She said, "You made the right choice."

"We're bringing her inside," Oraxis shouted up to Pip-Tau. "Come on, Alasie, let's get her changed and warmed up."

They ushered her into the new Telson Lodge, which smelled strongly of pine and burning wood. The stone fireplace in the back of the great room held a roaring fire, warming the interior nicely.

Pleasant smells. Cold, warmth. Comfort and discomfort. These were sensations to be relished. As wonderful as she knew it must've felt to be a Specter, she had no actual memories of the experience. Enoch had done his best to recreate it for her using constructs, but without memories, the whole thing seemed like a story being told about her.

Losing so much time was unsettling. It definitely didn't feel like she had just reawakened after the Fall of the Specters. Time and memory are the sort of simple things that people take for granted until their perceptions of them get warped.

She didn't know what the sensations of mass-sense or pushing off from a gravitational field felt like. She could only imagine what it was like to sit in wait inside Varuna for four and a half years, listening to Alasie's poems from the dark waters under the ice. But she knew how it made her feel now, as a human, knowing how dedicated her lover had been.

Alasie introduced Zeta to Natasha-Eta Herrington and her tiny pooch, Elle, in the room where she had been sleeping. Natasha-Eta wiped her tattooed shoulder with a bloody scrap of cloth, stained with bluish-black streaks. She said, "Sorry I missed your grand entrance, but I couldn't leave this design almost-finished. I'm done now. Let's get you changed!"

Oraxis waited in the great room as the women used warm water from a basin to wash the viscous breathing fluid out of Zeta's hair and off her skin. They dressed her in a comfortable outfit, which seemed to be stitched together using discarded jumpsuits, then wrapped her in a coat of soft leather and downy furs.

Oraxis called into the room, "We're wanted outside, ladies. The burial ceremony is starting."

***

A SONG WAS PLAYING OUTSIDE, muffled by the lodge's thick log walls, punctuated by the rumble of distant sonic booms — rhythmic Specter syncopation. Zeta recognized it as the traditional burial ceremony music of her tribe. Heartbeat drums and a chorus of chanting voices called out to the spirits to welcome their fallen tribemate into the afterlife.

They hurried back out to rejoin the crowd, finding another holographic show playing in the air. It was an homage to The Scorpion Tail Tribe — images of angry duppy masks floating overhead and colorful sparks drifting into the sky from the bonfires. Artificial stars speckled the darkening gray sky, which continued to sprinkle a dusting of snow onto the hair and hoods of the Stalwarts.

Goosebumps formed on her arms. The skin on the back of her neck and scalp tightened as haunting, nostalgic memories arose — Wilhelm-pa's funeral, Charra's funeral. Zeta had helped plan the ceremony, but she still wasn't ready. You never are.

Alasie put her arm around Zeta's waist and Zeta put her arm around Alasie's shoulders as they walked.

The Telsons and their closest friends followed Pip-Tau and Pandora away from the lodge into The Thin Forest. They crunched through snow and pine needles, repeating funerary chants in her native tongue — some more skillfully than others. After a few minutes, they reached a small clearing. A hole had been dug in front of a carved stone made of black marble.

Pip-Tau brushed the snow off a perfect replica of Pip-Rho's black porcelain avatar, which lounged lazily atop the stone. Its white eyes glistened with an impish expression, making it look like it knew a secret it would never tell.

Zeta read the words, which were inlaid in the stone with white letters.

Pip-Rho Telson
GY436-12-21 or GY525-07-07 to
GY675-20-02 or GY680-12-11

That's the life of a snowflake.
Short life, shorter life...

Either way, it's still beautiful.

Zeta recognized the first date as long enough ago that it must've been Pip-Alpha's birth date. The second birth date had to be Pip-Rho's resurrection date before making her fateful trip up to bait a Specter. The first death date was what would later be called Zeta Day Zero, or The Fall of the Specters. Jamji's spellsong device had been parked in a drone near Pip-Rho's egg, and the device's effects had sent her Specter cells on a rampage. Many considered that to be her date of True Death, since everything afterward could be considered the transitional period when Pip-Rho metamorphosed into Pandora. The final date was recognizable as the date of the One-Day War, when Pip-Rho's orb was reunited with her Specter form, and Pandora emerged, declaring that Pip-Rho was no more.

There was a time when Zeta would have considered Pip-Rho's life to be unimaginably long, but immortality had skewed her thoughts on that. They had a fragile sort of immortality. She dreaded to think about the Stalwarts who had lost their orbs trying to fight off the Guardians. *Every* life was short when compared to the time scales of the universe.

The chanting ended, and silence fell over the crowd. Zeta could hear the sniffles and crunching feet of people in the forest, keeping their distance as they encircled the burial site. Overhead, the darkening gray sky was all but blotted out by Specter-Stalwarts. Handheld torches cast dancing shadows throughout the forest. A few holograms glowed among the crowd, with XT-Xenos taking his place by Oraxis's side.

A weathered headstone a few paces away marked Susanne-Beta Telson's resting place. It was over three hundred long Genesis years old but still well-kept. A fresh bundle of pine and winterberries rested in the snow at its base. Oraxis and Genevieve still visited the grave regularly, leaving flowers or other gifts for their long-lost Susie-Q.

At least her grave wouldn't be so lonely anymore.

Pɪᴘ-Tᴀᴜ sᴛᴏᴏᴅ beside Rho's gravestone, sniffing and wiping her eyes. She read the inscription, "That's the life of a snowflake. Short life, shorter life... Either way, it's still beautiful. Those were Pip-Alpha's last words. She died at a young age when she froze to death in a snowstorm. Pip-Alpha grew up knowing she would die young. She accepted her death with the maturity of an eld and cherished the short life that she had. None of her Noddite reincarnations forgot that feeling. We've lived our lives as if they could end any day. Us Pips, we truly... *live*... every moment of every day. Even the Greek progression was a sort of game we played with death."

She sniffed a sad little laugh, then continued. "Add to the mysteries of Pip-Rho's life and death the fact that I *was* Pip-Rho until our lives diverged. Pandora *was* Pip-Rho until CCDC destroyed her and this new... being emerged."

Pip-Tau looked over at the queen — a look of resigned acceptance. Her lip trembled. "We know there's some glimmer of Pip-Rho left in Pandora. But there's probably even more of her left in me. And, I'd like to think... in all of us. Every life she touched left a mark which can never be erased, as long as we all still live."

Pip-Tau broke into pained sobs. She rushed to the embrace of Oraxis and Genevieve, burying her face in her Gen-ma's fur coat.

Pandora stepped forward and spoke with the cold dignity befitting a queen. "I hold Pip-Rho's aposynchronic orb." A bulge rolled through Pandora's black, fluid body. A metallic orb emerged atop her outstretched tendril of a hand, held out over the empty grave. "Her eternal data now lives on within me, Enoch, and the Acolytes of Varuna. Her orb serves no further purpose."

An odd vibration thrummed in the air, punctuated by a crack. The orb atop Pandora's hand disintegrated. Silvery shards tumbled down into the grave, glistening in the torchlight. They tinkled as they fell into a pile in the dirt. Some of the crowd gasped at this. Zeta put her face in Alasie's hair and stifled a sob.

Pandora continued, "Ashes to ashes, dust to dust. May the memory of Pip-Rho Telson be honored among Stalwarts and Specters alike until the end of our days. Let those who wish to cast remembrances into her grave now do so."

The Stalwarts lined up behind the Telsons to drop their tokens of remembrance into the grave. A pile of black-dyed lilies was available for those who hadn't brought something.

Zeta reached into her pouch to pull out the brown egg she had procured for the occasion. It reminded her of Pip-Rho's holographic avatar — the brown egg with an afro and a cartoon face. Her choice of avatar was a self-deprecating joke about her orbital containment vessel. That was one of the things Zeta had loved about Pip-Rho. The woman was probably more intelligent than any human had ever been, but she was also approachable and genuine.

When it was her turn, Zeta bent down and dropped the egg into the dirt. It landed in the snow-dusted soil at the bottom of the hole without cracking, making her smile a little.

When Alasie stepped up to the grave, she cleared her throat. She looked down into the hole, then up at the black cherub on the grave-stone. Looking into the statue's eyes, Alasie recited a poem in a wavering voice.

> **Storyteller...**
> **Tell a wondrous tale**
> **About a fair maiden**
> **And a quest for a grail**
>
> **Storyteller...**
> **Can you make me laugh?**
> **With ironic twists,**
> **Or a jest, or a gaffe?**
>
> **Storyteller...**
> **Fill me with dread**

To make me cry out
At gruesome bloodshed

Storyteller...
Build a construct —
A world to entertain
And maybe instruct

Storyteller...
Please tell me one more
About that Pip-Rho
Of legend and lore

Storyteller...
At that story's sad end
I'll proudly proclaim
That she was my friend

The storyteller.

THEY STOOD in the cold for what must have been an hour. Night fell as the long stream of mourners shuffled by to mutter condolences. Once they were through, XT-Xenos's Specter descended from between the trees. He lowered two thick tendrils over the grave to scoop the dirt back into the hole.

Pip-Tau said some parting words of gratitude to close the ceremony, and they followed the crowd back to the Telson Cabin. Music played in the clearing — gentle, but not too sad. Sparkling, multicolored lights were holographically projected overhead. The Zeta Day celebrations weren't over yet — they had just taken a somber turn.

Zeta, Alasie, Natasha-Eta, and the Telsons picked a bonfire to warm up around. Pandora's miniature Specter and Enoch's hologram also joined them. The fires had dwindled, so the men and Specter-Stalwarts hauled in more wood. The wet wood hissed and popped as it was piled into the fire. Billows of smoke wafted her way occasionally, making her cough.

"I liked your poem," Zeta told Alasie, wiping her stinging eyes.

"Thanks," Alasie said. They squeezed together, side-by-side.

"Here, here," Oraxis said. "An excellent poem, Alasie."

"We're so proud of you," Genevieve added.

The rest of the group gave similar compliments, and then the conversation died down again. They stared into the fire in solemn silence.

A glowing hologram appeared nearby, walking as if it had emerged from the forest. Enoch's interfaces allowed Stalwart-Specters to connect to the holographic projectors discretely mounted throughout the lodge and forest and broadcast their avatars among the crowd. This avatar was a pale-faced young man with a bushy red beard flanking his cheeks and a clean-shaven chin. He wore black and gray furs and raised his arms to show his mittened palms.

"May I approach your fire?" the hologram asked.

"No need for formalities, friend," Oraxis chuckled. "Our fire is yours."

The young man stayed planted where he stood, fixing his pale gaze on Zeta.

She still wasn't comfortable with her celebrity. She wasn't sure what to say to put the Specter-Stalwart at ease, so she looked back at the fire and pretended not to notice his stare.

Alasie stammered, "I guess you don't... It's been five years, so... um, Zeta, you probably don't recognize..." She was looking from the man to Zeta and back again. The dancing firelight illuminated the trepidation on her face.

Genevieve gasped and clutched Oraxis's arm.

"Ow, Gen!" Oraxis half-laughed. "Careful with that iron grip! I did the same thing to Alasie earlier. These Guardian myofibrites..."

The rest of what Oraxis said faded to background noise as Zeta looked back at the holographic man, studying his features.

She breathed the question, "Rohito?"

As quiet as she was, everybody heard, and everybody fell silent.

The young man's eyes glimmered with unshed tears. He nodded slightly. If his avatar accurately reflected his prior physical form, the boy who sank with her to the bottom of the spring pool had matured into a tall, trim young man in the time she had spent as a Specter. His freckles were still there, but they had faded. Five years was a long time on Genesis. It would've been over eight years on Earth.

And now, Rohito was a Specter.

He stepped forward as he spoke. "I just wanted to say some things, and then I'll leave you alone."

Zeta was ashamed that she hadn't wondered about Rohito's fate — if he voted for the bill and got his orb shipped off for New Genesis or if he was a Stalwart. Alasie had probably known. She'd been friends with Rohito, but never talked about him with Zeta.

"You don't have to—" Zeta started, but Rohito raised a hand and cut her off.

"Please, Zeta. It took a lot to work up the nerve to do this. This is what Zeta Day is for — that's what EoE Telson said. I'm taking an emotional risk talking to you. Please don't make me regret it." He'd stepped closer but still wasn't quite a part of their bonfire huddle.

"You were wrong," He said, his voice strained with stifled emotion.

"Wrong? About...?" She looked to Alasie for some sort of guidance.

"Just listen," Alasie hiss-whispered, giving Zeta a reproachful look.

Rohito took a shaky breath and started again. "You were wrong about how I felt towards you. In that message you recorded and had sent to me after you were abducted, you said you knew I hated you and that I'd be happier knowing you were dead. You couldn't have been more wrong, Zeta. I've never hated you.

"I know I panicked when I saw you at your Beta Ceremony party. I was a dumb kid back then, and I was afraid. I still believed in spirits and thought you were there to drag me down with you to the land of the dead, just like I dragged you down to the bottom of that spring pool to die with me. I was haunted by our deaths for a long time — by the way I clutched onto you, the way you looked at me with so much... horror."

His expression held unspeakable pain at saying this. Zeta never thought about how selfish it was for Rohito to hold on to her, dragging her down with him, because it didn't seem like it could have happened any other way. She was a good swimmer and could've gotten to the surface if he hadn't clutched her so tightly. She may have killed Rohito, but he had also killed her.

Rohito continued, "Later, when I understood that you were alive again, it was like a blessing from the gods — our deaths had been *undone.* I hoped to meet you again and make peace, but I never got the nerve. Alasie tried to get me to reach out, but I kept putting it off. Then you died again. It was so much like your alpha death, I couldn't bear it — dragged down into Varuna's cold waters by those black monsters."

He looked at Pandora and amended his statement. "*Misunderstood... monsters.*"

This got a chuckle from the others and a huff from Alasie.

He continued, "When you were gone, I'd replay that message and wish I could tell you how wrong you were. So... now I've said it — you were *wrong,* Zeta, and I would've had a lot more peace these last five years if you hadn't put that on me. But I still never hated you for it — I... *adore* you. I always have since the first time I saw you. I know it's... *unwelcome* affection, but it feels good to finally say it. Don't worry — I'm going to leave you alone. I don't expect you to want to be friends or anything. I'm glad to see you and Alasie together. I'm happy just knowing that you're alive and that you're happy."

He smiled, addressing the whole group around the bonfire with open arms. "We're incredibly fortunate to be given these second and third chances. Most neoprims aren't — let alone the countless billions of people who died before us. I won't waste this opportunity by spending my days tortured by the past. I guess that's all I hoped to get from this — to put the past behind and move into the future with a clear conscience. That's all I had to say. Happy Zeta Day, everyone."

He started stepping away when Alasie shouted, "I knew you could do it, Rohito! I wish we could hug, but..."

"Hologram," Rohito laughed, shrugging. "And Specter hugs hurt. Hug Zeta, instead."

Alasie turned to Zeta and squeezed her with bone-crushing force. Zeta wheezed a laugh as she hugged Alasie back, wondering if the brutal squeeze was Alasie's secret way of punishing Zeta for putting Rohito through so much.

It was fine — she deserved it.

"Goodbye, Rohito," she said. "Happy Zeta Day."

THE NIGHT CONTINUED with moments of playful conversation and somber silence. Lively music emanated from the lodge as light and laughter poured from its windows. The clusters of people in the clearing thinned as they either went inside or called it a night. When someone wanted to leave, they'd hail a Specter and get slurped up into a breathing fluid capsule to be transported to whatever faraway destination they called home. Pandora took her leave of them, but Enoch stuck around.

The Telsons stayed at their bonfire, talking the night away. On more than one occasion, Zeta caught Pip-Tau staring across the clearing to where Veer Gladstone and several other Elds in the provisional Council of Ten were sitting on logs around a smaller fire. She was certain that Veer was returning Pip-Tau's glances.

Zeta wished they could have a private conversation using mindspeak. Instead, she settled for speaking in a hushed voice after making her way to Pip-Tau's side. "So, what happened between you and Veer?"

"What happened?" Pip-Tau laughed. "What do you mean, *what happened?*"

Zeta leaned in, whispering, "After... you know, after the war and everything. After you were together at the Crash Pad. Was that just a one-time thing?"

Pip-Tau pulled back and looked at Zeta with a scrunched-up face, crossing her arms. "Whatchu you talkin' 'bout, Zeta?"

Then it struck her. Zeta knew what Veer and Pip-Tau had done — she knew what she saw, though it was experienced through a construct after her bootstrapping. Enoch's visual representation of Specter mass-sense may not have been an accurate reproduction of the sensation itself, but the things that her Specter had seen were clear enough.

Zeta thought for a moment about the timing of Pip-Tau and Veer's coupling. It'd happened after the Stalwarts were disconnected from the Worldnet. Neither of them had stored the experience on their orbs! It may as well have never happened.

But wouldn't other Specter-Stalwarts have seen?

Zeta looked at Enoch, who was standing suspiciously close to Pip-Tau and grinning at Zeta. "Enoch, did you... hide their... *wrestling...* somehow?"

Enoch nodded proudly. "You said not to watch. I'm in all the Specters, so nobody watched."

"Wrestling?!" Pip-Tau squeaked. "Zeta, what are you..." A sudden, shocked understanding came to her face. Her jaw dropped, and her eyes bugged. She shouted, "VEER?! AND ME?!"

Zeta nodded. "After you and Veer told me about your Zeta's Army idea, before the Guardians in Syn-Cen killed everyone, you spent your last moments together... you know... enjoying each other's company."

Pip-Tau gaped at her with the same shocked expression for a few seconds before she squealed, "Shut up! You are *not* telling me this right now, Zeta Telson!"

Riotous laughter burst from their group around the bonfire. Carff's surprisingly loud cackle filled the forest. A hundred curious heads turned their way.

"That's impossible!" Pip-Tau squeaked. "He would never! With me?! Stop joking around, Zeta!"

"I saw you myself," Zeta laughed. "I didn't mean to. You were both really... um... I think the word I would use is *zealous*."

"Zealous!" Carff whistled, clutching his belly and wheezing out a laugh that Zeta was concerned might send his newly resurrected elderly body to an early grave.

"Shut up!" Pip-Tau shouted, shoving Zeta away. She immediately began pacing, staring forward intensely. "Oh-my-god, oh-my-god, oh-my-god," she repeated to herself, rubbing her temples.

"You've always had a crush on him," Genevieve said. "Maybe you confessed, and he said he felt the same way about you."

"Impossible!" Pip-Tau squeaked, stomping over to look up at Genevieve. "Do you see that man?!" She stabbed a finger in Veer's direction. "And do you see this face?!" She shoved a thumb at herself.

"What about your face? I think you're adorable," Genevieve giggled.

"My point exactly!" Pip-Tau squealed. "A face only a mother could love! I'm a bug-eyed stick-figure woman with mosquito-bite breasts! Veer would never *wrestle* with me, even if I were the last woman on Genesis!"

"Wrestle!" Carff wheezed, slapping a hand onto Oraxis's shoulder before doubling over with laughter.

Pip-Tau was back to pacing again. "Oh-my-god, I *was* the last woman on Genesis! You don't think he'd be *that* desperate, do you? Oh-my-god..."

"You should ask him for a kiss," Alasie huff-laughed. All eyes went to her. She shrunk at the attention. "I mean... you said it yourself — take bold risks. Do something stupid in the name of love. That's what Zeta Day is for, right?"

"Here, here!" Oraxis laughed.

"Go for it," Zeta said.

After several more minutes of cajoling, Pip-Tau finally worked up enough nerve to go to Veer's fire. They watched as she led him away from the others and stood together in the dark at the edge of the clearing.

Using your enhanced hearing to listen in on other people's private conversations was considered bad taste, but watching with enhanced optics seemed innocent enough.

The Telsons fell silent as they watched Pip-Tau gesturing and talking. Veer went down to one knee, taking Pip-Tau's hand.

Genevieve gasped, "He's proposing?!"

"You're showing your age, Genevieve," Carff chuckled. "That knee-and-ring ordeal died with Earth. The Black Lion just doesn't want Pip-Tau to strain her neck looking up at him."

Another minute went by. They talked. Pip-Tau gesticulated and laughed. Veer nodded and smiled. Just when Zeta thought nothing would happen between them, Pip-Tau did a little hop, threw her arms around Veer's neck, and smashed their faces together.

The Telsons burst into triumphant shouts, accompanied by other scattered groups around the clearing. Those others must've also been watching.

Pip-Tau fished something out of a pocket and put her hand to her ear. Oh — she was putting in an earbud.

"Hey, EoE Pip-Tau Telson here!" Came Pip-Tau's breathless voice over the hidden speakers. "I know it's getting late, so before everyone heads out, I just want to thank you all for coming! We laughed, we cried, we kissed our inhibitions goodbye. It's been a crazy year, right? We're still trying to decide what *normal* looks like on a post-One-Day-War Genesis. Um... what else? Oh, keep an eye out for the proposed charter I'll be sending. I want feedback, people! You don't get to complain about it if you haven't made your voice heard! Alright, good night, everyone! Happy Zeta Day!"

"Happy Zeta Day!" Zeta shouted back, along with the rest of the scattered Stalwarts.

Pip-Tau yanked the earbud from her ear and hopped into Veer's arms, putting her hand into his dreadlocks and kissing him again. The shadow of a Specter swooped down from the darkness and sent a thick tendril down to engulf the couple, pulling them into its breathing-fluid-filled transport vacuole.

The Specter rose, accelerated away, and disappeared into the cloud-shrouded night sky. Its distant sonic boom echoed like thunder rolling over the hills.

***

Carff, XT-Xenos, Natasha-Eta, and Enoch departed over the course of the next hour. This left only Oraxis, Genevieve, Alasie, and Zeta at the dwindling bonfire. After having been gone for most of the party, Penelope-pooch, Pinga, and Elle rejoined them.

"Think we should head in and assess the damage?" Oraxis asked Genevieve.

"There's still a raucous party going on in there," Genevieve sighed. "We'll never get to sleep at this rate."

"I'm sure our beds are occupied, anyway," Oraxis said.

Genevieve gave a disgusted, scoffing sound and shook her head.

Oraxis said, "No point in going in to ruin their fun." He walked towards the tree line until he found a patch of snow that wasn't muddy from foot traffic. He plopped down onto his back in the fresh snow. "Don't mind my snoring."

Genevieve went to join him, saying, "Thank goodness our placental mats still work. Sleeping out in the cold like this could kill you otherwise."

Zeta whispered to Alasie, "Do you want to lie down with them, or... maybe go inside and see what the party is like?"

"Well, we're young," Alasie huff-laughed. "People our age are supposed to love dancing and stuff, but... I never really got into that. But if you want to..."

Zeta whispered, "I want to do whatever you want to do."

Alasie hugged Zeta, then gave her a gentle kiss. When they parted, she met Zeta's eyes and said, "I want to lie in the snow and count the stars with you. I *love* staring at the stars."

"But..." Zeta looked up at the slate gray clouds.

"I can make stars for you," Enoch said, startling Zeta. His hologram had reappeared by her side, standing a bit too close. The SI-child didn't understand personal boundaries.

A brilliant holographic starfield lit up the sky overhead.

Alasie gasped in wonder.

Zeta brushed her hand through the air where Enoch's hair was projected, as if to tousle it. "Thanks, Enoch."

They went to where Oraxis and Genevieve lay in the snow and joined them, holding hands and squeezing close together. Their pooches snuggled up by their sides.

"They won't always be there," Oraxis said. "The stars, I mean. Or galaxies. It'll take trillions of years, but in time, all you'll see when you look out into space is a cold, black void."

"Oraxis always knows how to liven up a party," Genevieve said.

"I think it's poetic," Alasie said. "It makes me think... wow... we're lucky to live in a time when there are stars to see."

A falling star traced a brilliant line across the starfield above. Enoch was putting on a show for them. He's a good kid.

Alasie and Genevieve gasped as if it had been real.

"Make a wish," Genevieve said.

"Gen, it's a hologram—" Oraxis started, then gave an "oof" — he'd probably taken an elbow to the ribs.

"I don't need to," Alasie said, rolling to her side to kiss Zeta's cheek. "I don't need any more than this."

Zeta put her arm under Alasie's head to rest it on her shoulder. She looked back up at the starfield. She recognized it as a true-to-life representation of the actual constellations. Zeta spotted the tiger eye stars, one of which she now knew was Helios — the bustling home system of the Prolifera and Guard factions.

That's where Jamji's orb was heading.

Zeta did have a wish, but she wouldn't tell it.

Even after all that Jamji had done, like trying to kill Zeta and the entire Astrus hive with an antimatter explosion, Zeta still loved her sis-kin. She knew that Jamji believed all the lies the Guardians told about Specters and Astri. She'd been doing what she thought was right and hadn't believed that Specter-Zeta was actually Zeta.

She might as well say it — it's Zeta Day.

"I wish Jamji were here," Zeta said. She braced herself for an argument, yet none came.

"Me too," Genevieve said, her voice trembling with emotion.

"Yeah, I'd love to give that kid a stern talking to," Oraxis said. "And maybe some bacon and eggs for breakfast."

The mention of eggs reminded Zeta of Pip-Rho. She said, "And I wish Pip-Rho was... still around."

Nobody talked after that. The sounds of music and merriment drifted on the cold wind — a distant celebration of her spirit. Though she had returned, the memory of what she sacrificed for the faction had turned Zeta into a legend she could never live up to.

Many people had planned to vote for her as Provisional EoE — maybe enough for her to win. But before the voting started, she announced that she wouldn't accept any position in the Stalwart government. Nobody, outside of maybe the Telsons, appreciated that she was still just a young woman. Not as young or ignorant as she used to be, but still too young to be called an Eld, let alone Eld of Elds — the most powerful person in the Surya system.

Zeta was no chosen one, no legendary hero. All she had done was risk her life for the sake of her vows. People do that every day. Zeta's sacrifice domesticated the Specters, they said. And Pip-Rho's sacrifice elevated them to their ultimate form, creating Pandora. Zeta didn't do anything — it was Cain's seed for Enoch, embedded in her orb, that had done all the work of converting the Specters. But that didn't matter to the Stalwarts — they needed a hero. And Pip-Rho didn't choose her fate. All she could do with her broken mind was all she knew how to do — create a character, build a world. But the character became real, and the real Pip-Rho faded away.

Pip-Rho, flippant as she was, always took her status as a legend in stride. But Zeta's legend intimidated her. It was a larger-than-life illusion that people saw when they looked at her. So, she avoided talking to Stalwarts too much for fear of exposing her simplicity and ignorance and shattering their image of her. Let them have their myths, their heroes. It's important to have things to hang your hopes onto.

But her days of taking on the problems of the universe were over. All she wanted now was to pet Penelope-pooch, kiss Alasie, hug Genevieve, and listen to Oraxis try to explain things she could barely understand. She wanted to hear XT's gentle voice and Carff's tooth whistle. Pandora and Enoch were figuring out how to create a Specter-based Worldnet, and she couldn't wait to play in Pip-Tau's next gameworld construct.

Zeta wanted to live for the sake of living, and she was going to savor every moment of this incredible life.

And the next.

And the next.

Until she finally reaches her end, as everything must do someday.

Even the stars.

ACKNOWLEDGMENTS

First and foremost, thank you, dearest reader, for beta reading this final installment of the Zeta Trilogy! If you enjoyed this series, please-oh-please leave a review on your platform of choice.

Special thanks go out to my beta readers, with the steadfast Jessica Walker and Marlas Williams topping the list. Extra special thanks go to Gabrielle, my eternally supportive wife and the creator of the eye-catching cover art for the entire series. My love and gratitude for my kids overfloweth, and I thank them for their inspiration throughout the Zeta Trilogy adventure. Finally, join me in casting your eyes to the stars and allowing Ourania, the muse of celestial poetry, to fill you with wonder and gratitude.